THE MISSING GIRLS OF ALARDYCE HOUSE

HEATHER ATKINSON

Boldwood

First published in Great Britain in 2022 by Boldwood Books Ltd.

Cover Design: Alice Moore Design

Cover Photography: Shutterstock

This book is a work of fiction and, except in the case of historical fact, any resemblance to actual persons, living or dead, is purely coincidental.

Every effort has been made to obtain the necessary permissions with reference to copyright material, both illustrative and quoted. We apologise for any omissions in this respect and will be pleased to make the appropriate acknowledgements in any future edition.

A CIP catalogue record for this book is available from the British Library.

Paperback ISBN 978-1-80415-785-5

Large Print ISBN 978-1-80415-781-7

Ebook ISBN 978-1-80415-778-7

Kindle ISBN 978-1-80415-779-4

Audio CD ISBN 978-1-80415-786-2

MP3 CD ISBN 978-1-80415-783-1

Digital audio download ISBN 978-1-80415-777-0

Boldwood Books Ltd
23 Bowerdean Street
London SW6 3TN
www.boldwoodbooks.com

1

Amy caught tantalising glimpses of Alardyce House as the carriage climbed the long, winding driveway – drab grey stone, dull windows, slate roof shiny with rain. The entire estate was as cheery as the cold, relentless drizzle. In her fragile, grief-stricken state she felt as if it were playing hide and seek with her behind the trees, refusing to reveal itself fully. The trees were dense and thick with red-gold leaves, so weighed down by the recent rain that they hung over the drive, scratching the top of the carriage with their gnarled limbs. Amy shivered as a sense of foreboding settled in the pit of her stomach.

Hot tears shone in her bright blue eyes, which burned with anxiety. She had hoped this place would be welcoming but already she felt as though it didn't want her.

A turn in the drive brought them around the tree line and finally Alardyce House had nowhere left to hide. It was revealed to her in all its dreary, depressing glory. The house was large and – from what she'd already gathered – filled with all the modern comforts but it was just a square grey box. She was put in mind of a prison and shuddered.

Two figures stood in its doorway – a short, round man and a tall, slender lady, the latter standing as rigid as the pillar beside her. Amy hadn't encountered her aunt and uncle in ten years, since she was seven years old, but she had the vague notion that he was boring and pompous and she haughty and cold.

Amy wiped her eyes on the backs of her gloved hands. As she was in mourning the only colour she was permitted to wear was black, which depressed her spirits even more. Refusing to show any weakness to these people who were nothing more than strangers, she tilted back her head and held herself proudly.

* * *

'Amy's gone through a terrible time of it lately so I want you to make her feel welcome,' Sir Alfred Alardyce whispered to his wife, having to go up on tiptoes to reach her ear.

'That girl has the devil in her,' Lenora whispered back, eyeing the elegant, black-clad figure as she was helped down from the carriage by one of their footmen. 'I can't help but worry what we're letting ourselves in for.'

'It would be unchristian of us not to take her in – she's just lost both parents.'

'She's of an age to marry. I shall set about finding her a husband as soon as possible,' she replied with a cold smile.

'Then I anticipate she will soon be settled,' said Alfred. 'But please remember she's in mourning and can't even think about marriage for a year.'

'I haven't forgotten,' she said, her mind already mulling over ways she could get round that particular obstacle. A pair of blue eyes coyly swept up to them from beneath the black bonnet and Lenora felt nothing but loathing.

'Amy, welcome to Alardyce,' said Alfred amiably.

'Thank you, Uncle, and thank you, Aunt Lenora,' she replied. 'I appreciate you having me to stay. These past few weeks have been awful and it's comforting to be among family again.'

She said it very sweetly but Lenora's jaw remained set; she was as yet unconvinced of her sincerity. She looked Amy up and down, assessing her suitability for the marriage market – thick chestnut hair coiled into a neat bun, creamy skin. Her waist was narrow but her breasts were unfashionably large. Lenora anticipated it wouldn't be difficult to make a good match for her.

Alfred stepped aside to allow Amy to enter.

'You must be parched after your long journey,' he said with forced cheer. 'You must take some tea.'

'Thank you,' replied Amy, removing her bonnet and handing it to a waiting footman. She was surprised by the number of servants lined up in the hallway – having three footmen wasn't convenience, it was downright lavishness. Her uncle was rubbing the city's nose in it that he was a wealthy man.

Also lined up were a dour woman dressed in grey, who Amy assumed was the housekeeper, a doddery old man dressed in a butler's uniform and four young maids, all po-faced. She was very conscious of the portraits of forbidding ancestors staring at her from the dark walls. Amy felt centuries of disapproval pressing down on her.

A memory came upon her so suddenly she faltered. She was seven years old and she was walking down this very corridor with her mother and father, both young and beautiful and full of life. She hadn't been scared then because they'd been with her, her mother's gloved hand clasping her own. Amy was appalled when she thought she might actually start to cry in front of all these strangers.

'Amy, are you well?' said Alfred. 'You've gone awfully pale.'

She snapped herself out of it. 'I'm fine, just a little tired after the long journey,' she replied, forcing a smile.

They entered the drawing room, which was a huge vulgar monstrosity, every available space stuffed with expensive, tasteless furniture and trinkets. Each painting hanging on the wall had been created by a master. The house had been commissioned by Sir Alfred after he'd made his fortune in industry. Despite his declaring himself a good Christian who preached abstinence, his home was a gaudy temple to wealth.

Two young men of approximately Amy's own age rose to greet her. Both were tall and slender with dark hair and eyes and very pale skin, a striking combination. One was smiling and friendly, the other cold and arrogant, just like his mother.

'Amy, these are my sons,' introduced Alfred. 'Henry, my eldest,' he said, indicating the proud one.

'Pleased to meet you,' Amy said politely with a small dip.

Henry didn't speak, confining himself to a stiff bow.

'And Edward.'

'Lovely to meet you.' Edward smiled, stepping forward and shaking her hand, making her smile back.

'Edward, calm down,' chided Lenora.

He rolled his eyes behind his mother's back, broadening Amy's smile.

She was instructed to sit on a hideously ornate suite alone while the rest of the family took the remaining seats, forming a semicircle, surrounding her. Amy was handed tea and cakes, which she nibbled at daintily, doing her best not to spill any crumbs.

There was an awkward silence followed by stilted conversation as everyone was so busy trying not to mention Amy's recent loss that they couldn't think of anything else to say. Her parents had both been lost after their ship went down in the Atlantic while returning from France a few weeks ago and now the Alardyces were the only family she had left in the world. *A family of strangers,* she thought miserably. How she wished she'd been permitted to remain in London where she'd been born and raised, where she had friends, but the terms of her father's will dictated she was to come to Alardyce House should she lose both parents before she was married, a situation her father had never seriously considered might actually happen.

On the bright side, their gentle Scottish accents did provide some comfort. Her mother had been from Edinburgh, her father from

London. They'd met when her father had come up north to do business with Alfred and he had fallen for her immediately. They'd married six months later and she'd moved down to London with him.

Amy liked Edward immediately; he was amiable and the only one who seemed comfortable talking to her. Henry was the handsomer of the two brothers, a striking-looking man with lovely brown eyes that glittered in the light. He remained quiet and sullen and stared at Amy as though she were a curiosity in a museum, his penetrating gaze making her intensely uncomfortable.

Her uncle was rather sweet in a bumbling sort of way but she despised her aunt immediately. She was proud and arrogant and her once renowned beauty was fading, turning her bitter. Amy had a large pair of breasts that not even the stiffest of corsets could conceal and Lenora kept looking at them disdainfully. Amy ignored the looks, but Henry's brooding eyes kept shifting to her chest, making her furious. What right did he have to stare like that? Amy's temper, always close to the surface – even more so since the death of her parents – snapped.

'You must excuse me, Cousin Henry, if I've spilt something on myself,' she said icily, making a pretence of wiping the front of her dress.

'Spilt something?' said Alfred, genuinely confused. 'I see no spillage.'

'Neither do I, Uncle, but I think it's the only reason why Henry's eyes must continually slip to my chest.'

Embarrassed silence filled the room. Henry's white skin turned bright red and he looked away, eyes glimmering with suppressed anger while Edward sniggered.

Lenora was incensed, eyes flicking towards the two footmen standing sentry at the back of the room, gauging their reactions to this humiliation of the prince of the house. They were far too experienced to betray any emotion and continued to stare ahead in solemn silence. Lenora turned her attention back to this niece who she already loathed. 'You must be mistaken Amy,' she said, voice cold. 'Henry was not looking your way, he was looking past you. As you've only just arrived we'll forget all about your misguided comment but here at Alardyce House manners are never forgotten. Have I made myself clear?'

'Yes, madam,' said Amy, her cold hauteur matching Lenora's own. 'Forgive me if I caused any offence. It was not my intention.'

'It's up to Henry to forgive you, not I,' she retorted, green eyes flashing.

Henry forced his gaze to meet Amy's, humiliation and pride vying for supremacy. 'There's nothing to forgive, dear Cousin,' he said magnanimously. 'A simple misunderstanding on your part. Let's not mention it again.'

His voice was smooth and deep and not at all unpleasant to Amy's ears but eerily it was devoid of any emotion. Amy was acutely aware that she'd already made two enemies in this house. She'd only arrived an hour ago.

Desperately needing to escape, she got to her feet. 'If you'll excuse me, I would like to change.'

'Ah yes, of course.' Her uncle smiled, relieved. 'Mrs Adams, the housekeeper, will show you to your room.'

Amy left the drawing room with an inward sigh of relief and followed the sour-faced woman upstairs.

'The family wing is that way,' said Mrs Adams, gesturing to the corridor leading to the left.

Amy started to turn that way, naturally expecting her room to be down there. Instead the housekeeper turned right and Amy had to hurry to catch up.

'You're down here, miss, in the guest wing.'

'Guest wing?' Amy frowned.

'Lady Lenora thought it best you have privacy because Master Henry's and Master Edward's rooms are in the family wing. You have this whole corridor to yourself.'

Amy was both hurt and amused. Obviously her aunt and uncle had heard about the Mr Costigan scandal and assumed she was a whore who would try to seduce their innocent sons but it hurt that she was being treated as a guest rather than one of the family.

Her room was large and pretty, overlooking the gardens at the front of the house. Waiting for her was a bonny maid of eighteen arranging a vase of flowers on the windowsill. When Amy entered the room she turned to give her a curtsey.

'And who are you?' said Amy.

'Nettie, miss. I'm your maid.'

The frail little blonde shifted uncomfortably beneath Amy's assessing stare.

'Nettie will take care of all your needs,' said Mrs Adams before leaving. Amy surmised she was going back to her usual duty of haunting the house.

'I've already unpacked your clothes, miss,' said Nettie. 'I didn't want your dresses to crease.'

'That's very efficient of you, thank you. Please assist me to change.'

'Yes, miss. I've laid out the Henrietta cloth dress.'

Amy stared at the depressing black garment. She'd have to wear hideous items like this for a full year. The heavy material only served as a reminder of her pain.

She unfastened the mourning brooch that was pinned to the front of her travelling dress containing locks of her mother's plaited blonde hair. Both her parents' bodies had been lost at sea but her mother had given her a lock of her hair when she was very young and placed it inside a locket. Amy had transferred it to the mourning brooch and wore it constantly. Her eyes stung as she gazed at it, running her thumbs over the glass casing before handing it to Nettie. 'Pin that to the front of the dress and be very careful with it.'

'I will, miss.'

Amy watched with approval as she pinned it respectfully to the dress before smoothing out the material.

'Are you privy to all the downstairs gossip?' said Amy as Nettie assisted her to change.

She flushed. 'Well, I hear things, miss.'

Amy dipped into one of the compartments of her portmanteau to fish out a small velvet purse of monies, which she handed to her. 'If you hear anything of interest, no matter how trivial, I would be grateful if you could relay it to me.'

Nettie peeked inside the purse and her eyes lit up. 'Of course, miss.'

'And we'll keep this arrangement between ourselves?'

'Of course, miss.'

'You know, Nettie, I think you'll prove to be a treasure.' Amy smiled. She might just have found herself an ally in this awful house.

At dinner that evening Amy got a more accurate reading of what her extended family was like. She hadn't had much to do with them before as her mother and her aunt had despised each other. Now Amy discovered why. Lenora was a spiteful, venomous banshee who behaved as though she were the man of the house, her uncle seemingly happy to bend to her stronger will. Amy knew her uncle and mother had been very close until Lenora came along.

Henry and Alfred were discussing politics in very serious tones while Lenora and Edward talked quietly together. That left Amy sitting alone at the bottom of the table with no one to talk to and a ton of grief bearing down on her. A veritable army of servants cleared away their plates, Amy's meal hardly touched. In this house full of people she had never felt so alone.

Taking up the entire wall to her left was a portrait of the family – Alfred, Lenora and their sons – gathered together to listen to Alfred read from the Bible, suitably devout expressions on their faces. The artist must have been good because he'd managed to eradicate all trace of conceit from Lenora's image.

It was Edward who distracted her with a lopsided grin. Concluding his hushed conversation with his mother, he said, 'So, Amy, what's London like?'

She sighed wistfully. 'Loud, full of life, exciting.'

'Decadent and amoral.' Her uncle frowned.

'No, not at all. There are wonderful museums, libraries and art galleries,' she replied, eyes lighting up as she spoke about a place she loved.

'And brothels and opium dens,' said Lenora.

'I'm sure there are but I can confidently say I never saw any.'

'I say, how disappointing.' Edward smiled.

'Edward, I will not warn you again,' said Lenora, making him sigh and fling himself back in his chair.

'Amy, do you enjoy the theatre?' Henry said pleasantly, surprising her.

'Yes, very much. I used to go to the Adelphi and the Gaiety in the Strand every week.'

'We do not approve of the theatre,' said her uncle. 'All those disreputable actors and actresses. It's not a place for a person of proper moral character.'

Amy looked at Henry and wondered if he'd only asked her that question so she would incur her uncle's disapproval but his expression was inscrutable.

Some impulse urged her to look up and she found herself staring at one of the footmen, really noticing him for the first time. He was tall, dark and handsome, which wasn't a surprise as footmen were chosen for their good looks and strong builds. However this one had something extra that she couldn't define, something that drew her. His mouth could be described as sulky and his eyes were so dark they were black, reflecting back the lamplight. Amy looked back down at her plate but, unable to help herself, she glanced up again and found he was looking directly at her. Amy couldn't help but smile inwardly. This house wasn't all bad.

2

The following morning Amy was sitting in the parlour with Lenora in silence, both women engrossed in their needlework. Henry and Edward had gone into the city while Alfred hid in his study. Since Amy had entered the house the atmosphere had become less than convivial and he was closeting himself away more and more.

Rush, the large lumbering butler, entered the room and bowed. 'Excuse me, Your Ladyship, but there's a young gentleman in the hallway desirous of speaking with Miss Osbourne.'

Amy's head snapped up. 'Who?'

'Mr Nigel Fitzgerald, miss.'

Amy sighed and rolled her eyes.

'Amy, who is this man?' said Lenora.

'Just a friend from London. Rush, please tell him I do not wish to see him. Ever.'

'I'm afraid, miss, he said he will not leave until he's seen you.'

'What a nuisance. I didn't think he would find me here.'

'Has this man been harassing you, Amy?' said Lenora.

'He's been obsessed with me for years. He's proposed to me so many times I've lost count. I've done nothing to encourage him.'

'Of course not,' replied Lenora sardonically.

They were interrupted by a man pressing his face to the window, big doe eyes scanning the interior of the room until they settled on Amy. 'Amy, I'm here for you, my love,' he cried through the glass.

'I'll get rid of him,' she said, getting to her feet.

'Please do.' Lenora frowned. 'Quickly.'

'What's going on? I can hear shouting,' said Alfred, entering the room. He jumped when he saw the face pressed up against the window. 'Good God, what is that?'

'Mr Fitzgerald,' said Lenora flatly before returning to her embroidery.

'He pestered me for months in London but I didn't expect him to come here,' said Amy. 'I'll make sure he leaves and doesn't come back. Rush, if you could show him into the drawing room, I'll speak to him.'

'I will not have you seeing him alone,' said her uncle. 'Rush, get Matthew and Gerard to go with her. They can throw the fellow out if needs be.'

'Thank you, Uncle,' said Amy.

Rush left the room and the three of them did their best not to look at Nigel Fitzgerald's face still pressed up against the glass.

'Amy,' he called, but she resolutely refused to look at him.

'Who the devil is he?' said Alfred.

'We were introduced by a mutual friend one evening at the theatre,' began Amy.

'There you go, the theatre. I told you it was evil.'

'Anyway,' continued Amy, 'he proposed to me a month later and I said no. Then he made me the offer on a weekly basis. He seems to think we're destined to be together.'

'I take it you don't like this fellow?' said Alfred. Rush appeared on the other side of the window and after they exchanged a few words the face disappeared, Nigel's voice calling, 'I'm coming, Amy.'

'Not at all,' she told her uncle. 'I'm sure you can understand why. He is very strange.'

'He'd have to be,' said Lenora.

Amy thought it prudent to ignore this remark.

Rush didn't live up to his name, so it took him some time to install Fitzgerald in the drawing room then return to the parlour and announce he was ready to see her.

'Amy, make sure he never returns,' said Lenora, voice heavy with warning.

'I shall do my best,' she replied before exiting the room.

Amy waited in the hallway while Rush called two of the footmen and she was excited to see one of them was the tall, handsome one. Her eyes regarded him playfully and his gaze met hers, although his expression was unfathomable. She discovered his name was Matthew when Rush addressed him directly.

Rush led the way into the ugly drawing room, followed by Amy then Matthew and finally Gerard, the second footman. A slender man in his late thirties with ash-blonde hair and light blue eyes paced the room, wringing his hands. Amy cringed at the sight of his hands – they were small, girlish and damp with sweat from the anxiety that constantly plagued him. He stopped in his tracks when he saw her and his expression softened.

'Amy, my love. As beautiful as ever.'

'What do you want, Nigel?' she said in a bored tone.

'I've been scouring the country for you and now I've finally found you,' he responded ardently.

'Then you've wasted your time. I thought I'd made my feelings perfectly clear the last time we met.'

'You were distraught over your parents' death. You didn't know what you were saying.'

It made her furious that he would try and use that to explain her lack of feeling for him. 'I knew exactly what I was saying,' she hissed. 'And it bores me to have to repeat myself. I have no interest whatsoever in marrying you. Is that plain enough?'

He looked crestfallen. 'But... I love you.'

'No, you don't, you're obsessed with me, which is an entirely different thing. Now go away, you're making a fool of yourself.'

His expression darkened and he glowered at the servants. 'Leave us,' he told them imperiously.

'No,' she retorted. 'They stay.'

'I wish to speak to you in private.'

'I've no wish to speak to you. This conversation is over.'

As she made for the door he released a bellow of anguish and ran at her but Matthew and Gerard put their towering forms between them.

'I think Miss Osbourne has made herself quite clear,' said Matthew, coldly polite. 'I suggest you leave.'

'Stand aside,' yelled Nigel, lunging for her.

Matthew grabbed him by the shoulders and held him firm while Nigel protested, still trying to get at Amy, who regarded him with a satisfied expression. She was enjoying seeing him finally put in his place.

'Escort the *gentleman* out,' boomed Rush.

'With pleasure,' said Matthew.

They had to drag Fitzgerald kicking and screaming to the door.

'Amy, please,' he cried.

'Don't come here again, Nigel,' she warned, noting how strong and masculine Matthew looked as he manoeuvred the intruder out of the door.

'I love you. I'll never give up.'

'And I'll never agree to marry you. Go back to London and don't come back.'

Her uncle and aunt emerged from the parlour to watch the spectacle, their mouths hanging open.

'She really needs a husband,' said Lenora.

Alfred nodded in agreement.

* * *

Amy was deathly bored at Alardyce. She wasn't permitted off the estate without one of the family accompanying her and when she asked if she could have her best friend, Lily, to stay her request was refused on the grounds that any friend of hers was bound to be of dubious moral fibre. If it hadn't been for Edward and Nettie, she would have gone mad. She and Edward grew close and enjoyed each other's company.

'I want to see the city tomorrow. Will you accompany me?' she asked him one day as they strolled through the grounds together. The Alardyce Estate included working farmland, a trout stream and a small forest. The gardens were huge and an army of gardeners worked to maintain them.

'Of course,' he replied. 'We'll have fun.' Edward cringed. 'Sorry, I don't suppose you feel up to fun at the moment.'

'Not really, but I certainly do feel up to getting away from Alardyce House for a few hours.'

'What do you want to see?'

Amy was actually looking forward to something for the first time since she'd learnt of her parents' deaths. Edinburgh was a vibrant, thrilling city, at the forefront of so many cultural and medical advances, and she couldn't wait to explore it. 'I've no idea, I'll leave that up to you but it's time I finally got back out into the world. I've been here almost two weeks and I haven't left the estate once.'

'There's plenty to see. Edinburgh's a beautiful city. There's the castle, the museums, the graveyard...'

'Graveyard. Sounds ghastly.'

'It's supposed to be haunted,' he said with a hint of mischief. He cringed again. 'I suppose you've had enough of those recently too?'

She nodded sadly and shivered.

'You're cold?'

'Yes, but it's better than being inside,' she said, pulling her black silk cape tighter around her.

He held out his arm to her, which she accepted, grateful for his warmth. It wasn't seemly for him to walk like this with her but Amy was so glad of his friendship that she didn't object.

'I know everything seems bleak right now,' he began. 'Especially in this house of strangers, but one day you'll wake up and you won't feel so bad and, you never know, you might come to like us.'

'I already like you.'

'And I like you. Things are actually interesting around here now you've arrived, but you might come to like the rest of them. Well, my father anyway.'

Once again he elicited a smile from her. 'How is it that you're not yet married, Edward?'

'I don't think it likely I'll ever marry.'

'Why on earth not? You'd be a fine catch for any woman.'

He stopped and turned to her with such seriousness it startled her.

'Have I said something wrong?' she said.

'Can I trust you to keep a secret, Amy, one that could be potentially devastating to me if it were ever to get out?'

'Of course you can.'

'The truth is that while I enjoy the company of women I do not – how can I put it? – desire them.'

'I see.'

'Are you shocked?' he said uncertainly.

'Not at all. I have friends in London who suffer the same dilemma.'

He looked relieved.

'It must be very difficult for you,' she said sympathetically.

'It's intensely frustrating. How I long to go to London where no one knows me.'

'Why don't you?'

'Money. Father would cut me off without a penny. He thinks the capital worse than Sodom and Gomorrah and as the younger son I will forever be reliant on his or Henry's charity,' he said bitterly.

'Has your father ever been to London?'

'Once or twice on business. He hated it.'

'So you're trapped here?'

'I am and I don't know how to escape.'

Amy felt dreadfully sorry for him. 'It won't always be like this. One day something will happen to change things but, I must say, it's a sad loss for womankind,' she said playfully.

'My parents know of my... tendencies, so they've pinned all their hopes on Henry, the prince.'

'Henry.' She frowned.

'What do you think of big brother?'

'He is terribly handsome but that's where his charms end. I find him proud, arrogant and a little strange.'

'He is that.'

'Which one?'

'All three.' He grinned and they both laughed. Edward's expression turned serious again. 'You should be careful around Henry.'

'Why?'

'It would be better if you were never alone with him.'

'Edward, what on earth do you mean?'

'Nothing. Sorry, I don't mean to frighten you, it's just that he's always been rather an odd sort and I've noticed how he looks at you.'

A chill ran down Amy's spine. 'I pity the poor woman he marries.'

'I believe Mother has some heiress in mind for him. He'll make a good match but a poor husband.'

She nodded in agreement.

'Forgive me for asking,' he said a little awkwardly. 'But I've heard my parents talking about you and a Mr Costigan.'

Amy stared down at her hands, which were encased in black kid gloves. 'Oh.'

'Sorry, I shouldn't have mentioned it.'

'I suppose you might as well know, everyone else does. At least if I tell you I know you've had the truth.' She took a deep breath before continuing. 'Mr Costigan was a friend of my father's thirty years my senior and I'd known him all my life. He was always kind to me and brought me little presents when he came to visit but as I reached adolescence I noticed he started to look at me differently. One day when I was fifteen we took a picnic by the river – myself, my parents and Mr Costigan and his wife. They'd never had children, consequently I was the only child there. I went off by myself for a walk in the woods, leaving them all to talk. He followed me and asked to kiss me. As I'd been raised to always be polite, I consented. It was my first ever kiss and it was very nice.

'After that, whenever he came to visit he would somehow get me alone and kiss and touch me. A few weeks later we went to stay at his house for the weekend. I noted I'd been given a room quite a distance from the rest of the guests and I admit I was a little excited by what I thought might happen. You see, I'd always had a little crush on him. He was handsome and charming as well as an athlete, so he was in excellent shape. That night he came to my room. After that things progressed rather quickly. The next night he, well, he touched me more intimately.'

'He took advantage of you,' Edward said, outraged.

'No. He always asked my consent first and he never made me do anything I didn't want to do.'

'You were so young.'

'Plenty of girls that age are married.'

'True.'

'Anyway, this went on for a few months. Whenever he came to our house or vice versa we would somehow find a way to be alone together and no one had the slightest idea. One night when he was staying at our house he came to my room and took my virginity.'

Edward's eyes widened. 'Weren't you afraid of pregnancy?'

'No. He'd suffered a serious illness as a child and was infertile, which was why his wife had never had a child.'

'He dared seduce a young girl with his wife under the same roof?' he exclaimed.

'She'd been an invalid for years so quite often he came alone. He took great care of her, but he was a vital man with needs and he thought I could fulfil them.'

'Don't make excuses for him.'

'I'm not, it's just how it was. Well, a month later he spent the night at our house again and came to my room. Unfortunately another family were also staying and when their daughter came to my room to talk she caught us together.'

'Good gracious.'

'The stupid girl was so shocked she screamed the house down and everyone came running in so fast I barely had time to throw on my gown.'

'What happened?'

'My father struck him and threw him out of the house, although it was the middle of the night and snowing outside. I never saw him again. His wife died a year later and he moved abroad.'

'Were you punished?'

'No. My parents were good people. They believed it was entirely his fault and I was just an innocent girl he'd taken advantage of. However the girl who caught us blabbed about it to everyone and my reputation was ruined. My father had been negotiating a good marriage for me but my prospective fiancé's family pulled out the moment they heard of the scandal. After that I went off the rails a bit. I knew I was damaged goods and no respectable gentleman would want me, so I got in with a disreputable set and caused my parents more heartache and worry.' Her voice cracked and she put a hand to her mouth to stifle the sobs. 'I can't bear how I treated them. I was a dreadful daughter.' Edward wrapped an arm around her and she wept into his chest. 'I miss them so much.'

'I know,' he said softly, stroking her hair as she continued to cry on his shoulder.

3

Four months after Amy's arrival, Lenora was indecent in her haste in arranging a gathering designed to introduce her to some eligible bachelors. She wanted her niece married off as soon as possible so she would be her husband's problem. However, as Amy and the whole house was supposed to be in mourning, the gathering had to be called a business meeting with Lenora inviting single men Alfred did business with, young men she deemed worthy of marrying into her family. She didn't like Amy but that didn't mean the girl couldn't be useful in enhancing their family's status with a good match.

Amy wasn't fooled, especially when she was led into the drawing room to find it filled with men who were all supposedly there for a meeting with her uncle. Food and drink were laid out, giving the room a distinctly festive atmosphere. It was a huge breach of protocol on her aunt's part but no one dared object. What Lenora wanted, Lenora got.

Amy stood at the back of the room with her mourning veil over her face, making it clear she wanted none of these strangers to approach her. But this only added a mysterious quality that intrigued rather than deterred and the guests were determined to see her face. Lenora made sure everyone present was aware of the considerable fortune Amy would inherit when she married, in accordance with her father's will. All this, combined with her novelty value and ample bosom, had every man in the room extremely interested. All she could do was stand there and tolerate being stared at, her grief and anger seething inside her. She was grateful for the veil – it disguised the tears that shone in her eyes.

Edward sidled up to her with a smile. 'My mother's matchmaking is legendary. I anticipate you'll be wed within the month.' His teasing was amiable. Edward hadn't a bad bone in his body, unlike his cold brother.

'Not if I have anything to do with it,' Amy replied. 'This is intolerable. Anyway, I'd make a terrible wife. I'm far too selfish and hedonistic.'

'I don't think you're selfish, Amy. Rather you know what you want and unfortunately it doesn't tally with what my mother and father want for you. Besides, enjoying the wilder side of life isn't a fault. I think it's rather courageous.'

'Which is exactly why I do not wish to be saddled with one of these dull lumps.' She sighed, indicating the room.

'Oh dear. Poor Mother's going to be disappointed. Arranging marriages is all she has to keep her occupied.'

He flashed a wicked smile. 'It will be very interesting to see who emerges the victor from this struggle.'

'I can tell you that now. It will be me,' she said, glaring at her aunt through the heavy black crape veil.

Edward's eyes flicked across Amy's prospective suitors. 'Pity really for there are some fine-looking specimens here tonight.'

'Who do you favour?'

'Mr Morris. Give me tall, dark and handsome every time.'

'I quite agree,' she said, more to herself than Edward, glancing at Matthew, who moved about the room refilling empty glasses. He looked very smart in his black tails, white shirt and white gloves.

Edward followed her line of sight. 'Puts all the others in the shade, doesn't he?'

'Who?' she said innocently.

'You know full well who. I'm guilty of such thoughts too. Unfortunately he's completely off limits.'

'If he was one of the men your mother had gathered here tonight then I might be reconsidering what I said earlier.'

Edward's smile was gleeful. 'My, he has had an effect on you.'

'I have eyes in my head.'

They watched Matthew sweep through the room then out of the door carrying an empty wine bottle.

'Here we are in a room full of money and titles and we're admiring the servants,' said Edward. 'We must turn our attention back to the task in hand. Mother will quiz you relentlessly about which man you favour. If you tell her you liked none of them then she will only redouble her efforts. Give her one or two names and she will be content to let nature take its course.'

'You are quite the tactician, Cousin. You would fit in well in London.'

'One day,' he wistfully replied.

'Thank you for your friendship, Edward. It's very much appreciated.'

'No, thank you, Amy. You've livened up this old place.'

'It's a pity you're not attracted to women because I think I could marry you.'

'We would be good companions yet be content to let each other do as we please.'

'That would be a most satisfactory arrangement. The respectability and security of marriage with none of the fuss. But I fear your mother would faint if we suggested such a thing.'

'Oh, I don't know. Henry's the one she's set all her hopes on and I think she would be so relieved I'd chosen a woman that she would give her consent. Then we could live in peace in our own home and hire Matthew to attend to your every need.'

'That is a thrilling prospect indeed.'

They both knew their talk was idle because his parents would never countenance it, although the arrangement would suit both Amy and Edward.

'Look at poor old Henry.' He laughed, indicating his brother standing awkwardly in a corner. 'Never was very sociable.'

'I've never met such a distant, arrogant man in my entire life.'

'Don't be too hard on him. He's had Mother telling him how wonderful he is since the day he was born. Now he thinks he's far too good for us mere mortals.'

'He's a pompous prig if you ask me. What that man needs is a strong drink and a cheap woman. Loosen him up a bit.'

'Amy, you really are the most scandalous gossip. I love it.'

At that moment Henry, sensing he was being talked about, looked over at them and his cold face flickered with irritation. Amy scowled back at him.

'Oh hell, here comes that tiresome fool Frederick Stanway.' She sighed, indicating a short, round man with a determined expression.

'I'll intercept him while you escape,' offered Edward, stepping forward to greet him while Amy melted into the crowd. Unfortunately Frederick was more determined than either of them thought and he managed to sidestep Edward and make chase.

Amy hurried out of the room, down the corridor and through a door on the right. She froze when she found Matthew alone, clearing glasses.

'I need somewhere to hide,' she told him. 'Quickly.'

'Err, yes, miss. Through here,' he said, indicating a side door.

She ran through it, pulling the door closed behind her, and found herself in her uncle's study.

Frederick entered the room a moment after Amy had hidden herself and his smile fell when he saw she wasn't there.

'Where's Miss Osbourne?' he demanded of Matthew, who was coolly loading glasses onto a tray as though nothing had happened.

'I believe she's in the drawing room, sir.'

'Funny, I thought I saw her come in here.'

'I'm afraid you're mistaken, sir.'

'Oh, right.' He sighed before leaving.

Matthew gave it a minute just to make sure he'd gone before he entered the study. 'It's quite safe now, miss.'

'Thank you for your assistance, Matthew. Tell me, is my uncle likely to come in here tonight?'

'No, miss. Lady Lenora bans him from the study when they have company.'

'In that case I shall remain here for a while.'

'You require a break, miss?'

'I do. I'm tired of being studied like a piece of meat in the market.'

'May I get you anything while you wait?'

'Scotch, please.' Her aunt, disapproving of Amy's favourite tipple, had banned her from touching it in front of company, ordering her to consume more ladylike drinks such as sherry, which she loathed.

If Matthew was surprised by her choice, he didn't show it and poured her a drink from the decanter on her uncle's desk.

'Do you drink?' she said, accepting the glass from him.

'I do, miss, but not on duty.'

She poured a second glass and held it out to him. 'I won't tell.'

'Thank you, miss,' he replied, the mischief in his eyes reflecting hers.

She was excited to be alone with him, and Amy lived for excitement. She'd had precious little since she'd moved to Alardyce House. Danger kept at bay her thoughts and feelings about the loss of her parents, which was always lurking in the background, a huge shadow over her life. As she looked at Matthew she felt the shadow briefly dispelled.

'How long have you worked here?' she said.

'Two years, miss.'

'Do you like it?'

'Sir Alfred is a most generous employer but I confess I don't wish to be a footman forever,' he replied, taking a swig of Scotch.

He didn't seem to be at all disconcerted by her questions and she admired him for it. Everything about him spoke strength and confidence.

'What would you like to be?' she pressed.

'I'm not sure yet. I'll just keep looking until I find it.'

'You live in the house?'

'Yes, miss.'

'Does your wife live with you?'

'I'm not married.'

'A sweetheart?'

'No, miss. I'm kept far too busy with my duties.'

Amy couldn't help but smile inwardly. 'What a waste.'

'I don't think I have much to offer a prospective partner,' he said rather endearingly.

'Don't sell yourself short, Matthew. You're far more interesting than any of the men out there.'

'Thank you, miss, and may I say that not one of them is worthy of you.'

Amy was emboldened by the large Scotch, the side of her that her parents had always tried to tame emerging as she smiled alluringly. 'You were very impressive ejecting Mr Fitzgerald from the house.'

'Thank you.'

Their gazes locked and excitement rushed through Amy. Finally she was starting to feel alive again.

'I must return before Aunt Lenora misses me,' she said, putting down the empty glass. 'Would you replace my veil for me, please Matthew? It's difficult to manage on my own.'

'Yes, miss,' he said, standing directly before her.

Amy's pulse raced when she felt the warmth of his body against her own, he was so close. His eyes remained fixed on hers as he gently replaced the veil. She shivered when his fingers brushed her cheek.

'Cold, miss?'

'No, not at all,' she replied, gazing up at him through the thick net of the veil.

Gently she separated herself from him and walked to the door. 'Thank you, Matthew.'

'Miss.' He bowed.

She felt guilty for smiling as she returned to the drawing room.

'Where have you been?' demanded her aunt the moment she saw her.

'For some fresh air.'

'Both Mr Morris and Mr Stanway have been asking for you.'

'And?'

'Now, listen to me, young lady. No one wanted you here, we felt obliged to take you in out of consideration for your mother's memory, so the sooner you marry and get out of this house, the better, and take that thing off your face,' she said, throwing back the veil.

Amy was so taken aback by her venom that she gaped at her, the hurt bright in her eyes before they cleared and narrowed. 'Yes, madam,' she muttered.

'That's better. Now pick one and get over there.'

Lenora watched Amy walk over to Mr Morris with a satisfied smile. Matthew, who had entered the room shortly after Amy, watched the episode with a frown.

As Amy chatted with Mr Morris she couldn't stop herself from looking in Matthew's direction. His eyes kept meeting her own and she found it difficult to keep her attention focused on the man she was supposed to be talking with.

* * *

When the interminable night was finally over and Nettie was helping Amy get ready for bed, Lenora strode into her bedroom without bothering to knock.

'Get out,' she ordered Nettie, who curtseyed and obeyed. Lenora waited until she'd gone before speaking. 'You did well tonight, Amy. Mr Morris was rather taken with you. I hear he extended an invitation for you to dine with him at his house tomorrow night?'

'You hear correctly, madam,' she replied dourly. 'Even though I'm in full mourning and I'm not supposed to pay any calls.'

'Sometimes circumstances dictate that we can't follow etiquette exactly.'

The prospect of dining with Mr Morris overwhelmed Amy. She wasn't ready for it; she was still far too raw. 'Aunt Lenora, please, I can't go out into society yet. I've just lost both my parents...'

'From what I hear you led those same parents a merry dance. You made their last days miserable with your selfish antics.'

Amy sucked in a breath and her eyes filled with tears.

'I will not allow you to do the same thing to us. Do you hear me, girl?'

A tear slid down Amy's cheek and she nodded.

'Excellent. Keep this up and we shall see you happily settled before the year is out and your mourning is over.'

Amy couldn't picture herself happily settled with Mr Morris, but she took Edward's advice and played along. 'Yes, Aunt Lenora.' She sighed. 'Now, if you will excuse me, I'm very tired.'

'Yes, of course. Goodnight, Amy,' she said in a grim, unfriendly way.

When Lenora had gone Amy finally released the tears that had been building up all evening. She took out the silver locket she wasn't permitted to wear in her mourning and opened it to reveal the portraits of her parents, which made her cry harder. They had been so good and loving and she had not appreciated them. Instead she'd indulged her hedonistic ways, dragging their good name through the mud in the process. Rather than treat her unkindly for it they'd tried so hard to understand and help her mend her ways, but she hadn't been interested. She'd put them through worry and shame and now they were gone she could never make it up to them. She had loved them so much and the pain of their loss was unbearable. Now she was an unwanted guest in this unwelcoming house.

She rested her head in her hands and wept.

* * *

Matthew was serving at breakfast the following morning. As Amy took her place at the table he set a plate of food before her, catching her eye, and they smiled at each other, which went unnoticed by everyone else.

'Thank you, Matthew.'

'You're welcome, miss.'

He returned to his place at the back of the room while Amy picked up her fork and tucked in.

'May I take the carriage this evening as I'm dining at Mr Morris's?' she said in a flat tone, indicating it was the last thing she wanted to do.

'Yes, of course,' replied her uncle.

'It's Strachan's night off,' said Lenora. 'Matthew can take you. He fills in when Strachan's away.'

Amy tried to hide her elation, unbelieving of her good luck. 'Thank you,' she replied, not daring to look in Matthew's direction in case someone noticed.

From the other end of the table Edward gave her a goofy grin.

'Aunt Lenora,' she said. 'Will you be accompanying me?'

'No. Why on earth would I?'

'Because I can't go alone.'

'Yes, you can.'

She couldn't believe what she was hearing. 'Madam, I can't be alone with a single gentleman all evening.'

'Things are much more relaxed out here in the country. You can't discover if you truly like each other with one of us in the way.'

'I would feel much more comfortable if—'

'I said no, Amy.'

'I'm not doing anything tonight, Mother,' offered Edward. 'I could go with her.'

'Has everyone suddenly become hard of hearing?' she demanded. 'I said Amy goes alone.'

'Uncle Alfred, please,' said Amy, turning to him for support. 'Surely you see I can't go alone? What about my reputation?'

'What reputation?' Lenora laughed. 'You ruined that years ago.'

Amy ignored the hideous woman's taunts. 'Uncle Alfred, I'm an unmarried woman. I must have a chaperone.'

He looked from Amy then to his wife and wilted beneath the latter's commanding gaze. 'Your aunt's right. We do things differently out here. You'll be fine.'

She stared at them both in outrage before looking to Edward, who shrugged apologetically. Henry had heard the entire exchange but remained silent.

'And you'll wear colours,' continued Lenora. 'You can't go to Mr Morris's wearing those awful drab clothes.'

For Amy this was the limit. She slammed her cutlery down on the table. 'I am mourning the death of my parents and I *will not* wear colours until the appropriate time.'

'You will do as I say.'

'I'm already breaking enough rules as it is and I will not break this one. I won't dishonour my parents' memory.'

'Do not speak to me like that,' yelled Lenora. 'Tell her, Alfred.'

'I'm sorry, but I agree with Amy. She can't wear colours yet.'

'I'm only trying to do my best to find her a husband.'

'I'm well aware of that, dear, but Amy's mother was my sister.'

Lenora went silent and pouted, knowing she couldn't argue with that.

'I'm tolerating you sending her unchaperoned because I trust your judgement, but I will not see her in colours before her year of mourning is up.' Alfred's voice rang out loud and clear but sweat popped out on his forehead and his hand holding the spoon shook slightly, belying his nervousness about standing up to his redoubtable wife.

Lenora huffed and stalked from the room.

'Thank you, Uncle Alfred,' said Amy when she'd gone.

'You're very welcome,' he replied, taking out a handkerchief and dabbing at his forehead.

Amy got the feeling he was going to pay for that rebellion.

4

Amy climbed into the carriage with a flutter of excitement as she wa
going to be alone with Matthew. However, that was scuppered whe
her uncle clambered in beside her. Only his nose and eyes were visibl
a thick scarf wrapped around his face, hat pulled down low against th
chill of the evening.

'I'm visiting Major Bridgestock tonight,' he told her. 'His house i
just down the lane from Mr Morris's.'

'I see,' she replied, trying to keep the disappointment out of he
tone.

'You can drop Amy off first then take me on,' he called t
Matthew.

'Yes, sir,' he replied.

The journey was conducted in silence, her uncle not knowing wha
to say to her without the rest of the family present. The only words h
uttered were, 'Good luck,' as the carriage came to a halt outside M
Morris's.

Matthew opened the door and offered her his hand to climb dowr
which she accepted. He ran his thumb over the top of her hand and hi
eyes caught hers.

'I'll send Matthew back after he's dropped me off,' called Alfred from inside the carriage. 'He'll wait for you and take you home.'

'Enjoy your evening, miss,' said Matthew and she gave him a playful smile.

Reluctantly she approached the front door as the carriage headed back down the drive, wishing she were still in it.

Amy rang the bell and was surprised when the door was opened not by a servant but by Mr Morris himself.

'Amy, you look enchanting. Please come in.'

Taking a deep breath, she stepped over the threshold and received her second shock of the evening. There was no maid or footman waiting to take her cloak, no butler offering drinks. It was just the two of them.

'Through here,' said Mr Morris, extending an arm towards a door on the right. She took timid steps towards it, the silence making her nervous, every part of her screaming to leave but she couldn't. If she did Lenora would make her life a living hell. All she could do was pray she got through the evening unscathed.

* * *

From the moment she set foot inside the drawing room Mr Morris was plying Amy with champagne and as soon as her glass became half empty he topped it up again. Fortunately she had a very strong tolerance for alcohol, so she was able to keep a clear head while he grew florid and his speech slurred.

At dinner – which was already laid out so there was no need for a servant – he talked only about himself and she was forced to listen, never getting the chance to respond as he droned on and on. Her thoughts kept straying to Matthew waiting for her outside. He should have returned for her by now and she hoped he wasn't getting cold.

After dinner she was more than ready to return to Alardyce House but Mr Morris insisted she share a nightcap with him.

'I'm really very tired,' she protested. 'I shouldn't be out in society so soon. I'm still in mourning.'

'Just one little drink. I'm so enjoying your company.'

'Fine,' she sighed, not wanting him to give her aunt a poor report.

He led her back into the drawing room, sat beside her on the couch and pulled her to him.

'What are you doing?' she demanded, pushing him away.

'I've done some checking up on you and I've heard some very intriguing stories. Does the name Costigan ring any bells?'

'How did you find out about that?'

'It doesn't matter. I've shown you a nice evening, treated you well. Now it's time you were nice to me.'

His mouth went to her neck while his hand attempted to push up her skirts.

Amy pushed him away and slapped his face. 'I'm leaving,' she said, getting to her feet and running from the room.

'Not yet, you're not,' he yelled, pursuing her.

He grabbed her, tearing her dress in the process, and she screamed. Lashing out, she grazed his left cheek with her fingernails, drawing blood.

He drew back his hand to strike her but the door burst open and Matthew charged in. So surprised was he by the scene before him that he paused on the threshold. Fortunately his presence was enough to make Mr Morris release Amy, who stumbled towards the door. Matthew caught her and glared furiously at Morris.

'You mention one word of this to anyone, Amy, and I'll tell everyone you led me on,' said Mr Morris, torn between anger and panic.

'I think your face will reveal your lie,' retorted Matthew.

'I do not converse with servants.'

'Miss Osbourne, would you wait in the carriage?' said Matthew, eyes not leaving Mr Morris.

Trembling, she nodded and lurched down the steps into the darkness. Matthew turned back to Mr Morris with blazing eyes, making the man recoil. He grabbed him by the scruff of the neck and threw him against the wall.

'Servant or not, I ought to beat you senseless for what you've just done,' bellowed Matthew. 'If you go anywhere near Miss Osbourne or Alardyce House again then I will come back and put you in the ground. Do you understand?'

'Yes,' he replied, cowering before him.

'Good. And just in case you think I'm bluffing, here's a little taster.'

He punched Mr Morris in the gut, and he crumpled to the floor. Matthew glared at him before turning on his heel and striding outside into the cool night air. He took in a couple of deep breaths to calm himself before opening the carriage door. 'Are you all right, miss?'

She regarded him with wide eyes, her face pale. 'Yes, I'll be fine. Thank you, Matthew.'

'You're welcome. Shall I take you home?'

'To London?'

Her tone was so childlike he smiled. 'I meant Alardyce House.'

'Oh. I suppose you better had.'

On the journey home shock started to set in and Amy started crying uncontrollably. She knocked on the side of the carriage and called to Matthew to stop.

'Could you pull over for a few minutes? I need to get myself together.'

He found a small dirt track that led off the main road and pulled onto it. Although it was pitch black the moon was full, casting some light. He jumped down from the trap, opened the carriage door and peered inside to find Amy sobbing into her hands. He held out his handkerchief to her.

'Thank you,' she said, accepting it and dabbing at her eyes.

He watched as she closed her eyes and took in a few deep breaths until the tears subsided. Feeling calmer, she turned her attention to her torn dress, which was ripped at the shoulder.

'I have a pin, miss, if it will help?' he said, producing one from his pocket.

'Please,' she replied, taking it from him. Because of the angle of the tear she couldn't manage the repair herself.

'Miss, if you will allow me?'

She hesitated before nodding. Matthew climbed into the carriage beside her, closing the door, and took the pin from her. After the fright she'd had she instinctively drew back from him.

'It's all right, miss,' he said, holding up his hands. 'You're safe with me.'

'Yes, of course. Forgive me.'

He gave her a reassuring smile before moving closer so he could attend to the repair. 'There, miss,' he said softly, stroking out the black fabric with his rough fingers. 'Not as good as new but it'll hide the damage until it can be repaired. Nettie works miracles with a needle and thread. I don't wish to pry, but are you hurt?'

'No. Just a bit bruised and shaken. I don't know how I can thank you for what you did tonight.'

'There's no need, miss.'

His kind tone undid her and she burst into tears. Instinctively he put his arm around her and she buried her face in his shoulder.

They sank back into the seat together and he held her in his arms.

'Do we have to go back yet?' she said, feeling comfortable and at peace for the first time in months with this strong, strapping Scotsman.

'Not if you don't want to, miss.'

She looked up at him. 'I feel safe with you.'

'You are, miss,' he said, his thumb tracing the line of her jaw.

He kissed her forehead, her cheek, then her lips. She allowed herself a moment to enjoy the kiss before pulling away.

'Morris was right,' she muttered. 'I am a slut.'

'No, you're not. A kiss doesn't make someone a slut.'

'You don't know what I've done,' she said so quietly he almost missed it.

'Excuse me, miss?'

'Nothing. I would like to go back to Alardyce House now.'

'As you wish.'

He climbed out of the carriage and back into the driver's seat and within ten minutes they were back at the house.

Amy sat in the carriage, gazing up at the imposing building, knowing she would face an interrogation from Lenora about her evening. She just prayed it would wait until morning. Matthew opened the door and assisted her to climb down on wobbly legs.

'Goodnight, Matthew,' she said.

'Goodnight, Amy,' he whispered as he watched her enter the house.

Amy was so pleased the family were all in bed that she could have cried again but this time with relief. Wearily she trudged upstairs to find Nettie waiting to help her undress.

'Are you all right, miss?' she said with concern.

'I'll live,' she sighed. 'Let's just say this evening didn't go as planned.'

'I'm sorry to hear that... sweet Lord,' she exclaimed when she helped Amy remove her dress.

Amy hadn't realised that her wrists were bruised where Morris had tried to restrain her, as were her upper arms where he'd grabbed her.

'He hurt you, miss.'

'He tried, but fortunately Matthew came to the rescue.'

'This is terrible, miss. The master will be furious.'

'I'm not telling him, Nettie. In fact I'm not telling anyone and you won't either.'

'But the man is an animal.'

'Yes, he is, but my position in this house is tenuous enough. If I tell my aunt and uncle about this then they'll only blame me.'

Nettie's eyes filled with sympathy.

'I need you to swear that you will keep my secret, Nettie. You're not to tell anyone, not even the other servants.'

'Yes, miss,' she replied, a little afraid of the fire in Amy's eyes.

* * *

Exhausted by her traumatic evening, Amy quickly fell into a deep sleep, which was disturbed barely an hour later by an almighty racket from downstairs.

Startled, she sat bolt upright, for a moment confused as to where she was. She paused to gauge what was happening and realised her uncle and Rush were downstairs talking loudly, so as to be heard over the screaming and crying of a woman.

Throwing the covers aside, Amy jumped up, pulled a heavy shawl around her shoulders and crept into the corridor, where the noises were even louder. She padded downstairs and into the sitting room.

Amy halted in her tracks as the horror before her pushed all concerns about Mr Morris out of her head.

'Oh my God,' she cried.

Alfred whirled round to face her. 'Amy, what are you doing here? Go back to bed.'

She hardly heard him, too absorbed by all the blood and the young woman she recognised as a housemaid lying on the couch, shaking and crying with pain. 'What happened to her?'

'She... fell,' said her uncle, avoiding her eyes.

'Fell?' She frowned. 'On what, a knife? She's been stabbed.' The front of the woman's dress was riddled with small holes, through which blood seeped. Amy's eyes widened even more when they settled on the woman's wrists. 'Someone's bitten her. Who would do this?'

'Amy, go back to bed. I order you,' exclaimed her uncle. 'Rush has called for a doctor, she's in safe hands. Ah, thank you, Matthew.'

Amy almost jumped when she realised he was standing right behind her.

'Excuse me, miss,' he said as he strode past her carrying a bowl of water and some towels. He was the essence of professionalism, not betraying the slightest sign of surprise. Neither was Rush, which told Amy this wasn't the first time they'd been confronted by this scene.

The girl's eyes were fixed on her, begging her to stay. Amy understood why, because if she'd been in the same position she wouldn't want all these men around her, she'd want a fellow woman. But they crowded around her, blocking the girl from view.

'Oh my God, what's going on?' cried a voice. Edward sped into the room, tying his robe, hair all over the place, mussed up in sleep. His jaw dropped open at the scene. 'What the devil happened to her?'

'The devil indeed,' commented Alfred, looking troubled.

'We must fetch the doctor immediately,' said Edward, putting a comforting arm around Amy.

'He's been called,' snapped back Alfred, looking uncharacteristically angry.

In all the chaos Amy still managed to spot Matthew's eyes narrow as they flicked to Edward's arm draped across her shoulders.

'What's going on here?' said Lenora, striding into the room, an elegant emerald-green shawl wrapped around her. She stiffened when she saw the bleeding girl and lifted her head, lips pursed. 'Not again,' she said, voice tight with worry.

'Again?' exclaimed Amy.

Lenora was startled to see her standing in the corner of the room with her younger son. 'Amy, go to bed. This is nothing to do with you.'

'Nothing to do with me? I live here now. It is everything to do with me.'

'Not now, Amy, please,' said Alfred, his voice so full of heartbreak she was silenced.

'Go back to bed,' said Lenora. Her cold gaze settled on Edward. 'You too.'

Knowing protest was useless, Amy allowed Edward to steer her out of the room. She looked back over her shoulder at the girl but all that was visible of her were her booted feet as Rush and Matthew tended to her wounds.

'Edward, what's going on?' she said as he ushered her upstairs. 'Please tell me.'

'My father was right, the devil,' he muttered more to himself than her.

'The devil? You're making no sense.'

'Actually I'm making perfect sense.' For the first time since she'd known him his boyish, good-looking face was troubled. 'My brother's up to his old tricks,' he whispered.

'Henry did this?' she whispered back, feeling sick. He'd warned her not to get close to Henry, but she'd imagined nothing like this.

'It's not the first time.' Edward sighed and shook his head. 'I've already said too much. Don't tell Mother or Father what I said because they'll only deny it. They refuse to believe their prince is rotten.'

'Something must be done. He can't be allowed to hurt any more girls.'

'We'll discuss it in the morning but say nothing to anyone else. If Henry knows that you know...'

'You think he might hurt me too?' she said when he trailed off.

'You're my only friend, Amy, and I'm taking no chances with your safety. Go back to bed and try and get some sleep.'

'I won't sleep now,' she said, feeling cold, which had nothing to do with the chilly night.

'Try and remember what I said – stay away from Henry.' He hesitated before adding, 'And lock your door.'

With that he retired to his own room, leaving her alone in the dark at the top of the stairs with the sound of the rain beating against the windows.

A peal of the bell announced the arrival of the doctor and Amy stayed where she was to watch from the shadows. Below, Rush went to answer the door, taking so long about it that the bell was rung a second time. When it was eventually opened a grey-haired man practically ran down the corridor and into the sitting room and she heard her uncle's voice greet him. Rush shuffled back towards the sitting room, closing the door behind him, but she could still hear the murmur of voices. The maid's cries had turned to whimpers.

'What are you doing?' said a voice.

'Dear God,' she cried, jumping for the second time that night.

To her horror Henry emerged from the shadows and, unlike the rest of the family, he was fully dressed.

'What am *I* doing?' she exclaimed. 'What are *you* doing?'

'I saw a shadow up here. I didn't know it was you.'

As her eyes adjusted to the gloom she took in his rumpled, muddied clothes and something dark on his hands, something that made her stomach turn over. 'What is that?' she said, taking a step back.

He rubbed his hands on his jacket then hid them behind his back. 'I found the maid injured in the garden. I brought her inside.'

'Then why are you up here and not downstairs with the others trying to help her?'

'I came upstairs to change.'

'So why haven't you changed?'

'Because I heard voices then I came across you.'

Amy swallowed hard. He'd overheard her and Edward talking. He *knew* that she knew. 'I... I was just going to bed,' she said, taking another two steps backwards.

He followed her, matching her step for step. 'Then go. It's dangerous for you to be wandering around up here, Amy.'

'Are you threatening me?'

'No.' He frowned.

His sinister eyes glittered in what little light there was, the rest of his face in shadow. The darkness of the corridor surrounded them, isolating them from the rest of the house, and Amy had never felt so afraid in all her life. As she continued to retreat backwards down the corridor he followed, his hard eyes not leaving hers. When he grabbed one of her arms she screamed.

'Careful,' he said. 'You almost fell.'

Looking over her shoulder Amy was startled to realise that she was standing on the very top step, the hard wooden staircase rolling away behind her. If she'd fallen she would have undoubtedly broken her neck.

The door to the sitting room opened and her uncle bustled out. 'What's going on? I heard a scream.' He peered up the stairs towards them but was unable to discern them in the gloom.

'Let go, you're hurting me,' said Amy, snatching her arm from Henry's grip as his fingers dug into her flesh.

She was very conscious of him watching her as she raced back to her room, not stopping until she was safely inside, locking the door behind her and jamming a chair under the handle for extra security. Amy grimaced and rubbed her arm, still able to feel Henry's strong fingers digging into her flesh.

5

The following morning Lenora interrogated Amy relentlessly about her evening with Mr Morris. She did her best to answer as vaguely as possible, her thoughts fuzzy as she'd got no sleep, terrified Henry would come for her in the night. Amy assured her aunt that she had a pleasant evening, disappointing Lenora when she said she hadn't been invited back.

Once the interrogation was over Amy asked her aunt, 'How's the maid?'

'What maid?'

She said it so offhandedly Amy wondered if she'd dreamt the whole thing. 'The maid who was hurt last night.'

Her stomach dropped when Lenora's face contorted with fury. 'You will not speak of that again. You saw nothing and you will say nothing about it. Do you understand?'

'Aunt Lenora,' began Amy, desperately fighting her own fear and anger, 'I understand you don't like it but I do live in this house now and I have a right to know if I'm in danger.'

'How typical of you to make it all about yourself.'

'To make what about myself?'

'You don't need to worry and I don't want to hear another word of the matter.'

Amy was unable to help herself. 'If your son's rotten then you should do something about it, not leave him free to hurt another woman.'

There was a loud crack and Amy stared at her aunt in astonishment, cradling her stinging cheek.

'You will not speak of it again,' said Lenora. 'Have I made myself clear?'

Amy didn't reply, she was too stunned. All she could do was watch Lenora stalk from the room, slamming the door shut behind her. She started to cry. She felt even more depressed than she had the previous night. It seemed life was conspiring against her, building around her a wall of pain and humiliation that she couldn't escape.

Wanting to be alone with her melancholy, she retreated to the large conservatory that overlooked the gardens. It was her favourite room in the house and where she went when she needed privacy. Best of all, the rest of the family hardly used it.

Perching on the edge of the couch, her corset maintaining her in a bolt upright position, she closed her eyes. The rain was coming down in sheets and she loved the sound of it hitting the glass.

Footsteps on the black and white tiled floor caused her eyes to fly open. She relaxed when she saw it was only Edward.

He sat beside her, concern on his face. 'Here you are. I've been looking all over for you.'

'Sorry. I just wanted to be on my own.'

'What's wrong?'

'Nothing,' she replied with a forced smile.

'Don't give me that, I can tell something's wrong.' He frowned when he saw her reddened cheek. 'Who did that to you? Henry?'

'No. Your mother.'

'Mother, why?'

'Because I asked her about what happened last night with the maid and she didn't like it when I ignored her order to forget about it.'

'I told you to say nothing to anyone but myself. What if she mentions your conversation to Henry?'

The thought hadn't occurred to her. 'Do you think she might?'

'It's possible. She'd do anything to protect her prince from the consequences of his actions. Let's pray she decides to keep it to herself.' He spotted the bruising on one of her wrists, which had darkened and deepened overnight. 'Did she do that too?'

'No. That was Mr Morris.'

'He tried to force himself on you?'

The memory made her feel sick. 'He did.'

'The dirty swine, you must tell Father.'

'No. Mr Morris has powerful connections in the city, he could make trouble for your family. Besides, your mother...' She trailed off as she didn't want to offend him.

'Would blame you,' he ended for her.

'Yes,' she sighed. 'He'd heard about Mr Costigan and thought I was there for the taking. Fortunately Matthew saved me.'

His eyebrows went up. 'Matthew?'

'He heard me screaming and charged in, which was enough to shake Mr Morris up. He won't bother me again.'

'I'm sorry, Amy.'

'Nothing seems to be going right for me at the moment,' she said, trying to hold back her tears and failing.

'Amy, are you well?' enquired a coolly polite voice.

They both looked round to see Henry standing awkwardly in the doorway, his pale face impassive as usual. Startled, she shrank back in her seat, glad Edward was there.

'She's just feeling a little under the weather,' Edward replied for her.

'May I be of any assistance?'

Amy was surprised. 'I appreciate your concern but it's just a headache.'

He gave her a stiff bow before disappearing.

'That was strange,' she said. 'Maybe he's checking up on me, trying to find out exactly what I know?'

'He's a strange man. Very strange.'

'How is the maid he hurt?'

'Paid off and packed off somewhere. She'll be all right, physically anyway.'

'Edward, please tell me, how many housemaids have ended up bleeding on the floor of this house?'

'She was the first.'

'Oh,' she replied, experiencing a sense of relief.

'But before her were one kitchen maid, two village girls and the gardener's daughter.'

'What?' she said, feeling sick.

'All injured the same way as that maid, stabbed, beaten and...'

'And what?'

He leaned forward to whisper in her ear. 'Violated.'

Amy gasped and her hands flew to her mouth.

'Remember what I said,' he continued. 'Be careful. Don't be alone with him.'

Amy kept to herself for the rest of the day, only joining the family for meals before retiring early to bed. She hadn't seen Matthew all day because it was his day off, which made her even more miserable.

* * *

The next morning after breakfast Amy was reading in the library when Matthew entered. She looked up from her book and smiled, pleased to see him.

'Excuse me, miss, but I wanted to ensure you were all right after the other night.'

'I'm completely recovered, Matthew, thank you.'

'I thought you'd like to know that I heard Mr Morris had an accident. His carriage went off the road last night and he was injured.'

She sat up straighter and cast her book aside. 'Is he badly hurt?'

'Yes. I've been informed he'll never walk again. His legs were crushed when the carriage tipped.'

'Was anyone else hurt?'

'The driver managed to jump clear when it went over, so he has only some minor cuts and bruises.'

'God forgive me for saying it, but I'm happy. This is justice.'

'I quite agree. No less than he deserves.'

'Thank you for bringing me this news, Matthew.'

She clasped his hand in what she intended to be a friendly manner, but he raised her hand to his lips and kissed it. She watched with surprise and excitement as he knelt before her and stroked her palm lightly with his fingertips before kissing it again. His kisses moved up her wrist and forearm, making her shiver with delight.

'Matthew, this isn't right,' she said weakly.

'Yes, it is,' he replied before pressing his lips to hers.

She considered pulling away but his kiss was so delicious she couldn't. Wrapping her arms around Matthew's neck, she let him press her back into the couch.

'What if someone comes in?' she said as he kissed her throat.

'All the family are out and the rest of the servants are downstairs drinking tea.'

'You planned this?'

He smiled, stroking her face. 'Forgive me, but ever since our encounter in the study I've thought only of you. I'm aware this may cost me my position but it's a sacrifice worth making.'

This was too much for Amy, who gave up any pretence of resistance. His caresses were clever and exciting and – although she was painfully aware she was being intimate with a servant – she could not separate herself from him. It wasn't the first time she'd been intimate with a man but it was the first time she'd experienced such over-whelming lust.

He was the one to break the kiss.

'What's wrong?' she said.

'Your family have been good to me and I betray their trust in the worst possible way. Please forgive me, miss, I was weak and couldn't help myself.' He got to his feet, straightening his collar. 'I trust we can keep this between ourselves?'

She sat up and smoothed down her skirts, flushed and breathless. 'Of course.'

'Thank you. You're too gracious, miss.'

He bowed stiffly and left the room, leaving her frustrated and dissatisfied.

* * *

After word spread about Mr Morris's accident, Lenora gave up on him and invited a different man to the house for dinner. Amy didn't know of the trap until she entered the dining room to find a stranger sitting at the table with her aunt and uncle. Although not handsome he was pleasant-looking, in his late thirties with a light blonde beard, thinning hair of the same colour and blue eyes.

The men got to their feet when she entered. Her uncle was the one to make the introductions.

'Mr Rowan Dreyfuss, may I present my niece, Miss Amy Osbourne.'

'Pleased to meet you, Miss Osbourne.' He smiled.

'And you, sir,' she politely replied, even though she was furious about this ambush. Lenora threw her a look that warned her to be on her best behaviour. At least Edward and Henry were absent for this fresh humiliation.

There was something about Rowan Dreyfuss that Amy took an instant liking to, even though she didn't find him physically attractive. There was a good-natured mischief in his eyes and he had an excellent sense of humour, even making one or two quips at Lenora's expense. As her aunt had absolutely no sense of humour his comments went right over her head. Amy found herself at ease in his company, endearing him to her even more.

Matthew was on duty that evening, his silent presence like a beacon to her but she resolutely refused to look his way, even though she was aware of where he was at every moment. As Rowan was in the middle of relating an amusing anecdote, Matthew leaned right over her to refill her wine glass and she inhaled sharply at his closeness, stirring those powerful feelings again.

It was the pleasantest dinner Amy had known at Alardyce and the family and their guest retired to the drawing room for drinks and conversation, where Edward and Henry joined them after returning from dining in town. As usual Edward was lively and talkative but Henry remained quiet and remote, preferring to watch proceedings rather than participate. Amy caught him looking her way more than once, an enigmatic expression on his face, and she got the impression he was trying to intimidate her, so she did her best to ignore him. Her mind kept straying back to the injured maid.

Before he left, Rowan invited Amy to dine with him the following week. She swallowed hard as she recalled what had happened at Mr Morris's but she thought Rowan was not like that.

Matthew watched Amy and Rowan walk out of the room together, talking animatedly. She walked right by him without a glance. The rest of the family followed them out and Matthew and Gerard started to clear away the plates and glasses.

'Lucky bastard, eh?' said Gerard, referring to Rowan. 'Rich and surrounded by beautiful women. Life's not fair.'

'No, it's not,' sighed Matthew.

* * *

Matthew and Amy remained aloof with one another, although the
kept accidentally bumping into each other around the house. H
would bow to her, say, 'Excuse me, miss,' and swiftly move on while sh
in turn said nothing. Therefore, she was horrified to discover that o
the night of her dinner with Rowan, which again Lenora had refused t
chaperone her to, it was the driver's night off and Matthew was t
take her.

The journey to Rowan's house was concluded in stony silenc
which was eventually broken by Amy when Matthew opened the doc
to assist her out.

'Have I offended you?' she said.

'No, miss.'

'I do hope we can still be friends, despite what happened betwee
us?'

'Yes, miss. We can,' he said, managing to raise a small smile.

'I'm glad.' She smiled back.

He assisted her out of the carriage and she looked up at the hous
dread settling in the pit of her stomach.

'I'll be right here if you need me, miss,' he said, divining he
thoughts.

Her smile was grateful. 'Thank you.'

Matthew watched her enter the house, his expression black.

* * *

Amy's evening with Rowan was much more successful than he
evening with Mr Morris, but no matter how hard she tried she ju
wasn't attracted to him. Perhaps she would have been if she could g
Matthew out of her head, but he stubbornly refused to go.

Rowan was the perfect gentleman the entire evening and the onl
time he touched her was to give her a tender kiss on the cheek as sh
left, which unfortunately Matthew witnessed. He said he would call o
her at Alardyce House in a few days as he had to go away on business.

Matthew's eyes were black in the moonlight and full of anger. Amy received the full force of them as he assisted her back into the carriage. When he slammed the door shut behind her she regarded him questioningly through the window but he ignored her and took his place in the driver's seat. Once again they travelled in silence until they approached the track where they had stopped on the journey home from Mr Morris's. He veered off the road and came to a halt. After tying up the horses he tore open the carriage door.

'What are you doing?' she demanded. 'Take me home at once.'

Ignoring her order, he climbed in beside her and shut the door.

'How dare you? I order you to take me home.'

'No, Amy,' he replied, daring to use her first name.

'You're disobeying me?'

'Yes.'

He leaned in to kiss her but she put her hands to his chest and pushed him back. 'You forget yourself, Matthew. Remember your place.'

'My place is right here, beside you.'

When he kissed her, Amy's resolve disintegrated and she welcomed him into her arms. Now they had complete privacy they let go of their reservations and fell back into the seat together.

'You're so lovely,' he breathed into her neck. 'I want to see your hair down,' he said, removing the pins. Gently he ran his fingers through the coil, splaying it out around her. She released a sigh of pleasure as he continued to slide the fingers of one hand through her chestnut locks while the other disappeared under her skirts and started to creep up her thigh.

'You have the softest skin,' he said, voice a whisper, his fingertips gentle, caressing.

Amy released a whimper when his fingers moved even higher, so close to the very centre of her.

'You're shaking, Amy,' he said as she trembled beneath him.

She gazed into his black eyes, feeling the heat rise in her body,

Matthew creating feelings inside her she'd never experienced before, not even with Mr Costigan.

Finally he touched her *there* and she moaned.

Matthew closed his eyes and shivered. 'So deliciously wet. Would you like me to do that again?'

'Yes,' she breathed, every muscle in her body going rigid with anticipation.

He pressed slightly harder, making her arch her spine.

'Again, please,' she groaned.

He kept his touch light and gentle as her body grew hotter. Amy ground her mouth against his, sliding her hands beneath his clothes to touch the bare skin of his back, enjoying how strong and firm his body was. Needing to see him, she unfastened his jacket and tugged at his shirt, which he pulled off over his head before his fingers returned to their clever work.

'You're beautiful too,' she said, stroking his smooth, hard stomach. She sucked in a breath of air as his fingers started to play harder, faster. 'Matthew,' she moaned before pulling his face back down to hers and kissing him, welcoming his tongue in her mouth. 'What are you doing?' she demanded when he ceased his delightful ministrations.

'There's something I've been aching to do with you,' he said before kneeling on the floor of the carriage and raising her skirts.

'We can't do that,' she said, pushing herself up on her elbows.

'Just lie back. I had something else in mind.'

Amy couldn't have stopped now even if she'd wanted to and she noted how the tables had turned and he was master here. She lay back and watched as he dipped his head between her legs, crying out as a fire started inside her.

'Matthew, oh my God.' She'd never felt anything like it before.

She enjoyed watching him pleasure her, the sight of his strong arms wrapped around her thighs and the gleam of his back muscles in the moonlight. She climaxed forcefully and loudly but there was no one around to hear.

As they caught their breath they looked at each other and laughed.

'I can't believe we did that,' she panted.

After adjusting their clothing they cuddled up on the seat.

'Do you regret it?' he said.

'Not at all. You?'

'No.' He smiled, kissing the tip of her nose. 'So, are you seeing Rowan again?'

He tried to ask the question casually but they could both hear the tension in his voice.

'He's coming to Alardyce in a few days.'

Matthew's expression darkened. 'Did you enjoy kissing him?'

'No. I'm not attracted to him.'

'Then why are you seeing him?'

'Because it keeps my aunt off my back.' Amy was suddenly aware how their relationship had altered and it made her uncomfortable. 'You do realise that whatever this is between us can't go anywhere?'

'I do but it doesn't mean I like watching you courting other men.'

She imagined how she would feel if the situation were reversed and she realised she would be jealous too. 'We'd better get back before they send out a search party,' she said.

'I suppose. Just remember what we did tonight when you next visit Mr Dreyfuss.' He spat the man's name out.

Her gaze turned cold. 'And you need to remember that I am not yours to command and I never will be.'

To her surprise he smiled. 'You've a fire inside you. I like that.'

He jumped out of the carriage, leaving her slightly confused but feeling better than she had in months.

They completed the journey to Alardyce House, Amy just managing to finish pinning up her hair as they rolled to a halt outside the front door. It wasn't as neat a job as Nettie would have done but it would do.

As Matthew helped her down from the carriage he took her hand.

'Goodnight, Amy.'

'Goodnight, Matthew.' She smiled, gently squeezing his hand before walking inside.

* * *

Amy's stomach fluttered with excitement as she went down to breakfast the following morning. Breakfast was self-service but Matthew was still there, standing tall and proud as though nothing had happened. With barely a glance in his direction she filled her plate and took her seat at the table. Unfortunately only her aunt was there for company and demanded a breakdown of the evening. Amy smiled inwardly at what she didn't tell her. What she and Matthew had got up to felt like a pleasing revenge against this hideous woman.

Lenora was very pleased Rowan was going to call at the house and was almost amiable to Amy that morning. By the time Amy had been relinquished from the inquisition Matthew had disappeared from the dining room, so she strolled towards the library, intending to enjoy a couple of hours' quiet reading.

'Amy,' called a voice.

She glanced to her left and saw Matthew standing in the doorway of the billiard room. Grinning, he grabbed her hand and pulled her inside, closing the door behind them.

'I've not been able to stop thinking about you,' he said, holding her close.

'Me neither,' she replied, kissing him.

They spent a few minutes in each other's arms. No one saw them emerge from the billiard room flushed and breathless.

* * *

After that Amy and Matthew saw each other whenever they could – snatched moments in shadowy corners or empty rooms. Once or twice they got carried away and their heavy petting almost turned into more but they always forced themselves to stop. Amy was so afraid of pregnancy she didn't dare, no matter how much she wanted to. Falling pregnant to a man of equal rank would have been bad enough but things could always be arranged. Carrying the child of a servant would be an entirely different matter. However, with each encounter she found herself weakening. Her passion for Matthew was all-consuming but what bothered her about their relationship most was that he was undoubtedly the dominant one. She had always considered herself to be a strong woman and let no man rule her, even her father had struggled to control her, but there was something in Matthew's nature that made her pliable. She could see what was happening and was powerless to stop it. More than once she resolved to end the affair at their next meeting but when that time came and she broached the subject he would soothe her worries with sweet words and physical pleasure, both of which he was very adept at.

The prime example of the strange dynamic of their relationship was the evening of Rowan's visit to Alardyce a week later than he had originally promised. Lenora was almost driven to distraction with worry, even going as far as to blame Amy for not being alluring enough. Finally Rowan sent a message that he had been unexpectedly detained on some urgent business and would call on them the following evening if it was convenient.

As usual Rowan was relaxed and amiable and greeted them warmly. Amy was genuinely pleased to see him and enjoyed an evening in his company but she knew her feelings for him would never go beyond friendship.

Matthew was in attendance that evening, straight and stern as usual, his expression unreadable, but she didn't think anything was amiss. He understood the situation.

Rowan parted from Amy with a gentle squeeze of the hand and a promise to call on her again very soon. Her uncle and aunt were very pleased with her conduct and she retired to her room in an optimistic mood.

Just as she was about to climb into bed there was a knock at th
door.

'Come in,' she called, assuming it was Nettie.

She got the shock of her life when Matthew sauntered in.

'You can't come in here,' she exclaimed, clutching her nightgow
about herself. 'Leave at once.'

He smiled as he closed the door and advanced on her. 'The rest c
the family are asleep in the other wing and all the servants are in bee
There's no one up here but you and me.'

Although she was excited to be alone with him, she was unnerve
by this intrusion into her bedroom.

'You've gone too far, Matthew. You shouldn't be in here.'

'No one will know,' he said with a disarming smile. He snaked hi
arms around her waist and pulled her to him. 'I only want a goodnigh
kiss.'

'All right. One kiss, then you leave. Understood?'

'Yes, miss,' he said, bowing so formally she laughed.

He smiled sweetly and she felt a surge of affection for him. He too
her face in his hands and kissed her.

'There, one kiss,' he said.

But the damage had been done and she wanted more. 'Perhaps ju
another.'

'All right, one more.'

He kissed her again and she moaned into his mouth, losing herse
in him. Unfastening his waistcoat and shirt, she pushed them off hi
shoulders, needing to touch his bare skin. She was so caught up in he
physical desires that she let him push her back onto the bed, his hand
sliding up her gown. Using his knees to part her legs, he opened hi
trousers. He positioned himself over her and pushed against her bu
didn't enter her.

'No, Matthew,' she said weakly. 'We can't.'

'I know but it doesn't stop me wanting to.'

She nodded, shaking with lust. Her body was crying out for his bu she was afraid. Amy had only ever had full intercourse once before with Mr Costigan when she was fifteen but she knew he had been sterile.

'Let me inside you once,' he said. 'Just so we know what it feels like.'

She couldn't see the harm in that and she trusted him to keep his word. 'All right.'

Amy bit her lip as he slid inside her, causing a bit of discomfort. Her fingers dug into his back but he moved again and it eased. As he continued to move the pain was replaced by the most delectable sensation she had ever experienced.

'Do you want me to stop?' he said.

'Not yet,' she moaned, gripping his buttocks and pushing him further into her, making him growl. He moved harder and faster, his lips moving over her face and neck.

Without warning he stopped and sat up.

Amy pushed herself up on her elbows and frowned. 'What are you doing now?'

With a playful grin he took her hand and pulled her off the bed and onto the floor. He sat upright and gently pulled her down to him.

'Sit on top of me,' he breathed.

She sat astride him while he guided himself inside her and she groaned, her head falling back. Gently taking her hips, he showed her how to move. Amy was an eager pupil. He yanked off her nightgown, almost ripping it in his haste, so for the first time she was completely naked before him, and he stared at her in fascination as she moved on top of him. She was beautiful, all soft, smooth curves and he enjoyed exploring her large breasts, which were finally free of the restrictive corset. All too soon the sensations built to an unbearable degree and Amy speeded up her movements.

'Amy, you must move off me,' he gasped.

But she was too overcome with pleasure to pay any heed.

'Amy, please,' he implored.

His words were cut off as he climaxed. She felt his hands tighten on her thighs as he flooded inside her, which caused the most intense feeling to swell inside her until it claimed her entire body. At that moment she cared for nothing except this incredible pleasure pulsating through her. With a gasp she flopped forward onto him and he cradled her in his arms, shaking with exertion.

Gently he laid her back on the thick rug and stretched out beside her, stroking the curve of her hip.

'I was intending to pull out of you so I wouldn't get you pregnant,' he explained.

The enormity of what she'd just done struck her. 'I didn't realise,' she exclaimed, sitting up. 'What have I done?'

'It's all right,' he said pulling her back down to him. 'There's a woman in the village who makes special preparations to prevent such things. I will call on her in the morning.'

'You want me to take some potion made by the local eccentric?' she said doubtfully.

'Trust me, it works.'

'And how would you know?'

'My sister has gone to her before.'

'I see,' she said slowly.

'You really should have moved when I said.' He frowned.

Amy looked back at him steadily. He had told her to do something, she hadn't done it and he didn't like it. She got up to pull on her night-gown. 'It's late. You should leave.'

'All right,' he sighed, climbing to his feet and dressing.

She sat down before the mirror to brush out her hair. He stood behind her and rested his hands on her shoulders, his eyes catching hers in the glass, black in the lamplight.

'Are you seeing Rowan again?'

'Yes,' she replied.

His grip on her shoulders tightened. 'I don't like it.'

'Well, I'm sorry, but it's nothing to do with you.'

'I know. I'm only a servant but I care about you, Amy.'

His words were gentle but his grip on her shoulders was still firm.

Sighing, she put down the brush and turned to face him. He knelt before her so they were on the same level. 'I care about you too, Matthew, but there's no future for us. We're too different. If our affair were ever discovered the consequences don't bear thinking about for us both.'

He took her face in his hands and kissed her. 'Then we must make sure no one finds out.'

6

Amy didn't see Matthew again until the next afternoon. He found her in the dining room before lunch.

'I have it,' he said, handing her a small vial containing a viscous yellow liquid. 'Three drops twice a day for four days.'

She eyed it mistrustfully. 'Are you sure it will work?'

'Yes.'

'All right, I'll try,' she said, sliding the vial into her dress pocket.

He kissed her just as the door opened and they sprang apart when the brothers entered. Coolly Matthew turned to the sideboard, poured her a glass of claret and handed it to her. She accepted it then calmly walked over to Edward, and no one noticed a thing.

Torrential rain kept the family indoors for the next two days and Amy found the black oppression of Alardyce House bore down on her. She didn't think it was the house itself that made her feel this way, rather it was the occupants. Despite her doing her best to please her aunt with Rowan, Lenora was still offhand with her, making it even clearer that the sooner she was out of the house, the better. Her uncle shied away from her, spending more time in his study, Henry haunted the house like a ghost, popping out at her at unexpected moments, and Matthew was kept busy with his duties. If it hadn't been for Edward and Nettie she would have been very lonely indeed.

Despite the terrible weather, Amy thought she'd go out of her mind if she didn't get some fresh air, so she sneaked outside and rushed across the sodden lawn towards the small maze at the edge of the garden. Its high hedges offered protection from the rain and it was paved, so she could walk without her boots sinking into the ground.

Hidden away in the maze, Amy felt entirely alone and – for the first time since she'd arrived at Alardyce House – at peace. Without the pressure of the family she could just be herself, the person the Alardyces didn't want her to be. It felt nice.

The sky was black, pregnant with chilly drizzle. It soaked into her black dress and cloak, the black silk gloves doing nothing to protect her hands from the cold and her fingertips started to go numb. Her bonnet became heavy with water but she refused to return to the house; it was the freest she'd felt in weeks. Besides, she had to find her way out of the maze before she could leave.

The lush green hedges were high and dense, blocking out everything but the sound of the rain. As Amy journeyed towards the centre of the maze the hairs on the back of her neck prickled. Sensing she wasn't alone, she whipped round, expecting to see someone standing behind her, but there was no one.

Amy picked up the pace, wanting to reach the centre of the maze. She had to find the middle before she could find her way out because she had no idea which direction to go in.

Her boots made a sharp staccato as they banged off the path, making her cringe, the noise seeming to draw attention to her, even though logic told her she was alone.

Then she heard it. A second footfall.

Amy stopped in her tracks, holding her breath to listen. There it was

again, another footfall just after she'd stopped. She spun round
attempting to locate the source of the noise, but she could see nothing
except the high green hedges, like prison walls. Anything could happen
to her in here and no one would know. Images of the injured maid and of
Henry – white-faced and eerily quiet with blood on his hands – returned
and she started to run, the tight corset restricting her breathing, but she
didn't dare stop when she heard the footsteps pursuing her, matching
her step for step. The blood thundered in her head, almost drowning out
the muffled rain and those taunting, terrifying footsteps. She just knew
was Henry. He was here. Finally he'd come to silence her.

Every time she turned a corner she hoped to find the exit an
safety but each turn brought her more high, thick hedges, gloom an
the interminable pitter-patter of rain.

She was forced to pause for breath. The panic conspired with the
restrictive corset to cut off her air supply and she leaned back against
hedge, chest aching, a stitch in her side. Over her ragged breaths she
realised the footsteps had stopped too. Amy spun one way then the
other, expecting Henry to come striding around the corner but h
didn't. She appeared to be alone.

Not completely alone. Someone else was breathing. At first she
thought it was herself, until she realised the sound was deeper, hoarse
Male. It was coming from behind her but the only thing there was
hedge.

Tentatively she peeled back a branch and peered through the gap
A dark eye blinked back at her. With a cry she let the branch snap back
into place and she ran, the exhaustion forgotten in her fear.

The footsteps started up again, running parallel with her on the
other side of the hedge.

Amy made a turn and found herself at the very centre of the maze
the fountain a big grey fish with water spurting from its mouth. The
statue was monstrous, its thick mouth and bulging eyes repulsive
momentarily distracting her from what was following.

The footsteps drew her back to the present and Henry appeared before her, emerging from behind a hedge.

'Hello, Amy. What are you doing out here in this weather?' he said while slowly advancing on her.

'I... I wanted a walk,' she said, backing away, maintaining the distance between them.

'You'll catch your death out here,' he said, dark eyes glimmering, making his pale skin look ashen.

His words snatched her breath from her throat. 'I'll return to the house now,' she said, turning back the way she'd come.

'That's the wrong way,' he called. 'You'll end up stuck in this maze forever if you go that way.'

'I'll retrace my steps, I'll be fine.'

In two large strides he was beside her, towering over her. She stared up at him, her heart thumping so hard she thought she might faint. Beneath her dress the corset felt as if it was pushing the air out of her body and her legs trembled from the exercise.

'I'll escort you back,' he said, reaching for her arm.

She darted out of reach, clutching her cloak around her as though it could protect her. 'I don't need you to escort me back, I can find my own way. Anyway, what are you doing out here?'

'I saw you come in and thought you might struggle to get out. The maze might not be that big but you are completely isolated in here,' he said, his hand closing over her arm.

'Let me go,' she said, shrugging him off.

His dark brows knitted together over those intense eyes. 'What's wrong?'

'I want you to leave me alone,' she cried.

'Have I done something to offend you?'

'Your very presence offends me. I don't want you anywhere near me.'

'Why?' he exclaimed, displaying a rare bout of emotion.

'You know why. Just stay away from me,' she said with a courage she didn't feel.

'You need to come with me, Amy. Now,' he said, countenance darkening.

'I'm going nowhere with you,' she retorted before turning on her heel and running from him.

Looking back over her shoulder, she saw he was pursuing her but he wasn't running – his stride was so long he didn't need to. Amy – hampered by her clothing and already exhausted – faltered, her head swimming.

'I've got you,' he said, lunging for her when she slipped and went down, saving her from hitting the path.

'Get off me,' she screamed, lashing out, hitting his arms and shoulders but to no avail. He refused to relinquish her.

'Please calm down,' he said in his usual dead monotone.

Easily he lifted her. Amy could only stare into his cold, handsome face in appalled horror, his arms tightening around her like an unbreakable metal band. His strength terrified her.

'Amy,' called a voice.

Her hopes soared. 'Edward,' she called back, practically screaming his name.

He appeared from behind a bush, eyes widening at the sight of his brother's arms locked around her. 'Let Amy go,' he said, as though talking down a wild creature.

'Go away, Edward.' Henry glowered, his grip tightening, making Amy wince.

'Look at her, she's scared.'

Henry looked down into Amy's pale face, not a flicker of emotion on his. Amy found herself released and she dashed towards Edward. He caught her and hurried her away, keeping her close.

'Thank you,' she whispered, voice shaking as he led her towards the exit. She looked back over her shoulder and saw Henry following, his eyes hard and determined. 'He's following us.'

'I know, it's all right. He won't hurt you with me here,' replied Edward, casting a backward glance at his brother.

Amy staggered out of the maze, clinging onto Edward, constantly looking behind her. Henry maintained his steady pace, eyes riveted to her.

Finally they emerged and Amy felt liberated. If she'd been physically capable she'd have run across the lawn back to the house but only Edward was keeping her upright.

As they entered the house Henry stormed past them, throwing them both a glower before heading straight upstairs, long black coat sweeping out behind him.

The last thing Amy wanted was for Matthew to see her soaked through, hair springing out from its coil, clothes sodden, but he just happened to appear in the hallway at that moment.

'Are you quite well, miss?' he said in his professional tone.

'Miss Osbourne got lost in the maze,' replied Edward, pulling off his coat and shaking off the rain.

As Amy removed her bonnet she caught Matthew's suspicious gaze.

'Please bring Miss Osbourne a brandy in the library, Matthew,' said Edward. 'She needs to warm up by the fire. Tell Nettie to lay out some dry clothes for her.'

'Yes, sir,' he replied, giving him a small bow before walking away.

Amy watched him go longingly. She would have loved to feel his warm, comforting arms around her.

Edward seated her in the armchair by the fire and wrapped a shawl around her. Matthew fetched her brandy then quietly retreated from the room without so much as a concerned glance, which only pained her more.

'Did Henry hurt you?' said Edward.

'No, you came along just in time.' She took a big swig of brandy, feeling her nerves steady. 'Thank you.'

'I saw him follow you in. I would have got there sooner but I'm embarrassed to say I got lost. Ever since I was little I've been losing my way in that thing.'

'But Henry hasn't,' she said flatly.

'Oh no, not him. Mind like a steel trap, that one.'

'Would he have hurt me?'

'I really don't know. He's a queer fish and I've never been able to fathom him, but I wouldn't be doing my duty to you if I said no. You saw what he did to that maid.'

She took another swig of brandy. 'The look in his eyes...' She broke off with a shudder.

'You must be careful in this house, Amy. Henry knows Mother's displeased with you, which makes you vulnerable.'

'Surely he wouldn't get away with doing to me what he did to that girl? I'm not some timid little maid who can be easily silenced.'

'I'm well aware of that but what the prince wants, the prince gets. Mother and Father will always clean up his mess. He's the future of this estate.'

'You should be the future, not that monster.' She shivered, taking another sip of the fortifying brandy. Warmth was flooding back into her body, right down to her toes and the tips of her icy fingers. Steam rose from her clothes as they dried before the fire. If she'd been out there much longer she would have caught her death – perhaps in more ways than one. The memory of Henry's hard, resolute eyes caused her to drain the glass.

'I'm afraid that's never going to happen,' continued Edward. 'They want someone who's capable of providing an heir to the estate. I'll forever be the disappointing younger son.'

'I don't think you're a disappointment. You're the best person in this house.'

He gave her hand a squeeze. 'That means a lot. No one's ever paid me a compliment before.'

'I don't know why. You're so kind. I'm so glad you're here.'

'Cousins together, eh?' He smiled.

She kissed his cheek. 'Yes.' With that she got to her feet. 'I need to change before I permanently ruin this armchair,' she said, grimacing at the large wet patch she'd left behind. 'Do you think it'll be safe now?'

'Yes, I think so.'

Wearily Amy tramped to the door. Her legs were weak, her body exhausted and she was light-headed, whether from the fright she'd had or the alcohol she wasn't sure, but she staggered from the room.

'My God, look at the state of you, girl,' exclaimed a high-pitched voice.

Amy closed her eyes and sighed. Lenora was the last thing she needed. 'I got lost in the maze,' she said weakly.

'You've been in the maze in this weather? Sometimes I think you're quite mad.'

'I needed some fresh air.'

'There are better ways to get some fresh air than tramping about muddy gardens in the rain. Don't expect me to tend to you if you fall ill.'

Amy was sent hurtling back into the past again when she was eleven and she'd fallen ill with a fever. She'd been seriously ill for three days and her mother hadn't left her side. Amy could almost feel her cool hand pressing against her fevered brow, hear her gentle voice soothing her, smell her lavender scent.

Involuntary tears sprang to her eyes. She wanted her mother.

Lenora pushed her nose into the air and stalked past her. Amy knew her aunt wouldn't care if she did fall ill and die, in fact she'd probably prefer it. Her money would be absorbed into the Alardyce Estate if she died before she was married. Henry could murder her and Lenora would erase any trace of her older son's crime, as she'd been doing for him his entire life.

Amy staggered to the stairs, her head spinning so fast she had to grip onto the polished rail to prevent herself from falling.

At the top of the stairs her stomach lurched and she thought she was going to vomit all over the expensive carpet. She staggered down

the hall towards her room, sliding along the wall to keep herse[l]
upright.

'Edward,' she tried to call but what she had hoped would be a lou[d]
cry for help came out as a whisper.

Yards from her bedroom door her strength finally gave out and sh[e]
dropped to her knees. Her bedroom door opened and Nettie's hea[d]
popped out.

'Miss,' she cried, rushing to her side. 'Can you rise?' she said, takin[g]
hold of her arm.

Nettie tried to get her back on her feet but Amy fell onto her bac[k]
already insensible.

'I'll get help, miss,' said Nettie.

Nettie disappeared from Amy's line of sight and she listened to th[e]
girl's footsteps pounding down the corridor as she called for assistanc[e]

Amy lacked the strength to do anything except lie there, starin[g]
down the dark, lonely corridor, half hoping help arrived quickly, ha[lf]
hoping it didn't. The forlorn, injured part of herself wanted to die an[d]
be reunited with her parents. Her fingertips found the locke[t]
containing their images.

Approaching footsteps brought her back to the present but he[r]
blurred vision meant all she could make out was a tall black figure.

'Edward?' she said hopefully.

The figure didn't respond.

She almost said Matthew's name, until the part of her that was sti[ll]
lucid stopped her.

The figure knelt beside her and peered at her curiously.

'Henry,' she whispered.

Amy tried to roll out of his reach but her body wouldn't respon[d]
She was helpless to escape as he scooped her up and carried her int[o]
her bedroom.

'No,' she mumbled, trying to wriggle free.

He laid her back on the bed then loomed over her, fiddling with th[e] buttons on the front of her dress, his cold, dead eyes suddenly blazing with an emotion that frightened her.

'No,' she repeated, trying to raise her hands to bat him away but still her body refused to respond.

She almost cried with relief when she heard running footsteps and Nettie's voice saying, 'She was here a moment ago, honestly.'

Henry froze and his eyes locked with Amy's. That scary, burning part of him retreated and the coldness swept into his eyes once more. He backed away from the bed just as Matthew, Nettie and Edward burst into the room.

'What have you done to her?' Edward yelled.

'I've done nothing,' replied Henry. 'I found her lying on the floor outside the door, so I brought her in here. I was just about to call for assistance.'

'You devil, Henry. Why are her buttons unfastened?'

'She seemed to be struggling for air. I was merely attempting to help her breathe.'

Edward pushed past him to her side.

'Edward,' she said, reaching out for his hand, feeling safe once more.

'Nettie, call the doctor,' he called over his shoulder before turning his attention back to Amy. 'What happened?'

'Don't know,' she mumbled, tongue thick in her mouth.

'She appears to be in the grip of a fever,' commented Matthew from the back of the room.

Amy wanted him to come to her, to feel his gentle lips on her burning forehead, but he was remaining remote, professional, which was the sensible thing even if it still hurt.

'You'll be all right, Amy. You'll see,' said Edward, his voice fading as she drifted into unconsciousness. The last things she saw were Henry's dark, emotionless eyes.

7

When Amy woke she immediately noticed that the rain had stopped. Every part of her ached, her head thumped and her throat felt as if it were filled with sand. She tried to move, desperate for water, but she couldn't raise her arm.

Her head lolled to one side and she saw she was alone. Her wet clothes had been removed and she was in her nightgown. How long had she been here like this? Hours? Days?

'Hello?' she tried to call but it came out as a weak gasp. She spied the glass of water on the bedside table and the ache in her throat turned into an unbearable agony as the cool, clear liquid remained enticingly out of reach.

The door opened and Nettie scurried in. 'Miss.' She beamed. 'You're awake.'

'How long?' she murmured.

'Two full days. We've all been so worried.'

'Wa...water.'

'Course, miss,' she said, picking up the glass and putting it to Amy's lips.

Greedily she gulped down the cool liquid before sinking back into the pillows.

'You've had a fever, miss, but it's broken now. I'll let everyone know you're awake. They'll be so relieved.'

'I doubt it,' she mumbled but Nettie had already gone.

Amy drifted on the verge of sleep, the thud of footsteps entering her room rousing her again. Lenora peered over her, complete indifference in her eyes.

'So you're feeling better?' she said flatly.

'Not really,' rasped Amy, wincing at the fire in her throat.

Without waiting for her mistress to give her the word, Nettie stepped up and assisted Amy to take another sip of water.

'Thank you,' she said, settling back into the pillows.

Edward dashed into the room and his face lit up. 'Amy, you're awake.' He rushed to her side and took her hand.

'Don't touch her, Edward,' said Lenora. 'What if she's infectious?'

'The doctor said she's not. It was her exposure to the cold weather that made her ill.'

'It did?' said Amy. She'd gone out walking plenty of times in inclement weather and had never fallen ill like that. Her constitution had always been more robust. This was because she was rarely allowed out any more, as well as all the recent stress. Anger swelled inside her. This was her aunt and uncle's fault.

'He also said you could have a bit of weak broth when you woke, miss,' said Nettie. 'I'll get Cook to prepare some.'

'You'll be up and about in no time,' encouraged Edward. 'Just get plenty of rest.'

Already her eyes were closing, the short conversation exhausting her.

'She'll live,' said Lenora. 'What a shame.'

* * *

The next time Amy woke it was dark and she was once again alone. Slight strength had returned to her limbs, enabling her to turn onto her side and reach for the glass with a shaking hand. The glass was as heavy as stone but she managed to raise it to her lips and take a sip. As she returned it to the table she lost her grip and it smashed on the floor. There was the sound of footsteps approaching. Amy's gaze remained riveted to the door as it was slowly pushed open to reveal Matthew.

'Thank God,' she breathed.

'Pleased to see me?' He smiled, perching on the edge of her bed.

'Relieved actually. I was afraid you were Henry.'

'I don't blame you for being afraid. How are you feeling?'

'You shouldn't be here. Someone might come in. How long have I been asleep?'

'About nine hours.'

He was maintaining a professional tone again, indicating something was wrong. 'Have I offended you?'

He sighed and took her hand. 'I think we should end our relationship.'

'Have I done something wrong?'

His expression softened. 'No, but my feelings for you are growing, and I can't sit back and watch Lady Alardyce marry you off.'

'I understand,' she replied, disappointed.

'I do hope we can still be friends?'

'Of course we can.'

'Good.' Tenderly he kissed her hand before releasing it, making Amy think their relationship had meant something to him. However, while their affair excited her it also weighed heavily on her shoulders and it would be good to have that weight taken off.

'I'll clean up this mess. I don't want you stepping on it,' he said, kneeling on the floor to collect the shattered shards of glass.

'Thank you.' She flopped back into the pillows, and her exhausted mind picked up on something he'd said. 'Matthew?'

'Yes, miss?' he said, the equilibrium between them restored.

'What did you mean when you said I should be afraid of Master Henry?'

'Because you should. You're an attractive woman, miss, and Master Henry likes attractive women, too much.'

'Please stop being cryptic, I haven't the stamina for it.'

'Very well.' He collected the final shard, dropped it into the pile in his hand then got to his feet. 'I believe he has certain proclivities.'

'Such as?' she prompted when he went silent again.

'There have been whispers in the village that he enjoys hurting girls, like what was done to the maid.' His black eyes darkened, like a storm gathering. 'You saw what was done to her.'

Amy swallowed hard. 'It angers you?'

'Of course it does. He's a coward who hides behind his powerful parents but what can be done to stop him?'

'Someone has to or he's just going to go on and on.'

'Don't worry yourself about that now, miss. It's more important you rest and get well again.'

He stooped to plant one last kiss on her forehead. 'Get better soon, miss. This house is an empty shell without you.'

With that he turned and left. Amy closed her eyes and sank back into the soft pillows, trying to ignore the pang of regret. She was going to miss him.

* * *

Amy was woken by a presence in the room. She jumped awake, every tingling nerve snapping her back into full consciousness.

She lay still, trying to gauge who it was but all she could hear was their steady breathing, the slight creak of the floorboard that told her they were standing just a couple of feet to her right, between her and the door. Fear paralysed her. She could do nothing but lie there and

wait for them to make their move. She didn't need sight to tell her wh
was there. She already knew it was Henry.

Any moment she expected to feel a weight bearing down on her,
knife in her stomach, but the minutes ticked by and nothing happened
nothing but that low, steady breathing and that oppressive, smotherin
presence.

What was he doing?

The tension built up until she could stand it no longer.

'Who's there?' she said.

'Henry,' a voice whispered back.

'Why?' she said, trying to control the rising panic. It was the dead c
night. No one was coming to her rescue this time.

'I'm watching over you. Go back to sleep,' he replied, voice lifeless.

'You... you don't need to do that,' she stammered, unable to hid
the terror any longer. 'Please leave.' She shifted slightly on the bed, th
only physical movement she was capable of, and her powerlessnes
brought tears to her eyes.

'I can't do that.'

'No. Go,' she said, heartened when her voice came out slightl
stronger.

The floorboards creaked and suddenly he was by her side, starin
down at her, face devoid of all emotion, except his eyes that were s
bright they positively sparkled in the darkness.

'I can't,' was all he said.

When he sat on the edge of the bed and his hand reached out fc
her, all she could do was push her head back into the pillows, helples
to escape. It was almost a relief when he swept back a few sweat
tendrils of hair from her forehead. She went still, as though he were
wild animal and the slightest movement might launch him into
frenzy.

'Why are you so afraid of me?' he said, those unnerving eyes borin
into her.

Amy knew this was a test. If he had any doubt she was aware of hi dirty little secret then confirming it for him would surely be a death sentence. So she remained silent.

'Why?' he repeated more vehemently.

'Stop touching me,' she whispered.

He removed his hand from her hair but remained where he was, still unnervingly calm.

'Go away, Henry.'

But he wasn't listening. He had his ear cocked to something outside, in the corridor.

'What is it?' she said.

He waved a hand, indicating for her to be quiet. She watched with consternation as he rose and walked to the door, opening it to peer out into the darkened corridor.

While his attention was drawn she attempted to get to her feet. Using every ounce of her strength she pushed herself up to a sitting position and rolled to the edge of the bed. Glancing at the door, she saw Henry was half in her room and half out in the corridor. Now was her chance.

Carefully she planted her feet on the ground and hauled herself upright. Her head swam and her vision blurred and the next thing she knew she was in a heap on the floor, unable to get up. She found herself staring at a pair of shoes and glanced up to see Henry looking down at her severely.

'Amy, what are you doing?'

Trying to get away from you, she muttered inwardly but she was too weak to say it out loud.

With a sigh he picked her up, her weight nothing to him, and he laid her back on the bed.

'There, all comfortable again,' he said, tucking her in.

Amy stared back at him fearfully as something in his eyes changed again and his hand moved up to her face. He ran his fingers across her cheek then into her hair and she was forced to lie there as his fingers tightened in her hair and his eyes started to blaze again.

Amy thought she was hallucinating when Nettie entered the room.

'Master Henry,' she exclaimed.

Henry jumped, retracting his hand, and turned to face her, looking angry. 'What the devil are you doing here at this time of night?'

'That's just what I was about to say, sir,' she retorted.

'I've come to watch over Miss Osbourne as you were neglecting your post,' he blustered.

'I'm back now, sir, so you can go to bed. It's very late and you must be tired.'

Amy was impressed with this small, placid girl standing up to this monster.

'You're going to stay with her for the rest of the night?' he said darkly.

Nettie nodded. 'I won't leave her side, sir.'

Henry looked to Amy, who held her breath as his eyes narrowed and his jaw tensed. 'Very well,' he eventually said. With that he swept from the room, slamming the door shut behind him.

'Are you all right, miss?' said Nettie, rushing to Amy's side. 'Did he hurt you?'

'No. You came just in time.'

'I'm sorry, I never should have left you but I had one last duty to attend to downstairs. Master Edward asked me to watch over you. He was afraid Henry would do something like this.'

'Please stay with me tonight.'

'Of course, miss. I'll sleep in the next room but I'll leave the connecting door open and I'll lock this one,' she said, slamming the bolt home on the door Henry had left through.

'Thank you, Nettie, although I'm not sure I'll get any more sleep tonight.'

＊ ＊ ＊

Amy was delighted to be visited by Rowan the following morning. He brought her a beautiful bunch of wildflowers tied with a big red ribbon. His kindness dispelled the cold dread that had settled in her heart since Henry's nocturnal visit. Nettie hung around the door acting as a discreet chaperone, pretending to dust the small table beside it.

Rowan enquired after Amy's health then chatted about mundane things such as the weather and harmless local gossip but he seemed distracted, as though something was weighing him down, and he left after only half an hour. Amy soon forgot about Rowan's worries when Edward came to see her and her own problems resurfaced. Edward listened to her tale of the previous night with mounting horror.

'My God, he's a devil,' he said.

'He was frightening.'

'You're fortunate he did nothing more than touch your hair.'

'What does he want with me? Why won't he leave me alone?'

'He won't leave you alone because you're a young, attractive woman. I shudder to think what he wants from you but I have the feeling he's restraining himself because you're family. You're not some little maid who can be easily hushed up.'

'What can I do, Edward?' she said, hating herself for giving way to tears.

He sat beside her on the bed and slid a comforting arm around her shoulders. 'I'll keep watch tonight. He won't get near you again.'

'You can't stay in my room. I don't want to damage your good name.'

'What do I care about that? This is far more important. I'll stay awake all night if I have to.'

'It's very sweet of you to offer but Nettie can stay with me. At least there's a bolt on my door. That should keep him out.'

'I know the prince well,' he said bitterly. 'If he wants something he lets nothing stand in his way.'

Amy shuddered.

8

Locking her door at night did indeed keep Henry at bay, although Amy heard his footsteps outside her door more than once.

On the bright side, three days later she was strong enough to finally leave her bed. She was still weak but determined to get out of her bedroom, so Nettie assisted her downstairs to the conservatory and settled her into a heap of cushions with a cup of tea and some bread and butter, which she insisted would build her up. The grey clouds had finally cleared and the sun shone through the glass onto her face. Unable to concentrate on her book, Amy cast it aside and fell asleep, the sun's magnified rays dispelling the chill.

'I trust you're feeling well, miss?' said a voice.

Amy sighed inwardly. She hadn't seen Matthew in days and she wanted to ensure everything was harmonious between them. She forced her eyes open. God, he was handsome. Why did he have to be a servant? He had more grace and dignity than most supposedly great men she knew.

'Much better, thank you, Matthew.'

'I'm very glad about that, miss, because I feel I should warn you, there's been a terrible incident.'

She pushed herself upright. 'What is it?'

Before he could elaborate, Lenora strode in. 'Ah, you've found her, Matthew. Why didn't you call me?'

'Please, what's happened?' said Amy.

Lenora looked to Matthew. 'Leave us.'

He bowed before striding from the room. Amy did her best to keep her longing eyes off him as he left.

'It's Rowan,' began Lenora once he'd gone. 'No one had seen him for a couple of days and he'd dismissed his servants. Concerns for his welfare became so great that a group of men along with the village constable broke down his door. They found him hanging from a beam in the attic. He'd taken his own life.'

'My God,' said Amy, hand flying to her mouth. 'Why on earth would he do such a thing?'

'I've no idea.' Lenora regarded her with her head cocked to one side. 'You said he seemed distracted the last time you met?'

'He was,' she said, still trying to catch her thoughts. 'As though he had a lot on his mind.'

'Did he hint at what that might have been?'

'No, he didn't. Poor Rowan.'

'You must be pleased.'

'Pleased? Why on earth would I be pleased?'

'You're off the hook. You can't marry a dead man. Mr Morris doesn't want your company again either, not that we want him in the family now – there's no room for cripples. Over for two. Maybe your charms aren't all you think they are?'

Amy huffed out an impatient breath. 'Aunt Lenora, both my parents have recently died and I'm recovering from a serious illness. The last thing on my mind is marriage.'

'Well, get it on your mind because I want you out.'

'Why? What have I done that so offends you?' retorted Amy, too tired to get angry.

'Your mere presence offends me,' hissed Lenora, grinding her teet
together. 'You're just like your mother.'

'So that's what this is really about. I remind you of my mother an
you never could stand her.'

'You're just like her, thinking you're so superior to everyone else.'

'You couldn't stand her because she was more beautiful than you
kinder and more loved by everyone, including your own husband.'

Lenora's green eyes flared and she drew back her hand.

'Excuse me, madam,' said a voice.

Lenora hastily lowered her hand. 'Yes, Matthew?'

'Lady Kennedy is waiting for you in your sitting room.'

'I'd forgotten she was coming.' Lenora's cold gaze snapped back o
Amy. 'This conversation is not over.'

'Now I understand where Henry gets it from.'

Lenora's green eyes were like knives. 'What are you talking about?'

'You know exactly what I mean.' Amy's lethargy meant she didn
care what this monstrous woman thought of her.

Lenora released an angry snort before flouncing from the room
skirts rustling.

After she'd disappeared Matthew shut the door and took the sea
beside Amy, seemingly forgetting the renewed formality betwee
them.

'I hope you're not too upset about Rowan?' he said.

'I feel awful. I had no idea he was so depressed. I should have don
more to discover what was bothering him.'

'Don't blame yourself. Not even his closest family knew there wa
anything wrong.' He handed her his handkerchief.

'Thank you,' she replied, accepting it and dabbing at her eye
'You've had a lucky escape. Every man I get involved with suffer
misfortune.'

'You're a risk worth taking.'

He gave her hand a gentle squeeze before getting up and exiting th
room, leaving her puzzled.

* * *

Amy's recovery was slow but steady and soon she was able to walk through the gardens unaided, although she never strayed far, in case Henry decided to follow. Ever since his unwanted nocturnal visit he'd maintained a distance from her. If she did run into him around the house he'd just give her a small bow, before moving on. Edward said he'd warned him off by threatening to expose him if he ever scared her like that again and so far it seemed to be working.

Amy's legs suddenly went weak and she had to concentrate on keeping her steps slow and steady. The doctor had repeatedly warned her that she needed to rest but Amy ignored his advice. She'd been resting for days and all it seemed to do was sap her strength. She'd seen so many women simply waste away for lack of fresh air and exercise and she was damned if she was going to be one of them.

The sky darkened and rain started to spot her clothes. Not wanting to get sick again, she took shelter in the neglected summer house, which was a misleading name for the dark, squat building that occupied a depressing corner of the garden. Dead leaves were scattered all over the floor, curled in on themselves with age. Cobwebs were strung up around the windows. At least it was dry.

'What the...?' she began when the door burst open.

Matthew stood framed in the doorway, clothes saturated with water, rain dripping from his dark hair and running down his face. Despite his dishevelled appearance it was his eyes that were the most remarkable – black as pitch and bright with hunger. They locked on her and refused to let go.

Amy's blood surged. She still wanted him. Some nights when she was alone in bed she positively ached for him. So when he strode towards her and ground his mouth against hers she took a moment to enjoy it before tearing herself away.

'Amy?' he said, reaching out for her.

Her mouth opened and closed but she didn't reply, she couldn't.

They stared at each other from opposite sides of the room.

Amy started to get angry; he had no right to pursue her like this. 'I did not give you permission to come in here,' she yelled, furious.

Her objections were cut off when he grabbed her and kissed her. He shoved her back against the wall and pushed up her skirts while she yanked open his trousers. There was a small part of her that warned her against this folly but she wanted him so badly she ignored the cautioning voice, caring only for pleasure as she welcomed him inside her. He was rougher than usual, as he repeatedly banged her back against the cold stone wall of the summer house, her corset protecting her from the worst of it.

Within seconds the pleasure hit and she buried her face in his shoulder, welcoming the feel of him flooding inside her, of his hands gripping her bare thighs and the growl rumbling in his throat.

When they both relaxed he kissed her and pressed his forehead to hers. 'I'm sorry, Amy. I tried to keep away but I can't.'

'Don't be sorry. I've missed you,' she sighed with satisfaction.

* * *

Amy and Matthew resumed their affair with more passion and intensity than ever. They found it difficult to stay away from each other, taking ever greater risks for their liaisons.

There was a lull in the pressure from Lenora for Amy to find a husband, out of respect for Rowan's memory. Everyone knew he'd favoured Amy and for her to be courted by another man so soon after his death would have been unseemly. As long as Amy behaved herself no one really bothered with her, except Edward of course, so she was left with a lot of time on her hands and if it hadn't been for her affair with Matthew she would have gone mad with boredom.

The family attended Rowan's funeral, along with the whole village, and the church was packed to the rafters. The inquest into his death took a few weeks but the reason for his suicide was discovered. Rowan had massive debts and some of his investments had failed, consequently his wealth had dwindled to practically nothing. He'd been in dire straits and Amy was wounded for it seemed he had only been interested in her for her wealth.

* * *

Days later the family were taking a drink in the drawing room together after dinner while Henry expostulated some ridiculous theories on why Lord Beaconsfield's Conservative government had just suffered a crushing defeat in parliament at the hands of the Liberals.

'What nonsense,' interjected Amy.

They all gaped at her.

'It was the outrageous tax increases and loss of trade that lost them the election.'

'Amy, how dare you—?' began Lenora but Henry spoke over her.

'What do you know of politics?' he said, fixing her with those intense dark eyes of his.

Amy tilted back her head, refusing to be cowed. 'I read the papers, therefore I know just as much as you do.'

Lenora and Alfred gasped but Henry wore the faintest hint of a smile.

'Disraeli's a great man,' said Henry. 'He built houses for the poor, improved public health with—'

'With water to housing and refuse collection. He also abolished using young children as chimney sweeps, the Congress of Berlin, yes, I know,' she interrupted. 'I don't deny he did many good things but he's also an imperialist. All that nonsense about making Victoria Empress of India,' she said with a dismissive wave of the hand. 'She only wanted the title because she was jealous of her Russian and German cousins. What right has any British person to such a thing? It's ridiculous.'

'You consider the British Empire ridiculous?' he exclaimed.

'Yes, I do. It's boastful pride and we can't possibly hold it forever. One day it will crumble and fall.'

So heated was their debate that Henry leapt to his feet and bellowed, 'This is treasonous.'

She jumped up and yelled right back, 'If it's treasonous to consider the oppression of entire peoples in their own countries wrong then, yes, I am treasonous.'

He stared at her in surprise before shouting back and Amy was amazed because she hadn't thought him possessed of such passion. Alfred and Lenora hastily placed themselves between the pair.

'Enough,' roared Alfred over their yelling.

They both went silent, glaring fiercely at one another.

'In all my life I have never seen such unladylike behaviour,' said Lenora.

'I assume you're talking to your son,' snarled Amy, her temper still raging.

Henry's mouth fell open at her nerve while Edward stifled a laugh.

'How dare you argue with a man who is much more informed on these matters than you are?' continued Lenora. 'You really must learn your place.'

'He is not informed, in fact he's one of the most ignorant men I have ever met. Don't you see, Aunt, he's a philistine?'

It was evident Lenora had no idea what the word meant, which only compounded her wrath. 'Apologise to Henry at once.'

'I most certainly will not.'

'Henry was at fault too,' said Edward reasonably. 'He was shouting as well.'

Lenora turned her anger on him. 'I might have known you'd take her side.'

'Apologise to Henry,' insisted Lenora again.

Amy refused to reply and folded her arms determinedly across her chest.

Lenora turned to her husband. 'You see how she is, Alfred? She's impossible.' She turned back to face Amy, eyes burning. 'We give you a home, comforts, food and you repay us with insults and bad manners.'

'I appreciate everything you've done for me but that does not change the fact that he is frighteningly ignorant,' she said, jabbing a digit at Henry.

'That's it. I've had it with you, young lady. Go to your room.'

'Go to my room? I am not a child.'

'You could have fooled me. Now get out of my sight before I do something I regret.'

Furious and humiliated, Amy stomped upstairs to her room, sweeping past Matthew – who had witnessed the whole affair – with barely a glance.

Feeling utterly wretched, she flung herself on her bed but she refused to weep. She would not let Henry or Lenora make her cry.

That night when everyone was in bed, Amy sneaked out of her room clutching a small box and scurried down the back stairs to the servants' hall. At the bottom she paused to make sure it was deserted before moving to the figure asleep on the camp bed outside the plate room. She climbed on top of him, startling him awake.

'Amy?' said Matthew. 'What are you doing here?'

'I overheard Mrs Adams telling Rush it was your birthday, so I got you a present.'

'Really?' he said, delighted, pushing himself up on his elbows.

She handed him the box and he opened it and smiled.

'Do you like it?' she said.

'Yes, very much,' he replied, holding the gold-plated pocket watch up to the light. 'Thank you, Amy. No one's ever given me anything so nice before.'

'You're welcome.' She smiled, kissing him. 'I'm your present too. Want to unwrap me now?'

'Here?'

'Why not? Everyone's asleep.'

With a laugh he pulled her down to him, the small camp be
creaking beneath them.

* * *

Obstinately Amy refused to apologise to Henry, despite urging from
her aunt that went on for several days. Even Henry grew tired of it an
told them it did not matter, but, unbeknownst to Amy, he'd deduce
she was up to something and resolved to discover what it was. He ha
noticed that she disappeared for short intervals and he suspected a lia
son. He tried to take note of where everyone was when this happene
but there were so many servants scattered about the place that the tas
was impossible.

In desperation he waited until she had gone for a walk in th
garden and decided to search her room. He found it unlocked an
performed a thorough search, but the only suspicious thing he foun
was a small vial containing yellow liquid. He held it up to the ligh
attempting to discern what it was.

At every meal he watched Amy closely in an attempt to detect an
covert glances or secret communications but there were none.

He finally got his chance when Amy declared one Sunday mornin
that she was too unwell to go to church. Henry left with the rest of th
family as normal then returned to Alardyce ten minutes later, als
claiming illness.

Henry hurried back just in time to spy her enter the summe
house. He waited a few minutes to see if anyone followed her insid
and when they didn't he realised whoever she was meeting mus
already be there.

He crept through the bushes and approached the building from th
side. Peering through a window, he was stunned to see Amy with he
skirts pushed up, sitting astride a man. He saw the man's hands grip

ping her naked thighs as she moved on top of him but Henry couldn't see his face because Amy's body blocked his view. Her dress had been pulled down and the tops of her breasts were visible bursting from their corset. Henry's breath came out in ragged gasps and he felt himself harden as he watched. It was the pleasure on Amy's face that excited him the most and how he wished it were him making her feel like that. He was hypnotised, before recalling himself and he ducked down out of sight, feeling like a dirty voyeur. He was shaking from shock and lust. He heard Amy's distinctive giggle and peeked through the window just in time to see her get to her feet and pull down her skirts. Frustratingly the man remained in shadow as Amy kissed the figure and left first.

Being careful to keep out of sight, Henry peeked around the corner of the summer house and watched her return to the conservatory. He waited for the man to emerge and when he didn't, only then did he recall there was a rear exit to the summer house. Moving to the other side of the building, he was just in time to see a flash of the black and yellow livery enter the servants' hall. Amy was degrading herself with a footman.

Henry skirted the side of the house and entered by the front door where he was greeted by Rush, who took his hat and coat.

'Tell me, Rush, how many footmen are on duty today?'

'All three, sir.'

'Inform me the moment my father returns. I need to speak to him urgently.'

9

Amy was back in the conservatory, her mind only half on her embroidery as she relived her latest encounter with Matthew. She was interrupted by a polite cough from Rush.

'His Lordship requests your presence in the study, miss.'

Puzzled, Amy put aside her embroidery and headed to her uncle's study. When the door opened and she saw Henry and Lenora's grim faces she knew something was wrong. As she stepped inside and saw all three footmen lined up her heart sank. She'd been found out.

'What's going on?' she said, keeping her voice even.

'I've just been given some extremely disturbing information,' her uncle began gravely. He cleared his throat before continuing, as though embarrassed by what he had to say. 'Not an hour ago you were seen in a very compromising position with one of these men,' he said, indicating the footmen. Two of them looked surprised while Matthew continued to stare stoically at the opposite wall.

'I deny it utterly,' she replied. 'I've been in the conservatory the whole morning. Who dares slander me in this way?'

Lenora stepped forward, a smirk contorting her face. 'Don't bother to deny it. Henry saw you.'

Henry's sheepish look enraged her. Deciding attack was the best form of defence, she launched into him.

'Why would you make up such a filthy story?'

'Don't you dare call my son a liar, you dirty slut,' bawled Lenora. 'You repay our generosity by sleeping with one of the servants. In all my time I have never heard of such base behaviour.'

She was screaming in Amy's face, lips drawn back over her gums.

'Denial is useless, Amy,' said her uncle. 'We know Henry would not make up such a story. The only question is, which one?' he said, pointing at the three men.

Amy remained stubbornly silent.

'If you refuse to tell me,' he continued, 'I will dismiss all three this instant.'

Amy wavered. She knew they had families to support, and they wouldn't get employment in another house after being sacked.

'Well, we're waiting,' said her uncle impatiently.

She sighed and looked up at the ceiling, trying to think of a way out of this mess.

'It was me,' said Matthew. 'Don't blame them,' he added, nodding at his colleagues. 'They know nothing of this.'

'You have my apologies,' Alfred told the two innocent men. 'Your jobs are safe. Return to your duties and say nothing of this to anyone.'

They scurried from the room, their relief evident.

'You should leave too, Henry.'

His face fell but, realising his father wouldn't back down, Henry obeyed.

Alfred turned his attention back to Matthew. 'You admit to having an intimate affair with my niece?'

Matthew glanced at Amy before replying. 'Yes, sir.'

He was so cool and collected, Alfred appeared the most disturbed by the interview.

'How long has this been going on?'

Matthew again glanced at Amy, who just nodded resignedly.

'About five months, sir, on and off.'

'Five months?' screeched Lenora. 'So this started not long after she arrived?'

'Yes, madam.'

Lenora glowered at Amy so ferociously that she thought she might strike her.

'Who initiated it?' she demanded.

'I take full responsibility,' said Matthew. 'I pursued Miss Osbourne until she gave in to me.'

'Nonsense,' snapped Lenora.

'Matthew's trying to protect me,' said Amy, casting him a tender look. 'I'm equally guilty if not more because of my position.'

'It doesn't matter who started what,' blustered Alfred. 'The fact is that it has happened. Does anyone other than us know? Amy, have you told any of your friends?'

'How can I? I haven't been allowed to contact them since I arrived.' She frowned.

'Matthew, have you told anyone?'

'No, sir, however, all the servants probably know by now as you informed my colleagues of the purpose of this interview.'

'You fool, Alfred,' said Lenora.

'Don't fret, they can be easily hushed. Now here's what's going to happen. Matthew, you are dismissed. You will pack your things and get out of this house immediately. I will pay you until the end of the day. You will not get a reference.'

'Yes, sir,' he sighed, as though bored by the whole thing.

'If you return I will have you thrown off the estate.'

Matthew ignored him, his eyes locked on Amy. He strode up to her, took her face in his hands and kissed her. Amy returned the kiss, knowing it would be the last time she ever saw him.

When Alfred tried to prise them apart, Matthew rounded on him with such blistering fury in his eyes that he recoiled.

Matthew turned back to Amy and his expression softened. 'Good-bye, Amy.'

'Goodbye, Matthew,' she said sadly.

Straight-backed and proud, he left the room. When he'd gone Lenora marched straight up to Amy and slapped her across the face.

'You whore,' she spat, shaking with anger. 'You revolting, filthy whore.'

Amy stared back at her, cradling her stinging cheek.

'Have you any idea of the damage you've done? If anyone was to find out about this our whole family would be disgraced. Did you once think of your cousins? Their chances at making a good match would be ruined. We'll be fortunate to find a cheap merchant willing to marry you.'

'Your father was a merchant, wasn't he?' retorted Amy, reminding her aunt of her inferior birth.

'Now let's all calm down,' said Alfred reasonably. 'Only we know what has gone on and the servants will remain silent if they want to keep their positions.'

'Servants always gossip,' said Lenora.

'As long as it remains downstairs gossip and not upstairs, I don't care.'

'Aren't you forgetting someone?' said Lenora.

'Who?'

'Matthew. It's perfect blackmail material.'

Alfred thought furiously. 'We'll put it about that he's been sacked for stealing and if he does start making trouble everyone will think it's just sour grapes.'

'But how will he live?' said Amy, genuinely concerned.

'You should have thought about that before you started carrying on.' He sighed and pinched the bridge of his nose. 'Now, young lady, you will go up to your room and remain there until we've decided what to do with you.'

'Yes, sir,' she quietly replied and made a hasty exit, rushing upstairs

to her room, trembling violently. When the shaking and involuntar
tears eventually subsided she lay back on her bed and thought throug
her position.

Amy realised her own actions had put her even more at her aunt
mercy. Before, she had been in a position to demand a decent marriag
Now she would have to be grateful for anything she put her way.

She chastised herself for being so stupid and all this for a man sh
didn't even love.

Nettie found Amy still lying on her bed an hour later. She place
the lunch tray beside her and smiled sympathetically. 'Are you all righ
miss?'

'I take it you've heard?' she said without taking her eyes off th
ceiling.

'Yes, miss,' Nettie replied awkwardly. 'We all have.'

'How humiliating.'

'Please don't punish yourself, miss. Matthew can be very charming
'Has he left?'

'Yes, miss. He was escorted off the estate by the groundskeepe
Before he left he asked me to tell you he's sorry.'

'Yes, well, so am I. Where will he go?'

'I don't know. He'll have to go out of the area if he hopes to secur
another position.'

'What about his mother and sister?'

The maid frowned. 'He has no family, miss.'

'But he told me...' She trailed off.

Amy simply didn't have the energy to think through this ne
mystery. Instead she dragged herself up off the bed, pulled open
drawer in her bedside table, took out some coins and dropped ther
into Nettie's hand. 'I want you to tell me if you overhear anything c
interest about my aunt's future plans for me.'

'Yes, miss.' She curtseyed.

As an afterthought Amy added, 'Who attends to Henry?'

'Johnson does, miss.'

'See what you can discover from Johnson about his master. Any unusual habits, that sort of thing.'

Nettie's eyes filled with mischief. 'Johnson fancies me. He'll tell me anything I want to know.'

'Excellent. Thank you, Nettie.'

After she'd gone Amy went into the drawer to retrieve the vial. In all the fuss she'd forgotten to take her dose after her encounter with Matthew. She recalled it with fondness and sadness. Never again would she feel his touch.

Her hand went into the top right corner of the drawer but she found nothing.

Frantically she tipped the contents out onto the bed and sorted through them in panic but the vial was gone. Breathing hard, she rang the bell and Nettie appeared a minute later.

'Miss, what's happened?' she said, indicating the mess on the bed.

'In this drawer there was a vial containing a yellow liquid. Have you seen it?'

'No, miss. You told me not to go in there and I haven't, I swear.'

Amy closed her eyes and took a deep breath to calm her nerves. She knew Nettie wouldn't take the vial. Why would she? Amy's eyes flew open. 'Henry.' It was too much of a coincidence that her affair with Matthew was discovered on the same day the vial disappeared. He'd been snooping in her room.

'Excuse me, miss?' enquired a baffled Nettie.

'It doesn't matter. I need you to do something important for me, Nettie. I need you to go to Magda Magrath's and pick me something up.'

'Magda's?' she exclaimed. 'But she's a witch.'

'No, she's not. She's a very intelligent woman who ignorant men are afraid of and try to damage her reputation with ridiculous superstition. She is no more dangerous than Dr Woodrow and a lot cleverer. Don't fear her.'

Nettie swallowed hard and nodded.

'Tell her you've come on my behalf and you require another vial. She will know what you mean.'

'Won't I get into trouble, miss?'

'No, it's nothing illegal. I just have a condition that requires medicine to prevent me from getting sick.'

'All right, miss,' she said determinedly, pleased by her mistress's faith in her.

* * *

Amy hardly slept that night, fearing for her future. Her breakfast was brought up to her by Nettie, who informed her that she had the afternoon off and would go straight to Mrs Magrath's as soon as she had completed her chores.

After breakfast she was summoned back to her uncle's study. Although her aunt was present she was relieved to see that Henry was not.

'Amy,' began her uncle. 'Your aunt and I have been up all night discussing your future. We've decided that you shall remain in this house and marry as quickly as possible. It's vital we see you safely wed in case any of this sorry tale leaks out into society.'

Amy nodded, knowing she would have to go along with whatever they doled out to her. 'Very well,' she sighed resignedly.

'We've already selected a husband for you.'

'Who?'

The door opened and Henry entered. 'Sorry I'm late,' he said, taking up a position by the fireplace.

'Who?' repeated Amy, ignoring his entrance. Her uncle's eyes flicked to his eldest son and horrible realisation dawned. 'No, please, not him.'

'What's wrong with Henry?' snapped Lenora. 'He's a fine catch for any woman, much more than *you* deserve. You should be grateful.'

'Grateful? He hates me. We'll make each other's lives a misery.'

'On the contrary, Amy,' said Henry in a soft tone she had never heard him use before. 'You've clearly lost your way. I will help you find it again.' He stepped forward and tried to take her hand but she snatched it away, wondering what sort of sick game he was playing.

'I won't do it. My father left instructions that I was free to choose my own husband.'

Lenora opened her mouth to bellow at her but Alfred got in there first.

'Think about it, Amy. If your affair with Matthew ever got out, you would be ruined. Again. Even if you were married your husband could divorce you, taking all of your fortune with him.'

Her anger fizzled out as she realised he was speaking perfect sense.

'We were happy to let you choose your own husband. You've brought this on yourself,' he ended rather sadly.

Amy knew she was defeated. She'd enjoyed a few snatched moments of happiness with a man she'd genuinely liked and this was the price she had to pay. A lifetime with a dangerous man she despised.

'I see this is the only way,' said Amy, crushed. 'When we marry then Henry will get my fortune and when he inherits this estate he will be one of the richest men in the country.'

Lenora smirked while Henry looked back at her steadily. Only Alfred had the grace to appear embarrassed.

'I'll leave you to make all the arrangements,' she said. 'I have only one condition.'

'You're in no position to demand conditions,' said Lenora.

Amy ignored her. 'The wedding will not take place until I am out of mourning.'

'Amy's right,' said Alfred. 'If we break convention everyone will wonder why. Henry and Amy will marry in seven months when she's out of mourning and no sooner.'

Amy gave him a curt nod before skulking back to her room where Edward came to see her.

She took one look at the concern on his face and burst into tears. He took her in his arms and she sobbed into his chest.

'Oh, Edward, I've made such a mess of things. Now your parents are forcing me to marry Henry.'

'I know. Mother just informed me.'

'I can't marry him. He'll make my life a living hell and enjoy himself while he does it.'

'Don't panic yet. I've come up with a plan.'

'Plan?' she said hopefully.

'I'll tell my parents I will marry you instead.'

'You would do that for me?'

'It's not an entirely selfless act. I do it for myself too.'

She nodded, recalling the conversation they'd once had. 'Do you think they'll say yes?'

'I've no idea but it's certainly worth a try. I know Mother had her eye on some baronet's daughter for Henry. If I marry you he would be free to wed her.'

'Thank you,' she said, hugging him again.

'Let's hope she says yes, then we can both be free.'

She smiled and nodded.

'So, Matthew, eh?' he said, wiggling his eyebrows suggestively. 'Why didn't you tell me? Didn't you trust me?'

'Of course I trust you but I didn't want to get you into trouble.'

'All right, you're forgiven.' His eyes filled with mischief, making her smile again. 'Was he everything he promised to be?'

'Oh, yes, and more.'

'Come on, do tell.'

So she did. It was nice having someone to confide in.

* * *

Nettie didn't come to Amy's room until late in the evening and the look on her face told her everything she needed to know.

'You didn't get it, did you?'

'I'm sorry, miss, I tried, really I did. I went to Mrs Magrath's cottage and said what you told me to say. She said she knew what I was referring to but she couldn't help me.'

'Why not?' Amy said, sick with apprehension.

'Because she didn't have any left and it takes two weeks to brew a fresh batch, by which time it would be too late. Those were her exact words.'

Amy groaned, feeling faint.

'I'm so sorry, miss,' repeated the girl, on the verge of tears. She held out the coins Amy had given her but she shook her head.

'No, you keep them. You did your best. That's all I can ask.'

When Nettie had gone Amy's legs buckled and she had to cling onto the bedpost for support. Without that vial she could end up pregnant. God forbid. She would have to see Mrs Magrath personally. Perhaps there was something else she could do?

10

It was another two long, excruciating days before Amy was allowed t
leave the house. In the meantime Edward put his proposal to h
parents but Henry remained adamant he wanted to marry Amy. Th
brothers quarrelled and Edward struck his sibling. Henry retaliate
and their father had to prise them apart. As usual the prince got h
way and Edward was punished by being confined to his room for tw
days. As Lenora blamed Amy for the entire episode she was ordere
not to leave her room either.

When Amy finally began the short walk to Magda Magrath
cottage she knew in her heart it was a fool's errand. If she was going t
get pregnant it surely would have happened by now – it had bee
almost a week since Matthew left. However she had to try, no matte
how slim the chance.

Magda was a very tall, thin woman with a face that would hav
once been beautiful but was now heavily lined. Her hair was wild an
pure white and her fingernails impossibly long. In sharp contrast sh
spoke with a cultured, urbane voice and lived in an immaculately ke
cottage on the periphery of the village.

She smiled when she opened the door.

'I've been expecting you. Come in, dear.'

Amy was seated in the cosy parlour and offered tea and biscuits, which she declined as she was sick with nerves and worry.

'I know what you've come for,' began Magda before Amy had said a word. 'And I can only tell you what I told your maid – I've run out of my supply. I'm brewing more but it takes two weeks to ferment.'

'Surely you keep a back-up supply?'

'Normally I do but a client recently bought up everything I had.'

Amy's suspicions were aroused. 'Was this customer a man?'

'I operate a strict code of confidentiality.'

'Then let me guess. This client was a twenty-year-old man of above average height with dark hair and a smug face and he lives at Alardyce.'

'I can't say for sure. One of the servants was sent on his master's behalf and he didn't specify who sent him.'

'The dirty sneak,' she seethed. 'He's trying to trap me.'

'A word of caution, Miss Osbourne. It seems you have a redoubtable enemy.'

'My uncle and aunt want me to marry Henry. In fact they're forcing me into it.'

Magda indicated Amy's hands. 'May I?'

'May you what?'

'I have certain powers. I can tell you what the future holds.'

'I'm not sure I want to know.'

'I may have good news for you.'

Amy thought she could use some of that, so she gave her reluctant consent.

Magda grasped Amy's hands with her own. Amy gasped as Magda's hands grew warmer, heat seeming to pulsate out of her. She tried to retract her hands but Magda held her firm.

'I see much violence in your life. Blood and violence. And a prison. A fine house but a prison nevertheless. On the wall is a painting of a devil upon his throne.'

Frightened, Amy wrenched herself free, leapt to her feet and ran for the door.

'Wait,' called Magda.

Against her better judgement, Amy stopped.

'Please listen. I'm sorry I frightened you. Sometimes the visions come upon me without warning. Permit me to give you a word of caution – danger is very close and it wants to hurt you.'

'I'd worked that out for myself, thank you,' Amy replied icily. She forced herself to calm down as she recalled the purpose of her visit. She needed this woman on her side. 'I take it you know who I had an affair with?'

Another non-judgemental nod.

'Then you will understand why I'm so anxious to prevent that which I fear the most. Are there any other remedies you can give me?'

'I'm sorry, I've nothing else. That remedy was only supposed to be used in an emergency, not on a regular basis.'

'Matthew told me it could be.' Amy frowned.

'That was very wrong of him. I partly blame myself. I should have known better after the last time.'

'Last time?'

Magda gave her such a pitying look Amy flushed with embarrassment.

'As Matthew's left the area I see no harm in telling you. He had an affair with a local girl a few months ago. He was giving her my potion too in order to prevent pregnancy. The girl became worried about the long-term effects on her health, so she came to see me. I told her to stop taking it immediately and end her relationship with him.'

'He doesn't have a sister, does he?'

'No.'

Amy coloured with anger and humiliation. In all her life she had never felt so stupid and used. At least with Mr Costigan she'd had the excuse of her tender age. Instead of learning from that episode she'd made the same mistake all over again.

'You see,' continued Magda, 'my remedy, when used occasionally, does prevent pregnancy, but when taken regularly it has a different effect. Over a few months, it makes you incredibly fertile. Now, this is all right if you still take the potion after intercourse but if you miss a dose then it's more than likely you will become pregnant.'

'Did Matthew know this?'

'No.'

'So you're saying there's a good chance I could be with child? Is it too early to tell now?' Amy said, head spinning.

'I'm afraid so. Come back and see me if your bleed is late.'

Tears filled Amy's eyes. 'Oh God, what have I done?'

* * *

Amy kept herself to herself after that. Lenora tried to interest her in the wedding arrangements but she would leave the room whenever the subject was broached. Henry tried to initiate conservations about their future together but she would stare through him as though he were a pane of glass. He would swing from gentleness and amiability to anger, her silence infuriating him. Once he even tried to kiss her, but she repelled his advances as though they disgusted her.

Alfred spent most of his time closeted in his study or fishing by the river to escape the horrible atmosphere in the house.

As Amy faced another long, interminable night of worry, Nettie brought her some news that cheered her.

'I've just spoken with Johnson,' she said excitedly.

Amy looked up expectantly. 'And?'

'Apparently Master Henry had a secret relationship with a girl in the village.'

'Do you know who?'

'Johnson wasn't sure of her name but from what he told me I think I can guess. Anyway, Johnson said Master Henry has strange... habits.'

'How so?'

Nettie shifted uncomfortably. 'He likes tying up women and hurting them.'

'What?' she exclaimed even though she couldn't really claim to be surprised.

'One time he really hurt this girl. Her dad found out and kicked up a fuss but he paid him off and kept it all quiet.'

Amy's face lit up with a wicked grin. He'd exposed her so she would return the favour.

'Do you want me to speak to the girl, miss?'

'Yes, please. Ask her if she wants revenge for what he did with no risk to herself.'

'Yes, miss.'

* * *

Amy managed to cry off going to church by declaring she was unwell. After she watched the family and servants disappear down the drive, she waited ten minutes to make sure Henry didn't return. Peeking her head out of her room, she saw the corridor was deserted. She sneaked out, quietly closing the door behind her, crept down the hall, and into the family wing.

The door to Henry's room was shut but to her relief it opened beneath her touch. His room was opulently furnished, fit for a prince.

She started by rifling through his drawers, which was a pleasing revenge. She checked his clothes, rooting through the pockets of his coats and trousers, she even looked under his bed but found nothing.

Next she turned her attention to his writing desk. It was locked and she was still searching for the key when she heard voices outside. Peering through the window, she saw the family returning.

Frantically she speeded up her hunt for the key but for the life of her she couldn't find it. As the family entered the house she decided to retreat but when she went to the door she heard footsteps coming up the stairs. Briefly she considered rushing across the corridor towards

Edward's room, but she couldn't be sure it was unlocked and if it wasn't she would be stranded in the corridor. So she decided to hide in Henry's room and hope it wasn't him approaching.

She slid beneath the huge four-poster bed seconds before Henry entered the room. He gave a deep sigh, and she didn't dare breathe as she watched his shoes pad about the room. From what she could hear she gathered he was changing out of his church clothes.

When the gong sounded for lunch she experienced a thrill of panic because if her lunch was brought up to her room and she wasn't there questions would be asked.

Amy remained perfectly still as Henry walked to the door, which opened and closed. Then silence.

Exhaling shakily, she rested her head on her hands while her thudding heart slowed. She released a shriek when hands grabbed her ankles and she was dragged out from under the bed. When she was released she rolled over and found herself face to face with Henry, monster and her husband-to-be.

'Amy, what are you doing here?' he said. 'I thought you were an intruder.'

'I was just returning the favour. I know you went through my room.'

'I wanted to discover what you were up to and put a stop to it before it hurt you, but I was too late.'

'You were the one who hurt me. You saw Matthew and I together and you decided to run to Mummy and Daddy.'

'I only did it for you.'

'Nonsense. You're trapping me into marriage so you can get your hands on my fortune.'

'You think so little of me?'

'How could I think well of you after what you've done?'

His face twisted into an angry scowl. 'Oh, I see. You want the footman, don't you? Why don't you go down to the servants' hall? There's two more you haven't had yet.'

When she slapped him across the face he grabbed her wrist.
'Woman, you infuriate me. Why do you keep fighting me?'

'I will always fight you, even after we're married.'

'Why can't you see I'm only trying to help you?'

'Help me, like you helped that other girl?'

'What other girl?'

'You know exactly what I'm referring to.'

'I'm afraid I have no idea,' he replied, eyes darkening.

Amy was scared. She was in the weaker position on the floor and
he was knelt before her, blocking her escape. When his lips crushed
against hers she turned her head to try and escape but he refused to
stop.

'Let me go,' she cried.

He relinquished the kiss but still held onto her. 'I don't care about
what you did with the footman. I don't care,' he continued, voice practically a growl, 'I want you.'

'And what the prince wants the prince gets, but not this time. I
know what you've done and I will find a way to prove it.'

'So that's what you were doing in here? Hoping to discover something about me so terrible I will be disgraced and the wedding will be
called off? Don't you see how tenuous your position is, Amy? You're just
a woman with no status, power or income of her own. The best thing
you can do is marry me.'

'I will never marry you.'

'Be careful. My father is still your guardian and he and my mother
already think your behaviour odd. I mean, debasing yourself with a
servant and now all these strange moods. He could have you
committed to an asylum any time he likes.'

Amy had not even dreamt of this possibility and Magda's vision of
prison echoed in her head.

Finally he released her. She dragged herself to her feet, and
blinded by tears, she stumbled past him to the door.

'Are you not coming down for lunch?' he called after her, voice mocking.

She ignored him and fled back to her room.

* * *

Amy lay in an almost cataleptic state as the helplessness of her situation brought her to despair. These people hated her and would put her in Bedlam without a moment's pause. Henry was right. Who would help? Edward, of course, but as the younger son he was powerless, and she hadn't heard from her friends in London for months. She was completely alone.

When Nettie came into her room to help her undress for bed, Amy was lying so still and quiet that for a moment she feared the worst.

'Miss,' she exclaimed, breathing a sigh of relief when Amy slowly turned her head to look at her.

'Oh, hello, Nettie,' she mumbled.

'I've seen her, miss.'

'Seen who?' she said disinterestedly.

'Gemma. The girl Master Henry hurt.'

Life flooded back into Amy's eyes and she sat up. 'What did she say?'

'She confirmed everything Johnson told me. Master Henry is a very sick man.'

'But it would only be her word against his.'

'On the contrary,' said Nettie, handing her a pile of letters tied in a bundle with string. 'Letters written to Gemma by Master Henry.'

Amy untied the string and opened the first letter. It was Henry's hand without a doubt, declaring his love for Gemma.

'These aren't really compromising,' she said, disappointed. 'Yes, they are love letters but they're not enough to do him any damage.'

'You've got the first one, miss. The more they go on, the worse they get.'

Nettie took a letter from the bottom of the pile, opened it and handed it to her. Henry's elegant script had transformed into a spidery scrawl as he wrote about what he wanted to do to Gemma. Henry's sexual fantasies were revolting and very frightening.

'How could she meet with him when he wanted to do things like that to her?' said Amy incredulously.

'Gemma said he was kind and gentle at first and it was only when she was hopelessly in love with him that he showed his true colours. He started to hurt her but she put up with it.'

'Why?'

'Gemma's a miller's daughter and Master Henry's the future laird. He dazzled her and bought her expensive clothes and jewels. He even mentioned them marrying.'

'Which he had no intention of doing.'

'No, miss. Anyway, the last time they were together he lost control. He tied her up and burned her with a cigar, then attacked her with a horsewhip. She still has the scars on her back. Johnson fetched the doctor and got rid of all the evidence.'

'Evidence?'

'There was a lot of blood.'

'My God.'

'The scars will be very difficult for her to explain away to any future husband. In the last letter he wrote to her he apologised for what he did and offered her recompense but she turned it down. She wanted to go to the authorities but he did a deal with her father.'

'He paid him to keep her quiet?'

'Yes, miss, and Gemma is still very angry. She wants revenge and said she's willing to do whatever she can to help you.'

'She's very brave and you've been most helpful,' said Amy, holding out another coin to her.

Nettie shook her head. 'Gemma's a friend. It's reward enough to help you bring Master Henry down, miss.'

11

Amy asked Nettie to guard Henry's letters for her, but before she could decide what to do with them she had a more pressing matter to attend to. She had missed her bleed last month but put it down to the stress she was under. When her next bleed was two weeks late and she started being sick in the mornings she decided she couldn't ignore it any longer. She knew deep down that her worst nightmare had come true.

At breakfast she hardly ate, sitting at the end of the table looking washed out. She confided in no one, although she thought Nettie must suspect something because as her maid she was privy to every secret.

One morning Amy went to see Magda, who listened sympathetically before examining her.

'There's no doubt you're with child,' she said. 'I'd say between two and three months.'

Amy nodded, eyes filling with tears. 'I know exactly when it happened. The last time Matthew and I were together.'

'Just so you're aware, I am not one of those hideous old crones armed with a knitting needle.'

The prospect made Amy nauseous. 'I could never do that. It's out of the question.'

'I'm sorry for the mess you're in, you don't deserve it.'

Amy returned to Alardyce, shut herself away in her room and cried.

There was a knock at the door but she ignored it, praying whoever it was would go away.

'Amy, I know you're in there,' called Edward through the door. 'I can hear you crying.'

She didn't reply, too ashamed to even look him in the eye, but he walked in anyway.

'Amy,' he said with concern. 'Has Henry done something to you?'

She shook her head and burst into hysterical sobs. He rushed to her and gathered her into his arms.

'Please, Amy, tell me what's happened.'

'I'm... I'm with child,' she managed to gasp between sobs.

'Dear God. Matthew's baby?'

'Of course it's Matthew's baby.'

'All right, calm down,' he said, stroking her hair. 'You have to think of the child now.'

He handed her his handkerchief and she wiped her eyes.

'What do I do?' she said.

'There's only one thing you can do. You have to tell my parents.'

'They'll be furious.'

'Probably but you've no choice. I'll be by your side.'

'Thank you, Edward. You're so kind.'

'My reasons aren't entirely altruistic. If your engagement to Henry is called off you'll be free to marry me.'

'You still want to marry me even though I'm carrying another man's child?'

'You know me, Amy. What other way could I have a baby? We could raise it as our own.'

She clutched onto his hands. 'You really think we could?'

He kissed her cheek. 'Yes, I do. The only obstacle is my parents' consent. Are you ready to tackle them?'

She got to her feet. 'Let's get it over with.'

Edward took her hand and led her downstairs to the drawing room.

'Mother, Father,' said Edward. 'Amy has something she needs to tell you.'

She stepped forward, heart beating so rapidly she thought she might faint as her aunt and uncle expectantly waited.

'I...' she began, her words silenced when tears threatened to overtake her.

'Amy, what on earth is wrong?' said her uncle.

'I'm... I'm...'

'You're pregnant, aren't you?' said Lenora.

Amy regarded her with surprise. 'How did you know?'

'I've gone through it twice myself, remember. I saw you not eating.'

'Why didn't you at least warn me?' Alfred demanded of his wife.

'Because I hoped I was mistaken,' she replied, fixing Amy with an icy stare. 'It's Matthew's baby, I take it?'

'Yes,' she croaked.

'Excuse me for asking, but I want to be sure there haven't been any others,' Lenora said sarcastically.

'There haven't,' she snapped back, her fear outweighed by indignation.

'All right, please,' sighed Alfred, tired of the constant arguing. 'The question is, what is to be done now?'

'There's only one thing that can be done,' said Lenora. 'She'll have to get rid of it.'

'No,' exclaimed Amy. 'I will not kill my own child.'

'Quite right too,' declared Alfred. 'Such a thing is against God.'

'I meant she should have the baby, then give it away,' said Lenora.

Amy stared at her aunt, frightened and appalled.

'You can't do that,' said Edward.

'We'll make sure it goes to a good home,' said Lenora, as thoug[h] they were discussing a puppy.

Amy was snapped out of her stupor. 'You are not giving away m[y] baby.'

'You're marrying Henry. How do you expect to have any sort [of] marriage raising another man's child? A servant's child at that.'

'This is my baby. You have no right to take it from me.'

'No right? We're your legal guardians until you marry.'

Edward interjected before things grew even more heated. 'I thin[k] I've come up with a solution that will satisfy everyone.'

'You?' His mother laughed. 'What could you possibly think of th[at] we haven't already?'

Edward ignored the barb. He was used to her scorn.

'Let's hear it, Edward,' said his father kindly.

'Amy marries me instead.'

'Don't be ridiculous,' said Lenora.

'Please consider it,' he continued. 'Amy and I think we could b[e] good companions for each other and I would get a child because, let[s] face it, I'm not going to get one by the usual method.'

'I've no idea what you're talking about,' she replied but it was clea[r] from her eyes that she had.

'You've always known there's something different about me, but yo[u] choose to ignore it. Amy accepts me for who I am. It's the perfe[ct] solution.'

'Absolutely out of the question,' said Alfred. 'She's engaged to you[r] brother.'

'Nothing has been made official. The banns haven't even been rea[d] yet.'

'I said no, Edward, and that's final. Amy, I'm sorry but my wife i[s] right. I don't wish to sound callous but this family, your own fathe[r] included, have worked very hard for all this and I'm damned if I'll let [it] pass into the hands of a footman's child.'

Amy didn't reply because Henry's threat of the asylum flitte[d] through her mind. It wasn't just her own future she was fighting for now, it was her baby's too.

Alfred rang for Rush and asked him to fetch Henry from the library.

'What's going on?' he said curiously as he entered.

'Your fiancée here,' began Lenora bitterly, 'has just informed us that she's carrying the ex-footman's child.'

Henry regarded her steadily and Amy clenched her fists in anger because if he hadn't taken her vial then none of this would be happening.

'You're a man now, old enough to choose your own wife,' said Alfred. 'Do you still wish to marry Amy?'

'What will become of the child?'

'She will continue with the pregnancy and after it's born we'll have it adopted.'

Amy flinched as though in physical pain. Already she felt protective of the tiny life growing inside her, but she remained silent for now. She had another seven months to fight for her baby. The important thing was that she kept herself out of the asylum.

Henry looked to Amy before replying, 'I still want to marry her.'

'What?' exclaimed Edward and Lenora simultaneously.

'I think I can help her.' His demeanour was gentle but it didn't fool Amy.

'That's good of you, Henry,' said Alfred. 'You're a true Christian but consider the alternative. You would be free to marry Miss Bartley.'

'You don't want to help me,' Amy retorted. 'All you want is my fortune.'

'Amy, how dare you?' said Lenora. 'You're fortunate any man would want you, never mind one as fine as Henry.'

'He can have my fortune. I'll sign it over to him right now if you say I can marry Edward and keep my baby.'

Alfred sighed. He hated female histrionics. All he wanted was this conversation over with so he could escape to his study. 'You see, Amy,

Henry only wants to take care of you. You do him an injustice when you accuse him of being a fortune hunter. After all, he will inherit a considerable fortune of his own.'

'This marriage will make us both miserable.'

Henry stepped forward to take her hands. 'How can you say that when I'll devote my every waking moment to your happiness?' he said softly, accompanied by what she thought was a thoroughly malicious smile.

She snatched her hands from his grip and backed away.

'Let us settle this right now,' said a weary Alfred. 'Henry, do you wish to break off your engagement to Amy?'

'No.'

'In that case, I'm sorry, Edward, but Amy will marry Henry.'

Edward, who knew his brother better than his parents, frowned at him suspiciously. 'Why are you doing this?'

'You've heard my reasons.'

Amy knew she was defeated. Henry was determined to have her and all she wanted was to flee back to her room where she could think. Glancing at Edward, she saw his disappointment.

'In light of this news, I'll order the banns for Henry and Amy to be read,' said Alfred. 'We must step up the plans for the wedding, before Amy's condition becomes apparent. Then you can take an extended honeymoon abroad and Amy can have the baby there and when you return no one will be any the wiser.'

Amy hung her head so they wouldn't see her tears. 'And you'll give my baby away?'

'Yes,' said Alfred. 'It might seem harsh but there's no other way. You've brought this on yourself.'

Amy felt trapped. The room seemed to shrink and she struggled for breath, dragging in ragged gasps of air.

'Amy?' said Edward, moving towards her.

Panic seized her when the walls closed in and the room spun. As she pitched forward she just had chance to note that it was Edward and not Henry who caught her.

* * *

When Amy came round she could hear the soft murmur of voices somewhere behind her. She kept her eyes closed so she could listen to what they were saying.

'I tell you her behaviour isn't normal. Maybe we should call the doctor?' It was Lenora.

'Edward has gone to fetch him.' Henry.

'I don't mean that sort of doctor. I was referring to one who could have her committed. Clearly something's wrong with her. First she has an affair with a servant and now these hysterics.'

'I will not put my sister's pregnant daughter in an asylum,' retorted Alfred, appalled. 'Let me know when she wakes.'

She heard footsteps retreating, the door opening and closing and she assumed her uncle had left.

'You know, Henry,' continued Lenora maliciously. 'If your father doesn't have the guts to do it then you could when you're married.'

'I would prefer to manage her myself,' he replied.

They were interrupted by the door opening.

'The doctor's arrived,' said Edward. A few words were exchanged then Amy felt a hand on her shoulder.

'Amy?' said a gentle voice in her ear.

She made a show of coming round, as though she hadn't been awake for the last few minutes. It took her a moment to focus on the bald-headed man with the thin face.

'What happened, Amy?' he said, his expression kind. 'I'm Dr Parlow. Your family called me because you had an episode.'

Mercifully it wasn't Dr Woodrow, who'd helped cover up Henry's mistreatment of Gemma and the maid.

'I fainted,' she replied.

'Your aunt told me it was more of a fit after you'd worked yourself up into a state. Do you get upset often?'

'I merely fainted, sir.' Amy knew Lenora was paving the way to having her committed. Well, she wasn't going to give her the satisfaction. Amy broke into a sly smile as she looked at the doctor. 'I understand it's common for women in my condition.'

'Condition?'

'I'm with child,' she told him sweetly, ignoring Lenora's thunderous expression.

'Oh,' said the doctor, obviously shocked.

'Please don't think badly of me, Doctor. Although it hasn't been announced yet, Henry and I are engaged.' She looked to Henry and flashed a smile. 'Aren't we, dear?'

'Err, yes,' he replied.

The doctor smiled kindly. 'You're not the first young couple to succumb to temptation.'

'Thank you,' she said, hoping she looked like the radiant bride-to-be. 'You're very kind but I fear your trip has been wasted.'

'On the contrary. Did you hurt yourself when you fainted? Permit me to examine you. We can't take any chances with the future heir, can we?'

His words were kindly meant but Henry and Lenora looked infuriated while Edward frowned. The doctor turned to the latter. 'Perhaps you should leave, sir, for the examination?'

'Yes, of course.' He gave Amy a questioning look but she nodded, even though he was the only one she wanted to stay.

'Have you had any pain or bleeding?' said the doctor.

'Not today, although a few days ago I did have a little spotting and cramping.'

'It's probably just the baby settling in. How far along are you?'

'Mrs Magrath said about three months.'

'Mrs Magrath? You went to her?'

'I was more comfortable discussing it with a woman, especially as Henry and I are not yet married.'

'I understand, but I would like to take over your care. Some of Mrs Magrath's practices are dubious to say the least.'

Amy nodded, although she fully intended to see Magda again but that would be her little secret. She was amassing quite a list.

After questioning her he calculated the baby would be due in the middle of November. He took his leave after assuring them that his services would be available to them day or night.

When he'd gone Lenora stormed up to Amy and slapped her across the face while Henry looked on stonily.

'Why on earth did you tell him about the baby? We were going to keep it a secret.'

'He's a doctor. Had he examined me he would have easily discovered my condition. Better he thinks the child is actually my fiancé's,' she replied calmly.

'I told Alfred not to bring in a doctor,' she spat. 'Well, at least he's bound by his oath to keep the pregnancy secret. We can say you lost the baby on honeymoon. That will do.'

Amy wrapped her arms around her stomach, hating the thought.

'Get out of my sight,' said Lenora.

Relieved, Amy retreated to her room but was disturbed a few minutes later by Edward barging in.

'What was all that about?' he demanded. 'Why did you say the baby was Henry's?' The envy in his voice was clear.

'Because your mother and brother were discussing having me put away in an asylum.'

'No. They wouldn't do that.'

'Of course they would. I heard them myself. Your father is set against it and stormed out of the room. When he'd gone Lenora and Henry continued discussing it but Henry said he'd prefer to manage me himself. Now a respected professional outside the family knows that not only are Henry and I engaged but we're expecting a child, so any plan to put me away would look suspicious. Now I'm protected, at least until we're married.'

'So you believe Henry is marrying you for your fortune?'

'Yes.'

'But you offered to hand it over to him if he released you to marry me and he declined. Why would he do that?'

Her expression darkened. 'You know what he likes to do to women and he wants to do it to me. I've vexed him too many times and he wants revenge.' She swallowed down her tears. Now was the time to be strong. She held out Gemma's letters to him. Edward had to see them. 'He wrote these to a girl he beat so severely he almost killed her.'

Edward stared at the letters. 'I always suspected but I'm not sure I want to see the evidence.'

'Go on, read them,' she said, pushing them into his hands. 'I'm sure you recognise his handwriting.'

Edward retreated to his room to read the letters and returned an hour later, pale and shaken.

'I can't believe the depths he's fallen to.' He regarded her with haunted eyes. 'I can't help but think of Mary Hill.'

'Who?'

'She was a maid here two years ago, a sweet, pretty girl of nineteen. One night she was found by the gamekeeper stumbling around in the gardens, naked. She'd been beaten black and blue and her back was bleeding from some deep cuts thought to have been caused by a horse whip. She was brought into the house and revived with brandy and the doctor was called. Fortunately her wounds weren't life-threatening and she was patched up. At the time it was put down to a dreadful accident that she'd fallen into a pile of wood and nails from a dismantled shed in the garden, which was ridiculous. I mean, how could that explain why she was naked?'

'It was Henry?'

'I simply couldn't believe it was him, but she was the first. It was harder to explain the second maid's injuries as an accident.'

'Why?' she asked, on tenterhooks. 'What had he done?'

'The exact same thing. The shed had gone, there was nothing she could have fallen into to cause her injuries, but what really gave it away was when the girl looked up at the window and screamed. We all thought she'd seen her assailant outside and ran out to try and catch them but I knew she wasn't looking outside. Henry was standing by the window. It explains why so many maids left after just a few weeks' service. Looking back, it all makes perfect sense. Maybe once or twice a year a girl would suddenly leave and Mother would have to find a replacement. Once a maid served me with a glass of wine and her sleeve rode up. Her wrist was red raw, as though she'd been tied up. I asked her about it but she scurried away like a frightened mouse. Deep down I've always known but it's different actually having the evidence in my hand,' he said, indicating the letters.

'How old was Henry when all this started?'

'I don't know, sixteen, maybe seventeen. Amy, you can't marry him. He'll do the same things to you only...'

'Only I won't be able to leave.'

'Exactly. What are you going to do?'

'The only thing I can do. Run away.'

'Where would you go? How will you survive?'

'I'll find a position somewhere. I could be a governess.'

'A governess?'

'I've no choice. What sort of future do I have if I remain here? Gemma survived by the skin of her teeth and she'd only been seeing him for a few months. What chance will I have when I'm entirely at his mercy? And if I go I can keep my child,' she ended, her voice cracking. 'Please, Edward, you have to help me.'

He sighed. 'Of course I will, but what will you do?'

Between them they came up with a plan.

12

———————

Amy sought out Henry and found him reading in the library. Even though he was aware she was standing over him he didn't look up from his book.

'May I speak with you?' she said when he'd ignored her for a full minute.

'I'm listening,' he said, still not looking up.

She took the chair opposite him and started to talk. 'I realise now that this wedding is going ahead whether I want it to or not. So I think we should make the best of a bad situation. What do you think?'

Infuriatingly he kept on reading his book and she resisted the urge to snatch it from his hands.

'Have you been listening to a word I've said?' she demanded.

He sighed and cast the book aside. 'Are you saying you're coming round to the idea of marrying me?'

'I would use the word accepting. Just tell me one thing – why do you want to marry me, really? Is it my money?'

He patted the space on the couch beside him, and she sat with some reluctance, making him smile.

'Well, that is a nice bonus but it isn't the main reason,' he said. 'No woman has ever infuriated me as much as you but at the same time no woman has ever interested me or challenged me as much. Is it so hard to believe that I actually like you, Amy?'

For a moment she was nonplussed, he seemed so genuine. 'You don't mean that. You're just doing all this to annoy me. Well, I hope you're happy now.'

'I am. Very.'

His grin infuriated her. 'Then at least one of us is,' she snapped, folding her arms across her chest.

'Oh, you are going to be fun.' He smiled. 'Tell me, do you really mean what you say about us trying to get along? A woman as stubborn as you does not give in so easily.'

'I'm not a fool, I know when to concede defeat.' She paused before continuing, praying she wasn't making an error. 'I heard you and your mother discussing having me committed. You said you'd rather... how did you phrase it, Henry? Manage me yourself. I think that would be preferable to an asylum – marginally.'

He studied her suspiciously but she returned his steady gaze.

'Do you really mean what you say?' he repeated.

'I do. Unfortunately.'

'In that case, prove it.'

'How?'

'Kiss me.'

She flinched. Not because of his appearance, on the contrary he was a handsome man, but because every time she looked at him she remembered what he'd done to poor Gemma and Mary Hill and God only knew how many others.

He moved a little closer and she recoiled.

'Come on, Amy, you'll have to do a lot more than kiss on our wedding night.'

'All right,' she said shakily, taking a deep breath, knowing she had no choice.

She closed her eyes as he pressed his lips to hers, fully expecting some form of violence but to her surprise he was gentle. It still made her squirm, so she imagined he was Matthew. This relaxed her a little. She had to play this part to perfection. He kissed her harder, encouraging her mouth to open a little wider. Gently Henry cupped her face in his hands, his thumbs stroking her neck and she felt a little thrill of excitement in the pit of her stomach. She started to wonder if there hadn't been some terrible mistake and he wasn't the creature he was purported to be. She became all too aware that she was kissing Henry, the monster, but it was... nice.

He was the first to pull away and he smiled at her, the gesture failing to warm those brooding eyes. 'There, that wasn't so bad. In fact I'd go as far as to say it was rather pleasant.'

With that he got up and left the room, leaving her sitting there, tingling. Amy released a sigh and buried her face in her hands. What was wrong with her treacherous body? Men had always been her downfall – first Mr Costigan, then Matthew, and now she had just enjoyed kissing Henry, the brute. Mr Costigan had woken something in her all those years ago, something crude and foul that Matthew had fed and now it was desperate for another outlet. Well, she refused to give Henry the satisfaction. He might be playing nice now, but it was only a matter of time before he unleashed his darker self.

* * *

A few days later it was abruptly announced that all the family were going to a museum in Edinburgh to see an art exhibition. Amy was puzzled as to the suddenness of the trip but she was looking forward to spending some time away from the estate.

The dark purpose of the outing was soon revealed.

The exhibition was a narration on the changing morals of society. The first part was titled Angels in the House and represented ideal femininity. One of the paintings by George Elgar Hicks, called *Companion of Manhood*, showed a wife comforting her husband.

Another showed the wife fawning over her husband, a cherubic child between them, whilst the next was of a blind basket maker and his wife delighting over their firstborn child.

Amy dejectedly walked past these scenes of domestic bliss, aware of Lenora's gaze constantly upon her. It was obvious to her now why this outing had been arranged. Lenora wanted Amy to see how she should behave for her future husband – the perfect wife providing her husband with peace, contentment and an efficiently run home. Amy hoped there would be a painting of a husband beating his wife that she could show her aunt but of course there wasn't. This gallery only showed the vices of women.

The next section was called Fates of Corruption and Amy's spirits sank even lower. The first painting by Richard Redgrave simply titled *The Outcast* depicted a girl being thrown out of her home by her father, clutching her illegitimate baby, while the rest of the family wept at the disgrace she had heaped upon them. Tears prickled Amy's eyes.

The Awakening Conscience by William Holman Hunt showed a man with his mistress perched on his knee, an ugly leer on his face while she gazed longingly at a time when she was free of sexual sin, wishing she could return to that time, but it was too late.

Found Drowned by George Frederic Watts was by far the most evocative, of a woman washed up dead on the shore after drowning herself. The woman had discovered she was pregnant out of wedlock and this was a better option for her than prostitution, which was a common fate for women who found themselves in such a condition. She lay with one arm stretched behind her head, her face bathed in light while her lower half was in shadow. A single bright star shone overhead out of the black sky, hinting that this act had cleansed her.

Amy glanced to her left and saw a pretty blonde girl of her own age staring at the painting with the same intensity and dread in her eyes. She caught Amy's gaze and at once the two women knew that they were both suffering the same ordeal. A harsh-looking man whom Amy took to be her father put a firm hand on the girl's arm and moved her along.

She kept looking back over her shoulder at Amy, as though she didn't want to lose sight of a fellow victim, and Amy didn't look away until she was swallowed up by the crowd. Even though she had only glimpsed her for a few seconds Amy knew she would never forget that girl's face.

A hand grasped her own and, assuming it was Edward, she gave it a gentle squeeze. She got the surprise of her life when she looked up into Henry's face. She would have retracted her hand but she was so tired and dazed that she simply didn't have the energy.

Allowing herself to momentarily forget what he was, she let him lead her past the rest of the exhibition and out of the door, leaving the rest of the family inside. They sat down together on a bench in a peaceful garden.

'I'm sorry for that,' he said, once again surprising her. 'It was cruel of my mother to bring you here.'

Amy took in deep gulps of fresh air, feeling light-headed.

'Are you all right?' he said with concern.

'Fine,' she replied, bravely trying to hold back tears.

As he put a tentative arm around her shoulders, Amy saw the girl from inside the museum speed by in a carriage, her white face pressed to the window as she was whisked away to whatever fate awaited her. This was the final straw and the tears started to fall.

'It's all right,' said Henry so compassionately she leaned into him and cried on his shoulder.

'You're not alone,' he whispered in her ear as he stroked her hair. 'I'm here.'

* * *

The next day Henry asked Amy to join him for a walk in the garden as she still wasn't permitted to leave the grounds alone. He chatted away kindly, never once mentioning the wedding or the baby. He was even careful of her health and insisted she rest on a bench after they had been walking for a while. He made no physical contact with her other than holding her hand and when she was rested enough he offered her his arm and escorted her back to the house.

What surprised her most of all was that she had a pleasant afternoon. Amy had always wondered how Gemma could have been so blinded to his true nature. Now she understood how charming Henry could be when he wanted. Nevertheless she never let herself forget what he really was.

* * *

A week later, Amy asked her uncle if she would be permitted to go into the city to get measured for her wedding dress. It wasn't an errand she was relishing but she wanted to show willing.

'Certainly not,' retorted Lenora before Alfred could reply. 'You've not yet proven we can trust you.'

'I've done everything you've asked of me,' Amy replied. 'What more can I do?'

'Be fair, Lenora, how is she supposed to get her dress if she can't leave the house?' interjected Alfred.

Amy shot him a grateful look.

'Amy, you can go into the city,' interrupted Henry.

Everyone stared at him.

'I beg your pardon?' snapped Lenora, unused to such mutiny, especially from her prince.

'She's been cooped up in this house for weeks, apart from that trip to the museum. That's long enough.'

'It is not your decision to make.'

'She's going to be my wife, therefore it is.'

Lenora was appalled and looked to her husband for support. 'Alfred, will you please tell your son?'

'I agree with him. Amy has abided by every demand we've made.

She should be rewarded for that. You can take the Growler.' He smiled first at Henry, then Amy.

'Thank you, Father,' said Henry magnanimously.

'But you can't see my dress before the wedding,' Amy said, feigning a playful grin, which he returned.

'I could accompany her,' offered Edward.

Amy prayed this would be permitted but Henry smothered her hopes.

'No, I will go,' he practically snarled.

Edward glowered at him before looking down at his plate.

Lenora's eyes were fixed on Amy. 'I'm coming too. I'm not letting you out of my sight, young lady.'

'As you wish, Aunt Lenora,' she said sweetly, unable to repress a triumphant grin.

* * *

What should have been one of the most exciting days of Amy's life was dull and depressing. In the Growler – an enclosed carriage for four that made a distinctive growling noise when it ran over any cobbles – she was wedged beside Lenora and across from Henry, neither of whom uttered one word the entire journey.

On arriving in Edinburgh, Henry headed to see his tailor about his wedding suit while Lenora marched Amy to a dressmaker's. She found it difficult to muster any excitement and browsed the dresses half-heartedly. It didn't matter which design she chose because she knew she would never wear it. Lenora favoured some hideous flouncy thing covered in bows but, just for spite, Amy decided on an elegant white dress trimmed with lace with a small bustle.

Before the assistant took any measurements, Lenora discreetly took her aside to explain about Amy's condition. So preliminary measurements were taken instead and they agreed she would return in a month to be measured again.

Amy followed Lenora out of the shop more depressed than ever. Fortunately her aunt mistook her sullenness for fatigue, so Henry took her to lunch while Lenora went in search of her own wedding outfit.

Lenora's absence seemed to work a miracle on both their spirits and they chatted pleasantly while they ate in a nice tearoom. Henry spoke amiably about the wedding, and seemed to be rather excited. His enthusiasm cheered her a little and she found herself thinking that if he was everything he appeared to be on the surface she might be happier about marrying him, but she pushed those dangerous thoughts away. She must remember that he was really a monster.

After lunch they browsed the shops together until Amy was too tired to go on. As they walked back to the carriage Henry wrapped an arm around her waist to support her.

Once back inside the carriage she fell asleep almost immediately. She woke a few minutes from Alardyce House with her head resting on Henry's shoulder and his arm around her. He assisted her out of the Growler and insisted she go to her room for a lie down. Amy felt guilty for being suspicious that this was a ruse to get into her bedroom when he merely kissed her cheek and said he would see her at dinner before leaving.

After he'd gone she asked Nettie to fetch the letters he wrote to Gemma so she could remind herself what he was capable of. One day he would reveal his true self. What if she was still pregnant and something happened to her baby? She simply couldn't risk it. Nothing meant more to her than this child.

Amy slept right through dinner and woke at eight o'clock the following morning, still in her dress. Nettie assisted her to change and she went downstairs to find the house a hive of activity.

'What's going on?' she asked Edward, who was the only one in the dining room.

'They're making arrangements for the garden party next week,' he replied.

'Garden party? For heaven's sake, we're all supposed to be in mourning.' An idea occurred to her so startling she froze. 'Will there be a lot of guests?'

'A hundred at least.'

'That's it, then.'

'What do you mean?'

'That's the day I'll go.'

* * *

Amy went to her favourite spot in the conservatory to think through her escape plan. It was perfectly simple, just a matter of blending in with the crowd to leave the estate. She ran a hand over her swollen stomach. No one was taking her baby.

Her thoughts were interrupted by Henry sitting himself down beside her, making her jump.

'Excuse me,' he apologised.

'I didn't hear you come in,' she said as her heart slowed to a normal rhythm.

'You slept solidly last night.' He smiled. 'Nettie tried to wake you for dinner.'

'I think it was all the excitement yesterday. All the fresh air took it out of me.'

'You must be careful in your condition.'

'Henry, you've never told me how you feel about marrying a woman who's carrying another man's child, a servant's child at that.' Her heart was in her mouth as she asked but she simply had to know.

He shrugged. 'It doesn't really matter to me, to be quite frank.'

'How can it not?'

'Because I want to marry you. It's the only thing I've ever really wanted.'

'Why? I don't understand.'

He looked down at his hands. 'Forgive me, I'm not very good at conversations like this.'

Instead he reached out to take her hand and she allowed him. He leaned in to kiss her and she started to relax again. Suddenly he gripped her wrists and held her fast.

'Release me,' she exclaimed but he pushed her back into the couch, forcing his mouth upon hers. She managed to twist her face away and issued a scream that echoed loudly through the room. This had the desired effect and he released her. She shot to her feet, shaking. Henry rose too, once again the cold, impassive statue.

'Amy, what's wrong?'

'You are sick. Sick,' she yelled before rushing from the room, almost colliding with her uncle.

'What's wrong?' said Alfred. 'I heard a scream.'

She pushed past him and hurried upstairs to the refuge of her room. After locking the door and kicking off her slippers she climbed into bed and pulled the covers over her head in an effort to block out the entire world.

* * *

After that Amy avoided Henry as much as possible. He bought her flowers and jewellery and made every effort to make amends but she rebuffed all his attempts. All the while the wedding loomed ever closer. As the banns were read out in church one Sunday she stared resolutely ahead, as she listened to the whispers around her.

One morning Nettie brought her unwelcome news.

'I just overheard her ladyship and his lordship talking. Her ladyship says you're acting strangely again – she's talking of calling off the wedding and having you committed.'

Amy pushed herself upright on the bed. 'What?'

'Please, miss, you must make things up with Master Henry or dread to think what will happen.'

'You're right,' Amy sighed. She couldn't have her plan ruined now or she would be trapped forever. 'Is Master Henry at home?'

'Yes, miss. He's taking a walk in the garden.'

Amy threw on a shawl and hurried out of her room, down the stairs and through the conservatory into the garden, frantically scanning the area for Henry. She spied one of the gardeners tending to a flowerbed and rushed over to him.

'Have you seen Master Henry?'

'He went that way, not two minutes ago,' he said, pointing to the sunken garden.

'Thank you.'

As she descended the steps into the sunken garden everything went dark, the sunlight blocked out by the overhanging trees. Amy shivered and pulled the shawl tighter about herself. She had never liked this place.

Henry was sitting on a stone bench staring into the distance. Taking a deep breath, she approached him, her footsteps echoing on the stone flags. He looked up and regarded her with a frown.

'May I?' she said, indicating the space on the bench beside him.

Henry nodded.

Amy sat down and stared at her hands, trying to summon up the will to apologise even though she'd done nothing wrong. 'I'm sorry.'

'Excuse me?' he said, icily civil.

She sighed inwardly. He was going to make her squirm. 'I said I'm sorry for the way I've been acting these past few days.'

'I still don't understand what I did to offend you,' he said, confirming how deluded he was. 'Just when we were getting along so well.'

'You must understand this pregnancy is playing havoc with my emotions,' she replied, forcing a smile. 'Anyway, it's over and done with. Please don't dwell on it.'

'All right. It's already forgotten,' he said in a cool tone.

Amy shivered as the breeze picked up.

'You're cold?' he said.

'Yes. I'll return to the house.'

'I'll walk with you.'

They walked to the edge of the sunken garden but before they ascended the steps he stopped her, face inscrutable.

'These strange moods of yours, they have to stop, Amy. If you don't want to confide in me that is your prerogative but, I mean it, this hysteria will not be tolerated. If it persists then the consequences for you could be very dire indeed.'

'I can safely say you will never have to endure another one again.'

'Excellent,' he said, giving her a small smile.

He moved closer, resting his hands on her shoulders. A tree branch cast a shadow across his face so only his glittering eyes were visible. Amy glanced sideways at the steps leading up into the light – and safety.

'When we're married things will be better for you,' he said. 'You will belong to me, not them.'

'I know,' she said, despising the way he made her sound like property.

He held out his arm to her, the affable smile returning.

Reluctantly she took his arm and let him lead her up the steps, feeling as though she were being led to the scaffold.

13

The only pleasure Amy got any more was from seeing Lenora vexed. When she realised Amy and Henry had patched things up she was visibly irritated. Uncle Alfred, however, was over the moon and talked excitedly about the wedding. Amy even played up to Henry, holding his hand and giving him flirtatious smiles because it annoyed Lenora.

Edward managed to get a quiet word with her towards the end of the evening.

'Nettie's procured the uniform. Everything's in place.'

'Thank you. I don't know how I will ever repay your kindness.'

'Just go and be happy. I only wish I was coming with you.'

'Why don't you?' she said hopefully. 'You could finally go to London, like you've always wanted.'

'That's very tempting, but I could not be so cruel as to leave my father alone with my mother and brother.'

'You're quite right.' She smiled, trying to hide her disappointment. 'He would be nagged to death.'

When Henry saw Edward talking to her, he hastened to her side, wrapping an arm around her waist and leading her away.

'What's wrong?' she asked, curious as to his reply.

'Don't get too close to Edward. He is not a good man.'

Amy knew he was referring to his brother's sexual preference and it annoyed her, but she tactfully remained silent.

'Promise me you will never be alone with him,' insisted Henry.

She replied with a small nod, trying to hide her mounting fury.

Lenora hated seeing the smug pleasure on Amy's face, so she contrived to eradicate it. She took Amy to one side just before dinner to break the news.

'We've found a nice couple willing to take your baby when it's born.'

Even though she would be long gone when that time came the news still upset Amy and her hands flew to her stomach. 'Who are they?'

'A pleasant couple with a nice farm in Ireland.'

'So far away.'

'The further the better. Out of sight, out of mind.'

'You think it so easy?'

'For your sake it had better be. They're good people and, although they aren't rich, the child will be well loved and cared for. Despite what you may think, I'm not a complete monster.'

Once again Amy remained silent. She was learning to curb her insolent tongue and wondered if she was finally growing up.

Lenora was disappointed. She'd hoped Amy would work herself up into a state again. Alfred had been starting to relent to her repeated demands to call in a doctor when Lenora would have seen to it that they found one who would have been easily persuaded to compile a less than favourable psychiatric report. Her adored son would then be free to marry the much more socially desirable Miss Bartley and, as Amy's guardians, they would finally get their hands on her fortune. However, Amy was displaying an amazing degree of self-control. If she kept this up there would be no grounds for having her committed.

'You can go,' said Lenora, waving her hand in dismissal.

Amy turned and calmly walked from the room with her head held high, the very essence of restraint, and Lenora withstood the urge to strike her.

Sighing, Lenora poured herself a glass of wine to soothe her nerves. She had no idea what her eldest son saw in that girl, for Lenora knew his affection for Amy to be genuine, to her surprise. Of course Amy was very pretty but she was also disobedient, wild and, worst of all, a dirty whore who debauched herself with servants.

It was different with Edward. She could understand why he'd been so desperate to marry Amy. Lenora knew exactly what her younger son was, so him marrying Amy would have been the ideal way out. The family would still have got their hands on her money and Henry could marry Miss Bartley, but Alfred would not give his permission. He was adamant Edward would never be permitted to marry any woman. No, the priesthood was the only way to hide his dirty secret. At least she still had three weeks to save Henry from Amy.

* * *

Amy had talked her plans over with Edward and Nettie until they thought them perfect. Towards the end of the garden party Amy would make her excuses and retire to her room where she would don the servant's uniform. Then she would blend in with the rest of the servants who had been hired from the village, leaving with them and hopefully getting through the gates unchallenged.

The evening before the escape she was a bundle of nerves. She'd packed a bag days ago and Nettie had smuggled it to a friend of hers who would deliver it to Amy at the railway station. All Amy had to do was put her most valuable items in her purse, which she would take with her. She was terrified and she had no real idea what she would do once she had made her escape. Lily, her best friend, was the likeliest source of help. Nettie had posted a letter Amy had written to her requesting her assistance and she could only pray she'd received it.

The knock at her bedroom door made her jump. 'Who is it?'

'Edward.'

She breathed a sigh of relief, and ushered him inside.

'All set?' he whispered as she glanced into the corridor to make sure no one was hanging about, before closing the door.

'Just about. I'm terribly nervous.'

'Try and keep as calm as you can. Think of the baby.' He took an envelope out of his jacket pocket and handed it to her.

'What's this?'

'Something to help you on your way.'

She opened it to reveal a substantial amount of money. 'I can't take this.'

'How are you going to manage without it?'

'I have a bit put by.'

'Take it, please. I have plenty.'

'Thank you,' she said, kissing his cheek. 'I'll say goodbye to you now because I don't know if I'll get the chance tomorrow.' She smiled and took his hands. 'I don't know how I would have survived here without you. I cannot tell you how much I appreciate everything you've done for me.'

'There's no need for thanks. Just go and live a happy life. Live for us both,' he said, drawing tears to Amy's eyes. 'And remember, stay in touch. Nettie gave you the address of her parents' house?'

'She did.' Amy didn't add that she never intended to write. Although she didn't think either Nettie or Edward would betray her, letters could be traced and she didn't want Henry to find her.

* * *

Amy barely slept that night and rose early, feeling lethargic. Nettie wa
almost as nervous as she was.

'I've hidden the uniform under there,' she said, pointing to the bee
'I'm the only one with any business going under there so none of th
other servants should find it.'

'Thank you, Nettie. I want to give you something to show my appre
ciation.'

She pressed a diamond ring into her hand and Nettie's eyes lit up.

'Miss, there's no need.'

'Yes, there is. You've helped save me from having my baby take
away. I will be forever in your debt.'

Nettie's eyes filled with tears and she flung her arms around Amy
neck. Amy hugged her back.

'I'm going to miss you.'

'I'll miss you too.'

'Are you scared?'

'Absolutely petrified.'

* * *

Henry noticed how quiet Amy was that morning, so he was even mo
attentive than usual, enquiring after her health. She assured him sh
was perfectly well.

The day was warm but Amy still had to wear her black mournin
dress, the looser maternity corset disguising her expanding belly. Mo
guests arrived than expected and Amy rejoiced for it would be easy fo
her to disappear in the crowd.

She was escorted into the garden on Henry's arm. He led her fro
person to person, everyone offering their congratulations on th
approaching wedding. No one mentioned the fact that she was still i
mourning but she could see it in their eyes. They all thought th
wedding rushed and she'd noticed more than one pair of eyes flic
down to her stomach.

The day was interminably hot and by four o'clock Amy was exhausted and wondered if she would have the stamina for her escape, but every time she put a hand to her belly she was reminded of why she was doing this. She was careful to remain courteous and deferential to Henry. The last thing she wanted was to annoy any of her relatives and attract attention to herself.

By seven o'clock the party started winding down and she decided it was time for her to retire. Henry had hardly left her side all day, so she didn't need to seek him out.

'I do hope you'll forgive me but I'm exhausted,' she said.

'Of course,' he replied. 'You've done very well. Mother will be pleased. Would you like me to check on you before I retire?'

'That's very thoughtful but I'm so tired.' She kissed his cheek, which, despite the warm day, felt cold. 'I'll see you at breakfast.'

'All right. Goodnight, Amy.'

She tried to keep her step casual as she returned to the house, her stomach churning and legs weak. She caught Edward's eye and he gave her a nod.

Just as she entered the house she encountered Lenora.

'Where are you going, young lady?'

'To bed. I've already asked Henry for his permission.'

'Fine,' she relented. 'You conducted yourself with grace today, Amy. Perhaps you're finally learning to be a lady.'

'If I am it's down to your expert tutelage,' she retorted acidly, unable to help herself.

Fortunately Lenora didn't pick up on her sarcasm. 'Yes, well, get some rest. We shall see you in the morning.'

Amy gave a curt nod and continued upstairs.

Once safely in her room, Amy locked the door and sank onto the bed. She was so tired she didn't dare lie down for fear of falling asleep. Instead she undressed down to her corset and shift in case anyone came in to check on her, then she could slip under the covers and be ready to change into her servant's uniform.

She pulled a chair up to the window to look out into the garden where some guests still remained. The servants hired from the village would soon go home and the house servants would stay up until the last guest had departed.

She couldn't believe she was actually going through with this. She just wished she could see her aunt's face when they discovered she'd gone. Fifty thousand pounds within their grasp and they couldn't spend a single shilling. Neither could she but she didn't care, she'd much rather have her baby than her fortune.

Finally it was time.

With trembling hands she removed the maid's uniform from its hiding place and slid the coarse wool dress over her head. She twisted her hair back into a bun and pulled on the cap. She gazed into the mirror, pleased with the result. It made her look plain and anonymous. Now all she had to do was get downstairs and outside without being noticed.

Peeking through the window, she saw her uncle and aunt talking with an incredibly dull middle-aged couple she'd had the misfortune to be introduced to earlier and Henry was close by talking with Dr Woodrow.

After wrapping herself in her cloak and picking up her purse, which was stuffed with the money Edward had given her as well as her locket and mourning brooch, she cautiously pressed her ear to the door. The only sounds were voices drifting up from below. Slowly she opened the door a crack and peered out. Nothing to the right. Opening it wider, she looked to the left. It was deserted.

Taking a fortifying breath, she stepped out into the corridor and gently closed the door behind her. Assuming the demure stance of a housemaid with her hands clasped and head bowed, she hurried down the corridor. Rather than turning right, which she would normally do, she turned left towards the stairs the servants used.

At the bottom of the stairs she paused by the doorway and peered down the servants' hall. There was plenty of noise coming from the kitchen as the cook prepared supper for the remaining guests, but the kitchen staff were all too busy to notice her. Taking another deep breath, she rushed past the kitchen, moving towards the back door.

Just before she reached it the door was slowly opened by Gerard, who had been promoted to first footman to fill the gap left by Matthew. Fortunately he was balancing a stack of empty plates so he didn't see her. Amy ducked into the wine cellar until it was all clear. Poor Gerard was so laden down it took him a while to pass and she stood stock still, her heart thudding.

When Rush appeared at the opposite end of the corridor she was forced to hide behind a wine rack just before he entered the cellar, grumbling to himself.

'Bloody jumped-up ponces,' he muttered, his clipped accent dropping into a rough Glaswegian brogue she had never heard before. 'You want a bottle of wine? I'll give you a bottle right up your puckered arse.'

Amy clapped a hand over her mouth to stop herself from laughing. She hardly dared breathe as he approached the rack she was crouched behind. A bottle just to the left of her head was removed and she ducked down, so he wouldn't see her. To her surprise she heard a loud pop and a gurgling sound as Rush drank his master's wine. So the redoubtable Rush wasn't so perfect after all.

He took another bottle from further down the rack and stormed out of the room. Amy released the breath she'd been holding, got to her feet and peered through the gap in the rack. All clear.

Reluctantly she moved from her hiding place and returned to the doorway. The passageway was empty.

She practically lunged for the door leading into the garden, hurried through it and gently pulled it shut behind her. She paused for a moment to inhale the cool evening air and compose herself. Twilight was setting in.

Some of the servants were starting to file towards the gates. Amy struggled to keep her step casual as she tagged on behind them.

Her heart almost leapt out of her chest when she saw Henry

standing by the gates, speaking with the groundskeeper. Bringing forth a degree of self-control she didn't know she possessed, she forced her step to remain even and kept her eyes firmly fixed on her feet. She would have to pass within just a few feet of him to get through the gate. If he saw her it would all be over for her and her child.

Edward appeared out of nowhere and engaged Henry in conversation, drawing his attention away from the gate. The last things she saw as she left Alardyce were Edward's eyes, which glanced up at her. Then she was free.

* * *

The walk to the railway station was fraught. Amy expected to be discovered any moment, so she kept her head down, careful not to speak to anyone. As she reached the village she broke off from the group and caught the omnibus into Edinburgh. No one looked twice at her the entire journey and she got off at Waverley station.

Nettie's friend was waiting for her with her suitcase. The small, mousy girl seemed surprised to hand the expensive carpet bag over to a woman dressed as a servant but she accepted the coin Amy pressed into her hand, curtseyed and scurried away. Amy attempted to get lost in the crowd, head bowed, insides squirming with unease. She had just fifteen minutes to wait for her train but it felt like a lifetime. Constantly she scanned the crowd, expecting to see Henry arrive to drag her back to Alardyce or to the asylum.

Finally her train pulled in and she jumped aboard. First class was scarcely populated, so she managed to get a compartment to herself and sat by the window. She willed the train to set off and finally the whistle blew. As the engine picked up speed she released a long breath and sank back into the seat with a smile.

After her ticket had been collected she closed the blinds and changed into her black mourning dress. The ticket collector had looked suspicious to find a servant in his first-class carriage.

She stuffed the servant's dress under the seat and sat down. Finally she could rest. Lulled by the new six-wheeled coach, which was a lot smoother than its four-wheeled predecessor, she soon fell asleep.

* * *

Amy slept for much of the ten-hour journey, only waking to eat. When the train finally arrived in London it was completely dark outside. The broken sleep had done nothing to revive her and it was an effort for her to lift her bag and step off the train.

She found a carriage outside the station and asked to be taken to a discreet hotel close to her friend Lily's home. Although she had never spent a night in it, she knew friends who had. Besides, it was far too late to call on Lily now.

After ringing the bell she was greeted by the night porter, who was surprised to be disturbed by a young woman travelling alone late at night. Fortunately he didn't ask any questions and showed her to a comfortable room on the first floor.

As soon as he'd left she removed her dress and corset, and climbed into bed wearing just her shift. She curled into the foetal position, cradling her belly. Finally it was just her and her baby.

* * *

It was ten o'clock when Amy woke the following morning, feeling revived. She rose and dressed, discarding the corset now she had no one to assist her on with it.

Without the corset the gentle swell of her belly pressed against the silk of her dress, but she was proud of it and stood sideways in the mirror to admire her stomach. Already she loved this child more than anything.

As she'd missed breakfast she asked for some tea and sandwiches to be brought to her room. After eating she felt much stronger, so she started the short walk to Lily's house.

Lily lived in a beautiful four-storey town house owned by her wealthy husband. Amy stared up at it nervously before ringing the bell, wondering what sort of reception she was going to get. The door was opened by a butler who led her through to the drawing room.

Lily was waiting for her, as beautiful as always.

'Leave us,' Lily ordered the butler, who bowed and obeyed.

'Thank you for seeing me,' said Amy.

'I suppose I should give you the chance to explain why I've hardly heard from you all these months. I thought you were going to invite me to stay?'

'Did you get my letter?'

'I did receive a garbled communication that didn't make much sense. One letter in months. It's not good enough, Amy, we're supposed to be friends...'

She trailed off as Amy threw back her cloak to reveal her swollen stomach.

'You're... you're with child?' stammered Lily. 'So that's why you had to get married. I saw the announcement in the paper.'

'Henry's not the father and we're not married.'

Lily's eyebrows went up. 'Who is the father?'

Amy felt so ashamed she couldn't speak and burst into tears.

Lily hugged her then sat her down and listened in stunned silence as Amy related the whole sorry saga.

When she'd finished Lily was staring at her with such surprise that for a terrible moment Amy thought she was going to throw her out. Instead she embraced her.

'Here I am being petty and you've been enduring this.'

'I know I've no right to ask, Lily, but I really need your help. I don't want to give birth alone. I'm so scared.'

'I won't let that happen. Between the two of us we'll come up with something.'

14

The day after the garden party the family gathered for lunch and Henry frowned at Amy's vacant chair. 'Has anyone seen Amy?'

They all shook their heads.

'I'll check on her,' he said, getting to his feet.

'Leave her be,' said Lenora. 'She's probably worn out. Pregnancy does that to you.'

'What if she's unwell? No, I must check on her.'

He hurried out of the room, knowing something was wrong. He took the stairs two at a time and raced down the corridor to her room.

'Amy?' he said, pushing open the door.

Her room was empty and he wasn't sure whether her bed had just been made or if it hadn't been slept in. He flung open the wardrobe and gasped. Although her bulkier gowns remained, all her day dresses and travelling clothes were gone.

Frantically he yanked open the drawers and searched her dressing table and, although some things remained, most of her personal items had vanished.

He spun on his heel and tore downstairs to the kitchen. All the servants stopped what they were doing, surprised to see him there.

'Have you seen Amy?' he boomed at Nettie, making her jump.

'No, sir,' she replied. 'Yesterday before she retired she said she intended to sleep in and wouldn't require me until after lunch.'

'Damn,' he yelled before running out of the room.

'She's gone,' exclaimed Henry, bursting into the dining room.

Lenora froze, the fork halfway to her mouth. 'What?'

'Amy, she's run away.'

'No, she wouldn't do that to us,' said Alfred, shaking his head.

'Oh, yes, she would, the ungrateful little slut,' screeched Lenora, shoving back her chair and shooting to her feet.

'She's pregnant. She can't just leave,' said Alfred, his voice filled with genuine concern.

'No doubt she's in London,' spat Lenora, pacing the floor like a caged beast. 'Gone to seek help from her dubious friends. If anyone knows what to do about an illegitimate child, I'm sure they do.'

'Where do we start to look?' said Henry. 'We don't know who her friends are.'

'I can't believe she would do this,' repeated Alfred, more to himself than anyone else. 'Are we so terrible?'

Henry regarded his brother suspiciously. 'Edward, you don't seem surprised to learn that she's left.'

'I don't know anything,' he replied.

'Liar. I've seen the two of you whispering in corners. You turned her against me, didn't you?'

'You did that all on your own. She couldn't stand the thought of being married to you. She hates you,' Edward said with relish.

Henry stormed up to his brother, who shot to his feet, and the two squared up to each other.

'Boys, please,' said Lenora. 'This isn't helping.'

'I know you had something to do with this,' said Henry before stomping to the sideboard and pouring himself a Scotch with a shaking hand.

'Don't just sit there, Alfred,' cried Lenora. 'Do something. We must find the stupid girl and bring her back before anyone finds out.'

'Y... yes, of course,' he stammered. 'Edward, would you ring for Rush?'

'We can't involve the servants,' said Lenora.

'What choice is there? We can't scour the whole of London on our own.'

Edward rang the bell and the call was answered a moment later.

'Rush,' said Alfred. 'It seems Miss Osbourne has... err... disappeared and we're anxious to locate her. Will you please ask around the village discreetly? Start with the omnibus conductor.'

'Yes, sir.' He bowed, betraying no emotion before leaving the room.

'I'm going with him,' said Henry.

'No, you're not,' replied his father in a surprisingly firm tone. 'Rush is perfectly capable of handling it. If you want to do something useful, pour us all a drink while we wait for him to return.'

'Yes, Father,' he relented.

The family waited in anxious silence for Rush to return, the brothers casting each other black looks while Lenora fantasised about what she would do to Amy when she got her hands on her. An hour later Rush returned.

'Well?' said Alfred.

'A young lady answering Miss Osbourne's description boarded the eight-fifteen omnibus to Waverley station yesterday evening, sir. I can't be entirely sure it was her as she was wearing a servant's uniform.'

'Servant's uniform?' said Lenora. 'She is mad.'

'No, she's not, she's very clever,' said Alfred. 'With all the servants about yesterday, no one would have noticed her leave with them. It seems we underestimated her.'

'Where did she get the uniform from?' said Henry. 'One of the servants, no doubt.'

'You must be right,' said Alfred. 'Rush, send up each of the servants one by one. I will see them in my study. Start with her maid, Nettie.'

Despite harsh interrogations, none of the servants were able to tell them anything. Alfred and Henry tried coaxing, bribery and threats but they all appeared as confused as each other. Even Nettie seemed to be clueless.

Henry was out of his mind with worry and rage. Stormy-faced, he hunted down his brother and found him in the billiard room. He grabbed him by the shirt front and pushed him up against the wall.

'What did you do to her?' he yelled in Edward's face.

'We all have skeletons, don't we? I just let a few of yours out of the closet.'

'Where's she gone? Where?' Henry roared with sheer frustration.

'No idea, but it's my guess you'll never see her again.'

Henry drew back his fist and punched Edward in the face, knocking him to the floor.

Edward put a hand to his mouth and stared at the blood on his fingers in amusement. 'I thought you were such a cold fish, Henry. It seems Amy's started a fire inside you.'

Henry stood over him, breathing hard. 'I swear I'll get you back for this.'

Incensed, Henry kicked his brother in the back then knelt before him, grabbed a handful of his hair and yanked back his head. 'You know full well what I'm capable of.'

'Then it's fortunate for Amy that she's far from here.'

With a growl of rage Henry shoved him away and stormed out of the room.

* * *

Sir Hugh, Lily's husband, owned a pleasant cottage in Berkshire, which was where she took Amy to wait out her confinement. Fortunately Sir Hugh was away in India on business and wasn't due to return to England for another four months.

Amy made sure she didn't leave the grounds for the duration of her stay in case anyone saw her condition and assumed Sir Hugh was the father. She didn't want to tarnish his good name.

By the time the newspaper articles requesting information about Amy were circulated, she and Lily were safely ensconced in Berkshire.

Amy's life became the cottage and her ever-expanding belly. She loved the feel of life growing inside her and each movement and flutter brought fresh excitement.

Lily furnished her with clothes and a beautiful bassinette for the baby. She was just as excited as Amy about the imminent arrival, having not yet managed to conceive herself.

As the weeks ticked by Henry became more sullen, brooding endlessly over Amy's disappearance. They'd managed to track her to a hotel in Kensington then nothing. They'd thought she was incapable of surviving on her own but she had proved them all wrong. He admired her courage but what drove him mad was that he knew she'd had help from inside Alardyce House. Henry's blood boiled whenever he thought of his brother. He would get his revenge on him and he would find Amy and bring her back. He wanted her and what Henry wanted he always got.

Amy was reading in the parlour of Sir Hugh's Berkshire country retreat, stroking her stomach, which bulged beneath her grey silk dress. Finally she was in half-mourning and no longer had to be permanently draped in black. Her pregnancy was full term and she couldn't wait to meet her child.

A sharp pain in her stomach made her gasp and drop her book.

'Lily,' she cried.

Her friend dashed into the room. 'What is it?'

'I think it's started.'

After dispatching the maid to fetch the midwife, Lily helped her upstairs to her bedroom, which had been prepared for the birth. Amy lay on the bed, gripping onto her friend's hand as she experienced an agony she didn't think possible.

'Don't leave me,' cried Amy when Lily rushed from the room.

'It's all right, I'm here,' she said, hurrying back clutching a bundle of towels.

She knelt before Amy, pushed up her skirts and her eyes widened.

'What is it?' said an anxious Amy.

'I can see the head. It's coming,' she exclaimed, sounding just as frightened as her friend. Frantically she began to place towels on the bed beneath her. 'I think I'm supposed to get hot water but I've no idea what to do with it.'

'Me neither,' gasped Amy in a brief respite between the pain. Another one gripped her and she screamed with fear as it felt as if she were about to be split in two.

'The head's out,' cried Lily, her immaculate blonde hair springing out from its severe braid. 'Where is that midwife?'

In response the maid tore into the room followed by a small but formidable-looking old lady.

'Oh, thank God,' said Lily, moving out of the way.

The midwife glanced between Amy's legs and nodded. 'You're almost there, darlin'. Just one more big push and it'll all be over.'

Amy was so exhausted she wasn't sure she had the strength. As the next pain swelled up inside her she bore down and felt the tiny body slither out. A loud, lusty cry filled her with relief and Amy fought against the fatigue to get a glimpse of her child as the midwife expertly cut the cord then cleaned and swaddled the baby. With a smile she handed Amy the tiny bundle.

'Congratulations. You have a healthy son.'

Amy took the child in her arms and experienced an intense love

He was gorgeous with a little rosebud mouth, pudgy cheeks and a mop of black hair, just like his father's.

'He's so beautiful.' Lily smiled, tears in her eyes.

'What's his name?' said the midwife.

'Robert.' Amy beamed. 'For my father.'

15

DERBYSHIRE, ENGLAND – JUNE 1888

Amy, clutching Robert's hand, walked up to the imposing front door of the huge house in the heart of the Derbyshire countryside and rang the bell. Robert looked up at her and grinned his big beautiful grin but Amy could detect his nerves. He was even more anxious than she was about this interview. She smiled down at him and ran her fingers through his thick black hair. At nine years old he was the very image of his father with the same dark eyes, sharp cheekbones and pouty mouth. He'd started to ask questions about his father and so far she'd managed to satisfy his queries with vague responses, but she was painfully aware that soon he would demand the truth and she had no idea what she would tell him.

They were shown into a large, beautifully decorated hallway, a huge chandelier hanging over their heads, and Robert stared up at it in fascination. The butler led them into an equally opulent drawing room. The whole place screamed *we have wealth and we're not afraid to show it*.

The lady of the house, who had requested her services, waited to greet her, looking more nervous than Amy. She was a beautiful young woman, delicate and slim with willowy limbs and tiny hands and feet.

She had the biggest blue eyes Amy had ever seen, set in a sculptured face framed by silky light-brown hair.

'I'm Mrs Huntington,' she said. 'It's so nice to meet you, Mrs Parker. Would you like some tea?'

'Yes, please.' Amy smiled, removing her bonnet.

Mrs Huntington smiled at Robert. 'And I think you would like some milk and biscuits?'

'Yes, please, madam,' he replied, giving her his most charming smile.

'What a polite young man.' She beamed before asking the butler to fetch the refreshments. When he'd gone she turned her attention back to Amy and Robert. 'It's very nice to meet you both. Please, have a seat. You come highly recommended by Lady Williams,' began Mrs Huntington in her soft, gentle voice. 'You were governess to her children for three years, is that right?'

'Yes. I was sad to leave that position. She was an excellent employer and I was very fond of the children.'

'And they you, I'm told. Apparently they flourished beneath your tutelage.'

'They were extremely bright children.'

'Well, I would like to offer you a position here, effective immediately, on a trial period of course. I have a niece, Jane, who I took in when my sister and her husband died in an accident.'

Amy swallowed hard, feeling a well of sympathy for her new charge.

'I dismissed her last governess as I was not happy with some of her techniques, which were severe to say the least.' She frowned. 'Consequently Jane is now a little wary of another governess but I think you're the ideal candidate to bring her out of herself.'

'I do hope so,' she replied.

'I'll pay you the same rate as Lady Williams. You will of course have your own room and meals will be included.'

'Did Lady Williams mention that Robert lives with me?'

'She did and it's perfectly all right by me. I love having children about the house. I've arranged for him to have the room next to yours. They are joined by a connecting door.'

'He gets his own room?' said Amy with surprise. 'That's wonderful, thank you. We've always been expected to share before.'

'This house has eleven bedrooms. I think we can spare one,' she said with a smile at Robert.

'Thank you, madam,' he said, getting to his feet to give her his most graceful bow.

'Such a gentleman already.' She laughed with delight. 'It will be good for Jane to have you here, Master Parker. We are in an isolated position, so she doesn't have many playmates. You are how old?'

'Nine, Mrs Huntington.'

'Then you're about the same age. Jane is eight.' She looked back at Amy. 'Is all that acceptable to you, Mrs Parker?'

'Very much so.'

'Excellent,' she said with a nervous exhalation. 'Would you like to meet Jane now?'

'Yes, I would. Very much.'

They followed her to a room and as Mrs Huntington opened the door Amy smiled. It was a huge playroom filled with toys, books and a beautiful mahogany desk by the window. Facing it was a smaller desk at which sat a pretty girl with the same doll-like appearance as her aunt. Her hair was long, blonde and curly, tied in bunches, and she wore a white pinafore dress.

'Jane,' said Mrs Huntington. 'There's someone I would like you to meet.'

'Oh, yes?' she said disinterestedly, her eyes not leaving her drawing.

'This is your new governess, Mrs Parker.'

Jane looked up with a serious little face, suspicion in her beautiful blue eyes. 'Hello,' she said politely before returning to her drawing.

'Hello, Jane,' said Amy.

'I'm sorry,' began Mrs Huntington. 'She's been like this ever since the last governess.'

'It's all right,' replied Amy. She stepped towards Jane and said, 'May I see your drawing?'

Jane shrugged and leaned back for her to see, although it was clear she resented the intrusion.

Amy studied the sketch. It was a pretty woodland scene with careful attention to detail. 'Very good. You have talent.'

Jane regarded her with surprise. 'You don't think it a waste of time?'

'Of course not. I love to sketch myself, although I confess I prefer to use watercolours.'

'You use watercolours? I love fairies and I've always wanted to paint them in watercolours. Will you teach me?'

'Yes, if you wish. There's some astonishing countryside around here. Perhaps we could go on an outing and paint some landscapes? With your aunt's permission, of course.'

'I think that's a wonderful idea.' Mrs Huntington smiled, pleased to see her niece thawing.

'When can we go?' said Jane.

'In a few days, after we've had a chance to settle in.'

Jane's eyes settled on Robert. 'Hello.' She smiled shyly.

'Hello,' he replied equally shyly.

'Would you like to see my toys?'

While the two children began playing together, Mrs Huntington smiled. 'I haven't seen her so animated in days.'

'Perhaps the last governess dented her confidence about drawing, which she clearly loves,' replied Amy.

Mrs Huntington's smile fell. 'I feel dreadful for hiring that woman.'

'I've met women like her before. They think children flourish beneath a regime of harsh discipline and constant bullying. They have no right being anywhere near a child.'

Mrs Huntington looked at her niece, who was running around with

Robert, laughing. 'I think you will do much to repair the damage.' She smiled.

* * *

Amy's duties didn't start until the following day, so she and Robert took a walk around the estate. Huntington Manor was set in beautiful grounds, with their own stables and paddock, which fascinated Robert.

They returned to the house, Amy ensuring Robert washed his face and hands and combed his hair. She'd expected to eat in the school room with the children but a footman informed her that the mistress wished for Amy and the children to dine with her.

During dinner in the grand dining room, Mrs Huntington – after insisting Amy call her Esther – chatted pleasantly and asked Amy about her life.

Amy gave her well-worn story of how Robert's father had died in a mining accident not long after he'd been born and she'd been forced to become a governess to support them both. Amy hadn't told a soul who she really was. After her money had run out and she'd sold all her jewels she'd been forced to seek employment for the first time in her life. Lily had written her references so she could get a position as a governess with a good family in Southern Ireland and Amy had discovered she was excellent with children. The last three years had been spent in Lancashire, and she and Robert had both been very happy there, but she'd had to leave her position when the family had decided to move to France.

There were only two people who knew Amy's true identity – Lily, who she wrote to regularly, and Mr Buchanan, her father's solicitor. She wanted him to know she was still alive so the Alardyces couldn't have her declared dead and get their claws into her money.

A year ago Amy had read in the papers that Lenora had died after long illness. Henry had moved to London and married his heiress, Miss Alice Bartley. Unfortunately she'd passed away and he' remained a widower. Unsurprisingly Edward was still single. *The Gazette* had reported that he had recently returned from abroad and was living in Kensington, finally living his dream of the capital.

Esther surprised Amy again by inviting her to share a drink with her after the children – both exhausted by spending the day playing together – had gone to bed. They enjoyed a glass of wine together while they talked and Amy discovered that Esther was rather lonely.

'We're so secluded here,' she explained. 'We don't get much company and my husband is often away on business.'

'May I enquire what sort of business he's in?'

'It's my family's business. We have textile mills in the north of England but the majority are in Manchester. He took it all over when we married – I've no head for business. My parents died when I was young.'

'Mine too,' said Amy.

'It's hard, isn't it?'

Amy nodded, touching the locket at her throat.

'Jane and my husband are the only family I have left but, because of my husband's business commitments, it's usually just Jane and I.'

Her big eyes were sad and Amy got the impression Mr Huntington was rather neglectful of his wife. Esther was gentle and kind, easy for a strong man to walk over. Still, she refrained from judging Mr Huntington too harshly until she'd met him – after all, there were two sides to every story. She knew that better than anyone.

* * *

Jane flourished beneath Amy's encouraging tutelage and she got on wonderfully with Robert. Esther was so pleased she made Amy's position permanent after just two days.

The four of them dined together each night, and the two women started to become friends. Esther confided in Amy that the lack of children was a huge bone of contention between her and her husband.

Esther thought of Jane as a daughter but Amy could see her yearning to carry a child of her own, to feel it growing inside her and raise it from birth.

When coaxed out of her shell Esther could be rather witty and after the children had gone to bed she and Amy stayed up drinking wine, talking and laughing.

* * *

Then Mr Huntington came home.

The servants flew about the house, preparing for his return, and Esther ordered a lavish dinner be made. She apologised to Amy because now she would have to eat in the schoolroom with the children, but Amy didn't mind.

The arrival of Mr Huntington was heralded by the housekeeper scurrying into the schoolroom.

'He's here, Mrs Parker.'

'Thank you, Mrs Morton. Jane, stand up,' she said gently.

She obeyed. Robert was out with the gamekeeper searching for rabbits.

'Straighten your dress,' she whispered to the girl, moments before Esther entered the room.

'Mrs Parker, I would like you to meet my husband.' She beamed.

In he strode and Amy's entire body went rigid with shock. He too stopped in his tracks and his eyes widened with amazement, but he swiftly recovered and stepped forward to greet her.

'Pleased to meet you, Mrs Parker. My wife informs me you're doing excellent work.'

She heard herself reply in a steady tone, even though she had no idea how. 'Thank you, sir. Jane is an excellent pupil.'

He gazed at her for a moment before striding out of the room followed by a smiling Esther.

'Continue with your exercises,' Amy managed to tell Jane before collapsing into a chair, head spinning. How could he be here? She'd spent so long hiding she had begun to think herself safe and now her worst nightmare was coming true. She was desperate to speak with him, to beg him not to betray her. Perhaps she could get him to listen?

Fortunately she didn't have long to wait because Esther went out for a walk and Amy was summoned to the master's study.

'Hello, Amy,' he said when they were finally alone.

'Hello, Matthew,' she replied uncertainly, squirming before his impressive mahogany desk. He was speaking in an English accent. What had happened to his native Scottish?

He stared at her in wonder. 'I can't believe you're here, as a governess of all things.'

'Neither can I. First, I'd like to say that I didn't know you were here.'

'And why should you? I've been careful to keep my identity secret.'

'As have I.'

'I read in the papers that you fled Alardyce. What happened?'

His tone was gentle so she saw no need to keep it from him, all except for Robert, of course. Something urged her not to tell him he was a father.

'Esther told me you have a son,' he said when she'd finished her tale. 'Is... is he mine?' he said hopefully.

She shook her head. 'I married shortly after I ran away and fell pregnant straight away. My husband died when Robert was very young.'

His eyes bored into her and she met his look unflinchingly.

'You're certain of this?'

'Absolutely. I was taking Mrs Magrath's potion, remember?'

The hope died in his eyes. 'Of course. You're perhaps wondering how I came to be master of all this?' he said.

'It's none of my business, and I swear I will not give you away as long as you keep my secret. Perhaps it would be better if I found another position?'

'That will not be necessary,' he said quickly. 'It's so good to see you again I'm loath to part from you now.'

'Just so we're clear, we can't resume our affair.'

'Of course not. I always enjoyed your company, Amy, that's all I meant. Sharing my bed is not part of your duties.'

'Good.' She smiled. 'I'm glad you have a nice life here.'

'Look, I even kept the pocket watch you gave me,' he said, producing it from inside a pocket of his waistcoat.

Not knowing what to say, she smiled and nodded.

He got up and walked round the desk, eyes fixed on her, and for a moment she thought he was going to kiss her on the mouth but instead he kissed the top of her head and she experienced a pang of disappointment. He hardly seemed to have aged, just a few creases around his eyes denoting the passage of the years. His hair was still jet black and he looked fit and strong. There had always been a strong magnetism between them and she was dismayed to realise that there still was.

She took a step back. 'I must return to Jane,' she said, giving him a little dip before rushing from the room, finding it strange having to curtsey to someone who was once a footman.

Jane was still hard at work when Amy returned to the schoolroom so she sent her outside to play so she could consider her position. There was no way she could stay here now. She didn't think Matthew would betray her to the Alardyces, but what on earth was he doing here masquerading as Mr Huntington? What was he up to? What about poor Esther? Had he duped her into marriage for her money?

She pushed these thoughts aside. No matter how unsavoury or criminal it all was, she couldn't get involved. She had to get her son away before Matthew discovered the truth.

* * *

Amy returned to her room to change before dinner. Before she had the chance to undress there was a knock at the door, and Matthew sneaked in, quietly closing the door behind him.

'What are you doing?' she demanded.

'Forgive me but I had to see you before Esther gets home.' He gently held her by the shoulders. 'I've often thought about you, Amy, and now you're back in my life I can't get you out of my head.'

He kissed her and the feel of his lips on hers was just as potent as it had been all those years ago. She snatched herself out of his embrace.

'This is wrong. Esther is a good woman and has been very kind to me. I will not betray her.' She turned her back on him so she wouldn't weaken. 'I think you should leave.'

He came up behind her and kissed her neck. 'I missed you,' he murmured, his warm breath on her skin making her shiver with delight.

His hand slid down her dress and over her breasts. Amy hadn't allowed any man to touch her since Robert's birth but when Matthew touched her she burned for more.

'Matthew, don't,' she feebly protested.

He turned her to face him and kissed her, his tongue flicking into her mouth, and she moaned as the last of her resolve disintegrated. He pushed her up against the wall, one hand freeing her hair from its bun, sending it cascading down her back. When his other hand disappeared under her skirt she gasped with longing.

Esther's trusting eyes filled her head – that gentle woman who had been a friend to her after years of loneliness.

'No,' she said, putting her hands on Matthew's broad chest and trying to push him away.

'What's wrong?' he said, refusing to be moved.

She ducked under his arm and retreated as far from temptation as possible.

'You have a beautiful wife and we have both betrayed her.' She sighed and shook her head. 'I thought I wasn't that person any more.'

'There's always been something powerful between us. Don[t] fight it.'

He moved to kiss her again but she held up her hands.

'Please leave.'

'Amy...'

'No, Matthew. I was weak once but it won't happen again. I aske[d] you to leave. Please comply with my wishes.'

His expression hardened and he stomped from the room, slam-ming the door shut behind him. Amy perched on the edge of the be[d] and buried her face in her hands. One day back in his company an[d] already she was under his spell.

16

Matthew stomped downstairs in a black mood. Amy had always been his weakness and all the years apart had done nothing to dampen his desire. Women these days were so straight-laced but Amy had that unquenchable fire inside her. Only she would give up a life of wealth and privilege to work as a governess and he couldn't help but marvel at her nerve. He'd hoped he could have Amy under his roof as his mistress, but she would be tougher to crack than he'd thought. He had mistresses dotted about the country but he'd already lost interest in them now Amy was back. She was all he'd ever wanted but, thanks to his stupid wife, she was feeling guilty. He would have to drive a wedge between them.

His thoughts were interrupted by the gamekeeper entering the hall via the front door.

'What on earth are you doing?' demanded Matthew. 'You are not permitted to enter this part of the house.'

'Sorry, sir, but the mistress gave me permission to bring back Mrs Parker's son.'

A boy stepped out from behind the man and time seemed to freeze for Matthew. It was like looking at himself when he was a child – the same hair and eyes, the same everything. Matthew knelt before him and stared in wonder.

'And what's your name?' he asked while the gamekeeper hastily left, closing the front door behind him.

'Robert Parker, sir,' he politely replied.

'Pleased to meet you, Master Parker. My name's Mr Huntington but you may call me Matthew.'

He held his hand out to the boy, who shook it with such seriousness it made Matthew smile.

'Is this your house, sir?' said Robert.

'It is. Do you like it?'

'Yes. We've stayed in some nice houses but this is the best.'

'I'm very glad you think so. Have you seen the billiard room yet?'

'Mama said I'm not allowed.' He sighed.

'Come along, I'll take you.'

'Thank you.' He grinned.

She lied, thought Matthew as he led the boy into the billiard room.

* * *

After changing her clothes and washing, Amy felt a lot calmer, although she was dreading having to look Esther in the eyes.

It was then she realised she hadn't heard Robert return and it was only ten minutes until dinner.

Peeking into his room, she confirmed he wasn't there. Worry niggled at her. This wasn't like him; he was such an obedient boy. What if he'd had an accident?

She hurried downstairs to seek out the gamekeeper but at the bottom of the stairs she paused when she heard Robert's laugh and the click of billiard balls. She'd told him not to play in there. Furious, she flung open the door and stopped. Matthew was by her son's side, helping him draw back the cue. Robert managed to pocket a ball and they both cheered. When Robert looked up and saw her standing there his smile only broadened, breaking her heart.

'I did it, Mama. Did you see?'

She forced a smile. 'Yes, I did. Well done, sweetheart.'

Matthew fixed her with dark eyes just like her son's.

Sweet Lord, he knows, she thought with a sinking feeling. It had been naive of her to think he wouldn't spot the resemblance.

'Robert, there's only ten minutes before dinner. Please go upstairs and change,' she said, wanting to get him away from Matthew.

'But, Mama, we're playing a game.'

'Do as your mother says and we'll continue the game after dinner,' said Matthew.

Robert's face lit up. 'Really? Thank you, Matthew.' He grinned before racing out of the room.

Amy moved to follow him, anxious to escape Matthew's accusing stare.

'Stay where you are, Mrs Parker.'

Amy obeyed. She had no choice.

'Close the door.'

She did before reluctantly turning to face him.

'Well, the tables have turned, haven't they?' he said, his anger building.

She didn't reply.

'Why did you lie to me? The child is clearly mine.'

'I admit there's a slight resemblance but he's my husband's,' she said, desperately clinging onto her story.

'You're lying to me,' he said, resting the cue on the table. 'Why?' he thundered, slamming his fist down on the edge of the billiard table. 'I am not a fool, nor am I blind. My own eyes tell me he's mine.'

'You're seeing what you want to see. My only charge is your niece. You have no children of your own.'

For a brief moment his eyes filled with anguish. 'Esther has never conceived. I thought the fault may be mine but how can it be when you've had my child?'

'I repeat, Robert is not yours.'

'If I discover you're lying to me there will be hell to pay.'

His eyes filled with a cold fury that frightened her and she swallowed nervously. 'If that is all, sir, I must attend to the children.'

She stalked from the room, head held high, but inside she was quivering. He had discovered her lie. The only question was, what would he do about it?

* * *

Matthew watched Amy leave then stormed into his study and summoned Hobbs, his valet and right-hand man. He was a tall and broad ex-soldier with hands like shovels and a craggy face.

'I need you to find something out for me urgently,' Matthew told him.

'Yes, sir?' he said, face expressionless.

'I want you to find out if Mrs Parker has ever been married. Don't return until you've found out.'

Hobbs bowed and left, leaving Matthew to seethe behind his desk.

* * *

Matthew's black mood extended into the next day. Esther tried to talk to him but her presence irritated him more than usual. Last night she'd even tried to get him to sleep in her bed but he didn't want her needy lovemaking. He wanted Amy's fire in his bed, not Esther's ice.

Hobbs returned the following afternoon, just as Matthew was on the verge of exploding with impatience.

'I checked every record,' he began. 'There's no record of Mrs Parker marrying anyone.'

'I knew it,' said Matthew, eyes gleaming. 'You've done well, Hobbs. You're to say nothing about this to anyone.'

'Sir,' he replied, bowing before leaving.

Matthew heard the sound of laughter from outside and gazed out of the window to see Robert playing with Jane. The boy looked so happy and carefree it made him smile. Now he was positive the child was his he couldn't help but be proud of the fine, handsome boy. His smile fell when he spotted Amy sitting on a bench. Now was his chance.

Snatching his keys from his desk drawer, he hurried upstairs and into the west wing. He checked no one was around as he found the key to Amy's room, unlocked it and stepped inside. He paused to take stock of the room. A few toiletries and trinkets sat on the dressing table. He picked up a deep blue ribbon and pressed it to his face, inhaling her scent, and exhaled shakily. Replacing it, he went through the chest of drawers but found nothing. Getting on his hands and knees, he peeked beneath the bed and saw a trunk. He pulled it out and threw open the lid but, to his irritation, it was empty. The wardrobe was the only place left. He opened it to reveal her clothes and frowned. It was full of dowdy grey wool dresses. A woman of her pedigree should be in silks and satins. If she came round to his way of thinking he would buy her new dresses, just like the ones she'd used to wear.

He shoved the ugly clothes aside to examine the items secreted at the back of the wardrobe – some hideous clumpy shoes, a couple of dull hats and a battered carpet bag. He found these poor, tattered objects rather sad after the wealth he knew she had once enjoyed.

He took out the bag and laid it on the bed to examine it. Inside he found a pile of documents and photographs, Amy's birth certificate, images of her parents and their death certificates as well as the mourning brooch containing her mother's hair.

At the bottom of the pile was a folded-up piece of paper. He opened it up with bated breath and smiled with satisfaction before folding it back up and slipping it into his pocket.

Something else caught his eye. Tucked away in the corner wa
about a hundred pounds, which Amy had obviously carefully squi
relled away. He put that in his pocket too so she couldn't escape. Afte
all, she was good at disappearing.

* * *

Amy's nerves were stretched to the limit. She kept expecting Matthe
to confront her but she didn't see him all day. Perhaps she would g
away with it after all?

After settling Jane and Robert in bed, she returned to the schoo
room to tidy up.

As she stooped to pick up some pencils Esther walked in and aga
Amy experienced a rush of guilt. She had noted earlier that Esthe
looked tense, as she had ever since Matthew had returned, and sh
wondered if she suspected something.

'Hello, Amy,' said Esther with forced cheer. 'I wanted to ask ho
Jane's progressing.'

'Extremely well.' She smiled, always pleased to talk about he
charge. 'She struggled with her spelling today, but she worked ha
and didn't stop until she'd overcome the problem. Her watercolours a
very good too.'

'That's wonderful. I was worried about her but since you arrive
she's become such a happy girl.' Esther shuffled awkwardly in th
doorway, as though there was something she wanted to say but didn
know how.

'Is something wrong, madam?' said Amy encouragingly.

She opened her mouth to speak then closed it again and wrung he
hands.

'Esther, what is it?'

Tears filled Esther's eyes and Amy placed a comforting hand o
her arm.

'I apologise,' said Esther, wiping away the tears. 'I'm being ridiculous.'

'Has something happened?'

'Oh, just the usual pressures. I'm so silly. Forgive me,' she said before dashing off.

'Esther?' Amy called after her, but Esther fled upstairs.

Before Amy had the opportunity to follow her, a voice interrupted her thoughts.

'Finally. I thought she'd never leave.'

Matthew entered the room, closing the door behind him, and she backed away.

'We have pressing matters to discuss.' He removed Robert's birth certificate from his pocket and read it. 'Robert John Osbourne. Mother Amy Osbourne, Father Matthew Bettany.'

The colour drained from her face. 'You've gone through my things. You have no right.'

'That's nothing compared to what you've done. How could you keep this from me?'

Amy knew further denial was useless. With a weary sigh she said, 'I knew I should have put a false name but I couldn't bring myself to lie to him.'

'But that's what you've been doing, Amy,' he replied darkly. 'I am his father and you were going to keep it from both of us.'

'I thought it for the best.'

'Why?'

'Robert can only ever be your bastard and I will not do that to him.'

Gently he took her hands. 'There's another way. You remain here not as a governess but as my guest. You and Robert could have your own suites, you'd want for nothing. I would remain married to Esther but in name only. We would lead entirely separate lives. Or if you prefer I could find us a nice house where we could live together with our son.'

Amy snatched her hands away. 'You want me to be your whore?'

'If you prefer I could divorce her first,' he said almost casually. 'I'd get all the money and property anyway, although it would create a scandal.'

'You would do that to Esther? A woman who is nothing but kind and clearly loves you.'

'And dull. Don't forget dull. She bores me silly.'

'Then why did you marry her?'

'I did find her charming at first.'

'I will not do this. I like and respect Esther and I won't destroy her.'

She tried to stride past him but he pulled her towards him.

'Listen to me, Amy.' The words came out haltingly as he struggled to control his temper. He squeezed her arm, making her wince. 'We were meant to find each other again. You came to me with the son I have longed for all these years. We are fated to be together.'

He gritted his teeth in an effort to control himself.

'You're hurting me,' she breathed as he squeezed harder.

'I'm sorry,' he said, relaxing his grip. He led her to a chair, sat her down then knelt before her and kissed her hands. 'I wouldn't hurt you for the world. Will you at least consider my proposal, please?'

Amy had absolutely no intention of agreeing to his revolting idea, but she needed to keep him happy until she could think things through. 'Yes, I will think about it.'

'That's all I can ask.' He smiled. 'May I kiss you to sustain me until our next meeting?'

She disliked the idea of betraying Esther again but she had to continue the charade, so she nodded. Heat burned between them and she lost herself in the kiss, in the feel of his warm hands on her skin.

'Just a reminder of what you could have every night if you consent to my proposal,' he whispered in her ear.

With that he left the room and tears welled in Amy's eyes. She sat for a while in the schoolroom while the rest of the house went to bed. Only when everything was silent did she creep upstairs to her room. She looked around the little chamber with dismay. He'd been in here without her permission, rooting through her things just as Henry had at Alardyce and the same sense of violation crept over her. Why couldn't these men just leave her alone? She knew she'd locked the door, which meant he had a key.

After locking the door, she took a chair and wedged it under the handle. Satisfied she was secure, she changed into her nightgown and slid beneath the covers but sleep wouldn't come.

Amy wasn't a fool. She knew Matthew didn't want her, he wanted Robert. Amy also suspected he wanted her to give him more children but becoming his whore was not the future she envisioned for herself.

Her thoughts were distracted by a squeak and she watched with dismay as the door knob started to turn. When it didn't open she heard the jangle of a key and the click of the lock. The door was pushed open slightly, revealing a slit of blackness and a shadowy figure beyond but the chair prevented it from opening any further. She lay absolutely still, eyes screwed tight shut, while her heart thudded so loudly she feared he would hear it. There was a dreadful moment of ominous silence and she could feel his rage at being thwarted.

The door closed and footsteps padded back down the hall. Amy exhaled shakily, unaware she had even been holding her breath.

17

'Mrs Parker, are you unwell?' enquired Jane.

Amy jumped out of her reverie. 'No, I'm quite well.'

'You're very pale.'

Robert looked up from his work with a frown.

'I didn't sleep well, that's all. Thank you for your concern.' She smiled.

'I've finished another drawing, if you would like to see?'

Amy rose lethargically out of her chair and shuffled over to Jane's desk. The sketch was perfectly executed but rather than the bright colours Jane was so fond of she'd used varying shades of black and grey. The picture was of a young woman, with long blonde hair and blue eyes. Her expression was benign, tender even, but it was her ghastly pallor and blue lips that worried Amy the most. Surrounding the girl was a shaded mass of black, as though she had stepped out of the shadows, a startling ghost-like figure.

'Is she a fairy?' said Amy, nonplussed.

'No.' Jane laughed as though the idea were ridiculous. 'Her name's Sally and she visits me at night.'

Amy was now quite alarmed, all her problems forgotten. She glanced at Robert, who was staring at the drawing with unease.

'And what does she do when she visits you?'

'Most of the time she just stands at the end of my bed, smiling. Occasionally she tries to speak to me.'

'What does she say?'

'I don't know. Her mouth just opens and closes and she makes this strange sound, like she's choking.'

Amy shuddered and took a step back from the sketch. 'How long has she been visiting you?'

'A few weeks, but lately she's visited more often.'

'Has she ever hurt or frightened you?'

'Oh no, she's a nice lady. It's all right, she lives here.'

They were interrupted by the door opening and Amy's stomach lurched when Matthew strutted in.

'I'm going for a spot of fishing at the lake and I promised Robert he could accompany me,' he told Amy smugly.

She had to bite her lip to prevent herself from being impolite. 'That's very good of you, sir, but he's in the middle of some work.'

'Nonsense. The boy should be enjoying the fresh air, eh, Robert?'

'Oh, please, Mama, can I go? I've never fished before.'

'Never fished,' tutted Matthew, shaking his head. 'We must remedy that at once.'

'He can't simply abandon his studies, sir.'

'Please, Mama,' Robert begged, gazing up at her with eyes the same colour as his father's.

'Very well,' she sighed. She didn't think it fair he be punished because of Matthew.

'Thank you,' he exclaimed, throwing his arms around her waist.

'Be careful around the water,' she called after him as he ran out of the room.

'Don't worry. I won't let him out of my sight.' Matthew smiled.

All she could do was scowl at his retreating back and pray he didn't tell Robert the truth.

* * *

While Jane was eating her lunch Amy took the opportunity to speak to Esther. She found her alone in the dining room staring miserably at her untouched plate.

'May I speak with you?' said Amy.

Esther looked up and smiled, glad of some company. 'Of course Amy. Would you care to join me?'

Amy's stomach was too twisted with knots to eat. 'No, thank you I've already eaten but I feel I must show you this. Jane drew it today' she said, putting the sketch on the table.

Esther's eyes widened. 'Good heavens. Jane drew this?'

'Yes. She told me this woman visits her room at night.'

Esther appeared alarmed. 'What?'

'She isn't afraid of her. On the contrary, she seems to find her presence a comfort.'

'Why is this woman entering her room at night and who is she?'

'Jane told me she lives here.'

'Could she be an imaginary friend?'

'I don't think so. I've never seen Jane play games with this Sally and she's clearly a grown woman, not a child.'

'You didn't say the woman's name was Sally,' said Esther.

Esther looked down at the drawing again and turned deathly pale 'Sally. Sweet Jesus, she looks dead. I always wondered...'

'Who's Sally?'

Esther cast the picture aside as though it would burn her, shoved her chair back with a loud scrape and dashed out of the room, leaving Amy to stare after her in confusion.

* * *

Matthew didn't return with Robert until late afternoon, by which time Amy was frantic with worry. Shortly before dinner Robert burst into the schoolroom, ruddy-cheeked and bright-eyed with excitement.

'I caught three fish, Mama. They were enormous.'

'He's a natural.' Matthew smiled, following him in.

Amy ignored him and addressed her son. 'Well done, Robert,' she said, forcing a smile. 'Did you enjoy it?'

'Yes, it was fantastic,' he enthused. 'We've given the fish to Cook and she's going to make them for dinner.'

'You and the children must dine with Esther and I tonight,' said Matthew. 'So we can all enjoy Robert's fish.'

Amy gave him a hard look. 'That's very kind of you, sir, but we shall eat in here as usual.'

Robert and Jane immediately protested.

'It would appear you're outvoted, Mrs Parker,' Matthew said in his best lord-of-the-manor voice.

'Yes, sir,' she replied, defeated.

Amy glared at his back as he left the room. So he was going to try and take her son from her. Well, she was going to give him one hell of a fight.

Amy tramped upstairs to change for dinner. After ensuring Robert took his bath and dressed smartly, she returned to her own room to dress. The chair she had used to wedge the door was gone.

* * *

After dinner both Amy and Esther were quiet, only Matthew and the children enjoying themselves. Everyone enthused over Robert's fish, and the boy beamed with happiness. To Amy's dismay, Robert looked up at Matthew as though he were a god while he smiled benevolently down at the boy. He'd sat Robert beside him at the table and the resemblance between them scared her. She couldn't believe no one else had spotted it and she watched Esther carefully for a reaction, but she appeared to have too much on her mind to notice.

The other servants seemed to resent Amy's presence in the dining room. They hadn't minded when it was just her and Esther but with the master home they'd expected everything to return to normal. Their grumbles were the least of her concerns, and she returned their indignant frowns with furious scowls.

She noticed Esther's eyes kept flicking to Jane, who seemed so happy and carefree. Clearly the mysterious Sally wasn't worrying the girl but she was worrying her aunt. Amy resolved to speak to Esther about the matter further when they were alone.

After dinner, when Amy would normally be settling the children down for bed, Matthew insisted on taking Robert into the billiard room.

The sound of Robert and Matthew's laughter set Amy's teeth on edge. Normally the thick doors would be enough to block out the sound but Matthew had purposefully left them open so she could hear.

Finally Jane started to nod off in her chair, so Esther told her to go to bed. Amy was glad because now she could broach the subject of Sally again but, before she had the chance, Esther spoke.

'Matthew's very fond of Robert, isn't he?'

'Yes, he is,' replied Amy warily.

'I suppose it's understandable when he has no son of his own.'

Amy could hear the hurt in Esther's voice and her heart went out to her. 'Have you considered the fault may lie with him?'

'But look at me, I'm so thin and weak while Matthew is strong and vital.'

'I knew a man once who was a champion rower and he couldn't sire any children,' she said, thinking of Mr Costigan. 'I know childhood illnesses and infections can cause irreparable damage.'

'I appreciate you trying to cheer me up, but it must be my fault. Everything's my fault.'

'That's not true.' It was then Amy realised Esther wasn't just timid, she was beaten down with disappointment and a domineering husband. Suddenly Amy wanted to be away from this poor woman whose life she had unintentionally made even more miserable. Quickly she rose.

'If you will excuse me, it's past Robert's bedtime.'

'Yes. Goodnight, Amy,' Esther said sweetly, disappointed at being left alone again.

'Goodnight, Esther,' she replied, the poor woman's misery bringing tears to her eyes.

As Amy approached the billiard room she could hear Matthew and Robert still laughing together. She opened the door just in time to see Robert pocket a red ball.

'Well done,' said Matthew with obvious pride. He looked up and saw Amy. 'Here's your mother.'

'Did you see me, Mama?'

'I did, sweetheart, well done, but it's past your bedtime.'

'Aw, I'm not ready for bed yet.'

'We have to be up early in the morning to go to the park and you promised Jane you would go.'

Robert took his promises very seriously. 'I forgot about that,' he said, putting down the cue.

'How about one more game?' encouraged Matthew.

'Thank you, sir, but Mama's right. I promised Jane and I really am very tired. Goodnight.'

'Goodnight, Robert,' said Matthew, disappointed.

Amy gave him a triumphant smile as she followed her son out of the room.

Robert was asleep the moment his head hit the pillow. Amy retired to her own room, quietly closing the connecting door behind her. Knowing Matthew would try to get in her room again she looked around for something else she could use to wedge the door shut. There was nothing suitable in her own room but she remembered there was a small table in Robert's.

Being careful not to wake the sleeping boy, she carried the little table into her own room. She stood it on end to make a perfect wedge, and the door was impossible to open.

Sure enough, an hour after she'd climbed into bed she heard the soft pad of footsteps and the key in the lock. She'd left her key in the door in the hope that Matthew would be unable to use his own key but it fell out uselessly with a clang. Pressure was applied from the outside but the table was so effective the door didn't budge.

'Amy, I know you're awake. You can't keep me out forever,' he snapped.

She didn't reply, hardly daring to breathe until she heard his footsteps retreat back down the corridor. Once again she hardly slept that night.

* * *

While Jane and Robert ate breakfast, Amy prepared everything they needed for their trip to the park. She had arranged this outing because she felt Jane needed a change of scenery. Perhaps it would help dispel her nocturnal visitations. She wished it were so easy to rid herself of her own. Time was running out. Soon Matthew would lose patience.

As soon as the children had finished their breakfast she ushered them into the hall to get their coats and shoes on, eager to escape the house. Matthew came out of his study to see them off.

'Children, be good for Mrs Parker.'

'Yes, sir,' they replied in unison.

'If you're well behaved I'll take you fishing again. Would you like that?' he said, addressing Robert.

'Oh, yes, sir.' He grinned.

Amy could see Jane was hurt at not receiving the same attention from her uncle and her heart went out to her. 'Perhaps you could take Jane too, sir? I know she would love to try fishing.'

Jane's eyes widened and she nodded.

'Well, I suppose she could come along,' Matthew muttered.

'Thank you, Uncle.' Jane curtseyed with an ecstatic smile.

Amy was relieved. She didn't like Matthew being alone with Robert.

'Mrs Parker, may I speak to you before you leave? I have some stipulations about today's trip.'

Amy sighed inwardly. 'Yes, sir.'

She left the children waiting in the hall and followed Matthew into his study. He closed the door and regarded her sternly.

'I wondered if you'd considered my proposal yet?' he began. 'I'm growing impatient, Amy. What is there to think about? I'm offering to give you back the comforts and luxuries you're used to.'

'There's Esther and Jane to consider and this isn't just my future but Robert's too. I have to make sure it's the right thing for us both.'

'Jane and Esther will go along with whatever I decide,' he said, cupping her face in his hands. 'If you accept I will give you the life you've always dreamed of.'

'Please, just give me a little more time. There's so much to think about, so many people who will get hurt.'

His eyes flickered with annoyance but he smiled benevolently. 'Very well. You have one more day. Tomorrow Esther's taking Jane to her friend's house. She can take Robert too so we can have some privacy to talk. We belong together, Amy. We always have. Until tomorrow, then.'

He watched her leave, his eyes narrowed.

* * *

At the park Amy had some time to think as she watched Robert and Jane run around on the grass. Amy's mind worked overtime. She knew when she refused Matthew's offer tomorrow he would try and keep Robert with him. How he would achieve that she didn't know, but one thing she had learnt at Alardyce was that this was a man's world and

women were powerless. Matthew could use his wealth and position t
get anything he wanted. She had no choice but to leave. Amy looke
regretfully at Jane. She was very fond of her charge, Esther too.

Amy wondered if she was being selfish, denying Robert a life o
wealth and a relationship with his father, but she made a respectabl
living and he had a much better life than a lot of boys his age. True, h
wouldn't grow up with money and fine clothes but neither would he b
known as a bastard. If it was ever discovered that Matthew was a
impostor Robert would be forever tainted by association. Beside
Matthew was cold and controlling and she didn't want her sweet littl
boy moulded into his image.

So, how would she leave? She wouldn't tell a soul, not even Robe
in case he inadvertently told Matthew or Jane. She had her saving
and she thought she might return to Lancashire. Her reputation u
there was good, so it shouldn't be difficult to find employment. No
she wished she'd never left in the first place, they'd both been s
happy.

When they returned to Huntington Manor Amy was relieved t
discover that Matthew had left on business and she didn't see him fc
the rest of the day. The children went to bed early and Amy wasn't lon
after them.

Instead of going to sleep she went through her things, decidin
what to take with her. To make a quick escape she would have to leav
some of her meagre possessions behind. Sadness washed over he
She'd hoped she wouldn't have to do this again.

She opened her portmanteau, intending to count her money, bu
her stomach dropped when she saw it wasn't there. Frantically sh
tipped the contents out on the bed but it was definitely gone.

'Oh, please, God, no,' she breathed.

There was only one explanation. Matthew had taken her mone
and now she was trapped.

Amy sank to her knees, eyes blurring with tears.

'Pull yourself together,' she told herself.

First things first, she hadn't secured her door properly.

She stole into Robert's room to retrieve the little table and received her second shock of the night. The table had gone. Before she could give way to despair she smiled slyly as she came up with another idea. The connecting door to Robert's room locked and she had the key.

After hastily changing into her nightgown, she hurried into Robert's room, locking the connecting door behind her. Matthew wouldn't try and seduce her with Robert in the room and she wished she'd thought of this earlier.

While she waited to hear the dreaded footsteps on the landing she gazed at her sleeping son, the sight calming her.

'Don't you worry, baby, Mummy will protect you,' she whispered, praying she could keep that promise.

After what felt like an eternity, she heard Matthew approach. She held her breath as he passed Robert's door and went towards hers. There was the jingle of keys and the click of the lock followed by the creak of the door opening and footsteps, louder, closer.

She peered through the keyhole and saw Matthew approach her bed. His whole body tensed when he realised she wasn't there. He peered beneath the bed and looked in the wardrobe in case she was hiding. Slowly he turned with such a malevolent smile she flinched. He looked right at her, his eyes seeming to cut through the keyhole.

'You're in there, aren't you? Clever girl.' He knelt before the door and peered right back at her through the keyhole. 'I want an answer, Amy. This is the last reprieve you're going to get.'

18

Amy slept fitfully and woke with an aching back after having squeezed onto the edge of Robert's bed. She rose before he woke and sneaked back into her own room so he wouldn't know anything was amiss. She felt sick to her stomach, her hands trembling as she dressed, but she had to remain strong because she was fighting for her son.

She went down to the schoolroom with Robert where Jane was already waiting and they ate breakfast together.

All too soon Esther entered the schoolroom wearing her hat and coat, ready to take the children to her friend's house. She too appeared distracted and she studied Jane closely, obviously still fretting about her phantom visitor.

'Are we ready?' she said.

'Yes,' exclaimed the children excitedly, making her smile. She looked to Amy. 'You're welcome to come too.'

Amy longed to say yes but knew she must get this conversation with Matthew over with while everyone was out of the house. 'Thank you but I have work to do here and this room could do with a good sort out,' she said, indicating the schoolroom, which she had purposefully left a mess.

Esther studied Amy with concern. 'Get some rest too. You look awfully pale. That's an order.'

'Yes, madam. I do feel a little under the weather.'

'Well, you shall have some peace and quiet today. My husband is going out on business and most of the servants are off, so you will have the house to yourself.'

Esther intended this to please Amy but it only depressed her more because she knew full well Matthew had no intention of going anywhere today. She would be completely alone with him.

Amy followed them outside to wave them off, standing on the steps until the carriage had disappeared from view. She returned to the schoolroom and found Matthew already waiting.

'Close the door,' he ordered.

She did as bid then stood before him, hands clasped, head bowed.

'Time's run out, Amy. I want your answer.'

She lifted her head. 'My answer is no.'

This came as no surprise to him, but he controlled his anger believing he could still win her over.

'Amy, do you hate me that much?'

'I don't hate you but I will not condemn myself and Robert to ignominy.'

'You're worried about Esther but you will be helping her. You can give her the child she longs for. We could have another together and she could raise it as her own.'

'I could never give up a child of mine, not even to Esther. Don't you see what you're asking of me? I'm a woman with feelings, not a baby factory,' she responded passionately.

He took her hands. 'We could be happy together.'

She hated his pig-headed persistence and the way he seemed to think she was a complete idiot. The temper she'd reined in for so many years finally snapped. 'Why won't you listen? I don't want you,' she yelled in his face.

He just smiled. 'There's the Amy I once knew. I thought she was gone but now I see she was just buried beneath the demure little governess. You loved me once. I know you can again.'

'I never loved you,' she said, pushing him away. 'You were a diversion to stave off the boredom of living at Alardyce. How could I ever love a servant?'

His expression blackened. 'You vicious little bitch. Things have changed. I'm the master now and you're the servant. I want you and Robert and I will have you.'

'Never,' she retorted. 'Do you think I would allow *my* son to be raised by a cold, cruel creature like you? I will not let you have him.'

She was a tigress fighting for her cub and she would fight to the death. Fortunately he knew just how to tame her.

'Looks like you need a reminder of who is in charge here,' he said, shoving her to the floor.

She landed on her back and tried to scramble to her feet but was hindered by her skirts. When he tried to grab her around the waist she kicked out, her foot connecting with his chest. He was surprised to realise she'd winded him and she almost escaped but he grabbed her leg, dragged her towards him and succeeded in pinning her down. Teeth bared, she struggled against him furiously, which only made him want her more. He pushed up her skirts and used his knee to part her legs. She kicked and thrashed under him but she lacked the physical strength to free herself. She tried to scream but he clamped his hand over her mouth. He'd never seen such fury in anyone's eyes before and if she had been able to he knew she would have killed him.

'Listen to me, Amy.' He smirked, revelling in his power over her. 'I can have you whenever I want. I am wealthy and powerful and you are nothing. Who would miss you if you were put away in an asylum?'

The fury in her eyes was swiftly replaced with fear and her struggling ceased.

'If you keep defying me I'll put you away forever and I'll have Robert all to myself and you'll never see him again. Do you believe me?'

She nodded, unable to speak because his hand was still clamped over her mouth.

'From now on you don't leave this house without my permission and you certainly don't go out alone with Robert. You will also welcome me into your bed. If you try to run away I'll have you tracked down and locked up and Robert will come to live with me. Do you understand?'

She nodded, tears forming in her eyes.

He released her mouth. 'Say it.'

'I understand.'

He kissed her and she didn't pull away but neither did she respond.

'I won't take you yet.' He grinned, gleeful in victory. 'It will be when you least expect it.'

He got to his feet while she sat up and pulled down her skirts. Without another word he stalked from the room, leaving her shaking and tearful on the floor.

She remained that way for an hour, before slowly getting to her feet. Calmly she rearranged her hair and straightened her clothes before she set about tidying up the schoolroom, working unthinkingly as she tried to figure out what she should do.

There was the rumble of carriage wheels and she hoped it was Esther and the children returning but it was Matthew heading out. He gave her a satisfied smile from the carriage window while she glared back at him. She hated him more than she had ever hated anybody, including Lenora. She swore she would not let him win.

Amy sat at her desk to write two letters – one to Lily and one to Mr Buchanan explaining exactly where she was and what was happening. She sealed them and pondered the problem of how to post them. She wasn't allowed to leave the house and she didn't trust any of the servants to post them for her. Then she recalled they were going to Buxton to see an exhibition of fairy art in two days. If Matthew gave his permission for her to go, she could post them then.

Next she wondered whether or not to tell Esther a few home truths about her husband. The marriage was not a happy one and Esther suspected Matthew of many things. The more Amy considered the idea, the more it made sense and she desperately needed an ally in the house.

She never wanted Robert to know Matthew was his father and she didn't want either her son or Jane exposed to this sordid situation. was quite clear Matthew wasn't a full shilling. Any sane man would have been anxious to have her out of the house before the truth was discovered. But if Matthew was unhinged it would be difficult to predict exactly how far he would go.

Determination welled up inside Amy. She'd escaped from one prison and she would do it again.

* * *

Amy took Esther's advice and went for a lie down after she'd finished tidying the schoolroom. Catching up on all the sleep she'd missed, she woke at five, just as Esther and the children returned home. Although the latter were in high spirits Esther was pale and fretful.

'Amy, may I speak with you?' she said the moment she was through the door.

Amy nodded and swallowed nervously, thinking she must know something, but how?

While the children ran upstairs to change, Amy followed Esther into the drawing room.

'I'm very concerned about Jane,' she began.

Amy tried not to let her relief show. 'Has something happened?'

'She told me Sally visited her last night and spoke to her.'

Despite her worries, Amy's interest was piqued. 'What did she say?'

'Jane couldn't remember. She said it was a strange name.'

'How did she know it was a name?'

'I asked the very same question and she told me she just had feeling.'

Esther looked as if she was on the verge of telling her something but was unsure whether to or not.

'Is there something else?' Amy encouraged.

'I think I know who Sally is.'

'She's a real person?'

'Can I trust you to keep what I'm about to say entirely to yourself?'

'Of course.'

'We had a housemaid by the name of Sally Jenkins. Twenty years old, very sweet and pretty. She disappeared one day and no trace of her has ever been found.'

'Could she have run away?'

'I doubt it. She was engaged to be married to a young man she adored and she was the only carer for her sick mother. She wouldn't have left voluntarily. The picture Jane drew is a good likeness of Sally.'

'Did Jane know her?'

'Yes, she knew Sally and she appears to be dead in the drawing.'

Amy was unsure what to say.

'Do you believe in spiritualism?' continued Esther uncertainly, afraid of being ridiculed.

'I've never given it much thought.'

'Well, I do, very strongly. I think Jane is being haunted.'

'Haunted?' repeated Amy with surprise.

'As my husband is going to be away this evening, I've taken the liberty of inviting a medium who is an acquaintance of the friend I visited today. What do you think?'

'I'm not sure. It's something I have no experience of.' Seances were the current rage. It was common practice to hold one during a gathering and the last family she'd worked for had been involved with them to the point of obsession, but Amy had of course never been invited to watch what she thought was just a parlour trick.

'She's going to hold a seance and I would like you to sit in on it with me.'

'If you wish me to be there, then of course I shall.'

'Thank you. She'll be here at nine.'

Amy nodded. It was vital she remain on Esther's good side.

* * *

Shortly before nine o'clock that evening Amy assisted Esther in closing the curtains in the drawing room and clearing the table in preparation for the seance.

As Esther had dismissed all the servants, Amy answered the front door when the bell pealed through the house. She opened the door and her jaw dropped.

'Magda Magrath?' The woman hadn't changed, although her wild white hair was neatly combed, befitting a visit to a grand house.

'Amy. Amy Osbourne?' she exclaimed. 'Are you a servant now?'

Amy glanced over her shoulder to make sure Esther wasn't within earshot. 'My name is Amy Parker and I'm governess here. Please don't give me away. I'll explain later.'

'All right,' replied Magda, confused.

She followed Amy through to the drawing room where she was greeted warmly by Esther. Magda was an accomplished actress and behaved as though nothing was amiss.

They took their places around the table, Esther sitting between the other two women.

'Is there anyone specific you wish to contact?' said Magda.

'A girl named Sally,' replied Esther. 'She was a maid here about a year ago.'

'While I connect with the spirits I need you to sing a hymn.'

Esther and Amy glanced at each other.

'Sing?' said Esther uncertainly.

'Spirits love to hear singing. It draws them out,' explained Magda. 'Something sombre and respectful. "Ave Maria" perhaps.'

Magda closed her eyes and tilted her face to the ceiling while Esther and Amy, neither of whom had any singing talent, started up a hideous rendition of 'Ave Maria'. Amy thought their singing was more likely to keep any spirit at bay rather than encourage it to step forward. She glanced at Esther, who seemed to be thinking the same thing, her natural shyness making her cringe with embarrassment.

Magda's head snapped up and her eyes flew open. 'The spirits are here.'

Esther and Amy broke off singing, eyes nervously flicking about the room, but they could see nothing in the gloom, although the air did feel a little cooler.

'We are seeking the spirit of Sally Jenkins,' called Magda.

Nothing happened.

'Sally,' she called in a strange, ethereal voice. 'We know you've been attempting to communicate. Please step forward and reveal your message.'

The air cooled another few degrees and goosebumps rose all over Amy's body.

'I see something,' whispered Esther.

All three of them peered in the direction of the door where a small pinprick of light bobbed and weaved, growing larger the closer it got.

'It's very pretty,' whispered Esther in an effort to soothe her nerves.

Indeed it was, its movement hypnotic, and Amy and Esther started to relax. Suddenly the light seemed to distort and expand, accompanied by a great whoosh of air that nearly knocked them out of their seats.

The light burst into the shape of a woman, sprouting arms, legs and a head. A terrible scream erupted from its wide, gaping mouth, a scream filled with so much pain and fear that Amy had to fight the compulsion to run from the room while Esther clamped her hands down over her ears. As the scream died away the shape became clearer, blonde hair sprouting from its head.

'Sally,' Esther breathed in amazement.

The woman shimmered and rippled before them, her feet hovering a good two feet off the floor, eyes conveying a heartbreaking anguish.

'Sally, please tell us your message,' implored a calm Magda.

Sally's mouth opened and her lips moved but no sound came out.

'We cannot hear you. Use my energy to strengthen your voice.'

There was another great gust of wind and Magda gasped and threw back her head, hair streaming out behind her. The spectre's wide black mouth stretched open even further and screeched one deafening word.

'Alardyce.'

It was so loud and clear there could be no mistaking it and Amy felt as though she'd been hit by a large, heavy object.

Sally's head snapped backwards unnaturally, exposing her white neck, which was slit open by an unseen hand, blood spurting from the wound. Esther's scream filled the room as Sally vanished. The wind died down and silence once again reigned.

Amy sat frozen in her seat, her heart threatening to leap out of her mouth while Magda slumped backwards, and Esther fell forward onto the table in shock.

Recovering herself, Amy jumped up and ran around the room lighting all the lamps, casting a warm, comforting glow. She poured three brandies and rushed back to the table to revive the other two women.

'Esther,' she said, gently shaking her shoulder.

Esther came round with a groan before her head snapped up and she glanced about the room in fright.

'It's all right, she's gone,' said Amy.

While Esther gulped down her brandy Amy attended to Magda, who was quicker to recover but nevertheless consumed her drink just as eagerly.

'Such a strong spirit,' said Magda. 'She took almost all my energy.'

She was exhausted, so Amy assisted her to the couch.

Esther was trembling uncontrollably and it took a couple of brandies before she recovered the power of speech.

'Her neck.' She shivered. 'Why did that happen?'

'She was showing us how she died,' replied Magda thoughtfully.

'You've seen something like that before?'

'Yes, a few times, when the person has been murdered.'

'Who would do that to poor Sally? She was such a sweet girl,' said Esther, eyes filling with tears. 'She said Alardyce. Could that be the name of the person who killed her?'

Esther failed to notice the look that passed between Amy and Magda.

'I don't know,' replied Magda. 'But Sally is at peace now. She was unable to cross over until she'd conveyed her message.'

'So she will leave Jane alone?'

'I can confidently predict you will never see her again.'

'Well, that is some comfort.' Esther seemed to relax after this. 'Do you think we should tell the police?'

'I know from bitter experience that the police don't take too kindly to mediums.' Magda frowned. 'We would be laughed out of the station. Sally's at peace now and that's what's important.'

'I suppose you're right. Now if you'll excuse me, I have a dreadful headache, although I doubt I'll get much sleep tonight. Amy, would you be a dear and see Magda out?'

'Of course.'

'Thank you. Goodnight.'

When Esther had gone Magda said, 'Are you ready to tell me what's going on?'

Amy recited everything that had happened since she'd left Alardyce, leaving nothing out, knowing she wouldn't be judged. Magda listened attentively and without interruption. It was a relief to Amy to unburden herself and she felt a little safer knowing another person was aware of her dilemma.

When she'd finished she sank back in her seat, awaiting Magda's verdict.

'I never liked Matthew,' she said. 'He was surrounded by darkness.'

'The vision you had when you touched my hand, the one of blood and violence, was it this house you saw?'

'No. It was a house I have not yet seen.'

'Would you give me another reading?' she said, holding out her hands. 'Please.'

Magda nodded and took both her hands in her own. Once again Amy felt the warmth seeping out of Magda and into herself. Magda's head fell back and her eyes closed.

'I see the same house, rich and opulent. On the south wall is a distinctive painting of a grotesque figure. He sits upon a throne wearing a crown with two inert bodies at his feet. *Mammon.*' She released Amy's hands and slumped back in her chair. 'Sorry, that's all I can get. My energy's still depleted from the seance.'

'So my future is unchanged?'

'Yes. The same house, the same painting on the wall.' Magda sat up straighter and regarded her with piercing eyes. 'If you ever see that painting, run.'

The seriousness of her tone frightened Amy. 'What do I do? How do I get out of this without ending up in an asylum, or worse?'

'I wish I knew. Women are powerless in this world of men,' Magda said bitterly.

'I can't let him take my son,' Amy said, voice cracking.

Magda patted her hands. 'Of course not.'

'He wants me because he thinks I can give him more children but is that possible without the potion you gave me?'

'Doubtful, I think. Given that neither his wife nor any of his mistresses have ever conceived his child, I think he is the one with the problem, but as long as he thinks you can be useful to him you will be safe.'

'How do I keep him out of my bed?'

Magda's expression was sad. 'I fear you may be unable to.'

Amy bit her lip, fighting back tears.

'Perhaps it would be better to play along until you can find a way to escape?'

'I can't do it to Esther. I'm too fond of her.'

'Who is more important? Her or your son?'

'My son,' Amy replied without hesitation.

'I have one idea that may help.'

'What?' she said, desperate for the slightest sliver of hope.

'Your uncle...'

'No, I don't want him to know where I am. He's just as likely to have me put away as Matthew.'

'He's a changed man since Lenora's death. It was as though he was under a spell that has been lifted. He came to see me after she died asking me to help him find you, desperate to make amends.'

'It was probably all an act.'

'I believe he was genuine. He said he'd discovered some new information.'

'What information?'

'He wouldn't say but he was distraught about his treatment of you.'

Amy wasn't convinced. 'By telling him where I am I'll be exchanging one prison for another.'

'Or you could free both yourself and your son. He's a powerful man, more so than Matthew. He's the only one who can protect you.'

'What if he tries to force me into marrying Henry again?'

'The man who came to see me wanted what was best for you, I truly believe that.'

Amy knew her uncle must have changed if he was consulting Magda. 'Maybe you're right but I'm not allowed out of the house. I'm taking the children to the fairy paintings exhibition in Buxton the day after tomorrow. I could meet him there.'

'I shall pass on the message but I'll need proof that I've seen you.'

Amy handed her the locket containing the images of her parents. 'May I beg one last favour?'

Magda nodded.

'Would you post these letters for me?'

'Of course.'

Amy added a hasty postscript to each letter stating that she was meeting with her uncle and was communicating with him via Magda then resealed them and handed them over too.

'I won't let you down,' said Magda. 'One more thing before I go, about Sally.'

Amy shuddered at the memory of the spectre.

'Servant girls were hurt at Alardyce and now we know the same thing has happened here. Matthew's the link between the two houses.'

Amy's heart skipped a beat. 'You think he's responsible?'

'It's too big a coincidence to be ignored. Sally was giving us a warning.'

'But it was Henry who hurt those girls at Alardyce. I saw proof of it, and he hasn't been here. If he had then Esther would have recognised the name.'

'Perhaps he didn't act alone?'

Amy recalled Matthew's coldness and his attack on her in the schoolroom and felt sick.

'Be careful, Amy.'

'I will,' she quietly replied.

After seeing Magda out to her carriage, Amy locked the front door and hurried upstairs to bed, nervous about being alone in the darkened corridors after what she had just witnessed. She considered sleeping in Robert's room again but decided to take Magda's advice and not make Matthew angry.

She lay there in the dark, jumping at every sound, replaying the sight of Sally's throat slitting open. Matthew never came and eventually, overwhelmed by fear and exhaustion, she fell asleep.

19

Amy woke at dawn feeling refreshed after a night's sleep undisturbed by unwanted visitors.

Pleasantly surprised, she dressed and went downstairs to breakfast, relieved to find Matthew still absent. He'd been called away to attend to some business in Manchester and wasn't expected back until tomorrow.

Amy went up to her room to change after she spilt ink on her dress and found a commotion in Robert's room. On entering she found some of the servants clearing everything out.

'What is going on?' she demanded of one of the footmen.

'A pipe's burst and dampened the room. It's ruined your son's clothes,' he said, indicating the sodden bundle on the floor.

'Can they be saved?'

'I'm afraid not. Plaster and dirt have got in and spoiled them.'

Amy regarded the pathetic bundle with sadness. She'd scrimped and saved to provide him with the best she could afford and it was all ruined.

'I'll dispose of them,' offered the footman rather kindly and she nodded. 'The room needs to be remodelled.'

'He can stay in my room until the work's finished,' she said. That would keep Matthew at bay.

'The master has given orders that the boy be moved into the family wing until the work's finished.'

'How could the master know this has happened? He's away.'

'I don't know, Mrs Parker. Mr Hobbs gave us instructions.'

'Is there a problem?' enquired Hobbs, materialising out of nowhere.

'Mr Hobbs, a word,' she hissed.

He followed her down the corridor out of earshot of the other servants, who were watching them curiously.

'What is this?' she demanded, rounding on him.

'Didn't the footman explain?' he replied.

'Matthew arranged this before he left, didn't he? He's trying to isolate me up here.'

'I don't know what you're talking about, madam.'

'Don't give me that rot. You know exactly what's going on. I want my son by my side, where he belongs.'

'I obey the master, not you,' he said before turning on his heel and stalking away.

Amy flew into her room and slammed the door shut, feeling as though she was losing Robert and was helpless to stop it.

Well, that decided it. She had to tell Esther everything before Matthew returned.

After composing herself, she returned downstairs and set Jane and Robert some especially difficult spelling exercises that would keep them occupied. Then she went to find Esther.

She found her gazing out of the drawing room window, obviously as apprehensive about Matthew's return as she was.

'Esther, I need to speak with you on a very important and extremely delicate matter,' she said breathlessly, nerves making her voice tremble.

Esther caught her tone and regarded her with concern. 'Is it Jane? Is she all right?'

'She's fine. This is about your husband.'

When Esther paled and swallowed hard Amy realised she'd already worked out that something wasn't right.

They occupied opposing armchairs and Esther apprehensively waited for Amy to speak.

'Before I begin it's vital you know that I had no idea who lived here before I accepted the position. As you know you sought me out, not the other way around.'

'Yes, I remember,' replied Esther, voice tight.

Amy's heart fluttered wildly and her hands shook so badly she was forced to clasp them together. 'My name isn't Amy Parker. It's Amy Osbourne.'

'Amy Osbourne? Why the pretence?'

'My uncle is Sir Alfred Alardyce. I went to live with him and my two cousins after my parents died but I ran away. While I was there I...' She trailed off, too ashamed to continue.

Esther grasped her hand and smiled kindly. 'Go on.'

'I had an affair with... with a footman,' she said, the words tumbling out in a long jumble. 'And the result of that affair was Robert.'

'Is that why you ran away?'

'Not entirely. The Alardyces said they would forgive me if I married their oldest son, my cousin Henry. You see, my parents left me a substantial inheritance that would become my husband's property when I married. That was the only reason they wanted me as a daughter-in-law. They were arranging a hasty marriage so we could go abroad on honeymoon where I would give birth and my baby would be taken away. However, I was shown proof that Henry was a monster who enjoyed torturing servant girls.'

'My God.'

'If I'd married him I would have been at his mercy for the rest of my life. I would also have had to give up Robert. That's why I ran.'

'I can certainly see why you did,' Esther said sympathetically.

'I do not deserve your understanding.'

'Why on earth not?'

'Because that footman, Robert's father is... your husband.'

Esther's eyes widened, as though she'd been struck. 'Impossible. He's the son of a wealthy merchant...'

'Matthew's a confidence trickster. At Alardyce his name was Matthew Bettany and he's putting on that English accent. He's actually Scottish.'

'No, this can't be true.'

'I'm afraid it is.'

'Prove it.'

'You've seen the resemblance between them, I know it. Robert is the image of him.'

Esther screwed her delicate hands up into tiny fists. 'I can't believe this.'

'Esther, you must, because we are both in danger.'

'Why?'

'I'm the only woman who has ever conceived Matthew's child.' She hated to see the pain in Esther's eyes but there wasn't time to tend to her hurt feelings. 'You know how desperate he is for a son. He wants me to live here as his mistress and give him more children and he said you would pass them off as your own to make them legitimate. Or he said if I preferred he would divorce you and he and I could live together with Robert.'

'What?' she shrieked.

'I refused, of course. Now he's said if I don't comply he'll have me put away in an asylum and he'll have Robert all to himself. Esther, can't let him take my son from me. Please, you have to help me.'

Esther shot to her feet, fear vying with anger. 'I will not listen to this pack of lies.'

She tried to leave the room but Amy jumped up to block her way. 'Think about it. Where have you heard the name Alardyce before?'

This made her stop. 'Sally.'

'Servant girls were abused and even disappeared at Alardyce, just like Sally disappeared. What if Henry wasn't acting alone? Someone had to procure those girls for him and as first footman Matthew was ideally placed. Has Matthew ever hurt or scared you? I know he must have because he's done it to me.'

Esther stared off into the distance. 'Yes.'

'He's an abuser and possibly a murderer.'

'Sally,' she murmured, eyes filling with tears. 'I always wondered why he was so insistent on taking my name. He said it would be better for the business if he was called Huntington. It never occurred to me that he might be a fraud.'

'He wants us both to bend to his will and he will use the children to ensure our cooperation.'

This restored Esther's fight. 'No,' she said firmly before sinking back into the armchair, cradling her head in her hands. 'I've suspected him of something dreadful for so long, but I had no idea it would be this bad. What can we do?'

'I've arranged to meet my uncle at the exhibition tomorrow.'

'And you trust him?'

'I have to. What choice is there?'

'But you said your uncle tried to have you put away.'

'That was down to my aunt. She was an evil woman and after she died my uncle saw the error of his ways. He's a good man at heart, just weak.'

They heard a carriage approaching and Esther rushed to the window.

'Oh God, it's Matthew. He's come home early.'

'It's vital he doesn't know we've spoken about this. If he thinks we're in league we won't be permitted to go to the gallery tomorrow.'

'What do I do? I can't bear to look at him.'

'Just act normal, please, Esther, or we'll lose both Robert and Jane.'

Amy knew Esther would go to any lengths to protect her niece and Robert too.

'I must go,' said Amy.

She hurried out of the room, down the corridor and back into the schoolroom seconds before the front door opened.

As she checked the children's work she heard Matthew being greeted by the butler, then there was the opening and closing of another door and she could only assume he'd gone into the drawing room. With the door to the schoolroom closed she could hear nothing and she tried to keep her mind focused on her work, praying Esther's courage wouldn't fail them all.

A few minutes later there was the sound of approaching footsteps and the door to the schoolroom slowly opened to reveal Matthew. Robert jumped up excitedly while Amy and Jane looked mistrustful.

'Mr Huntington, you're back.' Robert grinned.

Matthew beamed benevolently. 'Now, what have I told you to call me?'

'Sorry, Matthew.'

'That's better. Here, I have a present for you.'

He handed him a box, which Robert tore open.

'A clockwork train set. Thank you so much. Mama, look what Matthew's brought me.'

Amy tried to be pleased about the toy, which she could never have afforded.

'That's much too generous, sir,' she said coolly. 'You shouldn't have.'

'Nonsense. Here, Jane, I have something for you too.'

Jane was both astonished and pleased not to have been overlooked. He handed her a beautiful white pinafore dress with a radiant golden fairy embroidered on the front. It even came with a matching doll sporting the same dress. Jane released a squeal of joy and hugged both items.

'Thank you, Uncle. May I show Aunt Esther?'

'Of course.'

Amy knew Matthew was trying to win them both over with trinkets and she found it impossible to keep the scowl off her face.

As the children ran out to find Esther he advanced on Amy, who forced herself not to back away.

'Did you miss me?' He smirked.

She ignored the question. 'This so-called burst pipe in Robert's room is all a ploy, isn't it?'

'He's my son and he belongs in the family wing.'

'He's my son too or doesn't that count any more?'

'Of course it does,' he said in a softer tone. 'But you've had nine years with him. Now it's my turn.' His eyes darkened. 'It's not going to be a problem, is it?'

She willed herself to relax. 'No.'

The darkness passed and he smiled. 'And now, with Robert in the family wing, you and I can have complete privacy.'

Again she just nodded, keeping her eyes firmly fixed on the floor, thinking it safer not to reply.

'Hobbs informs me all of Robert's clothes were ruined in the leak. I'll take him into town for some new ones after lunch.'

'That's most kind but you needn't waste your money. I will make him some new ones.'

'Make? No, no, no. I will not have my son going around in such garments,' he said distastefully. 'He'll have brand-new ones handmade by a tailor.'

Again she nodded meekly.

'You and the children will dine with Esther and I tonight. It will give you the chance to admire Robert's new clothes.' He smiled before stalking out.

* * *

Amy didn't see her son until she was sitting at the dinner table with Esther and Jane, the latter speculating loudly about what her present would be while the two women anxiously waited. Matthew had refused to take Jane into town but had pacified her by promising to bring her back another present.

After keeping them waiting for fifteen minutes, Matthew entered wearing a smart new blue suit that complemented his dark looks perfectly. To Amy's dismay Robert entered wearing the exact same suit. Now even a complete stranger could tell they were father and son.

'What do you think, Mama?' said Robert proudly.

For a moment Amy couldn't speak, her breath caught in her throat. 'I think you look quite the gentleman,' she said, the words almost choking her.

'Look what we got you, Jane,' said Robert, handing her a beautifully wrapped package.

Jane tore it open and her eyes danced. 'They're shoes to match my dress. They're beautiful, Uncle. Thank you.'

Amy chanced a glance at Esther, who was looking from Robert to Matthew with an appalled expression. If she'd had any doubts Amy was telling the truth they'd just been dispelled.

* * *

Amy retired to her room with a sense of impending doom. Although he hadn't said as much, she knew tonight Matthew would come to her room and this time he would get in. She changed into her nightgown and climbed beneath the covers, resigned to her fate. The thought of Matthew touching her no longer excited her, it repelled her.

As she recalled poor Sally's fate, a horrible thought struck her. What if this was all a ploy to get her alone so he could kill her? Then Robert would be all his.

Amy sat bolt upright, the idea growing more probable by the second. Alone in this wing she could scream and no one would hear.

She had to survive long enough to speak to her uncle, then at least there would be someone with the power to free Robert from his monstrous father.

Making a snap decision she wasn't entirely sure was the right one, she jumped out of bed, flung a shawl around her shoulders, slid her feet into her slippers and padded out of the room and downstairs. When she was halfway down she heard footsteps approaching from the family wing. Increasing her pace, she reached the bottom and hid in the shadows. Peering up the staircase she saw Matthew walking into the guest wing carrying a single candle. She hadn't brought a light to avoid drawing attention to herself, so she had to stumble along in the dark but she had to move quickly for in a minute he would discover she wasn't there.

As she quietly made her way along the corridor images of Sally's spectre haunted her and every shadow caused her heart to lurch sickeningly.

There was the thunder of footsteps descending the stairs and, panicking, she raced down the hallway and lunged for the door to the servants' hall, closing it softly behind her. The stairs down were mercifully lit by lamps, so she managed to reach the bottom safely.

Amy took a moment to compose herself before making her way towards the kitchen. She accidentally disturbed the footman guarding the plate room, so she told him she just wanted a glass of milk from the kitchen. He grunted and was snoring again in seconds.

Amy's hands trembled so violently she slopped some of the liquid all over the counter.

It was then she knew she had made a huge error of judgement. What if her absence made him so angry he cancelled the trip tomorrow? She would never get to speak to her uncle. She had no choice but to return upstairs.

Clutching her glass of milk, she retreated back down the corridor past the sleeping footman and cautiously made her way upstairs.

'Where have you been?' growled a voice.

She yelped, almost dropping the glass of milk. Matthew steppe
out of the darkness, his face a mass of shadows.

'I was thirsty,' she replied, holding up the glass.

'I see,' he said, his voice softening. 'I thought you were trying t
avoid me.'

'No, of course not.'

'In that case,' he said, taking the glass from her and placing it on
window ledge. 'Come here.'

He pulled her to him and kissed her. Her instinct was to recoil bu
she made herself kiss him back, surprised to realise she was enjoyin
the kiss and loathing herself for it.

He pushed her up against the wall and started to hitch up he
nightgown.

'Mama,' called a voice.

They both froze.

'Was that Robert?' whispered Amy.

'I think so,' Matthew whispered back.

'Mama,' called the little lost voice again.

'Please, I must go to him,' she said.

'Of course you must.'

He released her and she rushed upstairs, almost crying with relie
Robert was the only reason he would have let her go. She found he
bewildered son at the top of the stairs trying to find the door to he
room.

'Baby, I'm here,' she said softly, so as not to startle him.

'Mama,' he exclaimed, flinging his arms around her waist. 'I don
like my new room, it's too big. Can I sleep with you tonight?'

'Of course you can, my darling.'

She took his hand and led him back to her room. They cuddled u
together in her bed, Robert clinging to her. Amy kissed his mop of dar
hair in love and gratitude for his timely interruption.

* * *

Amy worried Matthew would be angry with her the following morning but instead he was very affable. They were setting off early to catch the train into Buxton for the exhibition and Matthew even gave Jane some spending money.

Robert was wearing one of his new suits, a grey one that made him look more like his father than ever, and Matthew was taking him into town to buy more.

Esther was silent throughout the train ride, only speaking when Jane addressed her directly. It was only when Jane fell asleep, rocked by the soothing motion of the train, that she spoke to Amy.

'Did Matthew come to you last night?'

'Yes, but fortunately Robert woke so he had to go away.'

'Did Robert see him?'

'No.'

Esther sighed with relief.

'I'm so sorry, Esther. I don't want him, really I don't.'

'I know. I realised long ago that my husband's rotten inside. He's always treated me abominably so there's no reason why he should treat you any differently.' Her mouth opened and closed, she seemed hesitant to ask before she said, 'Was he like this when you knew him at Alardyce?'

'No, but he was a footman then. He didn't like it when my aunt pressed suitors on me.'

'Footman.' She laughed. 'He acts so high and mighty when in reality he's just a servant.'

'He always did have ambitions and it seems he's willing to go to any lengths to achieve them. Is he aware you know all this?'

'No. He hardly bothers with me any more.'

Amy had to wonder at Matthew. He had a beautiful, sweet, loving wife and he cared nothing for her. It made her furious. 'Esther, you deserve someone much better than Matthew.'

'I blame myself. Even before I accepted his proposal I knew deep down there was something wrong with him, but he was so charming I fell for him.'

They both watched Jane fast asleep in her new clothes and shiny shoes.

'We won't let him take them,' said Esther with a determination Amy hadn't thought she possessed.

'No, we won't,' she replied with equal determination.

20

The Buxton Gallery was extremely busy. The majority of the pictures in the fairy exhibition were by Richard Dadd, painted from his cell in Bedlam after he'd murdered his own father. Jane was enchanted by the work, although Amy decided to tell her nothing about the artist. She'd be horrified to learn of the twisted mind in which these beautiful images had been born.

Jane enthused over *The Fairy Feller's Master-Stroke*, *Puck*, and *Titania Sleeping*. Amy found them a little dark for her tastes, preferring Joseph Noel Paton's work, which was lighter and brighter. *The Fairy Queen* was exquisite, as was his version of Oberon and Titania.

'Excuse me, miss,' said a voice in her ear, making her jump.

She turned and got the shock of her life. 'Rush,' she exclaimed, so pleased to see him she almost hugged him.

'I'm to take you to your uncle, miss.'

Amy turned to Esther. 'My uncle's here.'

'Is that him?' she said, nodding at Rush.

'No, that's his butler. He's taking me to him.'

'Good luck,' she said, eyes huge with anxiety.

Amy nodded and followed Rush through the throng. They took a back staircase up to the next floor, Amy following his doddery figure in silence. At the top of the stairs she found herself in a room full of sculptures.

Alfred was sitting on a bench staring down at the floor, seemingly oblivious to the beautiful art all around him. He was hunched over in a black greatcoat and looked much older, his hair now entirely grey and face lined, his demeanour beaten down.

'Hello, Uncle.'

Slowly he raised his head, regarding her with grey eyes that widened with surprise and hope. 'Amy. My dear Amy.'

The genuine happiness in his voice warmed her and she felt herself thawing to him. She sat on the bench beside him and he took her hand in both of his.

'I've waited for this day for so long,' he began. 'For years I've hoped to find you. I want to say how sorry I am for the way my family treated you. I've regretted it every day since you left and I hope you'll let me make it up to you.'

'You really mean that?' she said, still scared to trust him.

'I do. I swear to God I do.'

Her face crumpled. 'Oh, Uncle.'

He embraced her and she cried on his shoulder. When she'd recovered he began to explain.

'You know your aunt passed away a year ago?'

Amy nodded.

'Just before she died she confessed that she ordered Matthew to seduce you.'

Amy stared at him, thinking she had misheard. 'Excuse me?'

'Lenora ordered Matthew to lead you into an affair.'

'Why?'

'She wanted everyone to think you were mad and of loose morals so you would be put away and your wealth absorbed into the Alardyce Estate. Only Matthew took it further than he should have. He wasn't supposed to... err... lie with you.'

Her stomach lurched and she thought she might faint.

Alfred put his arm around her to steady her. 'Are you unwell?'

'No,' she snapped. 'Just angry.'

'I promise I would never have been party to such a diabolical scheme.'

'I believe you,' she said, and she did.

'I can't tell you how it pleases me to hear you say that.' He smiled.

'Please, Uncle, finish the story.'

'You were discovered with Matthew accidentally by Henry. That wasn't part of the plan. Lenora herself wanted to be the one to expose you. Henry tried to warn me something was wrong. He came to me first after he'd discovered you and Matthew together and begged me not to say anything to Lenora. He thought I'd be able to have Matthew discreetly removed and that would be the end of it.'

'Surely Henry knew of Lenora's plan?'

'No. He would never have countenanced it either. He told me Lenora was up to something but I wouldn't listen. I arranged that confrontation in my study on Lenora's advice. It was what she wanted and I handed you over on a platter.'

'I thought Henry was just as bad as she was.'

'Henry's a good man with a good heart.'

She looked back at him doubtfully.

'I know you may not believe it, Amy, but he truly cared for you. He wanted to marry you to protect you from her. Only he really saw how badly your parents' deaths affected you, how lonely and isolated you were, and Lenora used that.'

Amy remained silent. It seemed her gullible uncle was ignorant about his eldest son's true character but she said nothing, for now. She couldn't bear to hurt this old man again.

'Lenora told me she was actually pleased when you got with child,' he continued. 'Because it meant you were well and truly trapped.'

'I still don't understand why.'

'It was a condition of your father's will that you be allowed to

choose your own husband, so Lenora purposefully put you in the wa
of men who were unsuitable. Then, when you were put away, you
fortune would have belonged to us, leaving Henry free to marry h
heiress, increasing our wealth even more.' He buried his face in h
hands. 'Oh, the evil, vicious, greedy creature.'

'Why didn't she just let me marry Edward like I wanted to? M
wealth would still have been absorbed into the Alardyce Estate.'

'Trust me, Amy, when I say that my younger son is not normal. Yo
wouldn't have enjoyed the happiness you imagined.'

Amy thought it dreadful they considered Edward to be bad ju
because he preferred men but her uncle was a deeply religious man.
hadn't thought even Lenora was so evil.'

'Neither did I. When she confessed all this to me I was so sickened
refused to see her again. I let her die alone with just her maid to hol
her hand. Henry and Edward would have nothing to do with he
either. We're told we should forgive people their sins but sometime
those sins are just too great.' Pleading filled his old, tired eyes. 'Was m
sin so great, Amy? Can you ever forgive me? I saw you were sufferin
after the death of your parents but rather than try and comfort yo
Lenora insisted it was best to let you soldier on. Perhaps if we ha
shown more compassion all this could have been avoided? I kno
loneliness and melancholy drove you into Matthew's arms.'

'It did.'

'Lenora destroyed my relationship with your mother, my own siste
and she made me do the same to you. I should have been stronger an
stood against her.'

'You thought I was mad. You were going to have me committed.'

'That was Lenora's idea but I told her that would never happe
That was one thing I stood firm on. You weren't mad, just grieving.
understood that.'

Amy thought hard as some distant memory revealed itself the
disappeared before she could grasp it.

'If I'd known you were so against the match with Henry I woul have called it off,' he said. 'I didn't want you to run away and have to live as a governess.' He broke into fresh tears and Amy took his hand, realising he was being sincere.

'I forgive you, Uncle. You're guilty of nothing more than falling for Lenora's tricks, as did I.'

'You really mean that?'

'Yes.' She smiled.

'Oh, my darling girl, thank you,' he said, embracing her. 'Your mercy is more than I deserve.'

She smiled as she hugged him back.

'You'd better have this back,' he said, placing her locket in her hand. 'Magda gave it to me so I knew it was really you.'

'Thank you for taking good care of it.'

'I want to make it up to you. I want to sign your fortune over to you.'

She blinked with surprise. 'You do?'

'Although I'm no longer your guardian, legally I still control your wealth. I want to give you your fortune. I should have done it years ago. I have an appointment with Mr Buchanan, your father's solicitor, tomorrow. The moment Magda told me where you were I sent him a telegram advising him to draw up the contract. I shall sign it tomorrow and it will all be yours. With interest it is substantially more than it was. You will be an extremely wealthy woman and you can give up this life of servitude.'

'I can't tell you... how much this means to me.' She gasped, over-whelmed.

'I hope it goes some way to making amends.'

The relief made her giddy. Here was the solution to all her prob-lems. She and Robert would be free to live their own lives and as a rich, independent woman she could defend herself against Matthew.

'You can come back with me to Alardyce this minute if you like,' he said. 'You never have to be in service again.'

'I can't. I need to go back for my son.' If only Matthew hadn't taken

Robert she could have taken him up on that offer; they both would have been safe.

'Magda told me you had a boy.' He smiled. 'What's his name?'

'Robert.'

'For your father?'

She nodded then recounted how she was trapped by Matthew and he listened with mounting horror.

'The devil,' he seethed. 'The diabolical devil. Rest assured, Amy, you need fear him no longer.'

'But he still has Robert. As his father he could keep him and I would never see him again. Foolishly I put Matthew's name on the birth certificate. I must return to the house and get Robert away without him suspecting anything.'

'I will return with you and demand he hand over the boy.'

'Thank you, Uncle, but it will do no good. He is quite unstable and I am sure he would fight to the death to keep his son. Esther and Jane would suffer too. I'll return to Huntington tonight and ask Matthew if I can take Robert for a walk into the village after lunch tomorrow.'

'I'll meet you there and ensure you get away safely.'

'Can Esther and Jane come too? I dread to think what would happen if they were left behind.'

'Amy, you are your own mistress now. You can do as you please.'

'I can, can't I?' she said, delighted. 'You have saved me and my son. Thank you.'

'Tomorrow you shall be free. Just cling to that. If you like you're welcome to live with me at Alardyce.'

'Isn't Henry there?' She frowned.

'He lives in London now. He moved out of Alardyce shortly after you left. Too many painful memories for him, I think.'

This puzzled her but she was too spent to discuss it. 'I must find Esther and Jane. We have to leave soon or Matthew will be angry.'

They both got to their feet.

'I return to London to meet with the solicitor,' said Alfred. 'I shall meet you at the railway station tomorrow at two. Is that all right? It gives me time to get the contract signed.'

'That is wonderful,' she said, hugging him. 'Until then.'

'You promise you will be there?'

She handed him back the locket. 'I promise. You know I could never be parted from this for long.'

He clutched it to his chest, tears shining in his eyes. 'I shall take the best care of it.'

After bidding him goodbye she returned to find Esther, so happy she couldn't stop grinning.

'I take it your meeting went well?' said Esther.

Amy smiled and nodded. They didn't discuss it until they were back on the train and Jane had fallen asleep again with her head in Esther's lap.

'I'm so happy for you,' said Esther once Amy had finished relating everything she and her uncle had discussed.

Amy could see she was disappointed at having to say goodbye. 'You and Jane could come with us.'

'I couldn't impose.'

'I want you to come. You're my friend.'

Esther positively beamed. She hadn't had a true friend since her sister died. 'But I would be penniless. Matthew has my money.'

'You don't need it. As of tomorrow I'll be an extremely wealthy woman. We can all stay at Alardyce – my uncle has already given his permission. Anyway, Matthew tricked you into marriage. He made you think he was something he's not. He's a fraud and we can expose him as such and get your fortune back.'

Esther released a sigh of relief. 'Thank you. Thank you so much.'

'Now, listen. It's vital we act normal. Matthew must suspect nothing. We'll ask him if we can take a walk into the village after lunch tomorrow and that is when we'll leave. Take nothing with you. If he sees any bags he'll become suspicious. We can buy everything we need after we've got away.'

'That's fine. I want no reminders of my marriage.'

'My uncle will meet us at the station and ensure we get away safely.'

The women hugged, buoyed by the thought of freedom from their mutual tormentor.

The next morning Amy woke in a state of high excitement and for the first time in a long time she was optimistic about the future. She and Esther ate heartily with the children and there was no sign of Matthew. They stuck to their normal routine so as not to arouse suspicion and Amy took the children into the schoolroom to begin their lessons. It was only when Esther called her into the drawing room an hour later that Amy realised things weren't going to go their way.

'There's something you need to see,' said Esther, her skin a frightening shade of white as she handed her the morning newspaper.

'Oh, God, no,' cried Amy, her eyes filling with tears.

On the front page was a large, rather severe photograph of her uncle and the headline, *Sir Alfred Alardyce Murdered.*

According to the article he'd been mugged in London just a few hours after he'd met with Amy. The attacker had stabbed him through the heart.

Esther hugged her as she broke into panicky, heaving sobs.

'Oh, God, what do we do now?' said Amy.

'Would he have had time to visit his solicitor?'

'No. His appointment was this morning.'

'We can still leave. Goodness knows, we can't stay here.'

'What will we do for money?'

'We'll find a way. I'll become a governess too if I have to.' Esther had tasted freedom and couldn't bear to give it up now.

'He'll try to find us and without my uncle to protect us...' Amy let the words trail off.

'Who is your uncle's heir?'

'Henry,' she replied grimly.

'Matthew's partner in crime?'

'Exactly. We can't turn to him and with my uncle dead my fortune passes into his hands, although he can't touch it. I suppose I must accept that I will never get my money back.'

'Is there no one else we can turn to?'

'Perhaps Edward, my uncle's younger son. He's living in Kensington somewhere.'

'Shall we go?'

'Yes, now, before Matthew returns.'

They turned for the door, which was flung open to reveal Matthew and Hobbs.

'When did you get back?' said Esther, doing her best to remain calm.

'I never really left, except for a few hours yesterday,' he replied. 'I was curious to see what you would do without me here. Now I know.' His eyes were black with fury, his voice even and cold.

'We weren't doing anything,' retorted Esther, doing her best to look indignant but her shaking hands gave her away.

'Forget it, Esther. I overheard every word you just said.'

'You killed my uncle, didn't you?' said Amy with mounting horror.

He smiled malevolently.

'This is nothing to do with Esther.'

'That's very noble of you, Amy, but you can't bluff your way out of this one.'

'What are you going to do?' said Esther fearfully.

'You're both disobedient, and disobedient women need to be punished.'

Esther and Amy backed away as the men advanced on them.

'You can't do anything to us without the children and the servants overhearing,' said Amy.

'The servants have been dismissed and Mrs Crowle's taken the children for a walk.'

'Who is Mrs Crowle?'

'Their new governess.'

'No,' Amy sobbed.

Both women ran for the connecting door leading into the library but the men dragged them screaming upstairs. At the top of the stair Amy succeeded in kicking Matthew in the shin, forcing him to drop her. She scrambled to her feet but he struck her across the face with the back of his hand and she stumbled. He wrapped his arms around her waist, and carried her down the hall into the little-used west wing.

'Put her in there,' he ordered Hobbs, who had hold of a shrieking Esther.

The two women screamed even louder at the prospect of being separated. Matthew dragged Amy into the room next to the one Esther had been hurled into. He shoved her to the floor, stepped inside and locked the door.

'I tried to do things properly but oh, no, you had to spoil it, didn't you?' he said in a low, angry voice. 'We could have been happy.'

'I could never be happy with you,' spat Amy, dragging herself to her feet. 'My uncle told me how Lenora ordered you to seduce me.'

'It's true, she did, but she never wanted me to go as far as I did. I couldn't help myself.' He reached out to touch her face. 'You're the closest I've ever come to loving someone.'

Amy slapped his hand away and spat in his face. Enraged, he slapped her again, knocking her backwards.

'You will not behave in such a revolting way in *my* house. You will conduct yourself as a lady should.'

'I will start behaving like a lady when you start treating me as a gentleman should. What are you really, Matthew? The son of a farmer or a blacksmith? Oh, wait, I have it – the son of a prostitute.'

She saw she'd hit the mark when his eyes filled with a murderous rage. He grabbed her by the throat and pushed her back onto the bed.

'This is how it is, Amy. I want you and Robert. I need Esther but neither need nor want Jane. It would be terrible if she were to have an accident.'

'You wouldn't do that, not even you. She is just a child.'

'I would do anything if it got me what I wanted. Now you and Esther are going to stay up here until I think you've been disciplined enough.'

'Robert will miss me.'

'I'll tell him you're ill. Have no fear, I'll make sure he's kept too busy to worry about you. Jane is fortunate he's so fond of her. It disposes me to be kind to her.'

He tried to kiss her but she wrenched her head away, tears starting to fall.

He grinned. 'Don't worry, Amy, I'm not going to force myself on you. I don't need to. You will give yourself to me willingly,' he said, touching her face. 'In the meantime here's something to remind you of me.'

He sank his teeth into her left forearm, biting so deep he drew blood and she screamed with pain and disbelief.

* * *

Esther panicked when she heard Amy's terrified screams and banged on the walls, crying out her name. Suddenly it went deathly quiet, which she found even more frightening.

'Amy,' she cried.

A few seconds later the door opened and Matthew hauled a dishevelled Amy inside and shoved her onto the bed.

'Thank God,' said Esther, relieved to see she was still alive.

Amy reached out for her and Esther cradled her in her arms as Matthew manacled Amy's right ankle to the other side of the bed. It was then Esther saw the wound on her arm.

'You animal,' she spat at him.

'It's just about lunchtime,' said Matthew smugly. 'I think I'll dine with my son.'

Esther was surprised by the sheer fury in Amy's eyes, not the defeat she had expected. Amy pushed herself upright to glare at Matthew.

'I'll kill you. I swear to almighty God I will slit your throat, just like you did Sally's.'

He laughed before exiting, followed by Hobbs, who slammed the door shut. There was a click as the door was locked.

'I will kill him,' snarled Amy. 'I will.'

21

Esther did what she could for Amy's injuries, which was limited given that she only had a basin of water and a cloth. She'd sustained dark bruising to her face after being struck and the bite mark on her forearm took some time to stop bleeding, the outline of Matthew's teeth clearly imprinted in her skin.

They sat down together on the bed to discuss their options.

'We have to do as he says.' Amy sighed.

'Never,' said Esther passionately. She'd never dared go up against Matthew before but now she felt empowered, even though they were locked up.

'We can do nothing while we're stuck in here. If we play along he'll let us out. The most important thing is that we get back to the children.'

'Do you honestly think he'll let that happen?'

Amy's eyes filled with tears. 'We have to try. I can't stand the thought of him downstairs with them.'

To keep busy, they examined their prison. They'd been given enough length of chain to get about the room but not enough to reach the door or window. There were changes of clothes for them both and their toiletries were neatly arranged on the dressing table. There was also a jug of water and a ewer for them to wash. They also had a chamber pot each and nightgowns and slippers. A lot of preparation had gone into their gaol.

* * *

Matthew heaped fresh torments on them that afternoon when he took the children into the garden to play directly below their window. Amy and Esther could hear them laughing and chattering as they ran about, joined by Matthew's baritone. They strained frantically against their restraints to get to the window but no matter how hard they tried they couldn't reach it.

'I've heard of horror stories like this before,' said Esther as they gave up their efforts and slumped onto the bed. 'Women locked away for years by their husbands, never to see their children again, and the law permits them to do it. We are nothing more than slaves.'

'No one's going to help us so we must help ourselves,' said Amy determinedly.

Esther nodded in agreement.

That evening Hobbs brought their dinner up for them on a tray, depositing it with a silent scowl before leaving. After eating they helped each other change into their nightgowns. They found it awkward removing their skirts and petticoats over the leg irons.

Just as they'd finished changing the door opened and Matthew strode in. It was clear he'd been drinking. As he eyed them both fiercely they staggered back, falling over their manacles. He lunged for Amy and held her by the arm while Hobbs unlocked her leg iron.

'Esther,' she cried.

They reached out for each other but Matthew hauled Amy backwards and dragged her into the next room.

After locking the door he stood there staring at her, eyes unnervingly dead and cold while she shook with fear.

Finally he spoke. 'You hate me, don't you?'

'No,' she replied, teeth chattering.

'Don't lie,' he snarled. 'You didn't used to hate me.'

'You never locked me up before.'

'I wouldn't have had to if you'd done as I'd asked. I never wanted it to come to this.'

'You can't force me to do something I don't want to do.'

'I thought we could be like we were before, at Alardyce.'

'Those days are long gone.'

He looked genuinely sad. 'When I was with you I almost felt normal. I didn't need to hurt anyone.'

Amy was able to see through her fear to realise that he was actually opening up to her, so she decided to take advantage of it. 'Why do you think that was?' she said in a coaxing, gentle tone.

He thought carefully before replying. 'Ever since I was a child I've never cared about anyone. All I've ever felt for people is disdain but you, Amy, you're different. You treated me like an equal. I could talk to you. I would have done anything for you. I even punished Mr Morris for you.'

Her eyes widened. 'Punished him?'

'After he attacked you I sneaked back to his house and tampered with the wheels of his carriage.'

'You caused that accident, the one that left him crippled?'

'I did it for you.'

'And what about poor Rowan? Did you punish him too?'

'That was Lenora. She found out from a friend of hers that he'd been gambling with money that wasn't his and sent him an anonymous letter telling him she was going to the authorities.'

'Why?'

'She knew it would only take something small to make him crack and it worked. She hoped the shock would make you crack too but she failed to realise how strong you are. She really was desperate for you to be put away.' When her eyes filled with tears he took her face in his hands. 'Now fate has brought you back to me and I want it to be like was at Alardyce.'

'How can I treat you as an equal when you keep me locked up?' Sh swallowed down the abuse she wanted to hurl at him. 'Do yo remember when we shared our first kiss?'

'How could I forget?' he breathed, brushing her lips with his own.

'You told me I was safe with you.'

'And you are, as long as you do as I say.'

His lips moved to her neck and she forced herself not to flinc 'Matthew, how many women have you hurt?'

'I don't remember,' he murmured into her throat. 'Sometimes would hurt them and I didn't even know what I'd done until it wa over.'

'Did you hurt Sally?'

'Sally?'

'The housemaid who worked here, the one who disappeared.'

'Oh, her? Yes.'

She swallowed hard and a tear ran down her cheek.

'You don't need to worry about her. Kiss me and if you mak it like it was at Alardyce then I'll let you see the childre tomorrow.'

'Promise?'

'I swear it. You can have breakfast with them then go into th garden.'

'Esther too?'

'Yes, Esther too.'

The thought of what she must do made her physically sick but do she would if it meant she could see her son. She took a deep breath. 'A right.'

He smiled and ran his hands over her waist. 'Lovely,' he breathed.

Screwing her eyes shut, she kissed him and was startled to feel touch of the passion she had once felt for him still lingered eve though she despised the man. Picking up on her passion, Matthe kissed her harder and moaned, his hands sliding into her hair and pulling out the pins.

'Ow,' she gasped as he tore out a few strands.

'Sorry. I just love seeing your hair down, it's so beautiful.'

His hands slid down to her stomach. 'We'll make more brothers and sisters for Robert, lots of them to carry my name. We'll be one big happy family, won't we?'

She nodded, remaining tight-lipped.

'Keep this up and I might let you see Robert soon,' he said, running his fingers through her hair.

'You said if I kissed you like I did at Alardyce then I could have breakfast with my son.'

'Did I? I don't remember.' He released her, eyes hardening. 'Back to your room.'

'No, wait, please. You promised.'

He grabbed her by the shoulders and steered her towards the door. 'Back to your room.'

'I'm not going until you tell me I can see my son,' she yelled as he hauled her into the corridor.

He remained obstinately silent, nodding at Hobbs, who unlocked the door. He shoved Amy inside and she fell to the floor. She leapt to her feet and ran at the door, which was slammed shut in her face.

'Let me see my son. Matthew, do you hear me?' she screamed. 'Robert. Robert.'

When it was clear there was going to be no reply she slumped to her knees. 'Robert,' she breathed hopelessly.

* * *

Amy and Esther spent the night curled up together on the bed, frightened out of their wits. They never knew when the door was going to open and the torments begin again. Eventually they both fell asleep out of sheer exhaustion and were woken by the jangle of keys and daylight streaming through the curtains. They sat bolt upright, holding onto each other. Matthew entered with an almost pleasant expression while Hobbs lurked in the background.

'Come on, chop chop. You should be getting ready for breakfast.'

They stared at him in confusion.

'But you said...' began Amy.

'We made a deal. Dress and have breakfast with the children. We'll be back in ten minutes to collect you both, so I suggest you hurry.'

Hobbs unlocked their manacles then went to wait outside the door. The two women were almost exuberant as they hastily dressed.

When Matthew returned he laid down some ground rules.

'I've explained your absence to the children by informing them that you're both unwell, and when I give the word you will tell them you're feeling ill again and need to return to bed. If you disobey me in any way you won't ever see them again. Are we clear?'

They both nodded and followed him out of the room. They walked flanked by the two men as though they were prisoners being escorted.

Amy's heart soared when she heard Robert's voice and tears of happiness threatened but she blinked them away before Matthew saw.

As the door opened, Robert's head snapped up and his eyes widened with delight.

'Mama,' he cried, running up to her and flinging his arms around her waist. Kneeling down, she wrapped him in a big hug, kissing his face and breathing in his scent.

'I've missed you so much,' she said.

'I've missed you too, Mama,' he replied, hugging her so tightly she thought her ribs might crack.

Jane had leapt at Esther and was hugging her aunt.

Robert looked up at his mother with big, dark, innocent eyes. 'Are you feeling better, Mama? Matthew said you were ill.'

'I'm still unwell, my darling, but I feel well enough to see you.'

'You're hurt,' he said, eyes shining with concern at the bruising on her face. She'd done her best to conceal it with some of Esther's powder but it had come off on the boy's shoulder when he'd cuddled her.

'I fainted and banged my face when I became unwell. It's fine. Nothing for you to worry about.'

'Shall we eat before it gets cold?' interrupted Matthew.

Amy knew the warmth with which Robert had greeted her annoyed him. He was trying to sever the bond between them and it wasn't working.

Also seated at the table was a sour-faced, middle-aged woman draped in grey.

'This is Mrs Crowle,' said Matthew. 'She's acting as governess while Amy recovers.'

Amy tried to control the hostility she felt towards this woman, who must not only be complicit in what was being done to herself and Esther but who was also in charge of the children. She hated the thought of this wretch having mastery over her son. Amy stared at the plate set before her with disdain, the eggs making her knotted stomach squirm. She couldn't eat a thing. Instead she nibbled the corner of a piece of dry toast.

'Mrs Crowle,' she began and the woman fixed her with beady, suspicious eyes. 'How do Robert and Jane progress in their studies?'

'Tolerably well,' she said in a pinched, mean voice. 'I've made some adjustments to the work you set for them, cut out some of the trifles.'

'I wasn't aware I was teaching trifles.'

'The maths and spelling for Jane. Such things are a waste of time for a girl. She needs to concentrate on her sewing and music, which are much more useful to a young lady.'

Amy blinked in surprise. 'Are you saying it's not important for Jane to be able to read and count?'

'I'm saying it's not vital and she is lacking in other accomplishments. I've banned the watercolours too. Fantasising about fairies is no way to spend one's day.'

Amy and Esther regarded a downcast Jane with concern.

'But Jane loves her watercolours,' said Esther.

'That is beside the point, madam,' she retorted, addressing Esther with a distinct lack of respect as mistress of the house. 'She is here to learn, not enjoy herself.'

'I was under the impression the two go hand in hand.' Amy frowned.

'Which explains why Jane is lacking in so many areas.'

'And what of Robert? Have you altered his studies too?'

'Not particularly but there is less playtime and more serious work.'

Amy glanced at her son, who was glowering at his new governess. She could see he was unhappy but she was powerless to stop it. 'It's still important they both receive plenty of fresh air. Being cooped up in the schoolroom all day is detrimental to their health and learning.'

Mrs Crowle's gaze was cold. 'Once again, Mrs Parker, that is where we differ.'

Incensed, Amy opened her mouth to reply but Matthew shot her such a black look she closed it again. She would not give him the slightest reason to cut short this precious time.

As breakfast came to a close Robert looked outside at the bright sunshine.

'Matthew, may we play outside with Mama and Mrs Huntington?'

Matthew broke into a gentle smile, unable to deny his son anything. 'Of course, but not for long. Remember they're still recovering.'

He nodded seriously before getting to his feet and reaching for his mother's hand. 'Come on, Mama.'

Jane rose too and, taking Esther's hand, led her out into the garden.

Matthew went to the window to watch them, Mrs Crowle standing beside him.

'The boy's very attached to his mother,' she said, dropping back into her native Edinburgh accent. 'The bond between them will be harder to break than we'd anticipated.'

'Then we must try harder,' replied Matthew, his eyes fixed on Amy.

She looked radiant with happiness now she was reunited with Robert and a deep well of jealousy rose up inside him. He didn't want their mutual affection to detract from their worship of him. Superficially Amy wasn't as beautiful as his wife but whatever it was within her eclipsed Esther entirely. Keeping her caged and apart from what she loved most excited him unbearably. He was pushing her to the limit of her endurance and he was curious to see what the end result would be. When she'd threatened to kill him he had no doubt that if she had been able to she would have tried.

He permitted them all an hour in the garden together before he sent Mrs Crowle out to call the children inside for their lessons.

'Can't we stay out a bit longer?' Robert asked him when they were back in the house.

'Now, think of your poor mother and Mrs Huntington,' said Matthew gently. 'You want them to get better, don't you?'

'I suppose,' he mumbled. 'Get better soon, Mama. I miss you.'

'I'm trying, darling, believe me, I'm trying as hard as I can.' She hugged him one last time, hoping he wouldn't see the tears in her eyes. 'I love you so much,' she whispered in his ear.

'I love you too.'

After saying goodbye to the children, Amy and Esther were reluctantly led back to their room.

They let Hobbs manacle them without protest, their minds elsewhere.

'They know something's wrong,' began Esther when he'd gone.

Amy nodded. 'Matthew thinks because they're children they'll be easy to deceive. I dread to think what will happen when they start to question him.'

'You don't think he would go as far as to hurt them? I know he's a monster but...'

Amy couldn't bring herself to say it but when she looked at Esther she realised she already knew. *He wouldn't hurt Robert,* they both thought.

'We should have warned them to always do as he says and neve
argue with him,' said Esther.

Amy nodded. 'We must convince him to let us see them again, a
soon as possible.'

They looked at each other and grimaced as they realised what mus
be done.

'I'll do it,' said Esther. 'He's my husband after all.'

'He'll hurt you.'

'I don't doubt it, but it must be done,' Esther said bravely, althoug
her skin was ashen.

22

Amy and Esther were asleep when they were woken by a clinking sound. Confused, Amy sat up, her eyes searching the darkness, but it was so absolute she could see nothing but a vague shadow. She jumped when fingers brushed her ankle and the manacle was removed.

'Who's there? What are you doing?'

'Amy, what's going on?' said Esther, sitting up beside her.

'I don't know.'

Amy was dragged off the bed by her feet, her back hitting the floor painfully.

'Esther, help me,' she cried.

Esther grabbed her hands and for a brief, painful moment she was caught in a tug of war. The one taking her away – whom she assumed was Hobbs – triumphed, and she was hauled along the floor. Frantically she scrabbled at the floorboards in an attempt to gain purchase but her efforts were in vain, all the while Esther calling out her name.

The door slammed shut, silencing Esther's cries. There was a click as the lock was turned, then she was pulled to her feet.

'Master wants to see you,' came Hobbs's gruff voice out of the darkness.

This sudden abduction and journey through the pitch-black corridors was disorientating and by the time she was shoved into the study she was shaking like a leaf.

'Amy, glad you could make it.' Matthew smiled, rising from his desk as though this were a pleasant social call. 'Why you are shaking? Was Hobbs a little harsh? Here,' he said, pouring her a brandy. 'This will revive you.'

She accepted it and stared at the contents doubtfully.

'It's not poisoned, if that's what you're thinking.'

Shrugging, she drank down the fiery liquid in one go and felt the trembling subside.

'Better?'

She nodded.

'Good.' His eyes flicked to Hobbs. 'Leave us.'

The man nodded respectfully and left, closing the door behind him.

'I just wanted to say how well you did this morning,' said Matthew. 'Robert was very reassured.'

She glanced at the clock on his desk, which indicated that it was one o'clock in the morning. 'Could you not have told me that earlier?'

'I've been busy. I took Robert riding today.'

Despite everything, she smiled. 'How did he fare? He's never ridden before.'

Matthew was pleased with her enthusiasm. 'At first he was a little nervous, but I found him a lovely black riding pony and they took to each other immediately. He did very well.'

'I would very much like to see him ride, if you would permit it?' she said, spotting her chance.

'I don't know. It would mean a trip to the stables. Do you think you and Esther can behave yourselves?'

'I'm sure we can.'

He pretended to ponder on it for a moment to give her false hope before shaking his head. 'No, I don't think so.'

The hope died in her eyes, making him smile.

'Then could we have breakfast with the children again tomorrow?' she pressed, voice faltering.

'No.'

'You said yourself we behaved very well.'

'So I did but that was a treat. Don't expect it every day.'

'When can we see them again?'

'We'll see,' he ended dismissively, turning his back on her.

He watched her through the mirror on the wall before him, which he'd had placed there specifically for this meeting. Before her on his desk lay a razor-sharp letter opener, a paperweight and a vase. With these weapons to hand he had presented her with his turned back. Through the mirror he saw her eyes dance over each of the three objects before her hand covertly grasped the letter opener. Her eyes lit up with that inner fire and, as she readied herself to plunge the knife into his body, he whipped round and grabbed her arm, his other hand gripping her throat. He spun her round and slammed her, face up, on the desk, so she was pinioned beneath him.

'Drop it. Drop it,' he urged, squeezing her wrist.

With a grunt of pain she released the dagger and it fell to the floor with a clang.

'Were you going to kill me?' he said with interest rather than anger.

'Yes,' she snarled, erupting beneath him. 'With you out of the way I would get my son back.'

'You can be together again if only you will obey me.'

'I obey no one,' she screamed in his face, struggling beneath him.

She succeeded in freeing her right arm and in her fury she slapped him hard across the face.

His eyes darkened. 'Again.'

She hit him as hard as she could and he grunted with pleasure. Lifting her head, she kissed him and bit his lip, drawing blood, and he gasped with pain and surprise.

To his astonishment she gave him a slow sultry smile, the blood on her lips making her look predatory. When he released her left arm she ripped his shirt open with such force the buttons popped off all over the floor and she dug her fingernails into his back before dragging them down his skin, drawing more blood. Her eyes were heavy with delight; she was enjoying hurting him.

Pulling him down to her, she kissed him, thrusting her tongue into his mouth while her fingers continued to nip and pinch his flesh. Finally he'd broken through the demure governess persona and found the molten lava beneath that was the real Amy.

Overcome with excitement, he bent to retrieve the letter opener and held it over her. Rather than cringe in fear she stared up at him steadily, only the rapid rise and fall of her chest belying her agitation. He brought down the dagger and used it to slit open the front of her nightgown, then pressed the blade against the exposed flesh of her stomach. It would be so easy for him to end her and then Robert would be entirely his, but the world would be a lot duller without Amy in it. Besides, this was the stomach that had produced his only child, his miracle. He placed his hand on her abdomen, revelling in how warm and vital she was, how fertile and feminine.

Amy snatched the knife from his hand and hurled it across the room. He ground his mouth against hers while opening his trousers, his hand sliding up her thigh as her legs wrapped themselves around his waist. When he pushed into her she released a cry.

This time he could feel she was letting go, allowing herself to enjoy the pleasure he was giving her, and he drove into her roughly while she bit his neck and shoulders and clawed at his back and buttocks. She was a wildcat, all teeth and claws and spitting rage and she was moaning loudly with gratification.

Unable to hold back any longer, he thrust into her so hard she was pushed back off the desk, her head hanging over the edge, body shuddering violently as they climaxed together.

When it was over she went still, returning to her senses. Matthew got to his feet to watch as her eyes flickered open, still bright with anger. Slowly she sat up, drew back her fist and punched him, catching him in the left side of the face and knocking him to the floor. He was stunned, but rather than fury he felt only admiration and he remained on the floor and gently kissed her bare feet while she glared down at him like a furious Amazon.

Laughing, he got to his feet and started to dress and the fire in her eyes died, giving way to shame. She clutched the tattered remnants of her nightgown about her as she slid off the desk to stand on wobbly legs.

'See, we're not so different after all,' he remarked.

Amy hunted around for a retort but nothing came to mind. Her eyes flicked over the lacerations and bite marks she'd left on his body, saw the bruise on his face and realised he was right. This was what he had seen in her. He'd recognised that she was like him.

'Congratulations,' he said. 'You've just earned yourself more time with the children tomorrow.'

She nodded her gratitude, feeling dazed.

'You can return to your room. Hobbs is waiting outside. He will escort you.'

Slowly she shuffled to the door, fighting back tears. As she passed him he grabbed her arm.

'Hopefully our second child is already starting to grow in your belly.'

She didn't reply or even look at him as she left the room.

Matthew watched her go with a smile. She was defeated. Finally.

* * *

Esther was relieved to see Amy back in one piece. She frowned when she saw the state she was in. 'Amy, are you all right?'

She didn't reply as she sat on the bed and let Hobbs replace the manacle. When he'd gone she curled up in a ball, crying silent tears.

Esther crouched beside her. 'What did he do to you?' she said noting Amy's ripped gown.

'We can see the children again tomorrow,' she croaked in response.

'That's wonderful, but what did you have to do?'

'Please don't ask me, Esther. Please.'

'Amy, what has he done? Tell me.'

'I can't... I'm so ashamed... I'm sorry.'

With that she buried her face in the pillow and refused to utter another word.

* * *

Amy was still subdued the next morning, even at breakfast with the children. The only time she seemed to become animated was when one of them spoke to her. Esther was worried sick. If Amy decided she was going to give up she'd be trapped too. She couldn't do this alone.

Matthew watched all this with great interest. It was apparent Amy was struggling with some disturbing emotions after he'd shown her what she truly was and Esther had no idea what was wrong with her which meant Amy hadn't confided in her. If Amy stopped telling her things it would be easier to divide them. Amy, for her part, couldn't look him in the eye.

As he looked down at his plate, feeling very pleased with himself, he missed the malevolent glare Amy shot him, which was filled with everything but defeat.

* * *

After breakfast they all went out to the paddock to watch Robert take his next riding lesson. He was a bit unnerved to have such a large audience but, with a smile of encouragement from his mother, he bravely mounted the gleaming black pony. At once it was evident he was a natural and Amy watched on proudly.

Matthew mounted his own horse, a fine black stallion, and trotted beside the boy. Amy wished his powerful horse would throw him.

Once back in their cell Esther tried questioning Amy again but she remained lost in her own world, which terrified Esther more than anything that had happened so far.

To both their surprise they were invited downstairs for dinner that evening.

'Does this mean you're getting better, Mama?' said Robert, excited to see her twice in one day.

Amy glanced questioningly at Matthew before replying. He gave her a small nod.

'Yes, Robert,' she said. 'It does.'

'Good.' He beamed.

Robert insisted on his mother putting him to bed that night and Matthew allowed Esther to do the same for Jane. The children's bedrooms were next door to each other so it was easy for Hobbs to stand guard.

Amy read Robert some of his favourite story, *Robinson Crusoe*, before tucking him in.

'I miss you, Mama,' he said, eyes heavy with sleep.

'I miss you too, sweetheart, more than you can ever know.'

'I don't like Mrs Crowle. She's mean, especially to Jane.'

'Robert, it's very important that you do as Mrs Crowle says and even more important that you do as Mr Huntington says. Don't make him angry. Do you understand?' she said as gently as she could, not wanting to scare him.

Robert was a sharp little boy and he nodded. 'Yes, Mama.'

'Good boy.' She smiled, hugging him. When she glimpsed Hobbs scowling at her through the crack in the door she realised her time was up. 'Get a good night's sleep, my darling, and hopefully I will see you tomorrow.'

He hugged her again and she kissed the top of his head.

'Goodnight, Mama.' He yawned, already sinking into sleep.

Amy panicked when she returned to her prison and saw Esther wasn't there.

'Where is she?' she demanded of her jailer.

'Master wants to see her,' muttered Hobbs as he chained her up.

'Why?'

'None of your business.' He glowered before stalking out, locking the door behind him.

* * *

Esther watched her husband uneasily from across the desk in his study.

'How are you?' he began gently.

'Fine.' She frowned, wrong-footed by his kind tone.

He rose from his seat and perched on the edge of the desk before her. 'I'm sorry for the harsh way I've treated you. You don't deserve it.'

'No, I don't, and neither does Amy.'

'Amy.' He laughed. 'Everything was fine until she turned up. You don't know her, Esther. This is all her doing.'

'Are you saying she forced you to keep us both prisoner?'

'Not exactly. I know she's probably given you a pack of lies so I shall tell you the truth. Yes, we did have an affair when I worked at Alardyce House and the product of that affair was Robert, who I did not know about until they came here. Of course I saw the likeness at once. What she has probably failed to tell you is that she tried to blackmail me.'

'Blackmail?' said Esther doubtfully.

'At first she tried to seduce me and when that didn't work she said she would tell you I was Robert's father if I didn't resume my affair with her. She even tried to seduce me again in this very room last night. I just wanted to talk, to try and come to some amicable arrangement that would end all this, but she went mad, claiming she still wanted me. She went into a rage and hit me,' he said, indicating the bruise on his face. 'So I sent her back to her room.'

Esther listened uncertainly. Despite what Matthew thought, she knew all about his philandering and Amy was an attractive woman. Would he really turn her down if he was propositioned? But this would explain Amy's odd behaviour and her apologies to Esther.

'Don't let her fool you,' he continued. 'She's a harlot. Do you know that when she was fifteen she had an affair with a friend of her father? A man thirty years her senior.'

'I should think the blame for that lay at the man's door, not hers. She was just a girl.'

He continued, undaunted. 'For nine years she has lied about her identity. Do you know why she ran away from Alardyce?'

'Because they wanted to take the baby from her.'

'No.' He laughed. 'She ran because they wanted to put her in a lunatic asylum.'

'I know. She told me.'

'I'm willing to wager she told you it was because they wanted her fortune, but that's ridiculous. The Alardyces never needed her money. It was because she'd suffer strange fits of rage, which would sometimes become violent,' he said, again indicating his face. 'She was completely unmanageable and they'd had enough. If one of the servants hadn't betrayed their master's plans she would be locked up now.'

'If she was indeed insane, as you claim, it didn't stop you sleeping with her.'

'I was young and taken in by her allure and wildness. Now I'm older and wiser I know exactly what she is.'

'You were a footman at Alardyce and you told me you're the son of a wealthy merchant.'

'I never lied to you. My father was a wealthy merchant but he suffered some setbacks in business and I was forced to temporarily go into service. Fortunately he quickly resolved those problems and I left Alardyce.'

'She also said that you're really Scottish.'

His lips twitched with amusement. 'Do I sound Scottish?'

'Well... no.'

'Have you ever heard me speak with a Scottish accent?'

'No,' she was forced to admit.

'My family's from Kent, just like I told you. This is all part of Amy's madness. She always was a fantasist.'

'Why did you never tell me you were in service?'

'Because I was ashamed. Look at you, Esther, you're so beautiful, so accomplished. What would you have thought of me if I'd told you?'

'And why didn't you tell me who Amy was when she first came to this house?'

'How could I tell my dear, sweet wife that I'd fathered a child with the governess when I was working as a footman? It was so sordid I wanted to protect you from it. I was hoping to get her out of the house so you'd never have to know but she'd already got her hooks into everyone. That's how she works.'

'You bit her arm.'

'She did that to herself. I told you, she's quite mad.'

'None of this explains why you have kept us both locked up.'

'Because you were going to run away with her and expose the children to danger. I couldn't allow that,' he said, taking her hands in his. 'I couldn't bear to lose you. I know I haven't been the best husband to you, but I do love you and I don't want you to go.'

'You had me chained up like an animal,' she said indignantly. She was proud of herself. Never before had she spoken to him so forthrightly.

'I can only apologise but Amy knows how to get into people's heads. Yes, I admit I want Robert, he is my son after all, but I want him to be ours, Esther, yours and mine. A son of our own to raise together.'

He smiled inwardly at the flash of longing in her eyes. God, she was gullible. He kissed her and she released a little sigh of longing.

'I love you, Esther, I miss you,' he said, shifting his caresses to her neck.

Esther's insides twisted with desire. It had been so long since he'd touched her and she was aching to feel him again.

'Would you like to spend tonight in my bed?' he breathed in her ear.

Esther hesitated before replying. She wasn't a fool – despite what he thought – and she knew he was a clever manipulator, but what if Amy had been deceiving her all along and only wanted her and Jane to flee to punish Matthew?

'I want you, Esther. Now,' he whispered, making her swell with desire. 'Will you come to my bed?'

Taking her hand, he kissed it and led her upstairs.

23

Amy couldn't rest. Esther had been gone for two hours and she feare[d]
what Matthew was doing to her. Or what if Matthew had finally carrie[d]
through his threat to split them up? The thought of enduring captivi[ty]
alone terrified her.

Amy closed her eyes in silent prayer. *Please let her be all right.*

* * *

Matthew was bored. Esther lay beneath him meek and impassiv[e]
releasing little mewls of pleasure that irritated him. He used to like th[e]
submissive posture she always adopted, it appeased his domina[nt]
nature, but it had soon lost its novelty value. He wanted to bite her [or]
strike her, anything to get a reaction, but he reined in the urge becaus[e]
he was trying to woo her, not frighten her. There would be plenty [of]
time for all that once she was back under his spell.

He closed his eyes to block her out and thought of Amy. He recalle[d]
the look on her face last night, the fury and passion in her eyes, and th[e]
next thing he knew he was climaxing and Esther looked up at him wit[h]

delight. For her part she released a thin, reedy moan, her body gave a slight tremble and that was it.

He lay beside her and held her in his arms, grimacing as her pointy elbow dug into his ribs.

'I think Jane would like you to take her sketching tomorrow,' he said after a few minutes of silence.

She looked up at him with delight. 'Yes?'

'Yes.' He smiled indulgently.

She hugged him. 'Thank you.'

'You're welcome, my love.'

It was only as she was drifting off to sleep, her head resting on his chest, that Esther recalled the spectre of Sally screaming, her throat cut. Her eyes narrowed as she recalled Amy had been the one to accuse Matthew.

'Matthew?' she began uncertainly.

'Yes?'

She pushed herself up on her elbows to look at him. 'Do you know what happened to Sally?'

To her surprise he smiled. 'This is about the so-called psychic you invited, isn't it?'

'How do you know about Magda?'

'I bumped into your friend's husband the other day, who told me his wife had recommended her to you. Did you know that Magda Magrath is a resident of the village of Alardyce?'

'No.' She frowned.

'Amy didn't mention the fact that she met her when she lived at Alardyce?'

'She did not,' replied Esther, starting to feel silly and gullible.

'I can prove everything I have told you,' he said, climbing out of bed and walking over to a small desk.

He unlocked the desk, pulled out a pile of newspaper cuttings then padded back over to her. 'When Amy came here I thought something like this might happen, so I started gathering evidence to support myself.'

Esther thumbed through the cuttings. The first was a newspaper article about Amy's disappearance from Alardyce. Some of the villagers had been interviewed, including one Magda Magrath, who had lived in the village for over twenty years.

'This woman was a known charlatan in Alardyce,' he said. 'She came here in collusion with Amy to trick you with smoke and mirrors into thinking I was a monster.' He showed her more cuttings dating from when Amy first disappeared, all stating how mentally unbalanced she was.

'And her uncle?'

'Was killed by robbers. The police have even arrested someone for the crime.'

Esther's eyes filled with tears. 'I am such a fool.'

'Don't, darling.' He smiled, wrapping his arms around her. 'She's a very convincing actress.'

'Oh, Matthew, can you ever forgive me?' She wept, looking up at him with pleading eyes.

He wiped away her tears with his fingertips. 'Of course I can. You were under her spell but now I have freed you,' he said, kissing her and pressing her back into the bed.

* * *

Amy spent most of the night wide awake worrying about Esther. The absolute darkness of her prison was terrifying alone. She buried herself beneath the bedclothes, curled up into a ball and cried, wondering whether she would ever see another living soul again. She only fell asleep at dawn, when the first few reassuring rays of daylight started to filter through the gap in the heavy curtains. Consequently when she woke it was almost lunchtime. She was disturbed by voices drifting in through her window from the garden.

'Robert?' she said sleepily when she heard her little boy laugh.

Sitting up, she strained to hear. There was also Jane's voice, Matthew's, and another lighter one. Mrs Crowle's? No, it was far too happy. She sat bolt upright. Esther. It was Esther. She was all right.

Why was she outside in the garden with the children while Amy was still locked away in here? It didn't make any sense. She must have pleased Matthew last night, just as she herself had done the night before, to get them both some time with the children. But if that was the case she should have been let out too.

Tears filled her eyes as she listened to her son happily chatting and laughing.

'Robert,' she breathed.

Then she heard something that turned her blood to ice. Matthew and Esther were talking, their voices low murmurs, and Matthew exclaimed, 'Esther, my love.' This was followed by her coquettish laugh.

The shock made Amy feel sick. There was only one possible explanation – they had reconciled. Somehow Matthew had persuaded Esther against her and they'd decided to leave her here to rot. Frantically she tugged at the chain in an effort to reach the window, straining her ankle, but she fell short a few inches. Her fingertips brushed the windowsill as she fell, sobbing in despair. They had what they both wanted – a son of their own.

* * *

Robert was confused. 'So you're better, Mrs Huntington, but Mama's still poorly?'

'That's right, sweetheart,' she replied.

'May I see her?'

'She's resting, darling,' she replied. 'The more rest she gets, the quicker she'll get better. Besides, we're all going for a walk to the lake.'

'Yes,' he said excitedly.

Matthew and Esther looked at each other and smiled.

* * *

When Esther didn't return all that day Amy knew her worst fears had been realised – Amy had lost her only ally. If they wanted to they could just let her die and no one would know. Robert would enquire after her but they could make up any story they liked and in his innocence he would believe them. Esther would replace her as a mother figure and slowly he would forget she'd ever existed.

Defeat metamorphosed into screaming rage and she started to tear the room apart. She dragged the mattress off the bed, strewing the bedding everywhere then smashed all the bottles on the dressing table. She ripped Esther's dresses to shreds before hurling a vase at the mirror on the wall, shattering it. When her anger was spent she slumped to her knees and cried hysterically.

Her room was so far from the rest of the house that no one heard the commotion. They weren't even aware of what she'd done until Hobbs brought up her dinner tray. His eyes widened at the mess.

'What have you done, you mad bitch? I'll have to tell the master.'

'That's right, you run off to him like the obedient little doggy you are,' she yelled as he hurried from the room.

A minute later Matthew and Esther appeared in the doorway.

'See, I told you she was unstable, didn't I?' said Matthew.

'Amy, what do you think you're doing?' demanded Esther.

'I heard the two of you in the garden. How could you fall for his lies, Esther, when you know what he's done?'

'He's not the liar, Amy, you are. I know Magda's a friend of yours. You must think I'm really gullible to fall for the little show you put on.'

'He killed Sally.'

'No, he didn't. I thought I could talk to you but you used everything I confided in you against me,' she said, the genuine hurt audible in her voice. 'All this time you've been trying to split us up. You wanted Matthew for yourself.'

'Wanted Matthew?' She laughed. 'You bloody fool, Esther.'

'Amy, you're not well. You need help,' said Matthew in his best sympathetic voice.

Amy caught the triumph in his eyes, which was too much for her. She launched herself at him but he caught her and pushed her back into the room, straining to hold her.

'Hobbs,' he called.

The two men grappled with Amy, who was fighting with a strength born of fear and desperation, and they struggled to contain her.

'Esther, I don't want you to see her like this,' said Matthew, fighting to maintain his grip on her. 'Why don't you take the children out for a walk?'

'Esther, please help me,' screamed Amy.

'I'm sorry but Matthew's right. You're ill,' Esther said sadly before walking away.

'Esther,' she wailed.

Esther broke into a run at the desolate sound of Amy's voice following her accusingly along the hall and down the stairs.

Matthew kicked the door shut to block out the sound. 'Get the other manacle,' he ordered Hobbs.

'No, don't,' she cried, trying to wriggle free but her efforts were in vain as Hobbs snapped on the second leg iron.

With her legs tethered it was easy for them to push her back onto the bed and tie her wrists to the bed head.

'Don't leave me like this,' she cried. 'Please.'

'Leave us,' Matthew ordered Hobbs.

Obediently he left. Matthew climbed on top of Amy and stared down at her with glee.

'Congratulations, you've just convinced Esther that you're mad.'

'And you've got what you want – my son, Esther nice and compliant and me a prisoner up here.'

'Not quite. I want you willingly, like you were two nights ago, remember? Right then in that moment you were everything I've ever wanted. Be that for me again and you will earn your freedom, then we can be a happy family. Although Esther wears the ring you will be my true wife. Just be mine.'

He tried to kiss her but she wrenched her head to one side.

His eyes turned cold. 'Perhaps some time like this will change your mind.'

Matthew left her chained up, pushing her dinner tray within tantalising reach so she could see and smell the food but not touch it.

* * *

For the rest of the day Matthew kept thinking of Amy tied up and helpless upstairs and each time he thought about it he got more excited and impatient. He was relieved when Esther finally decided to retire to bed.

'Are you coming up?' she said, flashing him what she thought was a seductive smile that instead annoyed him.

'I'll follow you shortly. I have some paperwork to attend to first.'

'You're going to see *her* again, aren't you?' she said, eyes narrowing.

'No. That's Hobbs's job.'

'She needs help, a proper hospital. We can't manage her here.'

'As always you're right. I'll speak to Dr Forrest in the morning.'

Pleased, Esther trotted upstairs and he sighed before returning to the papers on his desk. He gave it twenty minutes before leaving his study and padding upstairs to the west wing, unable to wait any longer.

He entered Amy's room to find her in exactly the same position he'd left her only now she was asleep. The light from the lamp he carried shone on her face, disturbing her, and she raised her head and stared at him, bleary-eyed.

'Who's there?' she said, fear in her voice, unable to see because the light was shining in her eyes.

'It's just me,' he replied, placing the lamp on the table, lighting her up. He wanted to see clearly for what he had planned.

'What do you want?' she said, tugging at her restraints.

'You hurt me that night in the study. Now it's my turn.'

Amy stared in horror as his eyes seemed to roll over in his head and turn black, devoid of anything that could be called human. His lips stretched into a horrible leer and a low growl rumbled in the back of his throat.

She realised she was going to suffer more than she had ever suffered before.

* * *

Esther hadn't gone to bed, instead she'd been waiting for Matthew to go upstairs. She knew exactly where he was headed – Amy's room.

When he was out of sight she sneaked back downstairs and into his study. Something about his story didn't ring true and after hearing Amy's pleas for assistance she felt she owed it to her to make sure Matthew was being entirely honest. If there was any evidence against him, she knew it would be in his study. That was where he kept his secrets.

She began with his desk. Heart pounding, she reached out a shaky hand and tugged at one of the drawers and was relieved when it opened. She sighed with relief when it contained nothing more suspect than some writing implements and paper.

The next drawer was empty. The third drawer likewise appeared empty and she was about to shut it when she caught the glint of something metallic at the back. Reaching inside, she pulled it out and almost dropped it with fright. A silver locket. With trembling fingers she opened it to reveal the images of Amy's parents.

She threw it back into the drawer and slammed it shut as though it might bite her. Fear shot down her spine as she recalled Amy telling her she had given her uncle the locket, so how was it in

Matthew's possession? There was only one explanation – he'd had Hobbs kill Sir Alfred and take the locket, so no connection would be made to Amy or himself. It was true, all of it. She was married to a murderer.

Realising it was vital she return to her room before Matthew, she hastened back upstairs. As she ran her breath came out in frantic bursts, her chest heaving with exertion and fear.

* * *

Matthew swaggered out of Amy's prison, wild-eyed and breathless, fastening up the collar of his shirt.

'Go and tend to her,' he ordered Mrs Crowle as he strolled towards the stairs with a smirk on his face.

* * *

Esther dashed into her bedchamber, threw on her nightgown and dived beneath the covers. At least there was no maid to give her away as Matthew had got rid of all their servants. The only ones he permitted into the house lived in the village, and they were only allowed inside between the hours of eight and five to cook and clean. He was too afraid of someone finding out what he'd done.

She lay on her side, facing away from the door, taking long deep breaths in an effort to slow her breathing and her thudding heart. She closed her eyes and buried her face in the pillow as her door slowly opened.

'Esther?' Matthew whispered.

She didn't respond, desperately hoping he'd think she was asleep and go away but he didn't. Instead he climbed in beside her and wrapped his arms around her. She gave a little sigh and shifted, as though he'd disturbed her sleep.

'Sorry. Paperwork took longer than expected,' he lied in her ear.

'It's all right,' she mumbled, keeping her eyes shut, unable to look at this monster she'd married.

He stroked her hair back off her shoulder and kissed her neck and for a brief, horrifying moment she thought he wanted to have sex with her but instead he just turned over and went to sleep. She lay frozen in the foetal position all night, trying to put as much space between them as possible, flinching every time he touched her. Tears stung her eyes as she recalled the last words Amy had said to her. She had begged her for help and she'd ignored her. That would stay with her until the day she died.

* * *

Amy drifted in and out of consciousness, her body wracked with pain, which wasn't helped by Mrs Crowle's rough ministrations. She drifted into terrifying visions populated by strange devils and demons all with Matthew's face.

When she finally woke with a loud scream she found she was able to sit upright. It was bright daylight, which comforted her somewhat, and Matthew was nowhere to be seen.

Both her hands and one of her legs had been freed so she could at least move about the room. She was wearing a fresh nightgown, which Mrs Crowle had put on her after Matthew had cut off her clothes with a large knife.

Tears spilled down her face. Last night she'd thought she was going to die; he'd been more beast than man. He'd pressed the blade of the knife to her throat, his black eyes dead, and she'd been certain she was going to suffer the same fate as Sally but instead he'd beat her, interspersing the violence by clamping his hand down over her nose and mouth, cutting off her air supply until her heart had swelled against her ribcage and she'd verged on unconsciousness. Then he'd released her, allowing her to breathe, and started the torture all over again. He'd only stopped when she'd said that if she was pregnant he would beat the child out of her, and he'd left, his dead eyes slowly returning to life until they were bright with satisfaction.

Slowly she sat up to assess her injuries. Her bare arms bore numerous bite marks, some so light they'd only left a slight bruise, others so deep the outline of his teeth was visible. One of the bites on her right forearm had been inflicted so viciously that she had bled and she'd been horrified when he'd licked the blood off, seeming to savour the taste like some hideous vampire. A tray of food and drink had been pushed through the door. Amy staggered to her feet, fell down beside it and greedily drank down the glass of water, her throat parched.

She was so weak she knew she must eat, despite her churning stomach, but she didn't have the strength to carry the tray over to the bed. She pushed the tray across the floor, crawling behind it until it was close enough to the bed. She lifted the plate onto the bed and slumped down beside it. Although she hadn't eaten for a while she still had to force the food down. Her stomach rebelled, threatening to bring it back up again but she succeeded in keeping it down. She would need all her strength for the fight ahead.

* * *

Esther was doing her best to act normally but every time she looked at Matthew she shuddered. The desperation to know how Amy was drove her to distraction but she didn't dare ask in case it made him suspicious.

Fortunately Robert did the job for her.

'How's Mama?' he said at breakfast.

'I'm afraid she's not well enough to come down today,' replied Matthew.

'Mrs Huntington's better so why isn't Mama?'

'It takes some people longer to get over these things,' said Matthew smoothly. 'Don't worry, she'll soon be recovered.'

'You said that days ago.' He frowned. 'May I see her?'

'She's resting.'

'I want my mama.' Robert pouted.

'I said you can see her later. Why don't I take you fishing this morning?'

'I want to see her now,' yelled the boy.

'And I said later,' Matthew bellowed back.

There was a moment of silence as Matthew glared ferociously at the boy but, rather than be cowed, Robert stared back at him with the same fury in his black eyes. Esther smiled inwardly. He had his mother's defiant nature and he wasn't afraid of Matthew.

'I'm not going anywhere until I've seen my mama,' said Robert, folding his arms across his chest.

Matthew swallowed down his temper. For a moment the boy had so reminded him of Amy that he'd wanted to strike him. He forced a smile. 'I tell you what. If you're a good boy today for Mrs Crowle and do everything she asks of you without complaint, then you can see her after dinner.'

Robert studied Matthew carefully, as though assessing the truth of his words before breaking into his charming smile. 'Thank you.'

The boy got to his feet, bowed to Matthew then followed Mrs Crowle out of the room. Esther saw his chirpy smile fade the moment his back was turned and he looked anxious and suspicious. Of course he knew something wasn't right and he didn't trust Matthew an inch. Clever boy.

It reassured Esther that Amy must be all right if Matthew was going to allow Robert to see her. She was alive but for how much longer?

24

Matthew retreated to his study to brood. The boy was being obstina[te]
He had thought it would be easy to make him forget about his moth[er]
but he'd been wrong. He would let him see her to make up for h[is]
harshness. That should placate him.

Satisfied he had found the answer to one problem, he turned h[is]
thoughts to the other. He'd gone over the top last night. He hadn[']t
wanted to hurt Amy as much as he had but he'd lost control. Last nig[ht]
he'd pushed her too far and there was no going back. Now she wou[ld]
either have to be kept a permanent prisoner or be got rid of because [as]
long as she lived Robert would never be his. He'd considered keepi[ng]
her alive to give him more children but what if she was discovered? H[e]
would end up in Newgate. There were far too many loose ends. Now [he]
had no choice, she had to disappear and her absence could [be]
explained by the fact that she had died of her illness. Robert would [be]
the only one who missed her but he was young, he would forget.

* * *

Amy panicked when the door to her room opened and Matthew strode in.

'Please, not again,' she said, holding out her hands to ward him off.

'I only want to talk.' He perched on the edge of the bed beside her and tried to take her hand but she snatched it away. 'I can see I frightened you. I didn't mean to do that.'

When he ran his fingers through her hair she flinched.

'I'm sorry for what I did to you,' he continued. 'I went too far and I want to make it up to you, so I've come to tell you that you may see Robert today.'

'Really?' she said with suspicion in her eyes, fearing a trick.

'Really, but of course you can't see him in here. I'll take you back to your old room.'

Just the thought of leaving her cell, even for a short time, and being with her son filled her with elation.

'Aren't you grateful?' he said.

'Yes,' she replied. 'Very.'

'Mrs Crowle will tidy you up before you see him,' he said before getting up and striding out of the room.

When he'd gone Amy clapped her hands together with delight. Finally she was going to be with her son again.

* * *

Mrs Crowle took Amy back to her old room. She half walked, half stumbled her way along the corridor as her legs – used to being manacled – refused to cooperate.

It felt nice to slip into a fresh gown and wash her face. The sheets on her old bed had been changed and were fresh and crisp.

Mrs Crowle's demeanour was dour as she tugged the brush through Amy's tangled hair but Amy didn't complain, refusing to give them the slightest reason to stop her seeing her boy.

Mrs Crowle left and a few minutes later Robert charged into her room.

'Mama,' he cried, hurling himself at her.

'Oh, my boy,' she breathed, tears standing out in her eyes as she hugged him.

'I've missed you so much,' he said. 'When are you going to get better?'

'I'm trying, darling, I'm trying as hard as I can.'

'Mrs Crowle is horrid and mean.' He pouted. 'And Mrs Huntington, she's different.'

Amy's eyes narrowed at the mention of her former friend. 'You have Jane to play with.'

'She's my best friend.' He smiled.

'And what do you think of Mr Huntington?' she said in a low voice in case someone was listening at the door.

'He buys me nice things and takes me out but he hardly pays Jane any attention. I don't understand.'

'He's very fond of you, that's all. Remember what I said – you must always do as he says and never make him angry.'

'I remember, Mama, but I made him angry this morning. I told him I wanted to see you even when he said you were too sick.'

'I appreciate that.' She smiled, ruffling his hair affectionately. 'But you must be careful not to upset him again. Promise me?'

'Promise.'

She kissed him. 'That's my good boy.'

They were allowed an hour together and Amy listened to him enthuse over his pony, which he'd christened Midnight in honour of her colouring.

When their time was up, Mrs Crowle came to fetch Robert but he hung onto his mother for dear life.

'Come along, Robert,' snapped Mrs Crowle. 'You must finish your lessons before lunch.'

'I don't want to. Please, Mama, don't send me away,' he said, tears standing out in his eyes.

Amy cradled him to her. 'Of course I won't. I never want to let you go again.'

'Five more minutes,' hissed Mrs Crowle. 'No longer.' She left them, banging the door shut behind her.

'I don't like it here without you,' said Robert.

'Listen to me, darling. You've done tremendously well so far. I just need you to be brave for a little bit longer. Can you do that for me, sweetheart?'

He wiped his eyes on his sleeves and nodded, trying to control his trembling lip.

'My brave boy. I'm so proud of you and I love you so much.'

'I love you too, Mama.'

They hugged again and the door opened.

'Time to go,' said Mrs Crowle in a tone that said no second chances would be given.

Robert nodded resignedly and stood tall and proud.

'Good boy.' Amy smiled, attempting to control the rising hysteria, not knowing whether she would ever see him again.

She only gave in to her tears once he'd gone. Hobbs came for her and half-dragged her back to her cell, where she was again manacled by her right ankle to the bed. After seeing Robert again it was even harder for her to return to her prison. At least she now knew one thing – it hadn't been Matthew's so-called benevolence that had allowed her to see her son, it had been Robert's insistence. That would push Matthew to do one of two things – either he would be forced to give her more freedom to placate Robert or she would become an inconvenience that would have to be got rid of. Somehow she thought it would be the latter.

* * *

Matthew was managing to be genial at the dinner table but only just. Inside he was a seething mass of rage and resentment. Robert had stayed with Amy longer than he had permitted and now the boy was sulking at the table, picking over his food.

'Come on, Robert, eat up,' he said with forced cheer.

'I'm not hungry, sir,' he mumbled, staring at his plate.

'Are you ill? I've never known you to be off your food before.' He smiled.

'I miss Mama.'

'You've just seen her.'

'It's not the same. I want her back down here.'

Robert regarded Matthew with tears blurring his eyes. 'Will she ever get better? It's been so long. Is she going to be all right?'

Esther and Jane watched as Matthew smiled, put down his napkin and walked over to the boy. He crouched by his side and Robert looked at him with wide-eyed innocence.

'You know, Robert, sometimes people get sick and they want to get better, and they try so hard but they just can't. Do you understand?'

A tear slid down Robert's cheek and his lower lip wobbled. 'Yes.'

When he started to cry, Matthew held him tenderly and a chill ran down Esther's spine. Now she was certain of his plans for Amy. He was going to kill her.

* * *

Excitement gripped Matthew as he mounted the stairs to Amy's room. He knew Esther didn't like him visiting her but he had no choice. This time he was determined to control himself. He didn't want to damage Amy too much because he was going to allow Robert to see her one last time before she was disposed of.

He found her on her feet, pacing the room like a caged tigress. He took a moment to enjoy the look on her face – fear, foreboding and a little hope that he was going to let her see Robert again. He admired her optimism.

'You upset my son,' he began.

'You mean *our* son.' She frowned. 'I did nothing to him.'

'Then why was he crying at dinner?'

'That's not down to me.'

'Well, you must have done something. He was fine this morning.'

'Have you ever considered that he misses me?'

'He was fine until he saw you. Perhaps it would be best for him if he never saw you again?'

Amy swallowed nervously at the ice in his tone. She feared this dead-eyed coldness of his much more than his temper. 'Let me tell you something about parenthood, Matthew – you put the child's needs before your own. Maybe one day you'll learn that.'

'I've got plenty of time to find out.' He smiled.

Amy knew right then that he never intended to release her and no one was going to help her. Fighting down her fear, she decided to try one last time to appeal to him. He was her only way out.

'It doesn't have to be this way, Matthew. You don't have to keep me a prisoner.'

'You would run away if I didn't.'

'Where would I run to? I have no money, no protector. You saw to that when you killed my uncle.' What she was about to say made her feel sick but she had no choice. She was doing this for Robert. Keeping her boy firmly fixed in her mind, she smiled wickedly. 'To be honest, I was glad to learn of his death.'

'Really?'

'Of course. You remember how he treated me at Alardyce? I hated him and it was a pleasing revenge.' *God forgive me,* she thought.

'Even though you'll never get your money?'

'He never would have fulfilled that promise. It was just a trick to get me back to Alardyce.' She sashayed up to him. 'You saved me from that, just as you saved me from Mr Morris. Those days with you at Alardyce

were some of the happiest of my life,' she continued wistfully. 'And yo
gave me the most precious gift possible. Why do we fight over Rober
Can't we both be parents to him? Think how happy he would be.'

'I offered you the chance and you turned it down.'

'I was foolish and jealous. Now I see it would be beneficial to him
have both of us. Together.'

She snaked her arms around his waist and he stroked her chee
with his thumb.

'What do you mean by together?'

'Like this,' she said, pressing her lips to his.

Matthew kissed her as he used to, before this madness grippe
him, and she started to hope that she was winning him over.

'Turn around,' he whispered.

Apprehensively she obliged, not wanting to turn her back on hi
in case he hurt her again. She held her breath as his fingers brushe
the back of her neck, feeling them move further down her body. Gent
he unhooked the back of her dress, which pooled around her feet, the
he kissed her neck and shoulders with infinite softness.

Amy forced herself not to flinch when he knelt down before he
and pulled down her underskirt. To her delight he unlocked the man
cle. The skin was red and chafed and he kissed that too.

He got to his feet, kissing her stomach, the tops of her breas
protruding from her corset, which he removed so she was only in he
shift. Then he kissed her lips again, his expression soft and gentle as h
ran his fingers through her hair.

Amy's head was yanked back as his hand fisted in her hair, his ey
turning from caring to wild in an instant.

'Nice try,' he hissed in her ear. 'You must think me a fool.'

'No, just insane,' she spat back.

He threw her across the room and she hit the floor with a painf
bang.

'As if I'd fall for such an obvious trick.'

She watched, horrified, as he pulled off his belt and wrapped it around his hand.

'But as you have your clothes off we might as well have some fun.' He grinned.

Desperately Amy scanned the room for a weapon and spotted the vase sitting on the windowsill, the carnations in it long dead. She smashed it against the wall, arming herself with a wickedly jagged shard.

'God, you're exciting,' he exclaimed. 'If it wasn't for Robert I'd be happy to keep you up here just for my amusement.'

'I'd rather die,' she yelled, holding the shard out before her, determination carved into her face.

'Then you shall,' he said, advancing on her. 'Let's see if it will be today.'

* * *

Amy wept agonised tears as Mrs Crowle tended to the wounds on her thighs and back. Her shift lay discarded on the floor, shredded and bloodstained.

'Stop whining,' snapped Mrs Crowle. 'The wounds will heal well enough, unlike the master's arm. It could be a lot worse so stop grousing.'

Despite the pain Amy smiled. She'd succeeded in injuring Matthew's left forearm with the shard of vase. The hole had been deep and ragged and had bled substantially but her victory had earned her a punch in the gut that had crumpled her in two. The blow had killed the last of her hope. He hadn't cared that she might have a child in her belly, which meant he no longer had any use for her. She was going to die.

'All done,' said Mrs Crowle. 'Now get up. I need to change the sheets.'

When Amy didn't move fast enough for her liking she pushed her off the bed.

'Why do you do this?' Amy gasped. 'What have I ever done to you?'

'Nothing.'

'Then how can you treat me so cruelly, a fellow woman?'

Mrs Crowle regarded her with mean black eyes and suddenly Amy saw the truth.

'My God. Why did I not see it before?'

Without another word Mrs Crowle left the room, locking the door behind her.

* * *

'Sir Henry, thank you for coming.' Mr Buchanan, the man who had been solicitor to Amy's father, smiled.

'I must confess I'm curious as to the reason for this meeting,' replied Henry, settling into the seat opposite his desk.

'As you've probably guessed, it's regarding Miss Osbourne.'

The knot of muscle at the base of Henry's jaw pulsated at her name. 'I had, which is why I'm curious.'

'I'm aware of the history between the two of you,' began the lawyer diplomatically. 'But as Sir Alfred Alardyce's heir the trust of her fortune passes to you.'

'I see. And the guardianship?'

'Is now null and void.'

'Do you want me to sign some documents?'

'Yes, but I wondered if you wished to comply with your father's wishes.'

'His wishes?'

'About signing the money over to Miss Osbourne.'

Henry frowned. 'How could he do that when he didn't even know where she was?'

'Your father met with Miss Osbourne the day of his death.'

It was as though an electric shock had run through Henry and he sat bolt upright in his chair. 'What?' he practically yelled.

'Please allow me to apologise. I assumed he'd told you. The late Sir Alfred met with Miss Osbourne a few hours before he died. He wished to make amends.'

'Amends, for what?'

'The late Lady Alardyce using the footman to entrap her.'

Henry gave a weary sigh, and dragged both hands through his hair.

'You were unaware of your mother's plotting?' said Mr Buchanan.

'Of course I was. I only found out when she confessed on her deathbed. But are you saying my father knew where Amy was? So, where is she, then?'

'Sir Alfred didn't tell me.' Mr Buchanan found himself in an awkward position. Amy had sent him a letter detailing where she was but she'd stressed that under no circumstances was he to reveal her whereabouts or anything about her current situation to Henry Alardyce. As she was his client, he was bound by this order, unable to relieve the younger man's distress.

'Dammit,' Henry growled, jumping to his feet and pacing the room. 'Forgive me, Mr Buchanan, but Amy and I were engaged and the reason for her disappearance has haunted me for years.' He trailed off as his intense eyes flickered and his hands curled into fists. 'I must find her.'

25

Esther sat up anxiously in bed as she heard Matthew approach. She knew he had inflicted more pain on poor Amy. Was she even alive?

Esther recalled when she'd first met Matthew. He was the most handsome man she had ever seen. With her beauty and wealth she'd always known she would have the privilege of marrying for love. However, shortly after their honeymoon she'd realised her adoring husband was cold and distant. He took enthusiastically to the running of the family business, indeed he had a great flair for it. It had been a relief to hand it over to someone so capable. Unfortunately he became so concerned with business that he forgot all about her. When it became apparent she wasn't going to produce a child he lost interest completely, preferring the company of his mistresses. Then along came Amy, with his son.

Only now was Esther able to admit that part of the reason she had abandoned Amy to her fate was because she was jealous. Now she realised how petty that was. She'd wedded a monster and all of them, two innocent children included, were being sucked into his evil.

She closed her eyes in an effort to retain her composure as his footsteps drew nearer. There was a time when she'd ached to feel his touch. Now she never wanted to set eyes on him again.

The door slowly opened and in he strolled, looking so self-satisfied she wanted to slap him.

'I thought I might share your bed tonight, my love.' He smiled.

'You're most welcome,' she replied, hoping she sounded pleased.

She hated the feel of his hands on her body, evil hands that were capable of inflicting such suffering on another person. As he moved on top of her she knew he was thinking about Amy and what he had done to her. Bile rose in her throat as he held her in his arms afterwards. Then he said something that gave her hope.

'I intend to take a trip out tomorrow. Some business has cropped up.'

'And who's going to deal with Amy?' She sighed, attempting to keep up the pretence. 'I hope you don't expect me to.'

'Hobbs will be coming with me, but Mrs Crowle can attend to her needs.'

'I wish you'd do something about her. She's such an inconvenience.'

'I never knew you could be so ruthless.'

'That's because I feel like she has tried to take my place.'

'No one could ever replace you,' he said, kissing the top of her head.

Lying swine, she thought.

* * *

Matthew breakfasted before Esther was up and was just going out of the door as she came downstairs. After he'd gone she ate alone. The last thing she felt like doing was eating but she forced something down. It was vital she keep up the pretence of normality.

The children were subdued, not looking forward to their lessons with Mrs Crowle, and the house hung heavy with unhappiness. She had to set things right.

Esther paced from room to room, unable to keep her mind focused on one particular task. Finally lunchtime came around and Mrs Crowle left the children in the schoolroom to take Amy's lunch up to her.

Seizing her chance, Esther sneaked upstairs to her bedroom and removed the bottle of chloroform and a handkerchief she had secreted away specifically for this purpose. She'd been so afraid of Matthew finding out she'd made a special trip into Buxton to purchase the chemical.

She hastened into the west wing where the door to Amy's room stood open.

Cautiously Esther crept down the corridor. Mrs Crowle's voice drifted towards her, admonishing Amy for some minor offence. As she'd hoped she had left the key in the lock and Esther removed it before silently tiptoeing into the room. Mrs Crowle's back was to the door so Esther tipped the liquid onto the cloth, being careful to avoid inhaling the vapours, ready to strike but the older woman sensed her presence and whipped round to face her. Esther's courage failed as she stared into the woman's mean black eyes.

'What are you doing, you silly little creature?' demanded Mrs Crowle. 'Give me that,' she snapped, trying to snatch the bottle from her.

Amy, who had understood Esther's plan, wrapped her arms around Mrs Crowle's legs and the woman toppled to the floor.

'Do it,' she cried.

Summoning up every ounce of courage she possessed, Esther dropped to her knees and clamped the cloth over the woman's nose and mouth. Within seconds she was out cold.

Shaking, Esther snatched the keys off Mrs Crowle's belt and hastily unlocked Amy's manacle. Amy stared at her in amazement.

'We have to hurry. We don't have much time,' said Esther, washing her hands in the basin.

'What's going on?'

'Matthew and Hobbs have gone into town but they could come back at any time. We have to go now.'

Slowly Amy stood up on wobbly legs while Esther manacled both of Mrs Crowle's ankles. Together they heaved her onto the bed, gagged her and covered her with a blanket.

'Please can you help me?' said Amy, unable to bend down to put on her boots because of her injured back.

Esther obliged then wrapped her travelling cloak around her. Neither woman dared waste time collecting anything to take with them in case Matthew returned early.

They left Amy's cell, locking the unconscious Mrs Crowle in, and Amy had to lean on Esther's tiny frame as they descended the stairs, her legs unused to exercise.

As they reached the ground floor Amy frantically staggered towards the schoolroom, desperate to see her boy. She threw open the door and the two children looked up with surprise before breaking into delighted smiles.

'Mama,' cried Robert.

The children ran to her and hugged her while she showered the tops of their heads with kisses. 'How I've missed you both.'

Esther watched the scene with tears in her eyes.

'Do you have any money?' said Amy, turning to her.

'No, but I know where Matthew keeps some. I'll fetch it while you get the children ready to go.'

'What's going on, Mama?' said Robert.

'We're going away, darling. Would you like that?'

'Yes, please,' they both replied.

'What about Mrs Crowle?' said Jane.

'She's asleep, which is why we must go now.'

While the children hastily pulled on their shoes and coats Esther raced into the study, pausing on the threshold. The room hung so heavily with Matthew's presence that she half-expected to see him standing there. She ran to his desk and tugged on the bottom drawer where he kept some spare money. It was locked. Her heart almost burst with fear at the delay. She knew he kept his key somewhere but she was so scared she couldn't think clearly. Instead she jammed the letter opener into the lock and twisted. To her amazement the lock snapped with a clang and the drawer popped open. Inside were a considerable number of notes, so she gathered them up and stuffed them into her purse. Amy's locket was still there so she took that too then she hurried out, closing the door behind her, almost colliding with Amy.

'Did you get it?'

'Yes,' replied Esther. 'Looks to be almost a hundred pounds.'

Amy's eyes lit up. 'That should do us for a while.' It occurred to her that it was probably the money Matthew had stolen from her. At least she'd got it back.

'We'll have to walk to the station – he took the horses. Can you make it?' said Esther.

'Yes,' she replied, even though she wasn't sure how true that was. She was very weak but this was her chance and she wasn't going to let it slip through her fingers.

The fifteen-minute walk into the village was fraught. They walked in silence, alert to every sound, straining to hear the approach of a carriage. Halfway through the journey they heard the churning of wheels and they leapt into the undergrowth but it wasn't Matthew. The children walked pale-faced and silent, realising the peril of the situation without having to be told.

Even when they reached the village they still didn't relax. Amy could barely stand by the time they reached the railway station, so she sat on a bench with the children while Esther purchased their tickets to London.

'Is she all right?' said the concerned booking clerk.

'She's not been very well. I'm taking her to a doctor in Harley Street,' replied Esther casually, surprised at how easily the lie tripped off her tongue. 'How long will the train be?' she enquired, trying to keep the anxiety out of her voice.

'Twenty minutes, Mrs Huntington, or thereabouts.'

'Thank you.' She smiled, amazed she was able to act so normally when inside she was quaking with fear.

She sat beside Jane, who gripped her hand, and they waited in silence, their terror mounting by the minute.

Finally their train pulled into the station and they jumped to their feet.

'Mrs Huntington, there's your husband,' called the booking clerk, pointing through the window.

All four of them froze.

'Shall I call him?' offered the man.

'No,' snapped Esther. She paused to clear her throat. 'No, thank you,' she continued in a gentler tone. 'He will feel obliged to accompany us and I know he is very busy today. I do not wish to disrupt his schedule.'

Amy peered out of the window, her pain forgotten in her fear, and saw Matthew and Hobbs strolling down the platform towards the exit, their backs to them.

'Let's go,' she whispered when the two men had disappeared around a corner.

The four of them dashed across the platform and leapt onto the train, searching for a compartment trackside so they wouldn't be visible from the platform.

Then a fifteen-minute delay was announced.

* * *

Matthew was in low spirits as he returned home in the carriage. He'd concluded his business much quicker than anticipated and had purchased what he needed to dispose of Amy. He'd decided on fast-acting poison, because he didn't like to think of her last moments spent in agony, despite the pain he'd already put her through. He would get

Hobbs to put the poison in her food; he knew he wouldn't be able to do it himself.

He entered the house to beautiful silence. When Esther didn't come out to meet him he assumed she was upstairs, but he frowned when he saw the schoolroom was empty until he recalled that Mrs Crowle had said she would take the children for a walk. His breathing quickened as he realised he was free to pay Amy a visit.

Matthew took the stairs two at a time, rushed down the corridor, unlocked the door to her prison and stepped inside. He broke into a broad grin when he saw the prone form lying on the bed, curled up beneath the blankets.

He perched on the bed beside her and went rigid when he saw the grey hair poking out from beneath the bedclothes. He yanked them back and his eyes widened.

'Mother?' he said, shaking her awake.

The old woman screeched into the gag, eyes wild. He tore the gag from her mouth and she grimaced and clutched her head.

'Bloody hell, my head's thumping,' she replied, slipping back into her Scottish accent.

'Never mind that. Where the hell is Amy?' he demanded, his own accent slipping in response.

'Probably long gone by now.'

He closed his eyes and took in a few breaths to calm himself, fighting the urge to strangle the stupid old witch. 'What did she do?'

'It weren't her, it were that bloody sap of a wife of yours. Sneaked up behind me and chloroformed me, she did.'

'Christ,' he roared, leaping to his feet. 'When did this happen?'

'When I brought Amy her lunch.'

He glanced at his pocket watch. 'Just over an hour ago. We may still catch them,' he said, running for the door.

'Oy. What about my legs?' she yelled, indicating the manacles.

He threw her the key then raced out of the room, bellowing Hobbs's name.

* * *

Twenty minutes later the train was still sitting in the station and Amy, Esther and the children were choking on the stinking smuts accumulated from dozens of journeys. To preserve their money Esther had purchased second-class tickets, a decision she was already regretting as they were stuck on an uncomfortable wooden bench close to the engine. Her nice clothes were already streaked with black dust.

'He'll be back at the house by now,' whispered Amy, so as not to alarm the children. 'He'll know we've gone.'

'And he'll probably be on his way here,' Esther whispered back, dread settling in the pit of her stomach.

Jumping up, Esther opened the door to address the guard. 'How much longer are we going to be delayed?'

'Shouldn't be long now, madam.'

'How long exactly?'

'Hard to say. It's a problem with the engine.'

'Will it be fixed in the next ten minutes?'

'Could be two minutes or two hours.'

'Right, thank you,' she sighed, stepping back into the compartment. What do we do, stay on or get off?'

* * *

Matthew's trap tore into the station. Abandoning it, he and Hobbs dashed into the ticket office.

'Have you seen my wife?' he bawled at the surprised booking clerk.

'She just boarded the train with the governess and two children,' he replied, bemused.

'Dammit,' he yelled, racing back outside just as the train started to pull out of the station.

Matthew and Hobbs raced towards the train, hollering. They

managed to catch the attention of the guard, who opened one of the doors and they leapt aboard just as it started to pick up speed.

Methodically they searched the compartments one by one, Matthew taking the left while Hobbs took the right.

At the last compartment by the engine Matthew spied two women through the glass and smiled as he wrenched open the door.

'Found you, you bitches,' he cried triumphantly.

* * *

Amy, Esther and the children watched as Matthew and Hobbs jumped aboard the train. They'd just managed to hide behind the station wall as they'd arrived.

'Quick, let's go before they realise we're not on it,' said Amy.

'Go where?' said Esther. 'We don't have any transport.'

Amy spied Matthew's abandoned trap. 'Yes, we do.'

'We can't take that,' said Esther with a mischievous grin.

'Yes, we can. It was bought with your money and you can drive it, I've seen you.'

'Just around the estate grounds. I've never taken it out on a road.'

'You just need to drive to the next station, then we can catch a train from there to London without running the risk of bumping into Matthew.'

Esther was both daunted and excited by the prospect. 'All right, I'll try.'

'I can sit up front with you, Mrs Huntington,' said Robert. 'I've had some lessons on the estate.'

While Esther and Robert sat in the front of the trap, Amy and Jane took the rear seats, facing backwards.

'All right.' Esther swallowed, taking the reins.

With a gentle nudge she urged the horse to turn about and they slowly rolled out of the station onto the road. She gripped the straps so tightly her palms started to sweat.

'You're doing fine, Mrs Huntington,' said Robert encouragingly.

The boy's praise increased her confidence and she started to relax as they moved out of the village onto the quiet country road.

* * *

The two nuns stared at Matthew in surprise.

'Excuse me,' he muttered before exiting the compartment.

'Sir, they're not here,' said Hobbs.

'Fuck,' spat Matthew, seething with rage. Now he knew that bitch Esther had been putting on an act all along, gaining his trust so they could all escape. He'd make her pay for this.

Matthew marched up to the ticket collector. 'Where's the next stop? We need to get off.'

'Stop, sir? It doesn't stop. Goes all the way through to London.'

'Never mind that,' barked Matthew. 'Get us off this fucking train.'

The ticket collector's face hardened. 'I'm sorry, sir, but you should have thought it through before you got on,' he countered before stalking off, leaving Matthew and Hobbs to glare at his retreating back.

'At least we know where they're headed, sir,' said Hobbs.

'You're right,' replied Matthew. 'Amy's running to her posh city friends. We stay on this train and we track her down there.'

* * *

Esther guided the trap to a shaky halt. Robert had to take the reins because she was staring at them incredulously, unable to believe what she had just done.

Amy was ready for fainting. Her back was aching from the bumpy ride and she desperately needed to eat.

They found an inn where they could rest and eat. The large home-made steak and kidney pie and fresh vegetables Amy devoured went some way to restoring her enough to make the short walk to the railway station and an hour later they were steaming their way towards the capital, this time in a first-class carriage. Esther wasn't about to make that mistake twice. The children fell asleep, their nerves shattered, secure in the knowledge that the danger had passed.

'Thank you for freeing me,' said Amy. 'I'd resigned myself to dying in that house.' She stroked Robert's hair, his head in her lap.

'It was the least I could do,' Esther replied.

'So it was all an act to gain his trust so we could escape?'

Esther gritted her teeth. Amy deserved the truth. 'I wish I could say it was but I'm afraid Matthew had convinced me that you were mad. He made me think you wanted to take my place in the house. Forgive me for believing him.'

'What made you realise he was lying?'

'I found this in his desk drawer,' she said, handing Amy her locket.

Amy was delighted to have it back and opened it to gaze at the images of her parents, desperately wishing they were here to help her.

'I'm so sorry, Amy,' Esther said, tears welling in her eyes. 'Can you ever forgive me?'

'I'm alive with my son on a train bound for London and that's thanks to you. So yes, of course I forgive you.'

Esther sobbed with relief and the two women embraced.

26

It was late when they arrived in London, so they checked into the same discreet hotel Amy had stayed at when she had first fled Alardyce.

Feeling safer together, they booked into a large suite on the top floor with two king-size beds. Amy and Robert took one, Esther and Jane the other.

Robert clung onto his mother all night but rather than curl into her for comfort he held her to him, as though protecting her from anyone who might try to take her from him again, making her want to weep with love for him.

* * *

After a good night's rest, Amy felt much recovered the following morning. Esther assisted her to dress in the bathroom because she didn't want the children to see her injuries.

'My God,' gasped Esther when she saw the welts and bites covering Amy's body. She had to clap her hand over her mouth to stifle the sobs.

'It looks worse than it is,' said Amy in an attempt to comfort her.

* * *

While Esther took the children shopping for clothes, Amy called on Lily. Unfortunately she and her husband were out of the country and weren't expected back for two months, so instead she decided to call on Mr Buchanan but he wouldn't be in the office until late afternoon. Frustrated, she returned to the shop where Esther was arranging clothes for the children.

'Are you going to wait until Mr Buchanan returns?' said Esther as she studied a dress she was considering purchasing for Jane.

'I daren't. Matthew will be in the city too. The longer we delay, the more chance there is of him finding us.'

This thought shook Esther. 'Then what shall we do?'

'We need a protector, someone who is aware of our situation. I'll pay Edward a visit. I read in the paper he'd moved to Kensington.'

'Do you have his address?'

'No, but I can get it from the County Records Office. Carry on shopping and I'll meet you back at the hotel for afternoon tea.'

'All right, but please be careful.'

* * *

Amy walked the quiet, respectable street clutching the piece of paper the young man at the County Records Office had given her with Edward's address on.

Edward lived in a fine detached house set back off the road with a beautifully landscaped garden. Amy looked up at it and smiled, pleased he finally had the freedom he'd craved for so long.

She rang the bell and the door was opened by a tall, elegant valet.

'Is Mr Alardyce at home?' she said.

'Yes, madam,' he replied, standing aside to allow her to enter.

After giving her name she waited in the large hallway while he went into the drawing room to announce her.

Edward dashed out of a doorway and his mouth fell open. 'I don't believe it. Amy.' He beamed.

She was so happy to see him her eyes glistened with tears.

He held out his arms. 'Come here, dear girl.'

She ran to him and flung her arms around his neck. 'Thank God I've found you.'

'You're shaking. Come, sit down.' He led her into the drawing room and seated her on a couch. He popped his head out of the door, mumbled something to his valet then returned, sitting beside her and taking her hands. 'Where have you been all these years?'

'Oh, Edward,' she said, the tears starting to fall. 'I'm in such a mess and I don't know what to do.'

She recounted her tale and he listened with mounting horror.

'My God, it's positively primitive,' he said, appalled.

'Matthew's here in London. He'll be searching for us. Please, I know I have no right to ask you for anything but I desperately need your help.'

He patted her hand. 'Then you shall have it. Where are Esther and the children?'

'Shopping. We left Huntington with nothing.'

'Which hotel are you staying at?'

She opened her mouth to reply then froze as she caught sight of the painting on the opposite wall. It was by George Frederic Watts and portrayed a hideous horned beast draped in golden cloth sitting on a throne wearing a crown, crushing two figures – a man and a woman representing youth and beauty. It was entitled *Mammon*.

Magda's warning resounded in her ears – *if you ever see this painting, run.*

Edward turned to see what she was looking at. 'Magnificent, isn't it? I've always admired his work.'

'It's... it's certainly unusual,' she croaked, forcing herself to smile. 'Where's the tea? I'm parched.'

Edward frowned. 'Oh, that fool Walker, he's probably forgotten. I'
go and see.'

'Thank you.' She smiled.

The moment he'd left the room she jumped up and raced into th
hallway, making a dash for the front door, which opened just as sh
reached it. In strode Walker followed by Matthew and Hobbs.

'No,' she screamed.

Turning, she raced back down the hall, hoping to find the bac
door but Edward leapt out of nowhere, blocking her way.

She veered off through another door and found herself in a librar
Hearing pursuing footsteps, she didn't pause and raced through int
the billiard room. She hesitated, searching for another way out b
there wasn't one. She was trapped.

The four men stalked into the room. Bravely she turned to fac
them and snatched up a cue, ready to use on the first one who got to
close.

'Edward, why are you doing this to me?' she cried. 'I came to yo
for help.'

'I know, but Matthew's a dear friend of mine. He came to see m
last night and told me he was looking for you, so when you arrived o
my doorstep I sent Walker straight to his hotel to fetch him.'

'Friend? Edward, he tortured women, he had your own fathe
killed.' She recoiled when she noted his expression didn't alter. 'Yo
already know. You're a part of it, just like your brother.'

Edward broke into a delighted smile. 'Poor old Henry. He did h
best to protect you but everything he tried only pushed you furthe
away.'

'Protect me?'

'He was absolutely dotty about you from the moment you arrived a
Alardyce. The only problem was he had no idea how to talk to wome
Most of them mistook his shyness for coldness, as did you. He hear
Mother's talk of having you put away and he thought by marrying yo
she wouldn't be able to do it, but no one actually foresaw you woul

fall pregnant.' He paused to glance at Matthew. 'It seems he got a little overzealous in his duties.'

Her icy gaze rested on Matthew. 'Hold on,' Amy snapped, momentarily forgetting the danger she was facing in her need to understand. 'I thought Henry wanted to hurt me.'

Edward's smile was malign. 'You think that milksop is capable of hurting anyone?'

'But the letters, Gemma...'

'Ha,' he laughed. 'All entirely fabricated by me. I learnt to copy Henry's handwriting years ago, I got him into trouble more than once that way.'

'Gemma never existed, did she?' Amy said, everything making sudden, horrifying sense.

'No. That was Nettie's idea.'

'Nettie? My maid?'

'She was my lover for a long time. How do you think we procured all those servant girls? If Nettie came across a girl she thought we'd like she told them she could get them work in a grand house.'

It finally struck Amy what she had thought to be so unusual about her uncle's claim of innocence in the plot to have her put in an asylum. He'd said he hadn't known, but Nettie had told her she'd overheard him and Lenora planning it. Now she knew why. Nettie had been lying to make her run.

'By *we*, you mean you and Matthew?'

He nodded. 'At first the girls would be so eager to please. I was one of the family and they were so grateful, until they discovered what I liked.'

'So Henry never hurt those girls?'

'Of course not. Anyone who really knew him would think the idea preposterous.'

Amy thought furiously. Edward's confession explained Henry's pleasant kisses and his tenderness towards her that was so at odds with his monstrous reputation.

'Why?'

'My brother caught me with that girl, Mary Hill, before I could get too carried away, although he never knew Matthew was a part of it too. Henry told our parents what I'd done and after that they restricted my activities. I was angry. You were the only thing he ever wanted, so I resolved to separate him from you.'

Amy's head swam, bile clawing its way up her throat. 'You hurt that servant girl, the one I saw bleeding on the floor?'

He nodded proudly. 'Henry tried to catch me out but he was too slow. By the time he found her I'd washed and changed. He took her inside and called the doctor.'

Amy felt faint. Henry hadn't been lying when he'd said he was the one to discover the poor girl. He'd had blood on his hands because he'd carried her to safety.

'You were the one who followed me through the maze? Henry was trying to save me from you?'

'Yes. I'm afraid I had a little lapse. I'd done so well controlling myself but when I saw you enter the maze and realised you'd be all alone I couldn't help myself.'

Edward didn't notice Matthew's eyes slide towards his back and narrow but Amy did. 'Henry was protecting me,' she said, feeling completely bewildered. It hurt that their friendship had been such a lie. She shoved the hurt aside, her inner fire igniting. 'If you and Matthew were such great friends why didn't you tell him I was pregnant?'

'He left without telling me where he was going. Last night was the first time I had seen him in years.'

'So you told me you had a preference for men in case anyone mentioned your strange predilections?'

'Yes.' He grinned. 'Clever, wasn't it?'

'You sick, evil pig,' she screamed, infuriated when he just laughed.

'If you're quite finished with your trip down memory lane,' interrupted Matthew. 'Perhaps Amy would care to tell me where my son is?'

'Absolutely not,' she said.

The four men started to advance on her as one and she gripped the cue in both hands, ready to strike the first one who got too near.

'If you don't tell me I'll have to beat it out of you,' he said.

Amy swallowed hard. She knew this time there would be no one to come to her rescue. This was the house of blood and violence Magda had warned her about, but she was damned if she was going to give up her son, Jane and poor Esther, who had risked her own life to help her escape.

Walker was the first to reach her but rather than swing the cue at his head as he was expecting, she jabbed the tip of it into his crotch. When he sank to his knees she brought the handle crashing into the side of his head and he went down like a sack of coal.

Hobbs was the next to try and she swung the cue at him but he caught the end of it and punched her in the face. Her head snapped back and she saw stars. He picked her up and flung her over his shoulder.

'Excellent work, Hobbs,' said Edward, stepping over the unconscious Walker as though he weren't there. 'Take her down to my special room.'

As she struggled to cling onto consciousness Amy felt herself carried into the hallway and then they were descending a set of steps into what appeared to be the cellar. A large wooden table sat in the centre of the room, leather restraints hanging from the thick wood, which was stained with ugly dark blotches. At the sight of this hideous contraption Amy got her fight back and she started to writhe in Hobbs's iron grip but he hardly seemed to notice her efforts as he tossed her onto the table. He and Matthew pinned her down while Edward tied her down with the restraints. Once that was done Edward turned to a small furnace in the corner of the room and lit it.

Matthew's face loomed over her, pinched and severe. 'We don't need to do this, Amy. Just tell me where Robert is and you will be spared any pain.'

'You're going to kill me anyway. Betraying my son will not be my last act on this earth.'

Matthew sighed and nodded at Edward, who started to remove her boots.

'What are you doing?' she demanded.

He didn't reply as he lifted her skirts and removed her stockings, exposing her bare feet. He stroked her right foot. 'I love feet.'

'Edward, we were friends once,' she said. 'Do you remember?'

He gave her a look filled with such coldness it chilled her to the bone.

'We were never friends,' he said. 'You were a means to get to my brother, nothing more.'

Amy's heart broke. For months he'd been her only comfort and friend, she'd told him her most intimate secrets and the Edward she'd loved had never even existed.

All she could do was watch as Edward wandered over to a wooden cabinet bolted to the wall and unlocked it. Amy had to stifle a scream. Inside was a vast array of implements of torture, some sharp and metallic, others with vicious teeth and jagged edges. They all gleamed in the lamplight, as though he enjoyed polishing them over and over.

He selected a pair of pliers and returned to the bottom of the table, staring down at her bare feet, body twitching with excitement. Amy bit her lip and a tear trickled from the corner of her left eye.

Gleefully Edward used the pliers to grip her right big toenail. Amy's breath came out in shallow gasps, her whole body trembling as she focused her attention on the ceiling, not wanting to see what was about to be done to her. As she felt the nail torn from her foot she screamed.

'Amy, where's Robert?' repeated Matthew.

'Go to hell,' she rasped as the agony turned into a dull throb.

She screamed again when Edward ripped out the second nail and without pause the third nail. She thought she would pass out but unfortunately she clung onto consciousness.

'Amy, please,' exclaimed Matthew in a beseeching tone she had never heard him use before. 'Just tell me where Robert is and all this will stop.'

She stared up at the ceiling, refusing to respond. Edward took the remaining two nails from her right foot and Amy turned her head to vomit over the side of the table. She thought she would go mad with it all but the thought of her son kept her clutching onto sanity.

'Jesus, Amy, tell me,' bellowed Matthew, his voice filling the room. He forced her head up so she could see her ruined foot. 'Do you want more of that?'

Edward casually strolled to the fire and pulled out a poker, which was so hot the tip glowed red.

'Last chance,' said Matthew grimly. 'Where's Robert?'

Amy shook her head, staring fixedly at the ceiling, screwing her hands up into fists. There was an excruciating pain in the sole of her right foot. She heard her own cries fill the room and she could smell burning flesh.

'At least she can't run away now.' Edward laughed.

Picking up a bottle of whisky, he poured it liberally over her mangled foot and the agony was so intense that for a moment she thought he'd set her on fire.

'Enough of this. She's not going to tell us.' Matthew looked to Hobbs, who had been watching the proceedings impassively. 'She walked here so they can't be far.'

Matthew looked down at Amy and was surprised to see her blue eyes alert and fixed on him. In those eyes was pleading – she was begging him not to leave her here with this madman.

He experienced a flashback to Alardyce when he'd sneaked into her big bed and she had nuzzled into him, stirring feelings of affection he had thought himself incapable of. Angrily he pushed the memory aside.

'Goodbye, Amy,' he said as coldly as he could.

Forcing himself not to look back, he strode out of the cellar with Hobbs in tow.

'Alone at last.' Edward smiled, applying the poker to her right shin.

Matthew tried not to break into a run as Amy's screams followed him up the stairs. He felt nausea and also something that was so new he didn't at first recognise it. Guilt.

As he exited the house he slammed the heavy front door shut behind him but her cries still rang clear in his head.

* * *

Esther paced the hotel room. She had tried to keep her worry from the children but concern was shining from their innocent eyes. It was five o'clock and Amy still hadn't returned. Something was wrong – there was no way she would be parted from Robert for so long.

'Right, that's it. Get your coats on,' she told the children.

'Where are we going?' said Robert.

'We're going to get help.'

Mr Buchanan's offices were a twenty-minute carriage ride away and Esther was grateful Amy had shared the address with her. It was approaching six by the time they arrived and the clerk was just putting on his coat.

'I'm sorry, madam. The office is now closed.'

'Is Mr Buchanan here? It's of vital importance I speak to him.'

'He's just leaving. Perhaps you could come back in the morning?'

Normally Esther's natural timidity would allow her to be pushed out but she was so agitated she stood her ground. 'I'm not going anywhere until I've seen Mr Buchanan. It's about Amy Osbourne.'

The door to the solicitor's office popped open and a small, white-haired man with kind blue eyes emerged. 'Amy Osbourne?'

'Mr Buchanan?'

'Yes?'

'My name's Esther Huntington and I desperately need your help.'

'Please step inside. The children can wait with Mr Anderson.'

'I'm not letting them out of my sight.'

'We can remedy that.' He lifted the blinds in his office to reveal glass panels that looked onto the clerk's desk.

Looking put out at having to stay behind to babysit, Mr Anderson seated the children at his desk and set out paper and fountain pens for them to draw with before retreating to a corner of the room.

'Thank you,' sighed Esther, sinking into the chair in Mr Buchanan's office.

'Now, Mrs Huntington, you said you had information regarding Miss Osbourne?'

Her tale came pouring out in one long torrent of tears. He listened with growing astonishment, his furry white eyebrows rising higher the more she talked.

'Where is Miss Osbourne now?' he said when she'd finished.

'She went to see Edward Alardyce.'

He leapt to his feet. 'Edward?'

His outburst scared her. 'Yes. Was that wrong?'

'I don't wish to alarm you, Mrs Huntington, but at Alardyce House he was caught torturing one of the housemaids.'

'Torturing?' she shrieked. 'There must be some mistake. That was Henry Alardyce.'

'Sir Henry is a good man. He was the one who caught his brother in the act and put a stop to his activities. The late Sir Alfred Alardyce told me the whole story. No one outside the immediate family knew anything about it otherwise Amy's father would never have arranged for her to live there.'

'It was Edward who told her Henry liked hurting girls,' replied Esther.

'This explains so much. I mean, who would want to be tied to such a man? No wonder she ran away.'

He dashed to the door with the speed of a man twenty years his junior and yanked it open. 'Mr Anderson, I need to send an urgent telegram to Sir Henry Alardyce. No, that won't be quick enough. You need to go there yourself. Immediately. Tell him to meet us at the police station.'

'Yes, sir,' he replied, catching the seriousness of his employer's tone.

'You're certain Henry can be trusted?' said Esther.

'Sir Henry is a good man who has gone to great lengths to curb his brother's activities. Besides, he's the only one who knows where Edward lives.'

27

Amy struggled to draw breath. She'd screamed so much her throat was raw and her body was wracked with pain. Her legs were covered with burns from the poker but Edward had grown bored of that and got his pliers out again. Now she was missing all her fingernails and he'd broken some of her fingers in the process as he'd wrenched them so hard. Her hands and right foot were nothing but gnarled, bloody messes.

Amy could see Edward was taking great pleasure from her suffering. He kept releasing little moans and gasps, and there was a large bulge in his trousers, making her dread what else he had in store for her.

'You know, Amy, this is all your fault,' he said. 'If you'd just married poor Henry you wouldn't be here now. He loved you from the second he saw you. He was even going to fight our parents for your right to keep the child.'

Amy groaned with despair as she realised what she'd given up. 'You were the one who stole the vial from my room. It's your fault I got pregnant.'

'I think Matthew had something to do with it too but, yes, it's thanks to me you have Robert. I even bought up Magda's supply so you couldn't get any more.' He grinned.

'Your disappearance has haunted Henry for years,' he continued, enjoying rubbing it in. 'He knew I had something to do with it but I refused to say anything so he couldn't prove it. Whatever pieces of you are left when I've finished will join my other guests.' He yanked her head to the right by her hair and jabbed his finger at the corner of the room. 'You see over there. Beneath the floorboards are four servant girls.'

The fact that she was trapped in a room with four dead bodies sent her over the edge and she started to cry.

He slapped her across the face. 'Don't snivel. I hate that. Really, Amy, I thought you were made of sterner stuff.'

He wandered back over to the wooden cabinet and pondered for a moment before removing a sharpened, gleaming scalpel, smiling wickedly.

* * *

Esther, Robert and Jane listened intently while Mr Buchanan addressed a bemused desk sergeant at the police station.

'I tell you, she is in the gravest danger,' he insisted.

The door burst open and in strode a tall, slender man with brooding dark eyes and a scowl.

'Buchanan,' he called, stalking over to him. 'Your clerk asked me to meet you here. He said it was urgent.'

'Sir Henry,' he breathed with relief. 'Thank God you've come. We believe Miss Osbourne is with your brother.'

'What?' Henry said, the horror in his eyes frightening Esther.

'Do you know where he's staying?'

'I do. We must leave now.' Henry turned to the desk sergeant. 'You,' he said, jabbing a finger at him. 'Round up as many of your men as you can. We're going to need them.'

The man jumped and hurried to obey.

* * *

To Amy's surprise Edward untied the straps tethering her arms and legs to the table.

'Sit up,' he said.

For a moment she couldn't move, her back muscles spasming unbearably after being forced to lie on the hard wooden table for so long. She managed to push herself up to a sitting position on her elbows. This was it, her one chance to escape while she still had a little strength left. Her eyes darted around the room, seeking a weapon, but before she could act he slid a practised arm around her waist and flipped her over, and tethered her again.

Not being able to see what was coming terrified Amy more than anything so far. The back of her dress was slit open and she winced as the blade of the scalpel caught her skin, warm blood trickling down her back. He pulled her dress open.

'What are you doing?' she cried.

She jumped when he stroked her bare back but for once his touch was gentle.

'I always thought you had beautiful skin, Amy, and I was right.' His hands moved up to her neck then around her ribs to cup her breasts.

'Stop it,' she sobbed. 'Please.'

She felt his weight on top of her and suddenly his teeth were buried in her shoulder. She screamed again. This felt as if she were being attacked by a wild animal. He bit her shoulders, her back and her neck, drawing blood.

'Keep screaming for me,' he gasped in her ear.

Turning her head, she glimpsed him tugging at his clothing, face lit up with diabolical glee. Divining what he meant to do, she tried to close her legs but she couldn't because of the restraints.

'No, Edward, please don't,' she cried, giving way to fresh tears as h
pushed up her skirts.

Before he could do anything he groaned and sticky warmth spille
over the backs of her thighs. Amy retched over the side of the tabl
again.

'It seems you're just too damn exciting,' he whispered in her ea
before climbing off her.

Amy prayed to God, thanking him for the reprieve and beggin
him to release her, whether that was by a rescuer or death she didn
care.

* * *

Matthew hadn't even begun his search for Robert. Instead he wa
tramping the streets, lost in thought. Amy was in Edward's hands an
although they'd committed their crimes together at Alardyce, Edwar
had far surpassed him in perversity and he could only imagine what h
was doing to her at that moment. He kept being assaulted by memorie
of his time with Amy, of curling up together in her big bed, of he
sneaking down to the servants' hall to give him his birthday presen
while he guarded the plate. On top of all that she was the mother c
his son.

He didn't want her to die.

Matthew broke into a run, startling a nursemaid pushing a peram
bulator. He wasn't far from Edward's house, and within five minutes h
was hammering on the front door until it was opened by Walker.

'Sir, the master's busy,' said Walker with a meaningful look.

'Out of my way,' Matthew snarled, shoving him aside.

He stepped inside and Walker slammed the door shut behind him
Even up here Amy's screams were audible, albeit faintly. Thank God
At least she was still alive.

Walker put a firm hand on his arm. 'Sir, you really must leave...'

Matthew punched him in the face then grabbed the back of h

neck, spun him round and banged his head off the wall, knocking him out. He rushed to the cellar door and pulled it open. Amy's cries were ten times louder. The stairs were in complete darkness, leading to a faint orange glow from a lamp at the bottom.

Amy's desperate pain-filled cries concealed the sound of his approach.

At the bottom he paused to peer into the room. Amy was spread-eagled face down on the table, her dress ripped open, her back a mess of long deep wounds. Edward had his back to him and was whipping her with all his might.

He watched as Edward cast aside the whip, panting, then climbed between Amy's splayed legs and started to unfasten his trousers.

Matthew leapt out of the shadows, grabbed Edward and hauled him backwards off the table. With a grunt of rage Matthew grabbed a handful of his hair and slammed his head repeatedly against the side of the table, only stopping when he was out cold.

'Who's there? What's going on?' cried Amy with a mixture of fear and hope.

She screamed again when Matthew appeared beside her.

'Don't be afraid. I'm getting you out of here.'

'Why? So you can kill me instead?' she said, close to hysterics.

'I won't kill you, Amy. I couldn't,' he said as he freed her. 'Can you move?'

Her wounds were terrible but she determinedly pushed herself up onto all fours.

'Where's Edward?' she said.

'Unconscious. We've got to go before he wakes up. Can you walk?'

'No,' she groaned.

'I'll carry you.'

'Why are you doing this?' she said as he gently pulled her dress back up over her breasts to protect her modesty.

'Because I don't want you to die like them,' he said, indicating the corner of the cellar where the girls were buried.

She frowned doubtfully.

'Please trust me, Amy.'

She just nodded, realising she had no choice.

He held his arms out to her.

'This is going to hurt,' he said.

As gently as he could he lifted her off the table.

'I'm sorry,' he said when she cried out in pain. 'I'm so sorry.'

Despite the agony she was able to catch the sincerity in his voice.

Matthew put an arm under her hips and the other under her neck and she rested her head against his chest as they moved past an unconscious Edward towards the stairs. She didn't care where he was taking her, just as long as it was away from this hellhole. At least it wouldn't become her tomb.

They stepped into the hallway and Matthew froze.

'What is it?' she said.

'Walker. He's gone.'

Matthew spied movement out of the corner of his eye and moved out of the way just in time to avoid the poker being brought down on his head. Unfortunately he stumbled over a chair and went sprawling. Amy tumbled from his arms and landed heavily on her back with a holler of pain. She watched as Matthew avoided another blow from the poker and began grappling with Walker.

'Amy, go,' he yelled.

With a monumental effort she managed to drag herself to the door. She tugged at the handle, her breath coming out in hysterical puffs, but it refused to open.

'No,' she rasped.

Her head swam and she sank to the floor. The fight had tumbled into the drawing room and the house filled with bangs and crashes. She prayed Matthew would be the victor – she wasn't getting out of here without him.

The pounding of footsteps caused her to freeze. The cellar door flew open and Edward emerged, bruised and bloodied, wielding a large knife. His eyes settled on her and his lips drew back in a snarl.

With a cry of fear she flung herself into the drawing room but she had nothing left and her knees buckled and she fell. Edward loomed over her.

'Thought you could get away from me, you bitch? No one escapes. You're going to end up under my cellar floor with the other whores.'

Silence so thick it was almost deafening descended upon the house and it took Amy a moment to realise the sounds of the struggle next door had ceased.

Matthew entered the room from the direction of the billiard room brandishing a poker, and through the open doorway she could see Walker's lifeless body on the floor.

'Get away from her,' snapped Matthew.

'Matthew, what on earth do you think you're doing?' said Edward. 'She has to die. She knows too much.'

'Not Amy. She lives.'

'What do you think is going to happen? You're going to live happily ever after with your son?'

'I'm not a fool. All I know is she doesn't deserve this.'

'Come on, Matthew, I'll kill her if you can't do it.'

Matthew pointed the poker at him. 'You touch her, you die.'

Edward rounded on Amy with the knife and she tried to scramble backwards out of reach but her mangled hands and right foot wouldn't cooperate. Matthew hurled himself at him and they fell to the floor, fighting. Matthew succeeded in knocking the knife from Edward's hand but lost the poker in the process. Edward elbowed Matthew in the chest, sending him to his knees, and he made a move towards Amy but Matthew grabbed his legs and he toppled to the floor. The knife was just within Edward's grasp and he strained every muscle in an attempt to reach it, so Amy kicked it out of reach.

It was evident Matthew was tiring, his movements becoming slower and more lethargic. Edward whipped round and punched him in the face and he fell back to the floor. Edward leapt to his feet, ran for the knife and snatched it up. He stood over Amy with the weapon gripped in both hands.

'Now you can watch me gut her,' he told Matthew.

She flinched but Matthew threw himself forward and slammed into Edward. Matthew got him into a headlock and, with his arm firmly around Edward's neck, he started to squeeze. Amy watched with morbid fascination as Matthew throttled the life out of him.

Just before his struggling ceased Edward's eyes settled on her and he grinned before going still. Matthew let the lifeless body drop to reveal the knife protruding from his stomach.

'Matthew,' she cried.

He looked down at the knife then dropped to his knees and fell onto his back. Amy managed to haul herself to his side and he smiled gently.

'Amy,' he said weakly.

'Oh God,' she said, eyes riveted to the hilt of the knife.

'It's all right. As long as the blade stays in I won't bleed out.'

'You might live?'

'It's possible.'

Amy grasped the handle of the knife with both bloodied hands.

'What are you doing?' he rasped.

With the last of her strength she yanked the blade out of his body, making him groan. Blood bubbled out of the wound and started to stain his clothes.

'Why?' he breathed, skin already paling.

'You'll never let Robert go,' she said, face wet with tears. 'And I don't want him turning out like you. I'm sorry.'

To her surprise he smiled. 'You're probably right and you've saved me from a hanging.'

Her vision swam and she fell beside him. She knew she'd lost too much blood, the floor was slick with it.

Mindful of her injuries, he took her hand and raised it to his lips to kiss it.

'Better to die like this than down in that cellar.' She smiled through her tears.

'I'm sorry for everything I've done.' He paused to grimace, pressing a hand to the ragged hole in his stomach. 'Please say you forgive me.'

She hesitated for a moment, recalling every wrong he'd done her but now he was dying for her.

'I forgive you.' Her face crumpled. 'Robert.'

'Esther will care for him. She's a good woman, too good for me,' he said, desperately trying to stay conscious, just for a little longer, so he could say goodbye.

'One last kiss,' he whispered.

They pressed their lips together.

'I love you,' he breathed before falling unconscious.

Amy rested her head on his shoulder, his hand wrapped around hers as the blackness overtook her too.

She found herself in her childhood home wearing one of her favourite dresses of emerald-green taffeta. All her wounds and pain had disappeared.

It was evening and she walked into the drawing room to find her mother rocking in her chair by the window doing her needlework. Her father was standing before the fire, gazing into the flames, and they both looked up when she entered.

'What are you doing back so soon, darling?' said her mother in her soft, gentle voice. 'You're too early. Come back later.'

'I want to stay,' she replied tearfully.

'Not yet, sweetheart,' said her father. 'Not yet.'

* * *

Amy was woken by a loud banging, as though someone was hammering at the door. Confused, she tried to push herself upright but she lacked the strength. Looking to Matthew, she released a loud sob a the sight of his white skin. It was clear he was dead.

As a figure entered the room she thought Edward's ghost had come back to haunt her, until she realised who it was.

'Henry?' she murmured with wonder.

His mouth fell open at the carnage before him and he raced to he side, followed by a group of policemen.

'Amy, thank God.'

'Henry, I'm sorry.'

'It's all right. Don't worry about that now,' he said gently. He went t take her hand and winced. 'Sweet Jesus, what did he do to you?'

'This one's alive,' called a voice.

Amy managed to turn her head to see one of the officers takin Edward's pulse at his throat.

She was too weak to feel much of anything about this. 'Robert?'

'He's safe,' replied Henry. 'He's waiting at the police station wit Mrs Huntington and her niece. We're taking you to hospital. I'll mak sure they get to see you.'

'Thank you,' she said, a faint smile playing on her lips.

As she was smoothly transferred onto a stretcher she took one las look at Matthew's body.

'Wait,' she said. 'In the cellar... four girls... dead under the floor.'

'What?' exclaimed Henry and the policemen in unison.

'Edward... killed them. Please get them out of there. It's an awfu place,' she mumbled before passing out.

28

Henry sat by Amy's hospital bedside, watching her sleep. She'd been heavily sedated while she was patched up and was now sleeping off the effects. The nurses had rested her on her left side so she wouldn't put any pressure on her back and bolstered her with pillows to keep her in that position. Her face was bruised, and tears prickled Henry's eyes at the damage that had been done to her.

Mr Buchanan's head popped around the door. 'May I come in?'

'Please do.'

He crept inside and took the chair beside Henry.

'How is she?' said Mr Buchanan.

'She'll live but it's going to take her a long time to recover,' replied Henry. 'She's had all her nails pulled from her hands and right foot, she's been burnt dozens of times on both legs by what the doctor thought was a poker and she's been whipped.'

'Edward's calling card.'

'Indeed. Some of the wounds were so deep her ribs were exposed, which is why she lost so much blood.'

'Goodness. It really is a dreadful business.' The lawyer sighed.

'No wonder she ran away from us,' said Henry, eyes shiny with tears. 'Look what we've done to her.'

'At least she'll have realised the truth – that it was Edward and not you who hurt those girls. He's here, by the way. Will you see him?'

'No. He is no longer my brother.' He regarded Amy contemplatively. 'I thought at times she was afraid of me and I could never fathom why. Poor girl must have been frightened out of her wits. It explains so much. Father was too kind-hearted. I told him Edward should have been locked up but he couldn't bring himself to do it. I wanted to warn Amy about his true nature but Mother vetoed that. Why did I listen to her? If Amy had been warned none of this would have happened. We may even have married.'

'You really care for her, don't you?'

'I always have, from the moment she entered Alardyce House grief-stricken and scared. She's the only woman I've ever loved.'

Mr Buchanan was unsure what to say to this, Sir Henry was normally such a private person. He was saved from replying by the door opening.

'Can we see her?' said Esther.

'Come in, Mrs Huntington,' replied Mr Buchanan with a smile.

Shyly she entered followed by two pale and frightened children.

'Mama,' said Robert, his black eyes filling with tears. 'Is she all right?'

Henry stared at the boy in astonishment. He'd seen him at the police station but hadn't really paid him much attention. His resemblance to Matthew was astonishing and a little unnerving.

'Your mother's going to be fine,' said Mr Buchanan kindly. 'She's just going to need some time to get well again.'

He got up to free the chair for the boy. Robert sat and reached out to take her hand then stopped when he saw they were heavily bandaged.

Henry offered his seat to Esther, who thanked him and pulled Jane onto her knee.

'Would you like some tea or something to eat?' Mr Buchanan asked them.

'Please,' replied Esther. 'The children missed dinner.'

'I'll see what I can rustle up.'

'Thank you.'

'I'll come with you,' said Henry. 'I'm famished myself.'

The two men left the room.

'Has Edward woken up yet?' Henry asked Mr Buchanan as they walked away, finding it an effort to even say his brother's name.

'No.'

'What happened in that house? Amy couldn't have done that to them both.'

'Indeed not. Edward had been throttled by a man's strength. The police surmise he and Matthew attacked each other.'

'Or Matthew was defending Amy. She couldn't have got out of that cellar alone. When Amy wakes up I want you to fetch the paperwork so I can sign her money over to her. I don't want her worrying about supporting herself and her son while she recovers.'

'Leave it to me, Sir Henry.'

'Thank you. Now let's get those children something to eat.'

* * *

When Amy woke several hours later, through her hazy vision she saw a figure slumped beside her. At first glance she thought it was Edward and she yelped with fear.

The sound disturbed Henry, who jumped in his chair, his head snapping up.

'It's all right, it's me, Henry,' he said.

She relaxed. 'Where am I?'

'Hospital. How are you feeling?'

'Numb.'

He thought that was probably a mercy. 'The doctor said you're going to be fine.'

'Robert?'

'Curled up asleep at the foot of your bed.' He smiled. 'Esther tried to take him back to the hotel but he refused to leave your side.'

She attempted to sit up but was struck by a wave of pain, so she was forced to relinquish the effort.

'Don't move. You've got a lot of stitches in your back. You need to remain on your side.'

'Can I have some water?'

'Of course.'

He put the glass to her lips and held it for her while she drank.

'Thank you,' she said, settling back into the pillows. 'Edward?'

'Alive but he hasn't regained consciousness yet. Hopefully he never will,' he said darkly.

'I want to say... how sorry I am for what I did to you... Edward explained...'

'Shhh, it's all right. Just rest,' he said, stroking her hair.

'Not yet... I have to tell you... your father. Matthew killed him.'

Ten seconds later she was asleep again, feeling safe while Henry stared at her in shock.

* * *

The next time Amy woke Esther and Robert were by her bedside. Henry had gone.

'Mama,' cried the boy.

Very carefully he put his arms around her neck and kissed her cheek. 'The doctor said you'll be fine,' he said in a way that indicated he was reassuring himself more than her.

Amy thought of their lack of money and a home and experienced a pang of fear. How would they survive if she couldn't work?

'Are you all right, Mama?'

'I'm fine,' she said, forcing a reassuring smile. Would he still love her if he knew she had effectively killed his father? 'Where's Jane?'

'Staying with a friend of mine,' replied Esther. 'All this has affected her rather badly, so I thought she could do with a break.'

'Quite right.' It struck Amy that she had also killed this woman's husband and she started to cry.

'It's all right, it's over,' soothed Esther, misconstruing the reason for her tears.

Amy didn't have the heart to correct her.

* * *

Henry stared stonily at his younger brother. He'd woken an hour ago and Henry was his first and only likely visitor, other than the police.

'Hello, big brother.' Edward's voice was barely audible, his neck black and blue.

'Don't call me that,' replied Henry. 'You're nothing to me any more.'

'You mean you're not going to get me out of this mess?' said Edward, spitting venom.

'Not this time. I blame myself. I should have let them put you away the last time you hurt a woman but I was weak. Instead I convinced Father to send you abroad. But I'll never forgive you for hurting Amy.'

'You still love her? Pathetic.'

'You scared her into running away. You made her think I was you, that I would hurt her. She must have been terrified thinking she was going to marry a devil. The police have searched the house and found your little torture chamber, and as we speak they're digging up the floor. So far they've found two bodies. Will they find another two down there, like Amy said they would?'

Edward just stared blankly at his brother.

'I'll take that as a yes. Did you know Matthew killed Father?'

'No.' Edward frowned. 'I hadn't seen Matthew in years until he turned up on my doorstep yesterday.'

Henry had to own that he did appear to be genuinely surprised. 'Well, he did.'

With that Henry turned his back on his brother and left the room.

'Henry, come back. You've got to help me.' At first his pleas were loud and menacing, as though he didn't really believe his brother was going to abandon him. When he realised Henry wasn't coming back they turned into hysterical screams so wild that the staff were forced to sedate him.

* * *

Amy was feeling wretched. Every time she moved a fire started in her back and the only position she could tolerate was lying on her side. She couldn't even bear to sit up. Her hands were bandaged and she couldn't complete the smallest task herself, making her utterly dependent on others. The nurses even had to help her use the bedpan, which she found completely humiliating. The worry about what she would do for money also preyed on her mind and she wondered if she could throw herself on either Esther or Lily's mercy until she was well enough to work again.

On top of all that she couldn't get Matthew out of her mind, replaying over and over the expression on his face as she'd pulled out the knife.

Esther, sensing Amy needed some time alone, took Robert back to the hotel because the poor boy was exhausted. Consequently when Henry and Mr Buchanan entered her room that afternoon they found her alone, quietly crying. She hastily wiped away her tears and as they sat by her bedside it was Henry who spoke.

'Hello, Amy. How are you feeling today, or is that a silly question?'

'I'm all right,' she replied, forcing a smile.

'Very good. We're sorry to disturb you but I wish to give you something.' He gestured to Mr Buchanan, who produced a piece of paper.

'What is it?'

'On my father's death I became trustee of your fortune. This is the contract to say I have signed control of it over to you.'

Her mouth fell open. 'What?'

'You've been to hell and back and that's all down to my family. I know this can never repair the damage that's been done but I do hope it will go some way to smoothing the course of your future.'

'I... I don't know what to say,' she stammered. 'Thank you. Thank you so much.'

'It's the least I can do. Are you able to sign?'

'Yes,' she said determinedly.

Somehow, despite her broken fingers, she managed to grip the fountain pen, and with a great deal of resolve she signed the papers.

'Are you all right?' said Henry, as the white bandage was stained red.

'Fine.' She grimaced, handing back the paper and pen.

'Congratulations, Amy.' Mr Buchanan smiled. 'You're now a very wealthy woman.'

For the first time in weeks, she smiled.

'If you're happy with the arrangement I can continue to be your broker, or I could recommend a few names if you would prefer someone else?' said Mr Buchanan.

'I want you to do it. My father always said you were one of the most trustworthy men he knew, even though you were a lawyer.'

Mr Buchanan smiled at the jest and the compliment.

'Henry, there's something I need to tell you about your father,' she began.

'Matthew killed him,' he replied, causing Mr Buchanan's eyebrows to shoot up. 'I've already told the police and they've released the poor soul they arrested for the crime, just in time too – he was due to hang in three days.'

'How do you know Matthew killed him?'

'You briefly woke and told me.'

'I did? I'm sorry, Henry. I thought I was meeting with Uncle Alfred in secret, but Matthew must have followed me or he had Hobbs do it. Have you caught Hobbs, by the way?'

'No,' replied Mr Buchanan. 'The police are still looking for him.'

'I hope they find him soon. He's an evil man.' She swallowed hard before continuing. 'Uncle Alfred said he was going to sign my fortune back over to me. He was going to meet us at the railway station the following day and ensure we got to Edinburgh safely.'

Henry sighed and shook his head. 'Why didn't he tell me?'

'He probably thought any mention of you would have made Miss Osbourne nervous,' said Mr Buchanan. 'She still thought of you as a monster.'

'Yes, you're quite right,' said Amy, feeling dreadful for thinking so ill of this good man. 'Anyway, Matthew couldn't allow that to happen because it would have meant he lost us both. Uncle Alfred was determined to fight him for Robert. He did his best for me,' she said, voice cracking.

'Please tell me you forgave him,' said Henry, his eyes boring into her.

'Of course I did.'

'Then he died with a clear conscience, thank God,' he murmured, like a prayer. He cleared his throat. 'Matthew's dead and Hobbs will be tracked down by the police. Justice is already halfway there.'

Silence filled the room.

'If you would excuse us, Mr Buchanan,' said Amy, breaking the silence. 'I would like to talk to Henry in private.'

He nodded and got to his feet.

When he'd gone Amy slumped down into the pillows. 'Edward told me everything,' she began. 'How he took his sick crimes and said it was you.'

'Your behaviour makes perfect sense to me now. At the time I couldn't fathom the reason for your moods, they seemed so up and down. You must have been absolutely terrified of me.'

'I was and now I realise how unjust that was. Edward said you were trying to protect me by marrying me.'

'I was. I knew my mother was up to something. You were so vulnerable to her tricks, separated from everyone you knew. She took advantage of that.'

'Why didn't you tell me about Edward?'

'I considered it many times but would you have believed me?'

She didn't even need to consider her response. 'No. I would have thought you were trying to slur him.'

She paused before adding, 'So you wouldn't have put me in an asylum?'

'Of course not. I was just going along with Mother until we were married.'

'And when you came to my room when I was ill you were protecting me from Edward.'

He coloured. 'My intentions were entirely honourable, I assure you.'

Amy felt awful. If only she'd married Henry she would have avoided so much pain and suffering. She would have realised his true character eventually and they might have been happy together; he was a good man. An almost murderous hatred for Edward welled up inside her.

'What will happen to Edward?'

'The police are still excavating the cellar but my guess is he'll hang, which is no less than he deserves.'

'I'm sorry.'

'Why on earth are you sorry?'

'Because he's your brother.'

Henry marvelled at her. After everything she'd endured the kind, generous spirit he'd recognised in her all those years ago still blazed brightly inside her. 'Not any more. You and Robert are the only family I have left. I hope we can have some sort of relationship?' He blushed. 'Err, I mean, I don't consider us to still be engaged, I just mean...'

'It's all right. I understand and I'd like that too.'

The door opened and a short but serious-looking man sporting a large moustache entered the room.

'My name's Inspector Seafield from the Metropolitan Police. I need to ask you some questions, Miss Osbourne.'

'I've been expecting you.' She sighed.

'You can sit here,' said Henry, vacating his seat.

'Thank you,' he replied, accepting it.

'I'll fetch some tea.'

'Are you coming back?' called Amy as he walked to the door.

He hesitated. 'Would you like me to?'

'Yes, please, if it's convenient.' She found his presence a comfort.

'Then I will.'

She smiled her gratitude and he stepped outside as the inspector drew out his notebook and started to ask his questions.

'Sir Henry,' called a voice.

He turned to see two large men approaching, one of whom looked vaguely familiar.

'Sir Henry, I'm Inspector Marshall. We met at the station,' said the older of the two men, holding out an enormous hand for him to shake.

'Oh, yes, I remember,' he said, accepting the proffered hand.

'This is Detective Sergeant Evans,' continued Marshall, indicating the solemn young man by his side. 'We did intend to come sooner but this dreadful Jack the Ripper business is keeping us very busy. Is Miss Osbourne in any condition to talk to us?'

'Yes, but one of your colleagues is already interviewing her.'

Marshall frowned. 'Who?'

'Inspector Seafield, I think his name was.'

'There isn't an Inspector Seafield.'

The three men raced into Amy's room.

'Gillis, you damned cockroach,' thundered Marshall.

'What's going on?' said Amy, this fresh shock frightening her.

'I'm sorry to tell you, miss, that this horrible little man isn't a police officer,' said Marshall, shaking with anger. 'He's a journalist.'

Amy stared at the impostor, horrified. Gillis himself appeared totally unconcerned.

'Hasn't she been through enough without you pulling a low, dirty trick like this?' barked Henry, Amy's scared eyes breaking his heart.

'It's a good thing we arrived when we did,' Marshall said, grabbing Gillis by the scruff of the neck and hauling him out of his seat. 'Impersonating a police officer is a very serious offence. Would you like to press charges, miss?'

'Yes.'

For the first time Gillis was afraid. 'If you do I'll publish every dirty little secret I can dig up about your family. I'll destroy you all.'

Marshall sighed resignedly. This had always been enough to discourage his previous victims from prosecuting him.

Amy tilted her chin. 'I've endured imprisonment and torture at the hands of two lunatics. Do you think you scare me? Do your worst, I don't care.'

Everyone enjoyed watching Gillis's face fall. 'But—'

'Shut it,' snapped Marshall, shoving him towards his colleague. 'Take that back to the station.'

Gillis looked as though he might cry as he was led from the room.

'Well done, Miss Osbourne,' said Marshall. 'I've been after that piece of filth for years but no one has ever had the guts to press charges.'

'Don't worry, Inspector. I intend to see it through.'

'To save you suffering a similar incident, only I will come to speak to you. If anyone else turns up you can throw them out.'

'Thank you.'

'Here are my credentials, so you know I am who I say I am,' he said, drawing his decorated truncheon, which displayed his name and identification number. 'We can leave your statement until later if you like?'

'No. I'd like to get it over with.'

'Would you like me to stay?' said Henry, concerned about her after her shock.

Her smile was sweet and grateful. 'Yes, please.'

It was the first time Henry had heard the whole sickening story. The horror was clear in Amy's voice as she spoke of her imprisonment and beating by Matthew. At the point where she was cornered by four men in Edward's house she held her bandaged right hand out to him for comfort and gently he took it. She didn't break off from her story or turn to look his way, it was just one simple, silent gesture. Henry was pleased but forced himself not to read anything into it. Although he knew he was still in love with her, he told himself she was just seeking solace and friendship.

Telling her tragic tale exhausted Amy and at the conclusion of the interview she could barely keep her eyes open. By the time Inspector Marshall left she was already asleep.

29

Amy was tormented by her dreams. First she was chained to the table in Edward's cellar, only in the dream the cellar was transposed to Alardyce House and Lenora was wielding the pliers, Edward standing beside her staring with his mad eyes.

She woke with a start.

'Mama?'

Confused, she looked around and saw Robert sitting on her bed. She held an arm out to him and he nestled into her. Esther was sitting in the chair by her bedside.

'Esther, how are you?' said Amy.

'Fine. We would have been back sooner but this one here slept for twelve hours,' she said, smiling at Robert.

'And how are you, darling?' Amy asked him.

'Better now. Mama, when can you leave here?'

'In a few days hopefully.'

'I've been thinking, you won't be able to work for a while, so I could find a position as a houseboy.'

'Oh, sweetheart.' She smiled, kissing his cheek.

'Nonsense. I'll help,' interjected Esther. 'Now Matthew's gone my fortune is once more my own.'

'You're both so kind but neither will be necessary.' She grinned at them. 'Henry's given me my money.'

'That's wonderful.' Esther smiled.

'Is it a lot?' said Robert, wide-eyed.

'Yes. It's a huge heap of money.'

'And you don't need to work any more?'

'No, I don't.'

He hugged her with joy shining in his eyes.

'Henry signed it all over without a quarrel?' said Esther.

'He did. I think he sees it as reparation for everything that's happened.'

'It was the right thing to do. He certainly seems like a good man.'

'He is. I feel dreadful about the way I treated him. The shame he must have endured when everyone discovered I'd abandoned him. They must have thought he'd done something awful to me.'

'You mustn't reprove yourself. You've been through enough and he obviously forgives you so please forgive yourself.'

Amy's throat was dry and she started to cough, so Esther picked up the jug of water.

'Oh dear, it's empty.'

'I'll get some,' offered Robert, desperate to be helpful.

'Thank you, dear,' rasped Amy.

Amy was glad he'd left her alone with Esther because there was something she wanted to say. 'I'm sorry about Matthew.'

Esther, like everyone else, believed Edward had killed him and Amy was content to let them, for now.

'Even though he was a monster I still feel a little sad. Is that strange?'

'No. I do too.'

There was a moment of silence as they both got lost in their own thoughts.

'What will you do now?' said Amy. 'Will you return to Derbyshire?'

'I've no wish to return to that house but there's so much to sort out. I'm going to be a very rich and a damn merry widow, I can tell you.'

'Good for you,' said Amy, relishing Esther's new-found confidence.

'I'll employ someone to oversee the businesses,' continued Esther. 'I'll definitely sell the house. Although it's been in my family for years it holds too many unhappy memories and I'm fed up with the country. I might move to London, or perhaps the outskirts, so Jane will still be near the countryside to walk and sketch. Finally I'm going to live my life on my own terms.'

Amy smiled at the excitement in her voice. Dying was the nicest thing Matthew had ever done for his wife.

Esther's smile faded. 'Matthew's funeral's in a week. The police will have released his body by then.'

'Are you going?'

'I feel I must. I want to make sure they bury him nice and deep. Will you come, if you're feeling up to it?'

'I'll certainly try. He was Robert's father, after all.'

'And then perhaps we can put it all behind us?'

'That is an excellent idea.'

'I've had the most wonderful thought,' said Esther, her smile returning. 'I've found a lovely house in Piccadilly that's available to rent. I was thinking of taking it until I could find somewhere to buy. Perhaps you and Robert could stay with us when you're discharged? You'll need time to rest and get back on your feet and you can't manage on your own with your injuries.'

'That would be perfect, thank you. You're my best friend and I've no wish to relinquish you yet.'

As Esther smiled a tear escaped from the corner of her eye and slipped down her cheek. She pressed a kiss to Amy's forehead.

Robert returned carrying a large pitcher of water.

'What took you so long?' said Esther. 'Talking to the nurses again, were you?'

Robert blushed, making Amy smile.

'What's this about the nurses?' she asked her son.

'Nothing,' he shyly replied.

'You'll have to keep an eye on this one when he's older,' said Esther playfully. 'He'll have all the girls falling at his feet.'

The joviality in Esther's eyes faded and Amy knew she was thinking *like father like son*, because that was what she'd been thinking too.

'Robert, would you like to stay with Aunt Esther and Jane in their new house in London for a while?' Amy asked him. 'When I'm well again we can find our own house.'

'Yes,' he said, brightening. 'Can I have a horse?'

'Of course, you must. We'll find a house with a paddock and stables.'

Robert looked more cheerful than he had in weeks.

'If you like I can send Midnight down to you when you're settled?' offered Esther.

'That's most kind, Aunt Esther, but I would like to choose another if that's all right?' said Robert. 'I would like a white one this time.'

* * *

Amy was discharged from hospital five days later. Although the wounds on her back had healed to the point that she could sit up, her right foot was still painful and she left the hospital in a wheelchair.

The house Esther had rented was three storeys but one of the sitting rooms on the ground floor had been converted into a bedroom for Amy.

The four of them muddled along nicely together. Robert and Jane were the best of friends and a new governess was hired for them – a sweet, placid girl of nineteen, the complete opposite to Mrs Crowle.

Autumn arrived and Amy's recovery was frustratingly slow. Although her missing fingernails had skinned over she thought her hands looked ugly. The splints were removed from her fingers and it was clear they had suffered irreparable damage and would never again be straight. She hated the sight of her hands and always wore gloves, only removing them to sleep or bathe.

Her right foot had improved but, as it was still painful, she could only get around with a cane, which made her feel like an old lady. Her poor physical state depressed her and the only things that cheered her, other than the children, were Henry's visits. He would bring her books to keep her occupied and they would discuss them in the small parlour that overlooked the garden. When she was well enough he took her for a stroll around the garden, Amy limping alongside him with her cane, holding onto his arm as they talked about anything and everything, reminding them both of the talks they'd enjoyed at Alardyce.

Henry managed to coax her to take a stroll down the street, her health not permitting her to go any further. She was terrified of being recognised as her image was in all the newspapers. The scandal of what had happened had spread like wildfire across the country, attracting huge public interest.

It hadn't taken the vultures long to unearth her affair with Mr Costigan and all the lurid details – some real and some imaginary – were circulated for all to read, completing her humiliation.

The four girls in Edward's cellar had been identified as servant girls, and they had suffered the same terrible injuries as Amy, their lives ended by their throats being cut.

Lily came to visit the moment she returned to England, astonished by what she had read in the papers, and became a frequent visitor and the staunch friend she'd always been.

* * *

Just as Amy's health began to take a turn for the better and she started to feel as though she could face the world again, she had a fall and landed heavily on her back, opening up the deepest of the back wounds that ran from the centre of her spine to the right, over her ribs.

Esther heard her cry out and found her on the floor, her clothin
saturated with blood. The doctor was called and Amy was helped int
her bedroom.

'I have to stitch the wound closed,' the doctor told her. He gave he
some laudanum for pain relief but it didn't make a dent in her agony.

The governess was asked to take the children out for a walk whil
Esther held her hand. Lying on her left side, Amy bit down on a pillo
as the needle pierced her battered flesh.

Esther's eyes filled with tears as she witnessed her friend's distress.

'Miss Osbourne,' said the doctor, 'I know it's difficult but you mu
keep still.'

Esther caught a glimpse of the torn flap of skin and almo
passed out.

'I think you'd better wait outside,' said the doctor. 'I can't deal wit
you if you faint.'

'Amy, I'm sorry,' she said.

The doctor resumed the procedure when Esther had gone, and th
pain was even worse than when the wound had originally bee
inflicted, the skin of her back having gone through too much trauma.

The door burst open and suddenly Henry was there.

'Amy,' he exclaimed, rushing to her side. He knelt beside her an
clutched both her gloved hands in his own. 'Talk to me,' he urged in a
attempt to take her mind off it. 'Tell me about the book you're readin
Is it Poe?'

'Y... yes,' she said, straining to grasp her thoughts through the ha
of pain that had descended upon her. Instead she focused on Henry
voice and his dark glittering eyes.

'Which story are you reading?' he pressed.

'You're asking me now?'

'Tell me.'

'"Pit and... the Pendulum",' she managed to moan.

The doctor had reached the area over her ribs where the skin wa thinnest and she gripped Henry's hands tighter, tears forming in her eyes.

'What did you think about it?'

She held onto his words. 'It made me feel like I'm not alone.'

He was puzzled by her meaning. 'You're not alone.'

'Almost there, Miss Osbourne,' said the doctor, eyes focused on his work.

'I mean dungeons, darkness,' she mumbled, her eyes starting to roll back in her head as oblivion tried to claim her.

Henry stroked her sweat-soaked hair back off her face, over-whelmed with helplessness at his inability to relieve her agony. 'And rescue at the last moment, don't forget that. It's the most important part.'

'But he doesn't say... what you do after,' she said through gritted teeth, her eyes screwed shut in distress. 'The nightmare's over but nothing's ever the same again.' She broke off from what she was saying to cry out with the pain. 'Henry, help me.'

'I'm here,' he said, touching her face.

'There, all done,' said the doctor, tying off the stitches.

Amy gave a long, slow exhalation and her eyes slowly rolled open. Her skin was white and her eyes red from crying.

'What sweet rest there must be in the grave,' she murmured before passing out.

Henry watched her sleep, his mind troubled. Everyone had been concentrating so hard on her physical recovery that her mental one had been entirely forgotten. He resolved to restore a love and desire for life inside her, to encourage her to fight the melancholy with the will to go on. Robert had got her through the dark days of her captivity but it would be himself who restored her to this world, on that he was determined.

* * *

Henry made sure he visited every day. Amy was once again confined to her bedroom, which she hated, so Henry, with Robert and Jane's assistance, brought the outside world to her. They filled her room with wild flowers they picked from the garden. They went to a florist and arranged for the most beautiful and exotic blooms available to be delivered to her. The colours and scents delighted Amy and went a long way to cheering her low spirits. Jane produced dozens of sketches and watercolours for her, each one a colourful and eye-catching outdoors scene, and pinned them up on the walls of her room for Amy to admire.

They visited the seaside and brought her back shells and pebbles, which she studied with the children as part of their lessons. When she could get out of bed Henry led her into the music room, where a pianist had been asked to play for them all.

Robert and Jane composed a little play of their own, which involved putting on lots of funny voices and a vast amount of giggling and Amy laughed heartily for the first time in weeks.

Henry also visited various agents to discover what properties were available to buy. He knew she was in no fit state to even consider moving yet, but he wanted to keep her thinking forward to the future rather than back to the past.

Her health precluded her from attending Matthew's funeral, which she felt a little guilty about. Esther went alone and returned an hour later, pale and tearful. When Amy asked her how it went she just shook her head, not wanting to discuss it. Only later did she tell her that journalists had turned up too and spent the entire service whispering and pointing at her. She had been the only mourner.

* * *

'I really appreciate everything you're doing,' Amy told Henry one day when he came to visit. They were sitting on a bench together in the garden and it was the first time she'd been out of the house in two weeks. 'I felt so miserable before but I've been kept so busy of late I've not had time to dwell on it.'

'So you're feeling happier?'

'Much.' She smiled, patting his hand with her own gloved one. 'Thank you.'

The sparkle had returned to her eyes and he was thankful for it.

'Will you stay for dinner?' she said.

'I'm afraid I can't. I have to attend a Liberal Party meeting.'

'You're a Liberal now?' she said, surprised. 'You used to be the most staunch Conservative.'

'I was until that... err... debate we had in the dining room at Alardyce. I considered your opinions and saw you were speaking sense, although you did express yourself rather forcefully.'

'I'm astonished.' She smiled. 'I thought you disliked me back then, you were so furious.'

'Disliked you? I adored our debate. I could see how passionate you were about the subject and I admired you for it. If my family hadn't been in the room I think I would have kissed you.' His smile fell and his cheeks flushed. 'Sorry, I didn't mean... what I meant to say...'

'It's all right. I think we misunderstood each other so completely back then that we should start over.'

'Agreed.' He smiled, relieved.

'I read about your wife passing away. I'm sorry.'

Henry nodded solemnly.

'You must have loved her very much,' she said gently.

'Ours wasn't a love match. How could it be when Mother picked her for me?' he said bitterly. 'But over time we did become good friends. She died giving birth to our first child, a boy. He died too after struggling for two days.'

Her heart broke for him. 'Henry, I'm so sorry. I had no idea.'

'Well, these things happen,' he said tightly, staring at the ground.

Divining he wouldn't want empty words of comfort, she took his hand instead and they sat in silence for a while.

'So, a governess, eh?' he said with a smile, dispelling the shadow.

'Yes.' She smiled back.

'How did you find it?'

'Terrifying at first but I worked for a good family.'

'I've heard it can be a lonely position.'

'I had Robert so I was never alone.'

'I'm glad to hear it. He's a good boy – you did an excellent job raising him.'

'Thank you,' she said, pleased. Her smile faded. 'They want me to give evidence next week at Edward's trial.'

'Are you going to do it?'

'I must. Besides, I want to make sure my version of events is made public. There's been so much nonsense printed in the papers.'

'If you go you will have to see Edward.'

She felt sick at the thought but swallowed down her fear.

'Would you like me to accompany you?'

'Yes, please.' His presence would make the ordeal easier to bear. 'Aren't you giving evidence?'

'Apparently they don't require me. The trial's only a formality. Everyone knows what the verdict will be.'

This made Amy feel better. The bodies in his cellar alone were enough to send Edward to Newgate.

'I need your advice on a very delicate matter,' she began uncertainly. 'There's something that happened at Edward's house that I've told no one. I think perhaps I should have confessed it before but now it's too late and if I do I'll cast suspicion on myself.'

He frowned. 'What is it?'

She explained in a slow, uncertain voice about what she had done to Matthew. As she spoke silent tears trickled down her cheeks.

'Do you think I should tell Inspector Marshall?' she said.

'It was Edward who put that knife in him, not you.'

'He told me he might survive if it was left in. I knew he would bleed out if it was removed and that's what I wanted.'

'You wanted him to die?'

She nodded. 'Because as long as he lived Robert and I would never be free. In his last moments he begged me for forgiveness. Then he bled to death right in front of me and I feel such pressing guilt. He was Esther's husband and Robert's father after all.'

'Now, listen to me, Amy,' he began. 'You tell no one of this. The police are satisfied Edward killed Matthew, which he did. You did what you had to do to save yourself and protect your son. Anyone would have done the same. Please don't carry this unnecessary burden.'

She indicated her gloved hands. 'That's why they're so ugly and deformed, because there's blood on them. It's a punishment.'

He took her hands in his own and started to tug off the right glove.

'What are you doing?' she said.

'Trust me,' he urged.

Biting her lip, she nodded and allowed him to remove the right glove, revealing the fingers, thick red skin covering the area where the nails should have been, the index and middle fingers twisted and bent. Next he exposed the left hand, which was even worse, and she looked away in shame. He raised her left hand to his lips and kissed it.

'I see no blood and I see no ugliness,' he said. 'Only suffering.'

The threatening tears burst like a dam and he held her to him as she sobbed on his shoulder. When she'd collected herself she sat up, feeling lighter, the weight of her guilt lifted, all thanks to this wonderful man.

30

The morning of Edward's trial Amy dressed carefully, with Esther'
assistance. Some of the newspapers had made her out to be a whore
who'd consented to what had been done to her in that cellar, and the
prosecution barrister said this would undoubtedly be the stance the
defence would take. Therefore Amy wore a sombre grey dress with
matching gloves and bonnet and black boots. Her hair was scraped
back into a bun and she wore no make-up or jewellery, other than the
silver locket containing her parents' images.

Esther was staying with the children, and Henry and Mr Buchanan
were taking her in the latter's carriage.

Amy anxiously awaited her escorts, stomach knotted with nerves.
She was dreading seeing Edward again and prayed her courage would
not fail.

Henry and Mr Buchanan entered the house and the sight of them
made her feel a little better.

'Are you ready?' said Henry.

Reluctantly she nodded and got to her feet. Robert and Jane lined
up to give her a hug and Esther kissed her cheek.

'Good luck,' she whispered.

Amy slowly followed the men to the door, resting her weight on the cane.

During the carriage ride Mr Buchanan went over the last-minute details.

'The defence barrister is famous for his ferocity. He will try to bully you and trip you up. Don't let him. Just stick to your story and everything will be fine. This is the only line of attack they have. It's vital you stick to your guns.'

Amy nodded. 'I'm afraid of seeing Edward again. What if I break down?'

'You won't,' said Henry. 'Think of everything you've survived. This should be easy for you.'

'Thank you,' she replied with a fond smile.

As the carriage pulled up outside the Old Bailey they were astonished by the size of the crowd. Every eye turned to the carriage as they waited to see who would emerge.

Amy's chest heaved with panic. This was the first time she'd been out in public in weeks and the idea of all those people staring at her was petrifying and she retreated into the furthest corner of the carriage.

'I think if you walk between us it'll be all right,' said Mr Buchanan, nervously eyeing the mass.

'We'll be right beside you,' said Henry, holding his hand out to her.

Amy gazed into his dark eyes, which no longer seemed hard and cold but open and honest. Nodding, she accepted his hand and gripped onto it for dear life.

Mr Buchanan descended the steps first and everyone craned their necks to see who it was. A ripple of disappointment ran through the crowd when no one recognised him.

Henry stepped out next and his resemblance to his brother was such that everyone knew him. He assisted Amy out of the carriage; she struggled down the steps and everyone started talking excitedly. The crowd pressed forward to get a closer look at the woman who was at the centre of it all. The police formed a ring around them, linking arms with each other to form a defensive barrier. Henry's arm went around Amy's waist protectively as some members of the crowd tried to move closer, jostling the police.

Amy heard her name being called and the shouts of the eager journalists. One man even screamed the word 'whore' at her and she heard a woman yelling back at the culprit, admonishing him, which heartened her. At least they weren't all against her.

The police officers guarding the main door hastily ushered them inside and the door closed behind them, blocking out the noise. An usher escorted them to seats outside court number one.

'Is the defendant already in there?' enquired Mr Buchanan, gesturing to the courtroom.

'Yes, sir. The trial's been going for over two hours already. Don't worry, he's sat between two big, hefty jailers. You're as safe as houses,' he told Amy, giving her a reassuring smile.

They waited in anxious silence for Amy to be called. She removed her coat and bonnet but kept her gloves on. The left middle finger joint ached and she rubbed it absently, going over in her head what she was going to say and preparing herself to see Edward again.

'He can't hurt you any more,' said Henry, taking her aching hand. 'Don't even look at him.'

She was about to ask for some water when her name was called.

'This is it,' she said, her heart starting to race.

'Soon it will all be over,' said Henry. 'Then you can go home, and if you find your courage failing, just look up. I'll be there.'

He gave her a shy smile and she patted his hand before following the usher inside.

The room was smaller than she'd expected. Directly opposite her was the raised judge's bench, an imposing wooden monstrosity. A hawk-like man sat behind it, frowning down at her.

The court was packed and every eye turned her way as she walked towards the witness stand. The people in the gallery craned their necks for a glimpse of her while all the men in the jury regarded her with cold, unsympathetic eyes.

Edward glowered at her from the dock, which was on her right, his eyes burning into her lacerated back, and she started to tremble. Looking up, she was reassured to see Mr Buchanan and Henry take their places in the gallery and the trembling subsided. She sat down and resolved to ignore Edward's presence.

As expected, the prosecutor went easy on her, even though he was as unsympathetic as everyone else in the court. His job was an easy one, there was already so much evidence against Edward. Her testimony was simply the icing on the cake.

The temperature in the room seemed to rise as her story went on, the tension in the room increasing along with the heat and smell. It seemed she wasn't the only one sweating. As Amy explained what had been done to her in the cellar shame and humiliation swept over her, so she looked down at her feet, unable to face the audience. The judge, who was rather deaf, yelled at her to speak up and her head snapped up. Immediately she sought out Henry, relieved that his eyes were warm and reassuring. He wasn't disgusted by her. When she started to falter, emotion threatening to overwhelm her, he gave her another encouraging nod and she lifted her head proudly. She had nothing to be ashamed of.

When she reached the worst of the tortures there was a loud sigh followed by a bang from the direction of the gallery and a woman lay on the floor in a faint.

There was a brief pause as the woman was roused and led out, her face ashen.

When proceedings resumed Amy continued her tale.

As she reached the part where Matthew fell to the floor with the knife in his stomach she paused to look up at Henry. He leaned forward in his seat and gave her an almost imperceptible shake of the head, telling her not to say what was running through her mind. So she skipped over it and ended where Henry found her.

Then it was the turn of Mr Laroche for the defence and she could tell by the resolute set of his mouth that he was determined to make her crack.

She looked up at the gallery again seeking Henry, but this time her gaze alighted on a blonde woman sitting at the front. Amy's breath caught in her throat. It was the same woman who'd been at the exhibition of the Fates of Corruption, who had been in the same situation as herself. She had aged well, her blonde hair framing her face like a halo and her smile was gentle and encouraging. Their eyes met and the woman gave her a nod of acknowledgement.

Knowing she was there fortified Amy's nerves and she faced Mr Laroche with renewed confidence.

His stare was assessing, sweeping over her as he decided how best to attack.

'So, Miss Osbourne,' he began in a booming voice that would have been more at home in the theatre. 'When you lived at Alardyce House you and Mr Edward Alardyce were friends?'

'We were,' she replied slowly. Everyone's eyes were on Mr Laroche who, although a small man, demanded attention, his personality naturally magnetic.

'In fact you were closer to him than you were to Mr Henry Alardyce, his older brother, to whom you were engaged?' he continued.

'I was.'

'And in all your time there you never once witnessed anything to hint at, shall we say, Mr Edward Alardyce's dark side?'

'Nothing.'

'Yet you had an affair with Matthew Crowle, who was first footman at Alardyce House?'

There were a few disapproving murmurs from the crowd but she willed herself to ignore them. 'I did.'

'How long did this affair last?'

'About five months,' she said, voice growing weaker as her shame increased.

'An affair, might I add, that was so intimate it resulted in the birth of your son?'

'Yes.' Inwardly she prayed her mistakes didn't come back to hurt Robert's future.

'Yet Matthew and Edward were accomplices at Alardyce. You, Miss Osbourne, had an affair with one half of this partnership and were good friends with the other. So how can you claim you knew nothing of their actions?'

'Objection,' protested the prosecutor, shooting to his feet. 'Miss Osbourne is not the one on trial here.'

Laroche threw his arms wide, his eyes amused. 'I'm merely trying to establish whether she is an appropriate prosecution witness.'

'You may proceed, Mr Laroche, but be careful,' said the judge in a voice that rattled like a bagful of marbles.

'Thank you, Your Honour,' he replied.

Amy noticed the jury watching her carefully. She despised them all for their nasty little suspicions.

'I knew nothing of their activities,' she said, tilting her chin. 'Had I known I would have gone straight to the authorities.'

Laroche continued as though she hadn't spoken. 'And then coincidentally you apply for a position at a house in Derbyshire and who should be master of that house but one Mr Matthew Huntington, also known as Matthew Crowle.'

'I didn't apply for the position. When my appointment in Lancashire came to an end my employer knew Mrs Huntington was seeking a new governess, so she recommended me. I had no idea Matthew lived there.'

Once again he ignored her. 'Your Honour, I wish to call another witness to the stand before I continue to question Miss Osbourne.'

'Is this pertinent to the case?' He sighed, thinking how close it was to lunchtime.

'My witness is vital to ascertaining the validity of Miss Osbourne's statement.'

'Your Honour, I have not been informed of any witness,' proteste
the prosecutor.

But the judge was eager to move things along. 'Very well, I sha
allow it just this once. Please step down, Miss Osbourne, but remain i
the room. We don't want to waste any more time.'

Bewildered, Amy climbed down from the stand, fearing her knee
would give way. Looking up at Henry and Mr Buchanan, she could se
they were equally perplexed.

'Please sit here,' said the usher, leading her to a chair at the prose
cutor's table.

'You know nothing of this?' she whispered to the prosecutor.

Furiously he shook his head.

Everyone turned to look as the door opened and a figure clad all i
black entered with a confident stride.

'I don't believe it,' whispered Amy, stunned.

'Who is it?' said the prosecutor.

'Matthew's mother. She assisted in my imprisonment at Hun
ington Manor. She should be in the dock, not a defence witness.'

Mrs Crowle gave her a hard look as she passed, which Am
returned. She seated herself in the witness box, a dignified woman i
mourning for her only child.

'You are Mrs Crowle, Matthew Crowle's mother?' began Laroch
loudly, causing an excited murmur to ripple around the crowd.

'I am,' she coolly replied, reverting back to her Edinburgh accent.

'You were residing at Huntington Manor while Miss Osbourne wa
governess there?'

'That's correct.'

'What was the relationship between your son and Miss Osbourne?

'They were lovers,' she said with relish, causing another excite
murmur.

'Really? Miss Osbourne states she was a prisoner there.'

'Oh, she played hard to get at first, but I saw them.'

'Saw them?'

'Her and my son on his desk in his study, at it.'

'At what, Mrs Crowle?'

'Do I need to spell it out?'

'This a court so I'm afraid you do.'

'They were... being intimate.'

There were more gasps from the genteel women in the gallery. Amy cringed and closed her eyes, unable to believe this was happening.

'And was it consensual?'

'Oh aye. Loving it, she was. She said he hurt her but I saw her biting and scratching him. She even hit him in the face while he only treated her gently. When they'd finished she made him kneel before her and kiss her feet.'

Amy wanted the earth to open up and swallow her whole. She kept her eyes glued to Mrs Crowle, not daring to look at anyone else, especially Henry. What was he going to think of her after this? Out of the corner of her eye she could see Edward grinning.

'Really? So Miss Osbourne's stay at Huntington Manor wasn't as unpleasant as she made it out to be?'

'Mr Laroche, where are you going with this?' enquired the judge. 'This case is to do with Mr Edward Alardyce not Matthew Crowle.'

'Sorry, Your Honour, but the events at Huntington Manor directly led to what happened at Mr Alardyce's home.'

'All right but don't drag it out. I know how fond you are of theatrics.'

'Of course, Your Honour.' He smiled. 'I've finished with this witness and would like to bring Miss Osbourne back to the stand.'

'Very well,' he sighed.

Mrs Crowle stepped down looking very pleased with herself as Amy took her place in the witness stand, her cheeks burning with shame and anger. She looked up at the gallery and saw the empty space beside Mr Buchanan where Henry had been sitting and fought back tears.

'Miss Osbourne, is it true you had sexual relations with Matthew Crowle at Huntington Manor?' said Mr Laroche.

'Yes,' she flatly replied, her humiliation complete.

'You had resumed your affair?'

'No.'

'Then why were you in a compromising position with him?'

'It was the only way he would let me see my son. He kept me and his wife locked up in a room together and if I pleased him he would let me spend some time with my boy.'

'If all this was forced on you then why did Mrs Crowle say you enjoyed your time alone with her son?'

'I didn't enjoy it. She's lying so the world won't know her son was a monster,' Amy shouted, the spark inside her flaring. 'Matthew chained me up, beat me and tortured me and his mother was complicit in the whole thing. She should be in the dock with him,' she cried, pointing at Edward.

'That's quite a temper you have, Miss Osbourne. If Mr Crowle was the sadist you claim he was, then surely he would have been the one inflicting the pain, not receiving it?'

'He liked to hurt and be hurt. If I didn't do as he wished he said he would put me in an asylum so he could have my son all to himself.' Tears formed in her eyes and her gloved hands shook with rage and humiliation. She knew she must look wild but she could do nothing to control it.

'Put in an asylum? That's the same thing your own aunt and uncle threatened you with. I find that rather curious. All the newspaper articles appealing for information after you ran away from Alardyce House stated you're mentally unbalanced and a danger to yourself.'

'How could I have managed all these years working as a governess while raising a small child if I was unstable?'

'I put it to you, Miss Osbourne, that you enjoyed warped sexual games with Matthew Crowle and Edward Alardyce, which got out of hand and you were hurt. Now you want revenge.'

'That's a lie. They kept me locked up, they hurt me.'

'When you were fifteen you had a sexual relationship with a man thirty years your senior, a friend of your father's.'

'That was not my fault, I was young…'

'You're a severely unbalanced woman whose only concern is for pleasure.'

'Pleasure?' she exclaimed, shooting to her feet.

'Please sit down, Miss Osbourne,' said the judge.

Ignoring him, she tugged off her gloves and held up her twisted hands for them all to see. 'You call this pleasure?' she yelled.

Everyone stared at her hands in horror, the only sound in the room Amy's ragged breathing. Finally she worked up the courage to face Edward, whose eyes were cold and distant and fixed on her. 'He did this,' she continued in an exhausted voice. 'He killed those poor girls and he almost killed me and no matter how you try to twist the facts, Mr Laroche, nothing will change that.'

Laroche looked furious. 'No further questions,' he said in an icy voice before stomping back to his seat.

'You may step down, Miss Osbourne,' said the judge, hopeful that they might resolve things before lunch after all.

'Thank you,' she replied, wanting to cry with gratitude.

The hard part was over.

31

To Amy's relief Henry was waiting for her in the corridor with Mr Buchanan. As her eyes blurred with tears she practically fell into his arms.

'It's all right, it's over,' he soothed.

She clung to his neck, crying, and she felt his arms go around her. He hadn't forsaken her; he was still here.

'That was a fierce attack, even by Laroche's standards,' tutted Mr Buchanan. 'He hardly mentioned anything Edward did. It was all about Matthew, to try and distract the jury from why they're here.'

Amy sat down and dabbed her eyes with Henry's handkerchief. She was offered another glass of water by the kind usher and drank it down, her throat parched from shouting. It was then she realised she'd left her gloves in the witness box and attempted to hide her hands behind her back. Henry took her left hand and patted it.

'Don't be ashamed.'

A second usher exited the courtroom and handed her the gloves. Hastily she pulled them back on.

'You were very brave in there,' said Henry.

'I was useless. I let him tear me apart.'

'On the contrary, you did very well,' said Mr Buchanan. 'Everyone in the room forgot everything Laroche and Mrs Crowle had said when you showed them your hands. It was a very powerful moment, one they won't forget.'

'Besides, the prosecution has a surprise witness too,' said Henry, eyes twinkling.

'Who?' said Amy.

'Would you like to watch?'

'Yes, please.'

Taking her hand, he led her back into the courtroom, only this time she got to sit in the gallery. Although most people were paying too much attention to the proceedings to notice them, two women saw them enter and Amy looked back at them warily, wondering what their reaction would be. To her surprise they smiled. Amy looked to where the blonde woman had been sitting but was disappointed to see her seat was vacant. She wondered if she would ever see her again.

Peering over the tops of the heads of those sitting in front, she found the witness box and her jaw dropped open.

'Nettie?' she whispered in disbelief.

Henry smiled and nodded.

'So, Miss Day,' began the prosecutor, his voice ringing out loudly through the cavernous room. 'Can you confirm for the court if Miss Osbourne had an affair with Edward Alardyce?'

'Course she didn't. That's a load of rubbish,' she replied with surprising vehemence. 'He told her he preferred men and she believed him.'

'Why would he tell her that?'

'To gain her trust. He thought if he told her something about himself that was so personal and dangerous, she'd be inclined to confide in him, and it worked but it was a lie. He likes women.'

'Why did he want to gain her confidence so badly?'

'It was all to get back at his brother, Master Henry, who he hated.

Master Henry caught him hurting a housemaid. He threatened to go t
the police if he did it again.'

Edward glared at Nettie, loathing shining from his eyes.

'You see,' she continued, 'Master Henry was in love with Miss Amy

Amy glanced at Henry, whose cheeks reddened.

'Edward wanted to hurt him, so when they got engaged Edwar
asked me to help. He forged letters in Master Henry's hand supposedl
from himself to a made-up girl called Gemma saying all the sick thing
he wanted to do to her, but they were all Edward's disgusting fantasie
Then I pretended I'd got them from this girl and showed them to Mis
Amy. She trusted me and Edward so she believed Master Henry was
monster. Edward convinced her to run away to avoid becoming one
his victims once they were married.'

'Miss Osbourne must have been frightened?'

'She was terrified, sir. She was young and had just lost both paren
and Matthew took advantage of her. The master wouldn't let her leav
the estate or have her friends to stay. She was lonely, sir.'

Amy was astonished and couldn't fathom why Nettie wa
supporting her so passionately.

'And Master Henry was still willing to marry her even though sh
was carrying another man's child?'

'Yes, sir. He loved her.'

When Henry's face turned positively scarlet Amy grasped his hand

'Miss Osbourne couldn't have been mentally unstable if a ma
such as Sir Henry Alardyce was willing to marry her?'

'There was nothing wrong with her, she was just grieving for he
parents, that's all. The lady of the house wanted Miss Amy's fortun
and thought having her sent to the asylum would be the best way to g
her claws on it. She ordered Matthew to seduce her – she thought
she could make Miss Amy look like she had loose morals it would b
easier to get her put away. Master Henry was marrying her to prote
her.'

'So you assisted Miss Osbourne to flee?'

'Yes, sir. I got her a maid's outfit so she could sneak out with the servants.'

'Why did you agree to help Master Edward in such a scheme?'

'We were lovers, sir. I would have done anything for him.'

'So this elaborate charade wasn't about Miss Osbourne, it was about Master Henry?'

'Yes, sir. Master Edward hated his brother. Like night and day, them two.' She threw Edward a haughty look. 'And that's the night.'

'Thank you, Miss Day. No further questions.'

Laroche got to his feet and stared at Nettie as though he would devour her. She, however, appeared completely unconcerned and regarded him with a bored expression.

'Miss Day, when did your relationship with Edward Alardyce come to an end?' began Laroche.

'About two months after Miss Amy left Alardyce.'

'Why did it end?'

'There were two reasons. First, I caught him with another maid in the scullery. Apparently it was all right for him to have affairs with the servants because he's a man,' she said bitterly. 'Secondly, because he started hurting me too.'

'You mean physically?'

'Yes. It was small at first. He slapped me then it got worse and he bit me until I bled and he burnt me...'

He spoke over her when he realised where she was going. 'So you have plenty of reasons to be angry with Mr Alardyce?'

'Yes, I do.'

'Is testifying against him revenge?'

'I'll say.' She smiled. 'I'm enjoying it immensely.'

'Your Honour, I call for this witness's evidence to be dismissed,' boomed Laroche, throwing his arms wide. 'She's clearly making it all up to get back at her former lover.'

'Is that what you think?' sneered Nettie before the judge could respond.

With magnificent dignity Nettie got to her feet and started to remove her gloves, just as Amy had done, and Nettie held up her misshapen hands, missing their fingernails.

'Miss Amy was right,' she declared. 'It wasn't pleasurable.'

Edward, who had been very calm up until that point, erupted into a fury.

'You bitch. You filthy whore,' he roared at Nettie while attempting to leap over the dock, the two jailers dragging him back. 'I'll slit your fucking throat and piss on the wound.'

The room swarmed with police, and the exclamations of surprise from the crowd made Edward turn on them too.

'I'll kill all of you dirty sluts. It's all women are fit for.'

It took five men to subdue him and he was hauled back down to the cells, his taunts still ringing through the shocked courtroom.

'I hope they hang you,' Nettie yelled after him. 'I can't wait to see you do the Newgate jig.'

Mr Laroche slumped in his seat, a hand over his face, knowing he was defeated.

Henry's face was etched with sadness as he watched his brother and Amy's heart went out to him. He had suffered too at Edward's hands. She gave his hand an affectionate squeeze and he raised his head.

'Shall we leave?' she said.

'Yes, please.'

They rose and left the gallery, followed by Mr Buchanan. Outside it was still swarming with spectators and Henry kept her close as they hurried down the steps to the waiting carriage. Parallel to them Amy spotted Nettie leaving the court. Their eyes met and Amy gave her a nod of gratitude, which Nettie returned before she was swallowed up by the crowd.

Gratefully they clambered back into the carriage, and the journey home was completed in silence, none of them ready to discuss what had happened.

Amy's eyes soon grew heavy with the soothing rocking motion of the carriage and she woke to find her head resting on Henry's shoulder, his arm wrapped around her. At first he didn't notice she was awake and she was content to stare up at his handsome face as he gazed out of the window. When he saw she was awake he hastily retracted his arm.

'Excuse me, but you almost slid to the floor,' he said.

'It's all right.' She yawned, sitting upright.

'We're almost home,' Mr Buchanan told her.

The carriage rolled to a halt outside the house, her heart lifting at the thought of Robert, Jane and Esther waiting for her inside. Just before she got out she turned to Henry. 'It was you who got Nettie to give evidence, wasn't it?'

'I discovered her affair with Edward shortly after you left Alardyce and at the time I thought the manner of her leaving very odd. When I tracked her to a house in Dundee where she was working she was very eager to give evidence against him, especially when she was told if she did she would avoid prosecution for her part in procuring the girls. She regretted plotting against you and this was her way of giving reparation. Nettie's not a bad person, she was just under Edward's spell.'

She smiled and kissed his cheek. 'Thank you. For everything.'

'You're welcome,' he said, voice soft and warm.

'You're both more than welcome to come in for some tea,' she said, unwilling to relinquish their company just yet.

'Thank you but I have an appointment with a client,' said Mr Buchanan.

'I'm afraid I wouldn't be very good company right now,' said Henry. 'I'll call on you soon, if that's agreeable?'

'It is. Very. Goodbye.'

They assisted her down and she watched the carriage drive off with a feeling of regret, although she wasn't sure why.

* * *

Three days later Edward was found guilty on four counts of murder, for the imprisonment and torture of Amy, Nettie and three other girls who had come forward, including Mary Hill. He was sentenced to hang at Newgate the following week.

Amy was transformed in the papers from a whore into an innocent victim who had almost died protecting her son from his monstrous father. The Women's Suffrage Movement held her up as an icon of what could happen to a woman in a world ruled by men and her reputation was somewhat improved, although it could never be fully restored.

* * *

Henry stood alone facing the execution shed in the exercise yard of Newgate as he waited for Edward to be brought from his cell, the sight of the noose blowing in the breeze almost hypnotic. A few feet away stood two journalists who watched him closely, jotting things down in their notebooks, already composing their articles in their heads.

The hangman was the first to make an appearance. He was a huge flabby man with a shaven head, a reprieved felon himself. He tugged at the noose, testing its strength. Next he inspected the trap, checking the mechanism and walking around the scaffold, ensuring everything had been constructed to his satisfaction. The man might be odious but he was thorough. There would be no errors on his watch.

When he'd finished his morbid task the under sheriff climbed the steps to the platform, followed by the prison governor and the prison doctor. The chaplain came next, reading passionately from the Bible. Edward appeared behind them flanked by two jailers, his hands pinioned before him. He looked feral – unwashed, unshaven and wearing filthy clothes. As he surveyed the pathetically small audience his eyes flashed and his lips drew back over his teeth, baring them. His appearance so startled the journalists they took a step back, as though he was about to attack. Edward's eyes settled on Henry and the two brothers stared at each other across the yard, the noose swaying between them, before his gaze moved on.

As soon as Edward was placed directly before the noose on the chalk mark marking the trapdoor, his face crumpled and his lower lip wobbled. Watching his tears was more disturbing than his madness and Henry had a sudden flashback to when Edward was six years old and he'd fallen and cut his knee while they were playing together in the garden. He'd cried in the exact same way and Henry had assisted him to limp back to the house, where the nanny had cleaned and dressed the wound. As a treat she'd given them a cup of chocolate each. The memory caused a lump to form in his throat. He'd loved his brother once.

Edward tried to back away from the noose but the jailers pushed him forward, struggling to strap his ankles together with the leather belt.

'No. I don't want to die,' he wailed in a childlike voice. 'Henry, help me, please.'

Tears prickled Henry's eyes as the bag was placed over his brother's head, mercifully muffling his cries, the cloth of the bag moving back and forth in time with Edward's frantic breathing. A whimper of fear could be heard as the noose was placed around his neck, a puddle of urine forming on the wood of the gallows as it trickled down Edward's quivering legs.

The hangman placed his hand on the lever and Henry forced himself to watch as he pulled it. Edward dropped through the hatch with a bang that jangled Henry's already fraught nerves. The pathetic spectacle was over for his neck had broken. Edward was gone, his body hanging limply from the rope. They were all gone now – his mother, father and brother. He was the only one left.

Blinking back tears, Henry watched the undertakers he'd hired waiting with the coffin at the edge of the platform. He didn't want Edward buried in the prison grounds, so he'd arranged for his body to be taken away and placed in the family vault at Alardyce. Fortunately

the sheriff of the county had given him permission to take the bod
which became property of the Crown after execution. There would b
no funeral or mourning for Edward, but his father would hav
despised the idea of his youngest son being buried in this reekin
hellhole.

The black flag was raised over the main gates and the prison be
tolled, letting the huge crowd assembled outside know it was over.

Slowly Henry turned and made his way out, glad he had his cane t
lean on because his legs were shaking. He walked blindly, seein
nothing except the body of his baby brother hanging from a rope.

* * *

Amy arrived at Henry's house two hours after Edward had been due t
hang and found he still hadn't returned. His valet invited her inside t
wait and offered her tea and cake.

When another hour had passed and still no Henry she assume
he'd gone on to friends or his club, so she decided to go home.

As she walked down the front steps of the house she saw a figur
entering the grounds. Henry was dressed all in black. The breez
stirred his long great-coat, causing it to billow out around him, the onl
sound the thud of his silver-topped cane as it struck the ground in
solemn beat. He removed his hat and his hair blew back from his pal
face to reveal those dark, glittering eyes, which brooded at the groun
When he looked up and saw her standing there those eyes lit up wit
hope.

'Amy,' he pleaded, extending his hand out to her.

She ran to him and enveloped him in her arms. Letting his hat an
cane fall to the ground, he held her close and buried his face in he
hair.

'I'm sorry,' she said, able to feel his pain. 'I'm so sorry.'

He was shaking so she took his hand and led him inside, where sh
poured them both a Scotch, which he gulped down gratefully.

Henry managed to raise a weak smile. 'I always found your preference for Scotch rather entertaining.'

'Most men find it disconcerting that I can hold my liquor better than they can,' she replied.

'Well, I find it admirable,' he said, refilling both their glasses with a steadier hand. 'Thank you for being here. I've been tramping the streets for hours because I simply couldn't face coming back to an empty house.'

'Was it quick?' she asked as gently as she could.

He drained his glass and nodded. 'Mercifully his neck broke but he begged me to help him. It was hideous.'

'I think he was in torment. Now he's at peace.'

'I blame Mother,' he said, finally giving voice to thoughts he had mulled over for years. 'Ever since he was a young child she degraded and humiliated him. No wonder he grew up hating women.'

'Why did she do that?'

'His birth was long and difficult and she couldn't conceive again. She always blamed him. She was desperate for a daughter, someone she could dress up like a little doll. She was always jealous of your mother for having a girl.'

'That explains why she hated me so much.'

'You reminded her of what she could never have. Now Edward's gone.'

'Edward chose to do what he did.' She frowned. 'Plenty of people have overbearing mothers but they don't start torturing and killing people.'

He could hear the bitterness in her tone. 'It was his choice to do what he did, but I knew him when he was just an ordinary little boy, before he turned into that creature who died so pathetically today.'

When his voice cracked and he pressed a hand to his face she embraced him. She loved him.

32

When Henry next came to call, Amy found herself brimming over with a nervous excitement that was entirely new. She stood before the mirror smoothing down her dress while Esther watched with a smile playing on her lips.

'Yes?' said Amy with a twinkle in her eye.

'Nothing.' Esther grinned back.

Henry entered the room looking rather flustered. 'Esther, Amy.' He bowed. 'Forgive my intrusion but I've come to bid you goodbye.'

Amy's face fell.

'Goodbye? Have you grown tired of London?' enquired Esther, her concerned eyes flicking to Amy.

'Not at all. It's Alardyce. I haven't returned since I inherited the estate and now some problems have arisen that require my immediate attention.' There was an urgency about him that was exhausting to watch as he shuffled from one foot to the other.

'How long will you be gone?' said Amy, hoping her voice wouldn't quiver with disappointment.

'It's hard to say but it may be months.'

'Oh,' she replied, downcast.

Henry cleared his throat before saying, 'Amy, would you be so kind as to take a walk with me in the garden?'

'Err... yes,' she replied, picking up her shawl and wrapping it around her shoulders.

Esther's gaze caught Amy's and she smiled encouragingly but Amy tried not to raise her hopes as Henry offered her his arm.

'Have you ever wondered,' he began as they strolled around the garden, 'how we would have fared had we married?'

'Nine years ago I would have said we'd have been dreadful together,' she replied.

'Yes, you made that quite clear.' He smiled. 'And now?'

'Now I think quite the opposite.'

He stopped and turned to face her. 'Not marrying you has been the single greatest regret of my life and one that – if you will permit me – I would like to rectify as soon as possible.'

She broke into a smile, breathless with excitement. 'What are you saying?'

He took her hands and went down on one knee. 'Amy Osbourne, I have loved you from the moment we met. Will you marry me?'

Euphoria swept over her but she bit her lip to restrain the cry of *yes* wanting to burst forth. 'Please sit,' she said, leading him to a stone bench. 'Before I give my answer we have things to discuss. My reputation is ruined and that will affect you too – you'll be ostracised from society.'

He shrugged. 'So?'

'You may lose your friends.'

'If they're true friends they'll support me. Amy, I knew about Mr Costigan when you came to Alardyce and I don't care about that. Neither do I care about your relationship with Matthew. You're so strong and if people decide to ignore us what does it matter? We'll have each other and that's all I need.'

'Oh, Henry,' she rasped, eyes filling with tears. 'I don't care about society either, but I care about you and Robert, and any children we have will be tainted by association.'

'That's years in the future, times are changing. Everything will be fine, I promise.'

He was brimming over with positive energy and it gave her hope. 'You really think it will?'

He leaned towards her, his lips almost touching hers, pinning her with those beautiful eyes that reflected the sunlight. 'I do.'

Amy blushed, embarrassed by what she had to say next. 'There's something else.'

She took a deep breath. 'After everything that's been done to me I fear I've been ruined for any man.' When he looked puzzled she added, 'Intimately.'

'I see. Well, can you hold my hand?' he said, clasping both her hands in his.

'Yes.' She smiled.

'Can you kiss me?' he said before gently pressing his lips to hers.

'Yes,' she breathed when the kiss ended.

'Then that's all I can ask.'

She cast her eyes to the ground in shame. 'My body's badly scarred. It's not pleasant to look at.'

He tilted her face back up to his. 'It doesn't matter to me. I love you, Amy. Do you love me?'

'Yes,' she replied without having to think about it.

'Then marry me.'

'Oh, Henry, yes, I will marry you.'

He broke into a broad, beautiful smile. 'I can't tell you how happy you've made me.'

They kissed again and her stomach knotted with excitement.

'Will you and Robert come with me to Alardyce or does it hold too many bad memories for you?' he asked her.

'No, I think it will be all right,' she replied slowly. She wouldn't really know how she would feel until she was back there, but she thought it might be all right now Edward, Lenora and Matthew were gone.

'If you like you can bring Esther and Jane too. I'll be kept busy there while I sort out all those damn problems. I also want to begin the renovation work and would appreciate your opinion. The old place hasn't changed a jot since it was built. If you find you're comfortable there, then perhaps we could mould it into something that is entirely our own?'

The thought of such a project excited her. It would be nice to have a purpose again. 'That sounds wonderful.'

'I'm glad it pleases you.' He smiled, touching her face. 'I must leave this afternoon, but you can join me when you're ready, which I hope will be sooner rather than later.'

'Believe me, it will.' She grinned, unable to remember the last time she'd been so happy.

'Oh, and I intend to have a contract drawn up stating that your fortune will remain your own after we're married. I never wanted your money and I will not have my mother victorious from beyond the grave. Now I must reluctantly take my leave and I'll be eagerly awaiting your arrival.'

They walked hand in hand back to the house, sharing another kiss before he left.

* * *

Amy worried what Robert would say about her engagement. It had been just the two of them for so long she hoped he wouldn't regard Henry as an interloper trying to take his mother away from him.

She needn't have worried.

'So, what do you think?' she asked her son after breaking the news.

'Will we go to live with him?' said Robert.

'Yes. He has a nice big estate in Scotland.'

'Can I have a horse?'

'Yes.'

'Do I call him Papa?'

'That's entirely up to you but you don't have to decide that now. D
you like Henry?'

'Yes. He makes you smile.'

'Are you pleased we're going to be married?'

'Yes, Mama.' He smiled before embracing her.

Amy cuddled him, so relieved. Finally her life was coming togethe
and she had everyone she loved in the world around her.

* * *

Five days passed before Amy arrived at Alardyce with Robert, Esthe
and Jane. Henry met them at Waverley station, the same station sh
had used in her escape all those years ago. She longed to rush int
his arms but for Robert's sake they greeted each other mor
decorously.

When Alardyce House came into view, peeking out at her fro
behind the trees, she could appreciate what a fine house it was. It n
longer represented a prison. She was aware Henry was watching he
reaction and he seemed relieved when she smiled.

The house was exactly as she remembered it but without Lenora
malevolent presence it was much more welcoming. A shadow seeme
to have lifted off the house.

On arrival they headed upstairs to change out of their travellin
clothes, shown to their rooms by Rush, who even smiled at Amy as h
bowed.

This time her room was in the family wing, her chambers rig
next door to Henry's. Robert's room was across the hall and he w
thrilled to discover he had a view of the paddock and stables. Esthe
and Jane were put in the guest wing.

While everyone was changing, Henry followed Amy into her roo at her invitation. Now they were alone they could embrace more affectionately.

'I've missed you,' he breathed into her hair.

'I've missed you too.'

They kissed and Amy marvelled at the touch of a man she loved as well as desired. It was an entirely new experience for her. His kisses moved down to her neck and rather than the expected fear she felt only happiness, her stomach aching with longing. She felt so relaxed with him, knowing he would never use her like Mr Costigan or hurt her like Matthew. He just wanted to love her.

'Forgive me,' he said, holding her close. 'I know we're not yet married but I can't help myself.'

'Don't be sorry, it was lovely.' She smiled, stroking the back of his neck, her fingers curling in his hair.

With one final kiss he left her alone and she smiled, radiant with happiness. She studied the room, deciding what changes to make, refusing to be ashamed of the vengeance in her heart. She intended to eradicate every trace of Lenora from this house. She was Lady Alardyce now.

* * *

Esther took the children for a walk into the village so Amy and Henry could tour the house and decide what renovations they would make.

They decided to leave the layout of the rooms as it was but they would redecorate as everything was looking tired and old-fashioned.

Amy had worried this house would hold too many ghosts but to her surprise it didn't. By the time she and Henry were finished all trace of the previous occupants would be erased, they were both determined on that.

They looked up at the portrait of the family that still took pride of place in the dining room, the one that had made Amy feel so alone, and she experienced a pang of affection as she regarded the image of her uncle. He had tried his best for her and it had got him killed. She put her arms around Henry and he held onto her.

'I think I'll have this picture moved,' he said in that stiff, emotionless voice she'd once thought meant he was a cold, unfeeling monster. Now she knew it just masked his stronger emotions.

'Don't feel you must on my account.'

'I want to. I cannot bear to look upon it.'

'We'll make this a home for our own family and it will be a happy place again.'

'Yes, it will.' He smiled. 'Let's move on, shall we?' said Henry, taking her hand.

When they went into the garden Amy froze at the sight of the summer house. She knew Henry had witnessed her disgracing herself with Matthew in there, which made her burn with shame.

'It was a long time ago,' he said when she cast her eyes to the ground. 'Let it go.'

'If I'd known then what I know now I would have married you and not given Matthew the time of day.'

'What shall we do with it?' Henry said, indicating the summer house.

'Knock it down for all I care. It holds only bad memories.'

'We can replace it with another. The architect has a plan for one which is much more modern.'

'I like the sound of that,' she said, not bothering to hide her relief. She was determined to hide nothing ever again from this man.

They moved on to the sunken garden.

'This place always gave me the chills.' She shivered, huddling up to him.

'I thought I'd have the trees cut back to let in more light. It always was a sad, neglected little corner. I used to come here when I was feeling melancholy.'

She recalled the time she'd found him here after they'd argued and she knew she had made him sad. He'd probably been trying to fathom her odd behaviour.

'There's just the conservatory left to inspect,' he said, moving swiftly on.

Once again this room was just as she remembered. Her favourite seat was still there, faded and dusty.

'This was my favourite room,' she said. 'I thought it the most cheerful room in the house.'

'I noticed you used to come here a lot,' he said.

They sat down and he put an arm around her. When he kissed her she wrapped her arms around his neck and she felt a delicious ripple of desire. He pressed her back into the couch and she felt his hand slide up her left leg in exploration. She was seized by panic that he would find her damaged flesh ugly, and she pushed herself upright and smoothed down her skirts.

'I'm sorry,' he said, sitting up with her.

'The fault lies with me, not you.' To her horror her eyes welled with tears and she clamped her hand down over her mouth to stop herself from sobbing out loud.

'What's wrong?'

'I'm ugly,' she cried. 'My body's covered with awful scars. When you see them you won't want me any more.'

'That's not true. I love you. Nothing will stop me wanting you. May I?' he said, indicating her legs.

'I can't.'

'I'll only look. I won't touch if you don't want me to. Do you trust me?' he pressed when she appeared uncertain.

She took a deep breath and nodded. 'All right.'

Amy gripped onto the sides of the couch as he rolled down her stockings, revealing the shiny burn marks dotting her calves and thighs. She kept her gaze on the floor, unable to bring herself to look at his face, dreading seeing revulsion there.

When his lips brushed her calf her head snapped up. 'You don't find me hideous?'

'Not in the slightest,' he said, stroking her skin with his long white fingers.

'Beautiful girl,' he whispered in her ear as she hung onto him, trembling. 'Beautiful girl.'

33

The renovations to the house were still ongoing three months later, although the ground floor had been completed just in time for the wedding.

Amy and Henry were married in a small, quiet ceremony in the village church. Amy had had enough of being a public curiosity, so she wanted only close family and friends in attendance. As it was November and the wind was biting they had the reception inside the house. It was a very simple affair but it was what they both wanted and it went off without a hitch.

Robert had really taken a shine to Henry and the two were forming a close bond. Henry didn't try to buy the boy's affection with trinkets as Matthew had done, apart from a beautiful white stallion named Snow. Instead they spent time together riding or hunting and it was Robert who proudly walked his mother down the aisle. Esther and Lily stood as bridesmaid and matron of honour with Jane as flower girl.

The day was perfect but Amy couldn't help but fear her wedding night. She was simultaneously afraid and excited because she wanted Henry so much but she was scared of baring herself completely to him.

After everyone had retired for the night, Amy and Henry went

upstairs hand in hand. While Henry went to his chamber to change
Amy went to hers so her maid could assist her to remove her wedding
dress and put on her nightgown. Her hair was brushed and tied at the
nape of her neck with a dark blue ribbon. She climbed into bed and
anxiously awaited the arrival of her new husband, who appeared two
minutes later.

'That was quick.' She smiled.

'I didn't want to waste time when I could be here,' he said, climbing
in beside her.

He kissed her, which was lovely, but she couldn't relax knowing
where it was going to lead this time. So rather than think about herself
she concentrated on pleasing him. She pulled his nightshirt off over his
head and gasped. He had always appeared quite slender and gangly
with his clothes on but now she saw that, although he was wiry, he was
well developed and strong. She ran her fingers over the muscles of his
shoulders and arms and down his back.

'I hope that was a gasp of approval,' he said.

'Oh yes,' she breathed.

She kissed his chest, her insides aching with desire, but his beauty
only made her more ashamed of her own body. She had always had a
fine figure and pregnancy and childbirth had done little to alter it but
her skin was ruined and hideous to the touch. She couldn't bear for
him to see her shame, so when he tried to pull off her nightgown she
panicked.

'No, don't,' she cried, pushing it back down.

He sat up and hugged her. 'You're not ready for me to see you
yet?'

'No. Sorry,' she sighed, feeling ridiculous.

'It's all right. We have plenty of time. Do you want to continue?'

'Definitely.' She wanted their marriage to be consummated.

He pressed her back into the bed and pulled her gown up to her
waist. Although she was apprehensive it still felt good when he entered
her. It was the first time she'd ever made love and the difference aston

ished her. It was a profound experience that only served to strengthen the bond between them.

He respected her wishes and made no attempt to remove her clothing again but every time his hands brushed her back she would tense, terrified of him feeling her mutilation. Consequently she couldn't relax enough to climax.

He held off for as long as he could but eventually he had to give in to his own pleasure.

Afterwards he wrapped her in his arms and she snuggled into his bare chest. Henry knew exactly what had been going through her mind; he had seen it all in her eyes.

'The scars don't matter to me,' he said.

'I know. It's all in my head. I'm sure it will get better with time.'

They both heard the doubt but preferred to pretend it wasn't there.

* * *

Their marriage was a happy, loving one. Robert started calling Henry Papa just two months after the wedding and they enjoyed a close relationship.

Esther and Jane bought a house in London but came to visit Alardyce often. Esther met a handsome earl who was bowled over by her beauty and gentle nature and proposed four months later. She sold Huntington Manor to a merchant who had made his money in the Yorkshire wool mills and a few weeks after he'd moved in Esther was informed that work he'd commissioned to the gardens had unearthed a body. Although the body had been in the ground for months she'd been identified as Sally Jenkins by her family, her distinctive blonde hair and clothes still recognisable. Finally she was laid to rest in the village churchyard and her family were able to grieve.

Life at Alardyce was peaceful and content until one day they had an unwelcome visitor. Henry was out in the garden overseeing the construction of the new summer house and Robert was studying in the library with his new tutor, an eager, clever young man from Glasgow. Therefore, when Rush announced a visitor Amy greeted them alone in the drawing room. As she got to her feet to welcome them her mouth fell open.

'Rush, please fetch my husband,' she said.

'Yes, My Lady.' He bowed before leaving.

The wretch before her studied her with eyes that danced with triumph.

'What do you want?' demanded Amy.

Mrs Crowle's gaze was sly. 'This is a very grand house. You must have plenty of money.'

'So that's what you're after, you revolting creature. Get out before I have you thrown out.'

'I don't think that would be wise, not until you've heard what I have to say.'

'And what is that?'

'Let's wait until Sir Henry arrives, shall we, Your Ladyship?' Her tone was mocking, as though Amy didn't deserve the title.

They waited in silence, Amy paralysed by rage, while Mrs Crowle wandered around the room picking things up and examining them before putting them back down.

'Stop that,' snapped Amy. 'Those are not yours to touch.'

Mrs Crowle ignored her but fortunately at that moment the door opened and Henry walked in. He stopped in his tracks when he saw Matthew's mother standing in his drawing room and Rush almost walked into the back of him.

'Shall I fetch some tea, sir?'

'No, thank you, Rush. Our guest isn't staying,' replied Henry, dark eyes furious and locked on Mrs Crowle.

Rush bowed and left, closing the doors behind him.

'What the hell are you doing here?' said Henry.

'She wants money,' said Amy. 'I can't say I'm surprised.'

'You're not getting a penny, now get out,' he thundered.

'I think you should wait until you've heard what I have to say,' said Mrs Crowle, lips twisting into a crafty smile.

'And what is that?'

Her beady eyes settled on Amy. 'I know you killed my son.'

Amy felt as though she'd been struck but maintained her composure. 'Edward killed Matthew. I saw it.'

'He may have stuck the dagger in his gut but you pulled it out and because of that he bled to death.'

'What nonsense.'

'Hobbs saw you.'

'What?' exclaimed Amy.

Mrs Crowle flashed her evil grin. 'You didn't know he came back. When he couldn't find his master he returned to Edward's house just in time to see you yank that blade out of my boy.'

'If you're telling the truth then why didn't he help his master?'

'He thought the police had been called, so he fled. Besides, he knew it was too late.'

Amy could have felt a modicum of sympathy for this odious woman if she thought she genuinely grieved her son's death, but she knew it was just about money with her.

'You're here to blackmail us with this pathetic scrap of information?' said Amy. 'Matthew's dead and buried and the only witness to what you allege is a man the police are searching for. His word counts for nothing. Really, Mrs Crowle, I expected more from you. It would be your word against mine. Who do you think the police would believe?'

'Then I'll go to the newspapers instead. They'll lap it up.'

'You will do no such thing,' said Henry, advancing on the wicked woman. 'If you speak a single word of this to anyone I will ensure you are thrown into Newgate. You were just as complicit in what was done to Amy as your son and it's a travesty that you're still at liberty. If you continue to push us I will see you dangle at the end of a rope.'

'You can't do that,' she croaked, hands involuntarily going to her scrawny neck.

'If I can do it to my own brother then I can certainly do it to you.' He rang the bell and Rush appeared. 'Our guest is leaving. Please see she is escorted off the grounds.'

'Yes, sir.' He bowed, calling for the two footmen, who were wearing their new all-black livery.

Henry addressed Mrs Crowle in a low voice so the servants couldn't hear.

'I warn you, I will do anything to protect my wife and that includes having you silenced. Is that clear?'

Mrs Crowle's eyes filled with defeat and she nodded.

'Good. Get out.'

She shuffled to the door, suddenly looking much older, and was escorted from the house by the burly footmen with Rush looking on. Henry wrapped his arms around Amy as they watched her leave.

'Thank you,' she said.

'It was a pleasure to see off the odious woman. Are you all right?'

'Yes, just a little shaken up.'

'She's gone now and I doubt she'll come back.'

He strolled over to the sideboard. 'Scotch?' he said with a mischievous smile.

Amy thought her heart would burst with love. 'Yes, please.'

* * *

That night Amy lay awake in her bed, alone, thinking back over the confrontation with Mrs Crowle, but it was Henry she was considering. He had been so powerful and commanding, making terrible threats she knew he would have carried through to protect her. She loved him so much she couldn't understand why she couldn't even share a bed with him because she was so afraid of him touching her back. The problem was in her own head. She felt that everything she'd endured had been a punishment for being Matthew's whore. Common sense told her this was ridiculous, but a tiny irrational part of herself told her otherwise. She wanted nothing more than to allow Henry to hold her at night. She'd fought so hard to survive so she and Robert could be free yet she was still allowing herself to be ruled by the past. Well, enough was enough.

Emboldened by the Scotch and wine she had drunk that evening, she flung back the covers and climbed out of bed. Not bothering with her shawl or slippers, she sneaked out of her room into the darkened corridor and rapped on Henry's door.

'Yes?' she heard him call.

She stepped inside to find him sitting up in bed, reading. He smiled, pleased to see her.

'Amy, is something wrong?' he said.

Without replying she padded over to the bed, pulled back the covers and straddled him.

'What the...?' he began.

She silenced him with a kiss before sitting upright and taking a few deep breaths in an effort to remain calm. If she didn't do this now she never would. Gripping the hem of her nightgown, she pulled it off over her head and cast it aside, so she was completely naked before him.

Henry stared at her in astonishment. He could see the edges of the scars on her ribs snaking around from the back but he hardly noticed them. They didn't matter.

'You're so lovely,' he breathed.

When she felt his hardness pressing between her bare thighs and saw the longing in his eyes she relaxed a little. He still wanted her.

He could feel her trembling as he gently ran his hands over her body, careful not to startle her. This was a huge step forward for her and he didn't want anything to spoil it.

Amy let him kiss and stroke the front of her body while she ran her hands through his hair. Tugging off his nightshirt, she pressed herself against him, loving the feel of his bare skin against her own.

She guided him inside her and he groaned loudly. Barely two minutes later she climaxed with a cry of delight and a look of amaze-

ment. A moment later he did too and they fell back onto the be
together.

'May I ask what brought that on?' he panted. 'Don't get me wrong
I'm most glad it happened, but what has changed?'

She rolled onto her side to face him. 'I wanted to feel you touch m
and I want to sleep with you by my side.'

'And how I have longed to oblige.' He smiled. 'Turn over,' he whis
pered in her ear. 'This isn't for me. The scars don't bother me in th
least but if you want to rid yourself of this fear then you must do this.'

'All right,' she said in a small voice.

He kissed her. 'It won't change how I feel about you. I will love yo
forever.'

Slowly she turned onto her front and lay rigid as she felt his eye
on her back. The skin was a map of pain. Long deep ridges scored he
skin and he brushed her long hair aside so he could see everything
including the marks left in her shoulders by Edward's teeth.

She buried her face in the pillow, fighting back the tears. Tender
he stroked her back, and Amy looked back at him over her shoulde
eyes wide with surprise as he dropped his head to kiss her, slow
moving down her back. She released sweet sighs of pleasure and h
felt her muscles relax.

As he continued to kiss her body he slid his hand between he
thighs and she moaned and parted her legs for him. He took her in th
position, not ceasing his gentle attentions to her back, and he wa
ecstatic when she climaxed a second time.

For the first time since they'd married they fell asleep togethe
wrapped in each other's arms with nothing dividing them.

34

CHRISTMAS DAY – 1896

The drawing room filled with raucous laughter as the festivities got into full swing. Henry and Amy's children – six-year-old Lydia, five-year-old John and three-year-old Stephen – ran around with Esther's six-year-old twin boys – Christopher and Thomas. Esther and her husband, William, sat together holding hands. He worshipped her, still finding it difficult to believe that this beautiful woman had chosen to love him. Esther hadn't known she was expecting twins until she'd gone into labour and William had burst into floods of tears at being blessed with two strapping boys to inherit his title and estate. Everyone had been astounded that her tiny frame had been able to contain them. Another curse broken.

Amy, for her part, found herself pregnant three months after she'd overcome her reticence about her scars and for a few years had been almost constantly pregnant. Now she had no qualms about her scars and sometimes forgot they were even there. Henry still adored her and their relationship was as passionate as ever.

She watched her husband steer John away from some candles. His hair was a little greyer, he had creases around his eyes and he carried a little more weight but he was still so handsome. He caught her eye and smiled.

Hitching John onto his shoulders, he walked over to her, the little boy giggling delightedly. He sat beside her and put John down.

'Go and play with your brother,' he said and John ran off to join Stephen, who was playing with a toy horse.

Henry wrapped an arm around Amy and pulled her to him. 'Look what I've found.' He smiled, holding a sprig of mistletoe over her head.

As they kissed they heard Lydia release the sound of disgust that children always made when they saw their parents displaying physical affection.

They all laughed and Amy rested her head on Henry's shoulder, sighing with contentment as she surveyed the room. Happiness such as this had seemed like an impossibility only a few years ago.

Mr Buchanan and his wife, Mildred, had joined them for the holidays. They'd been staunch friends ever since the trial and had even stood godparents to Stephen. Amy's childhood friend, Lily, and her family were also regular visitors and were joining them for the New Year.

She watched Robert and Jane talking together. They'd maintained their close friendship, which had slowly evolved into something more over the years. Jane had blossomed into a very beautiful girl, her hair a mass of blonde curls, and Amy smiled when Robert covertly ran his fingers through them, thinking no one was watching. He looked so much like his father now that sometimes it startled her. At seventeen years old he was tall and well-built for his age, all the hours he spent horse riding and hunting contributing to his strong frame. Occasionally he would pull a serious frown or say something in such a way that it reminded her of Matthew and she would just feel sad.

When he was thirteen he'd asked about his father, so she'd told him the truth, leaving out the more horrific parts of the story. Robert had accepted what she'd told him with great maturity, some of his own memories confirming the truth of her words. He'd not mentioned it since and still thought of Henry as his father.

'More wine, My Lady?' said the maid, Daisy.

The servants with family had been allowed home for the day but those who had no one had chosen to work, preferring the festive atmosphere of the house to being alone.

'Why not?' Amy smiled, holding out her glass to be refilled.

As Daisy poured, her sleeve rode up to reveal some dark bruising around her wrist and Amy experienced a pang of horror. She knew that pattern of bruising all too well.

All the sounds of merriment fell away as she looked into Daisy's eyes and saw fear and desperation there before the maid scuttled away, leaving Amy sick and breathless. She looked from her husband to her son, wondering. Not Henry, he couldn't, he was far too gentle, but so was Robert. She couldn't believe it of either of them. One of the servants must be responsible. If that was the case, why was her gut telling her to look closer to home?

Everyone was watching the twins running round a bemused Mr Buchanan, who was trying to reach his chair while balancing a glass of sherry and a plate of mince pies. Amy looked at Henry, who was laughing heartily, then to her eldest son. He was whispering in Jane's ear and she giggled coquettishly as he twisted one of her golden curls around his finger. There was such love in his eyes.

At that moment Daisy crossed the room, walking with her head bowed and shoulders hunched and when Robert spotted her his eyes turned black, his mouth stretching into a grotesque leer.

Amy swallowed back her tears as her heart broke. Like father like son.

When Robert turned back to Jane his eyes returned to normal. They looked at each other, smiled and nodded.

Amy felt numb as she watched Robert get to his feet.

'If I could please have everyone's attention,' he called.

The room went quiet.

'I realise this isn't the traditional way of doing things,' he began in his deep baritone, flashing his charming smile. 'But yesterday evening I asked Jane to marry me and she accepted.'

Cheers and applause filled the room. Jane – beautiful, sweet, innocent Jane – gazed up at Robert with adoration shining from her eyes. As he bent to kiss her the applause grew even louder.

Tears stood out in Amy's eyes but they weren't born of happiness. She looked to Daisy, who stared back at her with pleading in her eyes before hurrying from the room.

Amy turned to Henry and when he caught her look his smile fell.

'What is it?' he said, taking her hand.

'We have a very serious problem,' she replied, a single tear rolling down her cheek.

MORE FROM HEATHER ATKINSON

We hope you enjoyed reading *The Missing Girls of Alardyce House*. If you did, please leave a review.

If you'd like to gift a copy, this book is also available as an ebook, digital audio download and audiobook CD.

Sign up to Heather Atkinson's mailing list for news, competitions and updates on future books.

http://bit.ly/HeatherAtkinsonNewsletter

ABOUT THE AUTHOR

Heather Atkinson is the author of over fifty books - predominantly i
the crime fiction genre. Although Lancashire born and bred she nov
lives with her family, including twin teenage daughters, on the beau
tiful west coast of Scotland.

Visit Heather's website: https://www.heatheratkinsonbooks.com/

Follow Heather on social media:

 twitter.com/HeatherAtkinsoɪ
instagram.com/heathercrimeauthor
bookbub.com/authors/heather-atkinson
facebook.com/booksofheatheratkinson

Boldwood

Boldwood Books is an award-winning fiction publishing company seeking out the best stories from around the world.

Find out more at www.boldwoodbooks.com

Join our reader community for brilliant books, competitions and offers!

Follow us
@BoldwoodBooks
@BookandTonic

Sign up to our weekly deals newsletter

https://bit.ly/BoldwoodBNewsletter

Made in the USA
Las Vegas, NV
17 November 2022

59689966R00197